Praise for The Racel Griffin Series

L. Jagi Lamplighter, a fantastic new voice and a fabulous new world in the YA market! Rachel Griffin is a hero who never gives up! I cheered her all the way!

—Faith Hunter, author of *The Skinwalker* series

The Unexpected Enlightenment of Rachel Griffin, a plucky band of children join forces to fight evil, despite the best efforts of incompetent adults, at a school for wizards. YA fiction really doesn't get better than that.

—Jonathan Moeller, author of *The Ghosts* series

Rachel Griffin is curious, eager and smart, and ready to begin her new life at Roanoke Academy for the Sorcerous Arts, but she didn't expect to be faced with a mystery as soon as she got there. Fortunately she's up to the task. Take all the best of the classic girl detective, throw in a good dose of magic and surround it all with entertaining, likeable friends and an intriguing conundrum, and you'll have *The Unexpected Enlightenment of Rachel Griffin*, a thrilling adventure tailor-made for the folks who've been missing Harry Potter. Exciting, fantastical events draw readers into Rachel's world and solid storytelling keeps them there.

—Misty Massey, author of *Mad Kestrel*

Books in the Series

THE UNEXPECTED ENLIGHTENMENT OF RACHEL GRIFFIN

L. JAGI LAMPLIGHTER

BASED ON THE WORKS OF MARK A. WHIPPLE

PALOMINO PRESS

HOWELL, NEW JERSEY

PUBLISHED BY

Palomino Press
an imprint of Dark Quest, LLC
Neal Levin, Publisher
23 Alec Drive,
Howell, New Jersey 07731
www.darkquestbooks.com

Trade paperback ISBN: 978-1-937051-87-7

Cover Art: Dan Lawlis
http://danlawlis.wordpress.com/

Interior Art: John C. Wright

Interior Design: Danielle McPhail
Sidhe na Daire Multimedia
www.sidhenadaire.com

TABLE OF CONTENTS

DEDICATION

To Mark A. Whipple
whose works inspired this one.

and

To: C. S. Lewis, J. K. Rowling, James Callis,
Stan Lee, Jack King Kirby, Bryan Lee O'Malley
and the many, many others who inspired Mark.

ONCE THERE WAS A WORLD

THAT SEEMED AT FIRST GLANCE MUCH LIKE OTHER WORLDS

YOU *MAY HAVE LIVED IN* OR READ ABOUT,

BUT IT *WASN'T...*

CHAPTER ONE:
THE UNEXPECTED BENEFITS
OF REMEMBERING

EVEN AMONG THE WISE, ANIMALS DID NOT TALK.

These two were talking.

Rachel Griffin awoke in her bunk bed in prestigious Dare Hall. It was her first night at Roanoke Academy, her first night in America, her first night away from home. The other girls in her dormitory room were asleep. She could hear their rhythmic breathing. Yet she distinctly heard voices. She opened her eyes and sat up.

The tall, arched window was open. A chill blew in through it. On the windowsill sat an enormous raven, jet black with blood red eyes. The raven addressed the familiar that belonged to one of Rachel's roommates. The girl must have been a fan of the new fad of shrinking wild animals and turning them into cute playthings. Her pet was a tiny lion the size of a house cat.

The raven croaked harshly, "You are not supposed to be here."

The lion sat regally beside his human, who lay sleeping across the room, on the other set of bunk beds. "I was called. Where I am called, I come."

"None of my people called you."

"You called one of my daughters. I am always in her heart."

"You need to depart."

The lion yawned. It turned in a circle three times and settled down to sleep.

The raven cawed raucously and flew away.

Rachel replayed the conversation in her head. She did not know what the phrases meant, but she was certain she had just overhead something crucial, something not meant for her, something not meant for any human ears. It was like hearing a door swing open to another world. She would never forget a word of it.

But then, Rachel Griffin never forgot *anything*.

The peachy dawn light peeked through the purple curtains. Rachel opened her eyes and stretched. A cold breeze blew in from outside. Rising, she padded across the room. The stone slabs were cold beneath her bare feet. Pushing back the curtains, she closed the window and pressed her nose against the pane. Her breath made little puffs of mist against the cool glass. Gazing about, she took in her surroundings: the paper birches with their curling parchment-like bark, the gravel paths leading toward the green lawns of the Campus Commons that ran between the many dormitories and buildings, the myriad towers and spires of Roanoke Hall rising above the trees in the distance. A few early risers flew down the path that led to the main hall. They flew on bristleless brooms—flying devices that had about as much in common with a sweeping implement as a mundane automobile had with a horse-drawn carriage.

Her roommates were still asleep. Normally, Rachel would have gone back to bed at this hour. But not today. Today, she was so excited, she could hardly keep her feet from dancing. Her heart raced with anticipation. She could no more return to sleep than she could walk to the moon.

All her life, she had waited to come here. All her life, she had gazed at photographs of her parents at Roanoke Academy for the Sorcerous Arts—the best arcane school in the universe. All her life, she had wanted to be part of this world, wanted it so badly that she would lay awake at night, her mind afire with hopes and plans.

She had imagined the friends she might make, the adventures she would have, the secrets she might learn. She wanted to study every Art the school had to teach. She wanted to entrap storm imps with her flute playing. She wanted to conjure roses and to walk with dragons. She wanted to do daring deeds and accomplish marvels never before known to human kind.

In her dreams, she had imagined accomplishing all these things.

All her life, she had waited to come.

Now she was here.

Rachel was done dreaming. She could not bear waiting even another instant.

Her academic robes and square, black scholar's cap were crisp and new. She dressed quickly, fumbling with the buttons in her eagerness. Flipping the cap's tassel out of her eyes, she grabbed Vroomie the Broom from under her bed and slipped out of the room. She pelted down two flights of stairs before becoming impatient and jumping on her broom. Leaning close over the handlebars, she flew down the rest of the staircase and outside, pausing only to open the front door. The windy wake of her broom blew papers around as she passed through the foyer. Outside, she gasped at the chill of the early autumn air and then shot upward, high into the sky.

Rachel loved to fly. Every morning, she spent her first waking hour in the air. Every day, she saw the same thing: the forests, moors, and rolling tenant farms of her family's estate, Gryphon Park, and the accompanying town Gryphon-on-Dart in Devon, England. Today, for the first time, there were new sights—her first glimpse of the place that was to be her home for the next eight years. Flying as high as she could, she drank in every sight.

The dawn colors still flamed in the east, gold and dusky rose. From up here, she could see the brown waters of the Hudson River, where it ran to either side of the once-floating Island of Roanoke. Storm King Mountain loomed on her left. She could see the path of the railway cut into its slope. Beyond it rose the Berkshires, their green rounded peaks rolling off to the west.

To the north, on the island, she could see the rocky tor in which the evil spirit, the Heer of Dunderberg, was imprisoned with his storm imps. To the south, she could see the spires of the Lower School, for elementary students, the campus of which was separated from that of the Upper School and the college. Beyond the Hudson, to the east, lay civilization.

Everything was so beautiful in the soft glow of the early morning light, as if not only the subjects taught here but also the very school itself was filled with magic. Up this high, the air was surprisingly still. A flock of geese passed by, getting a head start on their journey south. They flew in a V, honking loudly, their cheerful cries echoing off the side of Storm King.

Gazing down at the place that she now called home, Rachel's heart swelled with an unfamiliar longing, as if she yearned for something to which she could not give a name, something just outside her grasp, something she could not bear to go without.

Something wonderful was about to happen.

Or something terrible.

Or both.

From the sky, it all looked intriguing and yet alien. Yesterday morning, she had been at Gryphon Park—now she was part way around the world. It had not been a hard trip. Her parents had taken her to London, along with Peter and Laurel, her older brother and sister, and the three children had stepped through a Travel Glass—which turned out to be a really big version of the Walking Glasses they used to get around town.

The Travel Glass led to New York City. Her parents had taken them to see a few sights: the Statue of Liberty, the Empire State Building, the gilded Temple of Apollo on Fifth Avenue, the Shrine of the Goddess Amaterasu. These last two landmarks had been crowded with mundane folk who had come to worship. Rachel had never mixed with the Unwary before, those who were ignorant of the magical World of the Wise. She had kept her shadowcloak tucked around her and stayed close to her family.

After that, it had been a simple matter of stepping through a second glass that exited in a cottage near the dock along the Hudson River, where the ferry, the *Pollepel II*, picked them up to carry them to Roanoke Island.

The trip had not been difficult, but it had been disorienting. The worst part, the part that made her chest clench even now, as she soared on her broom, had been leaving Sandra behind. For years, Rachel had imagined she would arrive at Roanoke for the first time holding her oldest sister's hand. All those years, as she had watched Sandra leave for school each autumn, she had never bothered to do the math. Otherwise, it would have been obvious long ago that, by the time she was old enough to come to school, Sandra would already have graduated.

Rachel hoped when she grew up, she would look like Sandra, calm, stately, and as beautiful as a swan. Or even like her middle sister, Laurel, spirited, curvy, and appealing to boys. Right now, she looked nothing like either of them. Her shoulder-length black hair stuck out in all directions, no matter how she tried to tame it. Like Laurel and Peter, Rachel had the almond-shaped Asian eyes of their mother, who was one-quarter Korean. (Sandra looked more like their Caucasian father.) However, she had not yet inherited her mother's astoundingly shapely figure. At thirteen years of age, Rachel was still as slender as a boy.

She was very small and very young. She was also extremely intelligent. She knew a great many things people twice her age did not. She had inherited her mother's perfect memory. She only had to encounter a fact once, and she knew it forever. Because of this and her general scholarly prowess, she had been invited to come to Roanoke Academy a year early.

Rachel had read a great number of books in her thirteen years: novels, fairy tales, serious literature, nonfiction works on flight or farming or fishing. Her favorite books were her beloved grandfather's journals, the records he had kept of his life, his triumphs, and his tribulations during World War II. Now that he was gone, his journals were all she had of him.

She knew a tremendous amount about a great many things, but it was never enough. There was always some intriguing fact, some tantalizing notion, some fascinating concept that hovered just out of her reach. She was determined not to let any unlearned bit of knowledge escape her.

Rachel Griffin wanted to know *everything*.

As the sun rose higher, the September day grew warm and sunny. Rachel angled her broom upward. Up higher, it was not the Island of Roanoke she saw beneath her—with its virgin forests, its open campus lawns, its august stone buildings, and its rocky tor—but Bannerman Island, the Obscuration set in place to keep the mundane world from troubling the school. Bannerman Island was small and wooded, with an old mansion and a ruined castle. It was deserted.

Rachel put her broom into a hover and closed her eyes. She thought back on the last few seconds. The real island spread beneath her in her mind's eye. The ruined castle and the old mansion were still there, but there was a much vaster tract of buildings and forest between them.

Now, to see if she could accomplish a trick her mother had secretly taught her. She opened her eyes and gazed down at the false image of Bannerman Island. While looking down, she simultaneously thought back a second. The illusion popped like a soap bubble. Rachel caught her breath. She could now see the real island.

Letting go of the handlebars, she clapped her hands, delighted. Obscurations might fool the eye, but they could not fool her perfect memory.

She flew a few loops, a tight spiral, and a zig-zag design. Nothing was as wonderful as flying, nothing as thrilling, nothing as exhilarating. Up until her eleventh birthday, the most important thing in her life had been her pony, Widdershins. Then, a year and a half ago, her parents finally allowed her to have a broom.

It had been love at first flight.

Below her, something caught her attention. She dived down into the huge evergreens—her memory of a tree guide she had once read told her these were hemlocks. She bent low over her broom, gracefully dodging branches with consummate skill. The woods were particularly dark. Here and there, a single sunbeam broke through. These bright shafts of light looked so substantial against the darkened forest that Rachel imagined she could slide down one. She put out her hand, letting it pass through the ray, but found nothing but dancing dust motes.

Ahead, a single large sunbeam fell upon the face of a statue that stood otherwise in shadow. Rachel flew closer. A strange sensation overcame her, as if her heart was suddenly too large for her chest. The statue was of a woman with her head bowed. She wore robes that draped over her demurely. From her back sprouted wings.

Wings.

Flying on a broom was the most wonderful thing Rachel knew of, but...

Wings?

As if in a dream, Rachel landed her broom and walked forward. Coming to stand directly before the statue of mossy stone, she reached up and touched its cheek. It felt cold and smooth beneath her hand.

"What is it?" she whispered. "It's not an elf—it can fly. It's not a fairy—no butterfly wings. It's not a pixie—too big. And their wings look more like a dragonfly's. What could it be?"

The air was still, but the bough above her head bounced in the silence. Rachel stood before the statue and traced the moss that streamed like tears down its cheek. A hush had fallen over the glade, a feeling of expectation. She felt as if she had forgotten how to breathe. For the second time that morning, a tremendous sense of foreboding came over her, but what it foretold, whether good fortune or ill, she knew not.

CHAPTER TWO:

THE TREACHEROUS ART

OF MAKING FRIENDS

RELUCTANTLY LEAVING THE STATUE, RACHEL TOOK TO THE AIR. Enough sightseeing, she wanted her new life to begin. Zooming back to school, she went in search of the other broom-riding children she had seen from her window.

She spotted them flying along the gravel path between the dorms. There were three of them—blond girls about her age. They rode travel brooms. Their brightly-colored, sporty, metal flyers had handlebars, seats, and foot rests like a bicycle. Toward the back end of the flying device, the main shaft swept upward a hand's span, ending in an elegant metal fan consisting of three large blades that stuck out behind the device like a horizontal peacock tail. Travelers were practical and sturdy but not as maneuverable as Vroomie.

The first girl had striking green eyes and her straw-colored hair was pulled back by a gold-flecked headband. Her face was narrow with a spattering of freckles. The second girl was even prettier, though she wore lipstick and dark eyeliner, which Rachel did not think looked attractive on someone so young. She had an intelligent look to her face. The third girl was plainer and heavier than the other two, but her clothes were of excellent quality, with mother-of-pearl buttons on her white shirt and sapphires in her ears.

All three girls were dressed in subfusc—the most modern of the three forms of dress allowed at Roanoke—white button-down shirts, black skirts, long black ribbons that hung down from their necks like thin split ties, and a black half cape. They looked so smart in their handsome outfits, gaily chatting together.

Occasionally, one let go of her high handlebars to gesture expansively.

Girls who liked flying. Perfect for new friends!

Rachel had never had a proper friend. She was very fond of the cook's grandson, but Taddy only visited his grandmother for a few weeks each summer and at Yule. She also adored Benjamin, the son of her father's close friend, but again, the Bridges rarely came over. She often visited the tenant farmers on her family estate, but their children had school to attend and chores to do. They seldom had time to play.

Ever since her brother Peter left for school three years ago, Rachel had spent her free time by herself. Her days were spent wandering the long halls of Gryphon Park or roaming over the extensive grounds. She loved the enormous mansion as if it were a friend, but it was not the same as having a person for a friend. She had spent her time with nothing for company except her books, her pony, and, more recently, her broom.

Of all the things she had anticipated about coming to Roanoke, having a friend was the one she looked forward to the most. In the storybooks, school children had inseparable friends. Could these girls be destined to be hers? He heart thumping hopefully, Rachel flew next to the other children and waved.

The three girls turned and regarded her. Rachel's stomach tightened. She did not like their disdainful expressions. She gave them a big smile. When none of them returned it, the knot in her stomach grew tighter. It tightened six times more when she realized they were staring at her broom.

Rachel's broom was not a light weight aluminum device made by Ouroborus Industries, like the other girls were flying. Hers had been constructed in the old-fashioned way, by hand. The main shaft was deeply polished dark walnut. The ten, slender blades of the fan were alternating slats of mahogany and cherry wood. The shiny black leather seat was low to the shaft, to allow her to lean close and hook her feet up behind her if she wanted to steer manually; instead of using the levers next to the short handlebars. The fastenings, handlebars, and footrests were of black cast iron and shiny brass. In the early morning light, the three shades of reddish and dark wood gleamed brightly.

Rachel thought Vroomie was the most beautiful thing in the world.

"Hullo. Rachel Griffin. How do you do?" she called hopefully.

"Cydney Graves," said the girl with the green eyes, giving her a rather nice smile. Her American accent sounded strange to Rachel's ears. Cydney gestured at the pretty girl and then the plain one. "This is Belladonna Marley and Charybdis Nutt."

"Marley...as in Aaron Marley?" Rachel asked.

As soon as the words left her mouth, she regretted them. It was not good form to ask if a new acquaintance was related to one of the world's most infamous evil sorcerers, the archiomancer who had released the Terrible Five from their ancient prison and aided them in their reign of terror. Belladonna's eyes immediately grew hostile.

"He was my grandfather," she said coldly.

Rachel sat there, not certain what to say. How did one make friends?

"What kind of broom is that?" Cydney leaned sideways to get a better view. "It's too short for a traveler, too long and thin for a sports model, and it has far too big a fan for a racer."

"It's a steeplechaser," Rachel answered proudly. "They don't make many anymore."

"I can see why," Belladonna snorted in amusement. "It's made of wood! What's with that? Couldn't afford a real bristleless?"

"What is a steeple?" giggled Charybdis, as if eager to amuse the other two girls. "An animal they only have in England?"

The three girls snickered.

Pain slashed through Rachel's heart. Nothing had as much power to hurt her as insults to her precious broom. But she did not let it show. Keeping up a calm mask was a trick she and Sandra had learned from their mother at a young age. Her face remained thoughtful and solemn.

Rachel raised her head haughtily. "It is a very good broom. Much better than the ones you're riding!" Which also was not the right thing to say. But then, they had insulted Vroomie.

Cydney's eyes narrowed. "I will have you know that my broom is an O.I. Redbird Flycycle. You can't buy a better broom."

"She doesn't know a good broom from a bad one, Cydney. Look how tiny she is. She can't be a student. She must be somebody's baby sister." Belladonna moved closer, circling Rachel. "Are those even your robes? Or did you put your big sister's clothes on this morning?"

Cydney gave Rachel's garments a cynical look. "Full-academic is so old-fashioned. Nobody wears it any more. Is your family too poor to buy new clothes?"

"No one wears full-academic except royalty," giggled Charybdis. "Dread and his cronies dress that way. So do the Romanovs, and some of the Starkadder princes."

Belladonna rolled her eyes. "Well, *she's* hardly royalty."

Rachel kept up her mask of calm. Inside, she felt crushed but also sadly amused. This last slight had missed its mark. True, she was not royalty; however, Rachel's father was the Duke of Devon and her proper title was Lady Rachel Griffin. It was impossible to get closer to royalty than her family, unless one were of royal blood. Duke was the highest of noble ranks, and the Griffins could trace their lineage back sixty-four generations, all the way back to Hyperborea, during the Roman Republic.

Since the Wise lived much longer than mundane folk, sixty-four generations was a very long time indeed. Even the Dutch and Japanese royal families, the oldest royal lines in the world, could not trace their lineage back beyond the Middle Ages, much less the Starkadders of Transylvania or the Von Dreads of the Kingdom of Bavaria. She did not know who the Romanovs were, unless the girls meant the family of the long-deposed Russian Tzar.

She considered explaining but thought better of it. Such claims smacked of boasting. One did not win friends by boasting —well, not the sort of friends she wanted.

Rachel looked at the three girls again, with their gold-flecked headbands and mother-of-pearl buttons. Realization dawned. These were the American *nouveau riche*, famous for flaunting their wealth. Coming to riches so recently, they did not understand the principle of true elegance. Rachel's family owned a town, but the Griffins did not parade around with jewels on their robes. They had far too much class for that.

Not that Rachel disliked Americans. In fact, she much admired the spirit of bravery and independence they exhibited. But she was beginning to fear she might not like these particular Americans. She felt sorry for these girls. But the sorrow was tinged with a fear.

Perhaps she was not going to find friends here after all.

The four of them emerged from the forest and flew onto the emerald green lawns of the Commons, the fields that stretched from the main building down the length of the campus to the lily pond. The three girls veered left. Rachel veered right, putting a little distance between herself and the others. It was easy to remain unfazed while someone insulted her; that was part of her mother's training. It was more difficult to keep up the brave front once the initial onslaught was over. Sometimes, it felt as if the emotions she had deflected swung around like a boomerang and hit her from behind, bruising her all the harder on the return.

She bent low and clenched her handlebars. She suddenly felt very lonely.

With the forest and the western dorms behind them, the main campus stretched out in either direction. To their left lay the reflecting lake with its small pleasure boats. The boats had eyes painted on them and could move of their own accord. On the far side of the lake rose the main building, great Roanoke Hall. The dining hall was in the center. The right side housed the Upper School; the left side housed the college.

Roanoke Hall resembled the Chateau de Chambord, which Rachel's family had visited in France. Like Chambord, the hall had been designed by the great sorcerer Leonardo da Vinci. It was a massive castle with enormous round towers. Dozens of lesser spires and gables graced the roof. Six bell towers rose above the rest.

It seemed to Rachel as if the towers and spires called to her, as if they were whispering, asking her to fly between them— preferably at high speed. She gripped her handlebars tightly, smiling, eager to accept the challenge.

What a wonderful place to own a broom!

The forest flanked the main chateau and the reflecting lake. Through the trees—birches and hemlocks, she could see the towers of the other dormitories, including Dee Hall, where she had secretly hoped to be assigned, even though generations of her family had all lived in Dare Hall. Each dorm was devoted to students studying one of the seven Sorcerous Arts. Each had its own character and nature.

To the right, the Commons stretched several hundred yards to a lily-covered pond. On the far side of the lawns were walled gardens, ivy-covered out-buildings, the gymnasium upon which grew purple wisteria, and an Oriental garden. On the closer side of the Lily Pond, in the distance, were fountains, statues, and a tall, domed memorials. In the distance, beyond the pond, she could make out the double row of trees leading to the docks. She could also hear the creek, which ran through the woods to the east.

Near the reflecting lake, an astonishingly handsome boy with golden curls was chasing a long red and gold ribbon that whipped through the air. He charged forward laughing loudly as he went. The other girls flying with Rachel stared at him, mesmerized.

No. He was not chasing a ribbon. He was chasing *a dragon.*

"Sigfried Smith!" shouted the three girls in unison. Rachel feared they were going to swoon and fall from their brooms. She glanced at the boy with interest and saw they were correct. It was Sigfried the Dragonslayer, the most famous boy in the World of the Wise.

The girls began all babbling at once.

"They say he's an orphan. And raised in the mundane world, too!"

"In a truly Dickensian orphanage, in the worst part of London."

"And he's rich as Croesus!"

"Do you think he really killed a dragon in the London sewers?"

"A giant one. All scales and fire!"

"I saw a picture in *Mirror of the Wise.*"

"Where else would an orphan boy get a fortune?"

In unison, they all crooned, "And he's got a pet dragon!"

Rachel turned away with a pang of regret. The boy looked so charming and energetic, but there was no point in joining the gaggle. With so many pretty girls to choose from, a boy like that—handsome, famous, and rich—would never pick someone undersized and awkward with people, like Rache,l for a friend.

Instead, she zoomed forward and looked more closely at the dragon creature, as it zig-zagged along the edge of the reflecting lake. Its long serpentine body—which sometimes seemed to be ten feet long and sometimes twenty—was covered with soft golden fur on top and ruby scales on the underside. Its frippery—immensely long whiskers, tail puff, and the mane that ran down the length of its body—were flame red. Short horns curled above its almost wolf-like head. It was a *lung,* a river spirit from the Far East. Only, according to the News Glass, no one had ever seen one like Sigfried's.

It was so beautiful. She wished she could reach out and pet it.

The dragon turned and looked at her with its large jade eyes. Their gazes met. He looked so intelligent, so mentally active, Rachel could not help smiling.

"Flying brooms! Wicked cool!" Sigfried exclaimed behind her. He had an English accent, too, though it was working class. Still, the familiarity of it made her feel more at home. Turning, Rachel saw him peering closely at Belladonna's red bristleless.

"Where do you attach the bombs, then?" Sigfried peered at the device. "These things look like they don't even have missile bays! How do you expect to blow up a lecture hall during a dull class without missiles?"

Rachel burst out laughing. Behind her the three blonds giggled, but they seemed uncertain, as if they did not know what to make of him.

"What a cute accent!" exclaimed Charybdis, batting her blond eyelashes at him.

Watching the girls gush over the famous boy amused Rachel. She did not like them, but she had to admit they made a pretty picture, all giggling and blushing in their smart black and white uniforms. She bet the boy liked it.

Boys were like that.

Rachel herself was not much interested in boys, except for her enduring crush from afar on John Darling, the son of world famous James Darling, Agent. With a start, she realized that John, who was one of the school's stars at Track and Broom, must be somewhere on campus. The thought made her slightly breathless.

"How fast can it go?" Sigfried ignored the girls, his entire attention on their brooms. He leaned over them, poking at the levers and the fans. "If I fly fast enough, can I ram through a wall? Can it emit an oil slick and make people skid in mid-air? Do people freeze if they fly too high, so that their corpses circle the earth forever? Have any sorcerers taken a broom to the Moon? Mars? If not, I want to be the first person on Mars!" He stared up hungrily at the sky. Grinning again, he asked, "Can I have a go?"

Rachel laughed again. The boy was outrageous. If she had a friend like this, she would always be laughing. The other girls did not seem to be catching on.

"I...guess you can try it." Belladonna bit on a lock of her shoulder length hair. "Though if you've never flown before, it's tricky. You might want to wait for gym class."

"One of you could give him a ride," suggested Rachel.

The other students turned. The gazes of the three young women were not friendly. Rachel blushed. She had not meant to draw attention to herself. She started to pull back, but the boy gave her a grin so bright that the gleam from his teeth could have blinded sailors on passing flying ships. Perhaps, he, too, enjoyed hearing a familiar accent.

"I guess you could sit on the shaft." Belladonna gestured at the long pole behind her seat. "People used to do that all the time, before the idea of adding seats became popular."

"Great! I want to go see Stony Tor." Sigfried spoke with tremendous enthusiasm. His startlingly blue eyes glittered with manic delight. "I hear there's an evil goblin trapped there! The Heer of Dunderhead or something. Can we see him? Will he be cross if we poke him with a stick? What if we shoot him with fireballs? Do we learn to throw fireballs here? All magicians in stories throw fireballs—or so I've been told. Haven't read a lot of stories, outside King Arthur. Do we get to be knights?"

"We are not allowed to cross the wards that protect school grounds." Cydney spoke with haughty primness. Rachel guessed the harshness of her tone was directed at Belladonna, for being the first to offer to take the cute boy for a ride. "Crossing the wards without the proper precautions could let something unpleasant through the protections."

"How disappointing." Sigfried scowled in annoyance.

Rachel's heart went out to him. "Why don't you take him without crossing the wards?"

"Duh! Stony Tor is outside the school grounds," Cydney looked at Rachel as if she were a particularly unpleasant bug.

Undaunted, Rachel rolled her eyes. "Leave by the door. Go out through the ruined castle and down the green steps to where the ferry docks. Then fly around the island to the north. That's what my big sister Laurel says she does when she wants to sneak out."

"I don't think we're supposed to do that," Belladonna broke in hastily.

"Well, no one ever said that to me, so the rule doesn't apply." Sigfried spoke with extreme confidence.

"Besides," Charybdis said, a slight tremble to her voice, "If we fly away from the island, we might get confused by the Obscuration and get lost."

Rachel smiled a secret smile. She murmured, "*I* won't get confused."

She turned to where Sigfried stood on the damp morning grass, his bare feet sticking out from under his brand new robes. He looked so eager and so filled with enthusiasm. Similar to laughter and yawning, Rachel realized, enthusiasm was contagious.

Like two dappled roads cutting through a dark forest, the dilemma branched before her. Should she take the safe path and say nothing? Or take the unknown path and risk leaving school grounds—which was surely against some rule—to forge a bond with a boy she had just met?

In less time than it took a tongue of flame to flicker, she had made her decision—just like when flying.

Rachel leaned forward and patted the back of the long leather seat on her steeplechaser, her eyes sparkling with glee. "Come on, Sigfried Smith. I'll take you for a ride."

CHAPTER THREE:

TWINKLING OF AN EYE

RACHEL AND SIGFRIED FLEW ACROSS THE LAWNS, OVER THE LILY pond, and down the tree-lined pathway leading to the docks. Green boughs formed an arch above the mossy walkway. The sun shining through the leaves bathed them in a verdant light.

The archway of a ruined castle loomed before them. Rachel shot through it, bursting into the brilliant sunlight. Grass-clogged steps led from the ruins of the ornate castle to the dock on the brown waters of the Hudson. In a burst of gold and scarlet, Lucky the Dragon flew up beside them. He moved effortlessly through the air, almost as if he were swimming.

"Whoa!" Sigfried cried, holding onto her waist tightly. "This is incredible! Can we turn upside down? Can we spin? Can we twirl in a circle fast enough to churn milk into cheese?"

"I think you mean butter." Rachel grinned gleefully, eager to meet any broom challenge. "Here we go! Hold on tight!"

Angling Vroomie upward, she flew a full Immelman loop, then spun sideways—upside-down to right-side up again. That covered "turn upside down" and "spin." Next came: the butter churn. Spinning while diving was not a move Rachel had practiced, certainly not while carrying a rider. She paused and pictured it in her head, calculating the forces involved.

Confident she could pull it off, she dove. They plummeted down, spinning as they went—her best imitation of a butter churn. The dragon flickered along beside them like a flag in the wind.

"Woohoo! Ride 'em, Cowboy!" whooped the boy. He shouted to his dragon. "Lucky, this is the greatest ride ever!"

Pulling up, Rachel glanced over at the red and gold creature. "Do you talk, too?"

The dragon slipped backward until its head came level with Sigfried's and whispered. "Uh...Boss. The girl asked me if I talk, too. *'Too'*...in addition to what? What do I say?"

The boy hissed back. "Shhh." Aloud he said, "Of course not. Animals don't talk."

"I heard two talk last night," Rachel blurted out.

"Did you? Do animals talk in the world of the Wise? Isn't that what they call us magical folk? The Wise? As in anyone who doesn't know about magic isn't...wise, I mean? What do you call normal people? Ignoramuses?"

Rachel giggled. "No. We call them the Unwary."

"Unwary? Wouldn't Uninformed be more accurate?" Sigfried asked. "As to the Wise? Wise what? Wise guys? Wiseacres? Are your farms intelligent because they have such wise acreage? And where do these knowledgeable acres come from, anyway? Edinburgh? Oz? The moon?"

Rachel giggled so hard she almost could not answer. "If you mean: where do the members of the World of the Wise come from? We are descended from Immortals."

"Immortal...what?

"Fairies. Elves. Ogres. Gods. Selkie. Mermaids. All sorcerers are descended from immortal creatures. We Griffins trace our lineage back to Abaris the Hyperborean, who could ride through the sky on a magic arrow—which I like to think of as the precursor to our modern brooms. Maybe that's why I am such a good broom rider."

"We're all descended from something? That's ace! Do I get to pick? I want to be a dragon!"

"Why a dragon?"

"Then Lucky and I could be brothers." His voice sounded so fierce that Rachel twisted on the broom and looked over her shoulder. Sigfried's eyes gleamed with fiery intensity.

"Lucky?"

"Lucky is my dragon's name."

"Oh!" Rachel said, delighted that the boy was so fond of his furry serpent friend. The dragon flew along beside him, his long whiskers flickering as he gazed fondly at his master.

"What about you?" Sigfried asked. "What do you want to be?"

Now it was Rachel's turn. Her voice rang with fervent conviction. "I want to know everything!"

"Normally, I would assume that was impossible," Sigfried said seriously. "But a month ago, I thought sorcerers and flying brooms were impossible. Can it be done?"

"No," she admitted, smiling sheepishly. "Not even among the Wise. I figure if my goal is to know everything, I'll strive harder. In the end, I'll know more than if I had settled for less."

"Know everything?" Sigfried paused, perhaps thinking. She felt his body move as he nodded. "I approve. I give you my permission to continue your quest."

Rachel snorted, but underneath, she felt grateful. He had not laughed. No one else had ever taken her desire to know everything seriously.

"What about boring things?" Sigfried asked with great seriousness.

"I find nearly everything interesting. I read books on every subject I can get my hands on." Rachel paused and then added thoughtfully, "I guess what I really want is to know about the things that other people don't know."

"You mean secrets! So you can hoard them?" Sigfried bumped knuckles with his dragon, who curled in his claws. "I approve of hoarding."

Ordinarily, Rachel refrained from telling people her deepest desires. Sharing them made her feel as if she were opening her rib cage and trusting her beating heart to other people's grubby fingers. This time, the truth came tumbling out.

"So I can be the one to share these secrets," Rachel whispered softly. "Do you know what it is like? That moment when you look into someone else's face, and, suddenly, you have their full attention—their expression changes, their shoulders straighten, their pupils widen—because you've told them something they did not know, something that fascinates them, something marvelous or terrifying."

"But...if you tell them, you won't be the only person who knows."

"Then, I shall just have to find even more secret things, so I shall have even more things to tell." Rachel flashed him a grin over her shoulder. "You see how knowing everything would come in handy."

"Huh…" Sigfried said. Rachel could feel him shrug. "I guess so. But back to brooms. Your arrow-riding ancestor. Could he ride his arrow into his opponent and bash in his skull? And can everyone ride a broom? Or only your family?"

"Anyone can ride a broom," Rachel replied, "but very few people are as good as I am."

She flew up the coast, the wind in her face. As she rounded an outcropping of rocks, she skimmed too close to the river. The enchanted wake of the steeplechaser sent up a peacock's tail of spray. Cold drops fell on the bare skin of her neck. She squealed, as much in delight as in dismay. Sigfried shouted in surprise.

Thick forests of hemlocks grew along the shore. Beyond the trees rose the rolling hills that made up the northern portion of the island.

"So, Sigfried, ahead of us…"

"Call me Siggy. All my friends do. Or they would, if I had friends. I'm not sure that Freckles, Banger, and Shanks back at the orphanage count as friends. They were more like the enemies of my enemy."

"I've never had a proper friend before either," Rachel said shyly. "I realized today that I am not sure how it is done. Making friends, I mean."

"Let's just agree! We'll be friends. You can be my first ever real friend! Other than Lucky, of course."

"Very good." Rachel grew pink with delight. "We're friends! You, me, and Lucky! Well, Siggy…up ahead is the tor where the evil goblin is imprisoned. Shall we take a look?"

"You bet! Can we set him free?"

Rachel giggled again, a mixture of nervousness and joy. The sheer audacity of her new friend amused her. "Probably not today. We'd need to learn more magic first."

"Too bad. It's wrong to kill someone who's tied up. It's not sportsman like," Siggy said seriously. "I'd like to see him blast something. With lightning, right? That would be ace!"

Above the hills rose Stony Tor, bald and rocky. Rachel circled it, sure to glance at the entire landscape. Any detail her eyes fell on now, she could pull up in her perfect memory and examine at her leisure.

On the far side of the tor, a deep valley lay between its stony slope and the hills beyond. At the bottom, late summer flowers bloomed in a grassy meadow. The steep sides seemed to call to her, and Rachel could not resist. She dived down at high speed, slingshotting up the far side, Siggy whooping behind her.

As she circled back, an odd pile of boulders on the tor caught her eye. She flew closer. A cave mouth had been sealed with very large rocks. The stones surrounding the cave were carved with runes and arcane symbols. The place smelled of ozone.

"I bet this is the Heer of Dunderberg's prison." As she spoke the name, thunder crashed. The peal rolled out from behind the pile of boulders.

"It heard us!" she cried.

Shrieking in terror, the two children sped away. Rachel did not bother flying up and over the forest this time. She shot through the trees, darting around trunks at breakneck speed. Sigfried's grip around her waist grew tighter and tighter.

Flying through the woods at top speeds proved as much fun as barreling down long corridors and negotiating spiral staircases. Rachel's favorite flying was the kind that required split-second decisions. She pictured everything around her, calculating how moving the levers or tilting her body would affect the torque of the broom, the speed of her progress, the sweep of the tail fan. Siggy's grip became so tight that Rachel could hardly breathe. When they missed striking a gnarly oak by a splinter's length, he screamed.

"Don't be such a baby," Rachel replied cheerfully.

The moment the words left her mouth, she mentally kicked herself. Mocking her new friend was as bad as bringing up the subject of Aaron Marley. Apparently, this making a friend business was more difficult than she had expected.

To her utter delight, Siggy was not daunted.

"Right..." he muttered hoarsely, but the tone of his voice implied that he had accepted her implied challenge. He did not scream again, even when she deliberately took them directly at a giant oak, only swerving within a few inches of the trunk. She could feel him tremble, but he remained stoically silent.

Had she been alone, she would have flown even closer before she swerved, but she dared not put her passenger at risk. As Vroomie moved effortlessly, its cherry and walnut blades spreading and retracting as she moved the levers, Rachel grinned. She had not been boasting when she told the blond girls that hers was the better broom.

Ahead, trees grew so close to each other that they formed a vast bark wall. This marked the wards of the school. Rachel veered to the west and flew along the coast. As she rounded the rocky point, approaching the ruined castle, a flash appeared on the docks—a bright, narrow pillar of light that went up as far as the eye could see. It swirled, quicker than the eye could track, forming bones, organs, and then flesh, all made of glowing whiteness. Color flooded in, and a man stood there. He walked toward the stairs and the path to the school.

He was dressed in an Inverness cloak. The half-cape along the back billowed in the breeze. His dark hair was drawn into a pony-tail. Around his neck, he wore a medallion showing a lantern surrounded by stars.

"An Agent!" Rachel cried, delighted. She urged the broom forward. "My father is an Agent. I wonder what..."

The man turned toward them. He had a pleasant face with eyes of mild blue. There was nothing wrong with his face—except that Rachel had never seen it before—*which meant...*

A feeling like a thousand spiders crawled along her spine.

"Excuse me, Children," the man called to them. "I am looking for a student. Her name is Valerie Foxx. Can you tell me where to find her?"

A choice lay before her. Like deciding which lever to pull when flying at an oak at thirty-five miles an hour, she had to choose instantly. She had only the length of time it took a single flame to flicker.

Rachel chose.

Leaning forward, she let her eyes go wide and innocent. She was good at that. It was one of the few advantages of being so little. "Is that the girl with the short blond hair and the Norwegian

Elk Hound? She came yesterday, but she was an Unwary. She did not like it here. She went home."

The man scowled, muttered his thanks, and disappeared in a narrow pillar of light.

"Wow! That looked incredible!" Sigfried cried, "You could see his skeleton! And his liver? Or was that his spleen? If I grabbed something while he was like that, would he arrive all twisted? What was that, anyhow? The flashy-disappeary thing?"

"It's called Jumping," Rachel replied, only barely paying attention. She shot through the arch and barreled down the green wooded way, pushing her broom as fast as it could go. The trees whipped by. Wind streamed through her hair, pulling out her barrettes.

"That's weird..." Siggy shouted to be heard over the winds. "That Victory Flock, or whatever her name was, would go home without even staying the night, I mean."

"Valerie Foxx. She didn't. I lied."

"Do you lie a lot?"

Rachel shook her head and shouted back over the rush of air. "No."

"You did it very well for an amateur." Siggy sounded impressed. "If you like, I can give you some tips."

"Er...thanks?" Her broom picked up speed. "Now we have to go find Valerie Foxx! She was on the ferry with me yesterday. We have to warn her."

"Why?" he shouted back.

"Because that man was pretending to be an Agent."

"An Agent of what?"

"Of the Wisecraft."

"What's that?"

"It's the law enforcement branch of the Parliament of the Wise, our governing body. The Wisecraft is responsible for stopping rogue sorcerers and for hiding the World of the Wise from the mundane world."

"Why does this Kraftcheese do that—hide the magical world?"

"To keep us safe. And to keep the Unwary safe from us. Real witch hunts tend to leave a lot of dead in their wake," Rachel explained loudly. "The important thing is that Agents are our law enforcement guys. So don't cross 'em."

"You mean...they are the bobbies? The cops? The fuzz? The pigs? The rozzers? The police?"

"In part. They also keep the supernatural world from hurting humans. They are part soldier, part magical policemen, part animal control—if you take animals to include basilisks and chimera and dragons."

"So this guy was impersonating an officer?"

"Yes."

Siggy shouted over the wind, "If this agent is an impostor, let's go find him and kill him."

"We can't kill him!"

"Why not? I've killed a dragon."

"People are different."

"Not evil people. So, how do you know he's a fake?"

"Because I did not recognize him."

"You know all the policemen?"

"I went to a Wisecraft banquet recently with my father, who is an Agent," Rachel shouted, as the broom burst out of the forest and torpedoed toward the Commons. The lily pond flashed beneath them. She did not bother to explain that her father was no longer a normal Agent. He still worked for the Wisecraft, but he had been transferred to some clandestine project, the nature of which Rachel did not know. "All the Agents in the world were present. They said so. I made a point of looking at everyone's face."

"Any chance there was a bloke at the banquet whose face you don't remember?"

"No," Rachel answered grimly. "None."

CHAPTER FOUR:
THE AWKWARD RESCUE
OF VALERIE FOXX

THE TWO CHILDREN SPED ACROSS THE COMMONS, PASSING THE GYM and the walled garden. The doors of the main building were open for breakfast. Rachel shot by the startled proctors, rocketed through the dining hall, glanced rapidly from side to side, and zoomed out the other side into the grassy interior courtyard. As she soared upward over the many spires of Roanoke Hall, she reviewed her memory of the children eating breakfast, rapidly examining each face in the crowd. The girl she sought was not among them.

Rachel flew over the lawns of the Commons again, searching. She did not know which dorm Valerie lived in. If the girl was inside, Rachel would have no way to find her. At the far end of the Commons, she circled the memorial to Taliesin the Brave, flew over the fountain that looked like a young tree with water cascading from every branch, and buzzed the lily pond—sending the sea fairies who lived therein diving for cover. Wind rushed by her ears at a low roar. Behind her, Siggy whooped loudly.

There was no sign of Valerie Foxx. Rachel was not deterred. She seldom grew frustrated when she had put her mind to something.

"Hey!" Siggy called. "Did you say short blond hair? How about that one?"

Below them and to the right was a walled garden. Purple blooms of wisteria grew along the trellis-like fence that made up part of the stone wall. In the center of the garden, mosaics surrounded a marble basin. In the middle of the shallow pool, a fat-cheeked cherub with a curling fish tail blew a fountain out of its trumpet. To one side, sitting on a bench, two girls pored over the latest issue of *Wise Wear* magazine. One was pretty, with short flaxen hair and a squarish jaw. She had a pile of notebooks next to her. An old-fashioned camera on a red strap hung over her shoulder. A silver and black Norwegian Elk Hound, with thick fur and a curling tail, lay with its muzzle resting on her feet. Rachel recognized her as Valerie Foxx.

The other girl was gorgeous with long, wavy blond hair, impish cheeks, and eyes that seemed almost luminescent. She also was the most well-endowed young teen Rachel had ever seen, but this might have been because her black and white subfusc outfit had been tailored to display her figure to best advantage. Her white blouse strained at the buttons, and her black pleated skirt was shorter than the knee-length specified by the school handbook.

Out of the corner of her eye, Rachel noted that Siggy had noticed as well. When the young woman stood up and bent over, his face turned red, and he averted his eyes—an unusually knightly response from a low-born boy. Rachel understood that boys liked curves.

For Rachel's part, she found the girl's display vulgar. She shuddered. If she had such a figure, she would wear baggy robes. She had no desire to be ogled by boys. Still, Sigfried's reaction intrigued her. Rachel knew her own ideas of decorum were in a minority. She had spent her early childhood with her grandparents, who had been born during the reign of Queen Victoria. How had a boy raised in a horrid mundane orphanage developed such an old-fashioned sense of propriety?

"Were there any girls at the orphanage?" she asked curiously, as she zoomed toward the walled garden.

"Only the nuns."

"Really? What order were they with?"

"Hestia, Goddess of Home and Hearth," he replied bitterly. "They weren't home-like at all. They were horrid."

"Do you like girls?" she inquired teasingly.

He answered indignantly. "I like ladies. What knight would risk life and limb and third-degree burns to slay a dragon for a trollop?"

"Did the nuns teach you how gentlemen and ladies should act?"

Siggy snorted disdainfully. "Are you kidding? They never talked to us except to shout or hit us with a ruler. I learned about knights and ladies from a book I stole from the library and hid under my mattress so that the nuns would not confiscate it."

"What was the book about?"

"King Arthur and his knights."

The corner of Rachel's lips kept quirking upward despite her efforts to restrain her amusement. He spoke of knights and ladies and hid books under his mattress. "Sigfried Smith, I believe we shall be very good friends indeed."

Rachel landed in the courtyard. Sigfried leapt from the broom, threw himself down on the mosaics, and kissed the ground repeatedly. The two girls stared at him in fascination.

"Never rode a broom before." Rachel offered by way of an explanation. Both girls nodded. From their reactions, she surmised that Miss Foxx had never ridden a broom either, but that the other young woman had. "You're Valerie Foxx, right?"

The short-haired girl flashed a pixie grin. "That's me. Valerie Foxx, fearless girl reporter."

"There's a man looking for you!"

"Really?" She began gathering her magazines. "Where is he? Is he one of the tutors? That's what they call professors here, right?"

"No!" Rachel waved her arms, barring Valerie's way. "I mean, yes—tutors. But, no...don't go looking for him! He's not a good man. He's bad. I sent him off, but I'm rather sure he'll be back when he discovers I lied to him. You've got to hide."

"How do you know he's bad?" The second girl looked up from her magazine, her eyes fairly dancing with curious amusement.

"Because he was impersonating an Agent."

"But he wasn't an Agent?" asked the second girl.

"No."

"Are you sure?" she asked, even more curious.

"If he were an Agent, I would have known," Rachel replied firmly.

"Oh-kay," she drawled, glancing at Valerie. "What do we do now?"

Rachel blinked. She had only thought as far ahead as warning Valerie. She had not considered what to do next.

"Who are you?" Siggy asked the second girl, averting his eyes so as not to stare at her ample charms. Seated on the bench, Valerie noted this and pressed her lips together, amused.

"I am Salome Iscariot." The lovely blond put a hand on her hip, which she jutted out.

"Of Iscariot Enterprises?" Rachel stepped closer, intrigued.

"Of course."

"You've heard of her?" Siggy said, but he looked at Valerie, who gave him a pretty smile. He returned it with a blinding smile of his own. She blinked, a bit dazed.

"Of her family's business," Rachel said. "She's the richest girl in the world."

"Very likely." Salome's smile showed perfect white teeth. "There are blockbuster actresses who have less in their personal accounts than I do. It would be the greatest life possible, if I didn't have to contend with the most evil mother ever to breathe or shop. Who are you?"

Sigfried scowled darkly at Salome's complaint about her mother, as if the comment offended him personally.

"I am Lady Rachel Griffin, daughter of the Duke of Devon," Rachel replied primly, aware that her hair had escaped its barrettes yet again.

"Ooo! You're Ambrose Griffin's daughter!" Now it was Salome's turn to be impressed. To Valerie, she said, "Her father is a famous Agent."

"The one you were telling me about?" Valerie opened a notebook and flipped through it.

"No, that was James Darling. Darling is legendary. Griffin is merely famous."

"Speaking of famous," Rachel tried to keep the sparkle out of her eye and failed, "this young man here is Sigfried Smith."

Both girls squealed with joy. They moved close to him, asking a thousand questions about his life, his dragon, his gold, his fight against the dragon in the sewer. He answered with a casual, devil-may-care attitude. This only fueled their fervor.

Turning to look for the dragon, Rachel noticed for the first time that there was another girl seated in the walled garden. Long pale golden hair floated about her like spun sunlight. She had the most lovely face with blue eyes, a pert little nose, and rosebud lips. She sat motionlessly, reading a textbook, her expression so sadly sweet that it almost hurt to look at her. She looked like a princess from a storybook.

Like Rachel, she was dressed in full academic black robes with a golden crest over her left breast. Golden crest meant royalty—she was a princess! Rachel had the right to wear a silver crest, but her parents had only put crests on her very best robes. Leaning closer, Rachel frowned in consternation. She had memorized *Burke's Peerage* and *Registry of the Noble Wise,* but she had never seen this crest before. What nation had an emu on their heraldry?

Siggy straightened. "He's back! That man!"

"What?" Rachel cried. "How do you know?"

"I...saw a flash down the way we had come."

Rachel checked her memory. She had been looking that direction, but her eyes had not picked up a flash. But if he was lying about that, how did he know?

"He's coming," Siggy insisted. "Should I go kill him?"

"You can't kill people." Rachel stamped her foot. "I told you that."

Siggy spread his arm, gesturing toward the docks. "It's more difficult to burn someone's face off and keep him alive. Killing is easier. And you don't have to worry about retaliation."

Rachel glared at him. "No killing!"

"What about a very severe scalding?"

"No."

"Then what?"

Salome grabbed Siggy's hand. "Let's go talk to him. He's not looking for us."

"Okay!"

They ran off. Rachel sighed. Salome obviously thought she had scored points by getting the famous boy to herself. Rachel did not care. Siggy was her first friend, true, but he was not the kind of boy she would want for a boyfriend. Too wild for one thing. She did care about Siggy's safety, though. If the man searching for Valerie was willing to impersonate an Agent, what else might he do?

Valerie looked up, notebook and pen in hand. "A girl reporter must gather facts to be useful. What does this man look like? Did he have any distinguishing marks or tattoos?"

Rachel described him as best she could, wishing that she knew how to draw. She could picture him so clearly, could zoom in on every tiny detail in her perfect memory. Without a Thinking Glass, however, she could not convey to someone else what she had seen.

"Sorry. No idea." Valerie shook her head. "That could be a number of people. None of whom have a reason to come looking for me."

Rachel squatted down and let her fingers trail over the thick, soft fur of the Norwegian Elk Hound. The dog licked her hand. "What's his name?"

"Payback. And it's a her," Valerie drawled. "Because Payback's a bitch."

Rachel, who lived on an estate with a dog kennel that bred hunting hounds, understood exactly what Valerie meant. She began to giggle.

Siggy and Salome came running back, faces flushed. Salome's chest rose and fell rapidly.

"He is an Agent," she reported. "I saw his badge. It was legit."

"No!" Siggy interrupted her, scowling in annoyance. "That's not what happened. I just told you. The man held up a blank piece of paper. He told you it was a badge. I could feel it in my head, trying to make me think stuff. But I'm too quick for the coppers! I didn't let it get to me! Then, he asked you where Valerie was, and you told him. He's coming."

"Oh, that's right," Salome frowned in confusion. "Evil paper. You told me. But...he had an official paper, too, right?"

"She's ensorcelled." Rachel stared. She had never seen anyone under a compulsion spell.

"The guy is coming!" Siggy repeated.

"W-what should I do?" Valerie asked, her face going pale.

Fear gnawed at her stomach. Rachel thought and thought, but this was not like flying. She did not have a set of skills in place for hiding from bad men.

"Shouldn't we go get a proctor?" she asked.

"Never go to the grown-ups!" Sigfried cried fiercely "They will blame you, even if it's not your fault. They'll probably lock you in a closet and take your food away. Grown-ups are like that." Beside him, Lucky the Dragon bobbed his head in agreement.

"You may slip in here, if you wish." The beautiful princess spoke with a slight Australian accent. Her speech had an air of formality, her words measured and enunciated. Putting down her book, she opened her purse. Inside was a staircase.

"Wow! A staircase in a bag!" Siggy grabbed Valerie's arm and hustled her toward the purse. "In you go!"

Valerie ducked in and ran down the staircase.

"What's in there?" Siggy asked. "Is it safe? Will it eat her?

"A house," the lovely princess replied with good humor as she closed the bag. She gave them a sweet look that made the day brighter, as when sun had broken through heavy clouds. "A modest one, I fear, but fully furnished and provisioned. Your companion should be quite comfortable for the duration of her visit."

Rachel's eyes grew large. She had only ever seen purses with a space the size of a room inside. Siggy looked skeptical, as if he thought the princess might be teasing him.

The princess stood up and extended her hand. "Lady Rachel Griffin, as there is nobody here to present me, I shall have to introduce myself. I am Nastasia Romanov, Princess of Magical Australia."

Rachel shook her hand, curtseying. With a shy yet brave smile, the princess curtseyed in return. Salome made a noise of amused impatience.

Nastasia regarded Salome as if she were a quaint exhibit at a county fair. "Would you be so kind as to introduce the commoners to me?"

Rachel nodded. "This is Sigfried Smith."

"Mr. Smith." The princess shook his hand. "Your exploits are known to us in Magical Australia. I applaud your bravery."

"Why, thank you, your highness." Siggy bowed over her hand, looking pleased. "Are you a real princess? That's extraordinary! Do you get to be queen someday? Do you own hoards of gold? Or do you own flocks of servants who you could order to go out and fetch more gold? Or, being from Australia, do you prefer opals? Me, I want to be a dragon when I grow up!"

"Um…" The princess wet her perfect lips, taken aback by the barrage of questions. "I…don't think people can turn into dragons. Not and still be intelligent, at any rate."

"That's not fair!" Siggy said crossly. He stomped on the water in the little marble pool. Droplets of water sprayed up. A few struck Rachel's cheek.

She sighed and continued, "And this is Salome Iscariot."

The two girls shook hands. Nastasia's face went a bit pale. She withdrew from the other girl's grasp. Rachel thought she looked slightly ill.

"Commoners!" cried Salome, perhaps recalling the offence due to Nastasia's quick retreat. "I'll have you know my parents run the second largest private enterprise in the world."

"Nonetheless, you are a commoner," the princess replied, not unkindly.

"I am much richer than you could ever dream of being, girl from a country I've never heard of!" Salome announced, her eyes flashing.

"Undoubtedly true, Miss Iscariot. I never dream about mere money, and beyond the borders of my own kingdom I am a pauper, as no foreign nation recognizes the currency of Magical Australia. That fact is, however, irrelevant. Money cannot buy blue blood, nor does a lack of wealth diminish it." The princess spoke graciously, unfazed by the other girl's show of temper. "Royalty comes with duties and obligations not required of those of common birth. Though we enjoy many advantages, our lives are not our own, but belong first to our country and our subjects. No matter how much wealth your family gathers, it cannot make you royalty, nor even nobility.

"However, there is no shame in being common, no insult in the term, nor does being born to high station make me better than anyone else. Only our actions, how we measure up to the duties we were born to, determine our worth. If you allow yourself to be groomed to take over your parents' financial empire, you will, perhaps, assume duties similar to those required of a royal princess and might one day rise to be the greatest and most worthy of commoners."

Rachel donned the mask of calm she had learned from her mother. Underneath, she danced with mirth. Salome was so outraged. Most likely, she had never met anyone who did not treat the daughter of the Iscariot financial empire as royalty. Rachel's sympathies were with the princess. She did believe in judging men on their merit. As the daughter of a duke, however, she also understood the obligations that came with rank, something that egalitarian Americans—despite their many other good qualities—often failed to grasp.

Footsteps rang against stone. The man with the pony-tail strode into the private garden, his Inverness cloak billowing. He looked around, frowning. His gaze fell over Rachel.

"Sorry," Rachel mumbled, her cheeks growing hot. "I thought she'd left."

"Where is she now?" The man spoke in a pleasant baritone.

"She went to the loo," Rachel lied.

"I have a package for her, a present. Can you give it to her?"

"Of course." The princess held out her hand. The man's pupil's widened at the beauty of the picturesque little girl.

Recovering his aplomb quickly, he gave her a mild smile and handed her a small white box. "Please tell her that this is from her father."

"Her father!" Salome exclaimed, shocked. When the man glanced her way, she managed a rather weak smile.

The false Agent left without another word. The children gathered around the box.

"Should...we open it?" Rachel asked.

"Certainly not. It is not ours." The princess replied, mildly offended at the very idea. "We must always do what is right. No matter the cost. Virtue and honor requires this of us."

"But...that man is evil!" Rachel insisted.

"Evil is a very strong word," the princess said cautiously, "but I do agree that there was something less than straightforward about him. Even if he is as you say, that does not grant us the right to act wickedly."

"I'll open it." Salome snatched the box from the princess, whose eyebrows arched in indignation, and opened it. Inside was an emerald and gold brooch shaped like a scarab. Rachel took a step back. The jeweled bug made her uneasy.

"Ooo, pretty!" Salome exclaimed.

Lucky the Dragon swooped over the wall and landed next to Sigfried, curling his tail around his human. "Okay, he's leaving. I..." He looked at the startled faces of Salome and Nastasia. "Er...was I supposed to be pretending not to talk?"

Siggy rolled his eyes. "Yes."

"Oops," murmured the dragon.

"Your dragon talks," Salome murmured, her eyes larger and more luminescent than ever.

The princess opened her bag and spoke into it. "He is gone. You may come out."

Valerie climbed out, holding her camera. The lens cap was off. "Darn! I should have had one of you take a picture of him."

Salome showed her the box. "He left you this. He said it was from your father."

"M-my father." Valerie's face went pale. "But I haven't seen him in..."

She reached for the box. The princess put a hand out to halt her. Valerie stopped.

"I recommend we bring this directly to the proctors," the princess stated. "It might be booby-trapped or cursed."

"Proctors?" asked Valerie.

"Hall monitors," explained Rachel. "Campus security."

"I think that choice should be up to Valerie," Salome objected tartly.

The box trembled. The scarab darted into the air and straight at Valerie. Darkness spread from it. Shouting, Siggy leapt in front of Miss Foxx. It struck him in the chest. He shouted in pain and staggered. The scarab tried to dart around him. Sigfried dodged in its way.

Rachel wanted to help, but her limbs refused to obey. Besides, what could she do? She had no magic yet, no flute, no familiar. Watching her new friend's bravery, Rachel vowed silently that she would become the best sorceress she could.

Never again did she want to be helpless and unable to act.

With a deafening roar, Lucky the Dragon lunged at the sooty cloud containing the scarab. A plume of fire shot out of his mouth. Darting forward, he scooped the burning brooch into his mouth. The children cheered.

"Mot it, M-Boss," Lucky muttered. His eyes went kind of funny. "Oh, mo!"

"It's hurting Lucky," Sigfried cried. "Lucky! Spit it out!"

"Mot to mget it out of here mirst." The dragon slithered up into the air and over the wall.

"Quick! After him!" Siggy shouted, his voice rough with desperation. His face was pale and slightly greenish. "We have to help Lucky!"

The dragon was the orphan boy's only family, Rachel realized suddenly. Freed from her paralysis, she grabbed her broom. Sigfried swung up behind her.

Ahead, Lucky flew in a zig-zag motion, engaged in an internal struggle. Across the Commons, students looked up, startled. Rachel scanned the lawns. Everyone was gawking fearfully. No one looked competent to help.

Out of the forest strode a college student. He was extremely tall. His cold, discerning gaze took in everything, as if he were surveying the campus with an eye to its defensibility and finding it wanting.

Rachel nearly lost control of her broom. If the princess was the most beautiful girl Rachel had ever seen, this was the most exquisite specimen of a male. He was startlingly handsome and perfectly built. The sunlight glinted off the red highlights in his dark hair. He wore full black robes and black leather gloves so thick they practically looked like gauntlets. Upon his chest blazed a golden royal crest.

He strode across the lawns toward them. Other students scurried out of his way like mice before a tiger.

Lucky the Dragon somersaulted onto the green lawns, twisting and bucking. Opening his mouth, he regurgitated the jeweled scarab. Darkness still billowed from it. In a single fluid motion, the prince pulled out a black and gold Fulgurator's wand and shot the flying brooch. Crackling white fire burnished with a golden tinge leapt from the sapphire at the wand's tip.

Rachel leaned forward. She knew about Eternal Flame, but she had never seen it. Tended by the Vestal Virgins, it burned the wicked but did not harm the innocent.

The blast struck the scarab. The metallic insect twitched and went rigid. Rachel waited with bated breath. The prince shot it a second time. A bolt of lightning leaped from the sapphire tip. The scarab brooch lay charred upon the grass. Kneeling, he poked it with his wand. As the last of the darkness dispersed, he ran a finger through it and brought it to his nose, sniffing.

Raising his wand, he gazed speculatively toward Lucky. Rachel shouted, waving her hands. The prince glanced up at her, frowning. Their gazes met. Something Rachel had never felt before, akin to a shiver but both more wonderful and more terrible, passed through her. He nodded and turned away, lowering his wand.

"Wow! Who is that?" Siggy asked, his voice aglow with hero worship.

Even without seeing the details of the crest on his chest, Rachel knew the answer. There was only one person he could be.

"Vladimir Von Dread," she replied. "The Prince of Bavaria."

CHAPTER FIVE:

THE DUBIOUS PROCESS OF BONDING

WITH FAMILIARS

"REALLY! I'M FINE!" SIGFRIED OBJECTED FOR THE TENTH TIME.
Rachel watched with concern from the side of the bed upon which the nurse had insisted Siggy rest. On the far side of the bed, the princess perched gracefully upon a chair, her lovely brow furrowed with care. Siggy had been unnaturally pale and somewhat green when he arrived. The nurse had played some enchanted healing music on her flute. He looked considerably better.

Nurse Moth was from the French branch of the far-reaching Moth family. She was a nervous, quick, bird-like woman with a large nose. She wore a nun's habit and a wimple. Rachel recognized the white-on-white outfit as belonging to the Order of Asclepius.

The Infirmary had green marble floors. Arcane healing symbols had been traced in silver on the pale blue tile walls. Overhead, painted puffy white clouds decorated a domed ceiling of periwinkle blue. An orrery hung there, the clockwork sun and planets able to rotate independently, so that the date and time could be adjusted for the room, to alter the celestial influences for healing purposes.

Flame-colored curtains separated the cots. Purple and green dragon-vein agate set into the beds were imbued with healing enchantments. Above each headboard hovered a glass ball burning with green health-giving fire. Chimes hung by the open windows, ringing in the breeze. In the center, a fountain gurgled.

Nurse Moth held up her scrutiny sticks, two rounded lengths of wood that were carved with runes and set with gems of different colors. As the nurse ran the sticks up and down Siggy's body, various gems flashed brightly.

"It is always wise to check. With the black magic, one never knows," Nurse Moth said in her French accent. She pronounced *the* like *zee*. "Just be still. It will be over soon."

"Soon by glacier years," Siggy muttered through clenched teeth.

The nurse *tsked* and continued her examination.

Finally, an ice age later, she straightened, rubbing her back. "I find nothing. Sit. I will get you a drink."

"That...wasn't so bad." Siggy looked faintly surprised and rather pleased.

The nurse continued, "In fifteen minutes, if you still feel fine, you may go to the Familiar Bonding Ceremony. But if you feel ill today, so much as an itch or a cough or a sniffle, come see me immediately, *non*?

Siggy nodded. "No...er...I mean, yes."

The nurse bustled off to her office.

Sigfried leaned forward and spoke in a hushed voice. "Do you think we'll get in trouble?"

"For saving Valerie?" Rachel's brows arched in surprised. "Why would we get in trouble for *saving* someone?"

"With adults, you never know." Siggy looked around suspiciously, as if expecting accusing adults to pour out of the walls and come for them.

The princess lay a comforting hand on his arm. "Fear not, young man. If anything should go amiss, I will go speak with the Dean. She and the Grand Inquisitor of the Wisecraft are friends of my family."

"Wow," Rachel murmured, impressed. "Your family has some very highly placed friends! The Grand Inquisitor is my father's boss!"

At the far end of the room, Valerie and Salome were being questioned by two proctors, whom Rachel recognized, as she had met them the previous day. Mr. Fuentes was a rather good-looking Hispanic young man with a big friendly smile. Mr. Scott was shorter and blond with a more serious cast of feature.

"I wish I knew what they were saying," she mused. She hated

being left out of the loop, especially when something was happening right in front of her.

"Do you really?" Siggy's eyes gleamed. "We...are friends, right?"

"Right!" Rachel turned to Nastasia. "Would you like to be our friend, too?"

Nastasia tilted her incomparably lovely head and gave the proposition due consideration. "A well-born girl and a hero? Both appropriate friends for a young woman of my station." She gave a little nod, blushing slightly. "I believe our being friends would be most agreeable indeed."

"We are all friends, then," Rachel raised her eyebrows in hopeful inquiry.

"Right!" Siggy spat in his palm and held it out toward the girls.

Ah. Another flick of a flame decision. How was her friendship with Sigfried to be? Was she going to let her new friend daunt her? Or was she going to prove her mettle? Taking a deep breath, she grabbed his goopy hand and shook.

Siggy looked impressed. "Now you are one of the boys."

Rachel grinned. Surreptitiously, she wiped her wet hand on her robes.

"*Noblesse oblige,*" Nastasia murmured. Her blue, blue eyes twinkled with a mixture of amusement and revulsion. With the resolve of a martyr refusing to show weakness in front of a firing squad, she shook Siggy's still-moist hand.

"Very good. We're all friends!" Rachel grinned, relieved that making friends had not proved as hard as she had first feared. "Now we can do important things together, like figure out why someone was trying to hurt Valerie! About the proctors over there..." She glanced in the direction of the door. The two proctors had stepped aside and were speaking privately to each other. Or so they thought. "Siggy, you were saying?"

Siggy tipped his head down and half-closed his eyes. "The dark-haired guy is saying—"

"His name is Mr. Fuentes," Rachel supplied.

Siggy said, "Fuentes is saying: '...new kinds of magic. This en*sorcelling paper sounds like yet another new magic. Maybe the scarab, too.*'" Siggy paused. "Now the blond guy..."

Rachel said quickly, "His name is Mr. Scott."

"Scott is saying, *'How are the Agents supposed to keep people safe if they are constantly faced with magic no one has seen before. Some of it is very dangerous.'*

"Now, Fuentes is saying, *'I don't know, Buddy. But it sure makes our job harder.'*

"Now, Scott: *'You can say that again!'*" Siggy paused and then continued as Scott did. "*'Do you think there could there be something to that report—that someone on campus intends harm to the students?'*"

"Now, Fuentes: *'Nah. If so, why would've they risked something so obvious as sending an operative from outside? Why not just attack Miss Foxx surreptitiously?'*"

"Now, Scott: *'Could the last of the Morthbrood be behind this? It's rumored that the ones who turned State's evidence gave the total number at three more than were apprehended.'*"

Siggy whispered to the girls, "Does he mean Mothbrood? Like Nurse Moth?"

Rachel shook her head quickly. "No. The Morthbrood are an ancient organization of bad sorcerers. The Moths are a huge family of the Wise descended from Lord Moth, an intimate of the fairy king and queen."

Siggy continued, "Fuentes: *'Aw, I don't know. People have been jumping at the shadow of the Terrible Five for twenty years now. Isn't it time for a new Big Bad? Not every bad German is a Nazi. Not every black magician's a Morth Brood. Come on. Let's go report to the boss.'*"

Siggy's voice fell silent.

"How are you doing that?" Rachel whispered in awe.

Siggy grinned. "Let's just say I have sharp hearing."

The Familiar Bonding Ceremony was held in the Oriental gardens with its flowering trees and picturesque arching bridges. Tiny waterfalls separated a series of koi ponds. A traditional *shishi odoshi* made a rhythmic *tock* noise, as pooling water caused the bamboo arm to swing from its up to its down position. When the wind blew, Japanese bells chimed.

In the center of the garden stood an ivory archway. Ivy grew over it, except at the very top where the Roanoke coat-of-arms was displayed: a seven-branched tree atop a winged floating island. Standing torches, their flames dancing merrily, marked the pathway leading to the arch.

Rachel looked around eagerly, drinking in everything. In addition to a sixty Upper School freshmen—all of whom were older than Rachel, some by two years—there were college freshmen, who had not attended the Upper School. Also present were a handful of returning students who wished to bond with a new familiar.

A heavyset man with a short brown beard stepped forward. He was dressed in black and green robes, the color of professional Canticlers. A green tassel hung from his square, black scholar's cap. "Greetings, I am Mr. Hieronymus Tuck, one of the Language tutors here at Roanoke Academy. Yes, I am the descendant of Friar Tuck of Robin Hood fame. No, I do not know what a Friar is, either."

Rachel checked her memory of dictionaries she had flipped through—from libraries of the Wise and from mundane libraries her parents had taken her to visit in England. None of them explained the word *Friar*. The best definition she could find was: *a title of respect used in the past*. She frowned. This was not the first word of its kind she had come upon. Words no one—Wise or Unwary, magical or mundane—seemed able to explain. *Steeple*, for instance. Fingers could be steepled, and brooms could be steeplechasers. But no dictionary or encyclopedia explained the word *steeple* itself.

It was a mystery for her to ponder—similar to the mystery of why there was a statue of a woman with bird wings in the forest, but no mention of any such fey creature in any field guide or encyclopedia.

"Today, you will be bonded with your familiars. Your familiar is an essential part of Conjuring, one of the seven great Arts of sorcery taught at our esteemed institution. It is also useful for Thaumaturgy and Warding, two of our other Arts. Only at Roanoke can you study all seven of the Sorcerous Arts. The other magic schools in the world only teach one or two. To learn what is taught at Roanoke elsewhere, you would have to attend school for twenty eight years."

Groans rose from the assembled students.

Mr. Tuck continued, "This ceremony provides other benefits as well. I shall leave you to find them out for yourselves. Line up. When I call your name, take your familiar and walk through the ivory arch. When you reach the far side, you will be bonded."

With so many animals, Rachel was amazed that no dogs chased the rabbits, and no cats chased the birds. Most were well-behaved, though someone's ferret did chase someone else's tiny fennel fox. Of course, familiars were much more intelligent than the mundane animals they resembled, which made it possible to incorporate them into the society of the Wise.

Rachel stood in line with Siggy, the princess, Salome, and Valerie, who was snapping pictures of everything. Siggy had Lucky wrapped around him. Valerie was accompanied by Payback, who had a yellow bandana tied around her furry neck. A giant python slithered around Salome's shoulders and wrapped around her arms, giving all the boys something to pretend to stare at as they checked out its mistress.

Princess Nastasia explained with a gracious air that—while she had considered the three traditional familiars, devils, dingos, and roos—she had gone instead with the Tasmanian tiger, an animal extinct in the mundane world, but still very much alive in Magical Australia. Rachel found the creature terribly interesting. It looked like a cross between a tiger and a wolf. It even had a marsupial pouch.

Rachel held her black and white cat very tightly, lest he squirm out of her arms and vanish into the underbrush. Mistletoe was a rangy cat with huge jowls, a battered ear, and scars from many a catfight. The other students looked calm and expectant. Rachel was not so sanguine. Mistletoe's mother had been Moonbeam, the worthy companion of her beloved grandfather and a descendant of a long line of famous familiars. Many of Moonbeam's children had gone on to be outstanding in their own right. Rachel's father and her sisters and brother all had offspring of her grandfather's cat.

When it had been Rachel's turn to pick, she had fallen in love with the little black and white kitten that was the feistiest of the litter. He showed such spirit and curiosity. He immediately won her heart. When the time came to test for supernatural aptitude, little Mistletoe failed the tests. Grandfather declared him a sport, a throwback with no magical talent. He and her parents urged her to pick a different kitten, but Rachel would not abandon the little fellow. She was sure he would improve with time.

Only, he had not.

Three times in the last week she had dreamt the nightmare where, upon reaching the ivory arch, Mistletoe bolted, leaving her standing by herself, humiliated in front of her entire class— the children she was going to be living with every day for next eight years. With a sinking feeling in the pit of her stomach, she wished she had accepted her father's last-minute offer to buy her a different familiar.

To take her mind off her fears, she glanced around, pausing briefly on each student's face and filing it away in the well-ordered library that was her mind. The crowd was international. Rachel picked out American, Irish, French, Spanish, Egyptian, and Japanese accents. As they were called forward, she recognized many family names, some of whom were the children of high members of the Parliament of the Wise.

Everyone stared with interest when the lovely girl with piercing blue eyes and chestnut hair that floated around her like a cloud turned out to be Wendy Darling, the daughter of the famous James Darling—the star of the *James Darling, Agent* comics. The mischievous red-haired boy behind her was her cousin, Ian MacDannan, the son of Finn MacDannan, Darling's right hand man from his fight against the Terrible Five, when they battled the Veltdammerung, led by the Terrible Five. Rachel knew both these children. They had attended Yule Parties and other functions together since they were little. She waved, but they were looking the other way.

A dark boy with a sardonic expression and a wolverine at his side was announced as Wulfgang Starkadder, whom Rachel knew to be the seventh heir to the throne of Transylvania, or perhaps he was the fifth heir, depending upon whether women could inherit in his country. Two of his older siblings were sisters. Nearby, she saw Cydney Graves and her two friends. They were standing with several other children, including a rather mean-looking dark-haired boy. The whole group of them sneered at her when they caught her glancing in their direction.

The majority of familiars were cats, dogs, owls, or ferrets, though there were a number of magpies and snakes as well. Some students had large mammals that had been shrunk by magic. Juma O'Malley fed peanuts to a little elephant. Mei-Xing Lee, from China, carried a miniature panda, and a little polar bear played with Wanda Zukov's long dark-red hair. Rachel only noted two supernatural creatures among the crowd. Misty Lark, a girl with a dull, almost lifeless expression in her eyes and straw-colored hair that stuck out like hay, stood next to a tiny unicorn. A boy by the name of Mortimer Egg had a red-eyed rabbit that Rachel was sure was a phooka. Lots of phooka roamed Dartmoor, where Gryphon Park was located. Rachel had learned how to spot them.

One girl, Magdalene Chase, was even smaller than Rachel, a tiny dark-haired thing with skin so pale one could practically see through it. Rachel knew that she herself looked as if she might be ten; this girl could have been eight. Magdalene tried to present a porcelain doll as her familiar and was laughed at by the assembled students. Rachel did not laugh. She felt very sorry for the tiny girl and wished she had some way to protect Magdalene from the scorn of the crowd. Squeezing Mistletoe tighter, she wondered if everyone would laugh at her like that when her cat deserted her at the arch.

As Mr. Tuck called Mortimer Egg and his phooka forward, Rachel spotted the person she had been hoping to see, a short girl with straight brown hair and many freckles. She had an open, friendly face, but there was a glint of steel her eye, as if she was little but fierce. Standing beside her was the tiny lion.

Rachel joined her. Mistletoe squirmed. She grabbed him tighter to keep him from escaping. "Hallo. I'm Rachel Griffin. Um...do you mind if I ask you a rather peculiar question?"

"Not at all. I love peculiar questions." To Rachel's delight, this girl also had an English accent. She extended her hand. "I'm Jane. Jane Fabian, but everyone calls me Kitten."

"Kitten? That's a bit..."

"Odd?" Kitten gave her a knowing nod. "My family is like that. We are all nicknamed after animals and have rather unusual familiars. My brother Squirrel—Cyril is his real name—has a phoenix. My sister Panther has...a panther. A full-sized one, too.

And Bobcat has a psammead—a sand fairy. I have Leander, of course. Though, frankly, some days it might be more appropriate to say that he has me."

"Nice to meet you, Kitten. I would shake hands, but my cat will get away," Rachel apologized. "Do phoenixes and a psammeads make good familiars? My sister Laurel wanted a chimera, but Father said supernatural creatures were a bad idea."

"The phoenix is irascible, and the psammead is both cantankerous and shy, which makes for a horrid combination." Kitten replied. "Still, my brothers seldom complain. Both creatures are terribly good at conjuration. But here I am babbling on, and you haven't had a chance to ask your peculiar question. Do ask."

Rachel paused, gazing down at the tiny lion. "Does...does your familiar talk?"

"You mean Leander?" Kitten looked at her lion, who stared steadily back at her with large golden eyes. She looked back at Rachel. "What makes you ask that?"

"Just wondering." Rachel noted that Kitten had not denied it.

"It certainly seems to me as if he does." Kitten gave her lion a very kind smile, but it was not the sort of smile Rachel would have given her familiar. It was a look of respect, almost awe.

The tutor called Kitten's name. She threw Rachel a grateful look and ran off with Leander. The two of them walked down the line of torches and passed through the ivory arch, followed by Diogenes Flint, Claudia Ford, Zoë Forrest—whose hair was dark green, Warren Foster, Valerie Foxx, and the horrid Cydney Graves, whose familiar was a large fruit bat.

Then, it was Rachel's turn. She carried Mistletoe down the torch-lined walkway. The cat spilled over her arms, and *mrowed*, threatening to bolt. By the time she reached the ivory arch, her arms were shaking. She put him on the ground and held her breath.

He did not bolt. He sat down and washed his paw.

"Come on, Mistletoe," she called in a high sweet voice, her heart pounding. "This way."

Mistletoe stood and raised his tail. With perfect poise, he walked beside her. They passed underneath the ivory arch together.

The chatter and chimes and *tocks* of bamboo receded. Rachel walked forward, but she felt as if she were dreaming, as if she were floating weightless, as if she could walk forever and never reach the other side. Silvery light swirled over her and her cat. It happened so quickly that she might have feared she imagined it, had she not been able to recall the instant perfectly. Playful tingles danced up and down her limbs. A feeling of hope took hold of her, of excitement.

With the abruptness of waking, they had reached the other side. The noises came rushing back. Rachel breathed a huge sigh of relief. They had done it.

To her surprise, she discovered that she could tell where her cat was, even when she was not looking at him. Mr. Tuck chuckled merrily at her startled expression.

"One of the joys of having a familiar, Miss Griffin," he rumbled jovially. "One of the joys of having a familiar."

CHAPTER SIX:

UNFAMILIAR CLASSES

RACHEL'S FIRST CLASS WAS LANGUAGE. TO HER DELIGHT, SIGGY AND Nastasia were with her. Comparing their schedules, they discovered that they were in the same Core Group. This meant they would have all their classes together.

Freshman Language was on the second floor of Roanoke Hall, overlooking the lake. The windows were open. A cool breeze blew through the chamber. The room echoed slightly as the students tromped in and slammed their books on the large central table. The classroom was not like the schools she had seen in photographs, with small desks lined neatly in rows. Instead, straight-backed chairs surrounded one big polished wood table. Choosing a seat between her two new friends, she sat on the edge of it, bouncing with anticipation.

The tutor for Language class was Mr. Tuck. He strode into the room, his robes swishing, and ponderously lowered himself into a large arm chair in front of the blackboard. When all the students had arrived, he stood, sticking his thumbs behind the pleats to either side of his chest.

"As you already know, I am Mr. Hieronymus Tuck, Canticler. In this class, we will study the ancient works of magic and translate them from their original languages. We will be studying Aristotle's *On Magic*, Plato's *Arcanium*, the volumes of Pliny the Elder's *Natural History* that deal with Enchantment and the Wise of his day, as well as many other important texts.

"We will also be studying the Original Language, both words and gestures. There is more to a great Canticler than mere pronunciation and hand motions. How well you can command the natural and unseen world will depend upon your talent for sorcery, the confidence of your delivery, and the discipline with which you develop your skill."

He paused and then asked in his deep resonating voice, "Questions? Problems? Major dilemmas? No?" He looked to the left and right. "Everyone, open your books to page five."

Rachel did not need to open the textbook. Having glanced at it once, she could now recite it from memory. Yet she obediently opened hers like everyone else. Her mother had warned her that if others found out about her gift, they would expect her to take all the notes and answer all the homework questions. It was better, her mother had said, to let others underestimate her.

Rachel waited, tense with excitement. She loved the feel of new ideas pouring into her thoughts. It was like drinking knowledge, and her mind was always thirsty.

"Language class," Mr. Tuck explained as he paced back and forth, "is the study of the One True Language, the language from before the dawn of time, in which all objects were originally named. Our knowledge of it comes down from Ancient Sumeria. If one knows this language, one can speak to the very world itself and convince inanimate objects to do one's bidding. The sorcery performed using this language is called Canticle. Hence, I am a Canticler. A single act of sorcery performed using this method is called a cantrip. Cantrips use the sound and the gesture that represents each word of the original tongue."

Mr. Tuck pointed at a book on his desk with the first two fingers of his right hand and made an intricate sign with his left hand. He spoke some words Rachel did not catch. She played the memory back several times. It started with *Ti* and ended with *lu.* The syllable in between had been pronounced too softly for her to hear.

The book rose into the air. Mr. Tuck moved his right hand. The book followed his gesture, rising and dipping as it soared around the classroom. A girl shrieked and covered her head.

"Fear not, Miss O'Keefe. I have not brained a student with a flying tome yet," the tutor stated dryly. "Of course, there is a first time for everything."

"How...how did you know my name?" asked the girl. She had a heart-shaped face and mousy brown hair held back by a black and white checkered headband.

Mr. Tuck chuckled. "Miss O'Keefe. You are the seventh of that name whom I have taught. When the day comes that I cannot recognize an O'Keefe at a hundred paces, it will be time to put me out to pasture. Tell me, are you the last? Or are there more where you come from in the Land of Infinite O'Keefes?"

"I-I'm the last." Miss O'Keefe had pale skin. When she blushed, her entire face turned pink.

"Hmm. A seventh daughter. And your mother, if I recall, was also a seventh daughter, is that not so?" Mr. Tuck mused. She nodded. "I expect great things of you, seventh daughter of a seventh daughter. See that you do not disappoint me."

He lowered the book gently to the table. "Very well. Today, we will start with four simple words: up, down, open and close. Repeat after me: *Ti. Doe. Libra. Legare.*"

Mr. Tuck repeated the lesson a number of times, emphasizing both the sound and the gesture for each word. Rachel's eyes glazed over. She had understood the first time and would not forget. Waiting for him to move onto the next subject, she daydreamed about growing up to be a great sorceress who could call all things by their proper name.

Eventually, the time for the hands-on portion of Language class arrived. Mr. Tuck handed out small rectangular boards with a hinged door set into the middle. He instructed the students to practice by raising and lowering the piece of wood and opening and closing the door.

Rachel took a deep breath and tried it. A rush of excitement traveled from her toes and fingers through her limbs and out her mouth, leaving her feeling tingly and slightly breathless. The door opened slowly. She had to press her hand against her mouth to keep herself from giggling uncontrollably. She had done it. She had used magic. She had performed a cantrip. No matter what happened for the rest of her life, nothing would ever take this accomplishment away.

She was officially a sorceress!

Sigfried Smith, Princess Nastasia, Wulfgang Starkadder, and Joy O'Keefe, the seventh daughter of a seventh daughter, turned out to be naturals. Their doors flew open. Their boards zipped up and down. On the other hand, skinny Remington Blake, with his mop of dark hair, and pimply redhead Zachary Duff could not get theirs to do anything.

Rachel found herself somewhere in between: better than many, worse than others. She was a bit disappointed not to be among the best in the class. Apparently, she was not destined to be a great Canticler, like her sister Sandra. She noted with some small pride, however, that her control was excellent. Her block of wood might float slowly, but it went exactly where she directed it. Siggy's and the princess's swerved wildly. Siggy grinned like a maniac at the mayhem caused by his block, as it knocked into the chandelier and slammed against the window. When hers did not obey her, however, the princess grew impatient and glared at it imperiously.

The only student with better control than Rachel was Astrid Hollywell, a mulatto girl with a caramel complexion and a head of tight curls. She sat by herself guiding her piece of wood through slow lazy loops. Rachel watched, impressed. She smiled at Astrid, but the other girl ducked her head shyly.

When the class came to an end, the princess asked Rachel to introduce her to the other students they had been working near. Rachel introduced Princess Nastasia Romanov to Joy O'Keefe and Prince Wulfgang Starkadder. Joy gaped open-mouthed at the honor of shaking the hand of a real princess. Nastasia accepted Miss O'Keefe's admiration graciously, though Rachel caught the tiny crinkle of embarrassed amusement at the corner of her eyes. When the princess shook Wulfgang's hand, however, her lovely face went rather pale.

As they walked to Art class, Rachel whispered to her, "Princess, what's wrong? You look...distraught."

Gliding along gracefully, Nastasia spoke in a perfectly even tone. "I fear I may be losing my mind. Something most strange keeps happening to me."

"Strange...how? Like hearing animals talk?"

The princess threw her an odd look. "Occasionally, when I shake the hand of another student, I...go someplace else."

"Did you go somewhere just now, with Wulfgang?"

"Yes. I have shaken hands with eleven students since my arrival and upon six of those occasions, I have found myself in another landscape."

"The same landscape or different ones?"

"Different. But none of them pleasant." The princess looked beautiful even when she was frowning thoughtfully. "Something is always blowing up or burning or freezing. This last time, with Mr. Starkadder, it was a glacier."

"I wonder what that means?" Rachel mused.

"It gets worse."

"How could it be worse?"

"In the case of Miss Iscariot, I was standing on her grave."

"Her grave!" Rachel cried. "When does she die?"

"Twenty years ago," the princess replied. "According to the date on her headstone, she is already dead."

Rachel pondered the Princess's disturbing news as they made their way to class. She did not question whether Nastasia's visions were real—many sorcerers had visions—but she did struggle to comprehend what they could mean. Under what circumstance could a young girl have died before she was born? Could Salome be a vampire? But they met in bright sunlight. Or a revenant? Was that why she looked so much more mature? It made no sense...which meant that there was more to know.

Whatever the truth was, Rachel could not wait to discover it.

They arrived at Art class to find animals milling around the classroom. Dogs, cats, and ferrets sniffed at the cabinets where the arts supplied were stored. A magpie and a red-winged blackbird flew among the rafters. Apparently, Art was a class to which one brought one's familiar. Lucky was already with Siggy. The two girls ran back to their room. To Rachel's delight, Nastasia was one of her roommates. She had the bunk above Rachel's.

Even with her new familiar empathy, Rachel could not catch Mistletoe. He had slipped through a hole that was too small for her. She could sense the cat, but she could not get to him. She called, but he did not come. Mistletoe never came when called. Being a familiar did not change this.

Back in the classroom, Rachel was the only person without a familiar. She sunk as low as she could in her seat, hoping fervently that no one would notice. The tutor for this class was Mrs. Heelis, an old woman with round glasses, who wore her white hair in a bun. Her high-necked robe was black and red, like all Conjurers. She did not wear a cap. Her ancient cat slept beside her on the floor in a pool of sunlight.

Seated at the table, she spoke to the students with a lively gleam to her eyes. "Art is the basis of the Sorcerous Art of Conjuring. All conjured objects must be conceptualized in the mind," she tapped her head, "before they can be drawn into the world of the real. Here, your familiar will be a big help. Your familiar can see into the world of dreams from which conjured items come. It can help bring definition and perspective to your creation."

She made a gesture and glanced at her cat, who suddenly sat up alert. The two of them bent their heads toward each other. Straightening, Mrs. Heelis held her palm up and drew her fingers together until her fingertips touched. Then the cat raised his paw and batted, just as Mrs. Heelis moved her hand downward.

"*Muria*," she stated firmly.

As if she were waking from a dream, Rachel realized that a sweet white duck with a light blue bonnet that looked like a living version of Jemima Puddleduck waddled around the room. There were gasps of astonishment, and girls squealed with delight.

"It is only temporary. It will fade soon," Mrs. Heelis explained. "But you may all come over and examine it."

Looking up, Rachel realized that there were framed pictures of Peter Rabbit, Squirrel Nutkin, Jemima Puddleduck, and Benjamin Bunny on the walls. She smiled at the pictures. They seemed so charming and friendly.

The princess felt otherwise." I do not care to look at so many rabbits." Nastasia frowned fiercely at the walls, while the other students gathered around the living animated duck. "The rabbit is the enemy of my people."

"Your enemies are rabbits?" asked Valerie Foxx, who was with them in this class, though she had not been in Language. Her friend Salome was not with her.

"We are overrun with them in Magical Australia. Somebody once enchanted a top hat so that a magician could pull a rabbit out of it, and they just kept coming." The princess waved an admonishing finger. "Never pull a rabbit out of a hat! It goes badly!"

"As a knight, I vow to defeat your enemy for you!" Siggy announced fiercely, eager to perform deeds of derring-do. "Lucky and I will rid you of these rabbits, won't we, Lucky!"

The dragon remembered not to speak in public, but his eyes glittered with eagerness as his head bobbed up and down.

"Sigfried Smith," the princess replied with regal graciousness, "I would be honored if you and Lucky came to Magical Australia to defeat our rabbits."

Siggy grinned and gave Lucky a thumbs-up.

Heelis. Puddleduck. From the deep well of random information in Rachel's memory, pieces clicked into place.

"Beatrix Potter!" She jumped up and ran over to the tutor, who was feeding the animated duck imaginary corn. "You're Beatrix Potter. You married a Mr. Heelis and disappeared from public view. All these pictures on the wall. You painted them."

"Yes I did," Mrs. Heelis admitted with a kind smile.

"You must be very old," she blurted out and then blushed. It was not the kindest thing to say. The other students snickered.

Mrs. Heelis did not seem offended. "Those of us with the blood of the immortals running through our veins are not as tightly bound by time as ordinary folk. I am well into my second century. Now, pencils ready. Let us begin by drawing the basic shapes: circle, triangle, square."

Chapter Seven:

Encounter in a

Nigh-Empty Hallway

"VLADIMIR VON DREAD! HE'S EEEVIL!" SALOME EXCLAIMED, AS they all sat down to lunch together. Rachel had finally told the other girls the fate of the scarab brooch.

Lunch was held in the dining room, in the center of Roanoke Hall. The chamber was shaped like a plus sign, with a fountain in the center of the four wings. To one side were the kitchens, where students went to choose their food. While the main cooking was done by human employees, the pastries and other baking were done by brownies, little fey creatures closely related to the *bwbachs* that cleaned the dorm rooms—if one filled the bowl beside one's door with milk.

Familiars who ate human food were welcome in the dining hall. Here and there a dog or a monkey ate beside its master or mistress. All others were fed in their rooms or at the menagerie. Rachel suspected this was for the best. Watching a snake swallow a live mouse at lunch might not encourage hearty appetites.

The dining room itself consisted of long tables that sat twelve. The central table was occupied by Vladimir Von Dread and his companions. The rest of the tables were either assigned to various specific Arts or open to anyone. Rachel and her friends currently sat at one of these free tables. She had had the option of sitting with her brother or her sister, both of whom had waved her over—Peter smiling calmly and Laurel bouncing with enthusiasm—but Rachel had spent the entire summer with them. She wanted to get to know her new friends.

Their table was off to one side. It should have been out of the way, but a great many people kept staring at them. Rachel hated being the center of attention. She struggled to breathe. Her head felt light. Gripping the table hard, she was beginning to fear she would faint.

The air whooshed back into her lungs. No one was staring at her. The boys stared at Anastasia or Salome, and girls—and those boys who were more interested in heroes and dragons that ookie girls—stared at Siggy. Gaggles of girls drifted by and asked to pet Lucky the Dragon. Grinning his huge grin, Siggy always obliged.

Rachel breathed a deep sigh of relief and turned her attention to her food.

"Von Dread was incredible!" Sigfried exclaimed, as the latest gaggle departed. He had a huge tray of food with servings of everything the kitchen had to offer. He had cut each item in half and was sharing it with Lucky, who hid under the table. "You should have seen him. He destroyed the evil bug-thing with a blast of fire and lightning. Boom! Boom!" He pantomimed Von Dread drawing his Fulgurator's wand and blasting the scarab brooch.

"Evil but gorgeous." Salome heaved a huge sigh and lay her cheek against her hands, batting her huge eyelashes.

"Do you mean the Prince of Bavaria?" Valerie Foxx had been cleaning her camera lens. She gestured emphatically with the soft blue lens cloth. "Is his name really pronounced Dread, like dreadful? All this time, I assumed it was Von Dreed."

"Nope. It's Dread." Salome fluttered her extremely long eyelashes. "As in we dread him."

"I don't dread him, he's amazing!" Siggy tossed a sticky bun in the air for Lucky to catch. The dragon shot out from under the table, elongating like a Slinky, snapped it out of mid-air, and disappeared again.

"But he's evil!" Rachel echoed Salome's objection as she slathered more butter on a honey roll. "Father says the King of Bavaria is horrid. He says he's the worst tyrant alive today."

Valerie pushed her camera aside and took a bite of her sandwich. "Only ruler to actually nuke another country back into the stone ages."

"Wicked!" exclaimed Siggy. "I want to do that. Do we learn to do that here? Nuke stuff? Is there a spell for nuclear combustion? How about one for other kinds of combustion? Does the school get blown up a lot?"

"I've done research on his son, the prince," Valerie continued. "Did you know, Vladimir took off a year from school, a couple of years back, to participate in the Winter Olympics? He has won gold medals in fencing, skiing, and skating, and silvers in swimming and shooting."

Rachel recalled some old News Glass images she had once seen in Sandra's room. "He also took gold in septathlon—a sorcery contest not covered by the mundane news."

The princess took a sip of her cranberry juice and dabbed her lips with her napkin. "Aren't some of those summer sports?"

Valerie leaned forward eagerly. "He has competed more than once. The Summer Olympics did not conflict with his school schedule."

"That's a lot of different sports." Siggy's eyes goggled. "I *told* you he was impressive."

Salome rolled her eyes. "It's easy to get on a team when your father runs the country."

"Father or not, he must be an excellent athlete if he won medals at the Olympics," Rachel said thoughtfully. "He competed against the best athletes in the world."

"Good point." Salome pouted prettily.

The princess spoke up. "My father puts all sorts of things on our Olympic team: boxing kangaroos, wallabies, emus. They never win medals. Usually, they are not even allowed to compete." When the others stared at her, Nastasia gave a regal shrug, "My father is...a bit eccentric—in a friendly way."

"An emu?" Rachel asked, hardly sure whether the princess was teasing.

"On the track team." Nastasia nodded sadly, as if this were one of the great burdens of her life. "Once he even tried to put a croc on the swim team—at some Pan Asian Games. Scared all the other contestants out of the pool. But they still would not give the croc the medal, even when it was the only swimmer who finished the race."

"Enough about stupid animals nobody believes in, like crocs and emus," Siggy grinned at Valerie. "Tell me more about Von Dread, Fearless Reporter Girl!"

"You should ask Salome." Valerie tucked the lens cloth back into the leather case she wore on her belt. "She knows much more than I do."

Salome leaned forward, allowing an unobstructed view down her blouse. Sigfried started to look and then glanced away, scowling. She said, "He's the unofficial head of Drake Hall. Everyone kowtows to him. It's so ridiculous to watch that it's funny. I'm not afraid of him. I refuse to scurry around and be his little minion."

"Are you in Drake Hall?" Rachel paused mid-bite, honey dripping from her warm roll. According to her sister Laurel, no one good ended up in the Thaumaturge's dorm.

"All us rich kids are in Drake. No one else can afford to be." Salome giggled. "Those high-grade gemstones on the tips of the Fulgurator's wands are pricey."

"What are Fulgurators?" Siggy asked.

Rachel replied. "Soldier who wields lightning on the battle-field—the same way cavalry refers to soldiers who fight from horseback." She turned to the girls. "What dormitories are you all in?"

"I'm in Dee," volunteered Valerie.

"That's fabulous." Rachel ducked her head so the other girl would not see her envy.

"What are we talking about now?" Sigfried asked noncha-lantly.

Suspicious of his tone, Rachel checked her memory to see what trouble he had been getting into. Recalling back, she paid attention to the images that had been caught by the corner of her eye. A banana, an apple, and two sandwiches disappeared into the voluminous pockets of his robes. She wondered what he intended to do with so much food.

"The dormitories," Valerie replied. "I'm in Dee Hall. Salome's in Drake."

"According to my sister Laurel," Rachel leaned forward, "Dee Hall has bookworms and know-it-alls; Dare Hall is filled with musical show-offs; and those in Drake Hall are stuck-up or sneaky or just plain scary." Rachel stuck her tongue out at Salome, who looked extremely amused.

"What does your sister say about the other dorms?" Valerie pulled out her notebook.

Rachel tipped back her head. "Um...Marlowe Hall is all jocks and emos. The kids from Spenser Hall talk too much. Raleigh Hall has geeks and nerds, and those in De Vere are subtle and secretive."

"Oh. That is wonderful!" Salome clapped her hands. "I'll have to tell Ethan." When the others looked blank, she added, "Ethan Warhol. My boyfriend?"

Valerie waved her pencil in the air as she spoke. "He's the son of Felix Warhol, the controversial Senator from Maine? No? None of you have heard of him? Senator Warhol's famous!"

"Siggy and I are English." Rachel shrugged. "Do you know the names of anyone in the House of Commons?"

"Good point." Valerie flashed a mischievous grin. "Though being a Fearless Reporter Girl, I do know a few."

"So what are those of us in Dare? Musical show-offs?" Siggy grinned as he shoved two muffins into the pockets of his robes. Rachel was not certain, but she thought she saw him put a slice of bacon in there as well. "We can live up to that, can't we, Lucky? At least we can, as soon as we get an instrument."

Placing her glass of milk on the table, the princess murmured softly, "I wonder if I might be in the wrong dormitory."

"Me, too," Rachel murmured back. A sympathetic camaraderie passed between them.

There was something wonderful about having a friend with whom one shared common values. It filled Rachel with a warm glow. She had not expected, upon coming to America, to find someone who admired the understated things she had grown to appreciate under the tutelage of her grandparents. And yet, here was a real princess, someone raised to rule a nation. No doubt she had received the same kind of training as Rachel. Between Nastasia and the amusing Sigfried, Rachel was on her way to the inseparable friendships so common in novels.

Life could not possibly be better.

"Excuse me, Nastasia Romanov?" An older student approached the table. The hood of her robe covered her face, except her mouth. She spoke in a wry, sardonic tone.

"I am she." The princess rose graciously.

"Hi. I'm Xandra Black…Maybe you've heard rumors about me? Some people call me Flops-Over-Dead-Chick? My familiar is the fattest cat ever to lay around taking up space? No? No matter. Um. Sorry about this…"

The young woman's head jerked backward. Her hood fell off. She was pretty with long dark hair. Then, her eyes rolled up in her head, and a voice came out of her mouth, a deep eerie voice that sent shivers up and down Rachel's back.

"Nastasia Romanov! Touch not the Upper School junior, Joshua March."

"I don't much care for some unknown power ordering me around," the princess confided to Rachel as they walked to their next class. Despite her gentleness, a spark of defiance danced in her eyes. "It was kind of Miss Black to bring me a message from the supernatural world. But how do I know if that voice was friendly?

"Or, even if it was friendly, does that mean it was necessarily wise? Joshua March is the son of my father's friend. I have looked forward to meeting him. And, more importantly, where do unknown voices from the supernatural world fall into the hierarchy of command? Do they have sufficient authority to be giving orders to a princess of Magical Australia?"

Rachel giggled. The princess arched an eyebrow in regal surprise. Rachel realized that her friend was entirely serious.

"What does any of it mean?" Rachel whispered to her. "Your visions. This person who is after Valerie? Are they related? Is there really an evil operative on campus, such as the proctors spoke of?"

"I do not know."

"Have you touched Valerie?"

"Yes. I saw her as a young woman in her early thirties who was working for a major news corporation."

"Huh. That tells me…nothing." Rachel drummed her fingers on her books as she walked. Her thoughts whirled, pulling volumes from the library of her mind and flipping through them at high speed. But there was not enough information to click into place any of the puzzle pieces they had found so far. If she was patient and alert, the information she needed to figure this out would come to her. She was sure of it.

Still, it was frustrating not to know.

Lunch was followed by Music with Miss Himeropa Cyrene, a thin birdlike lady who had the most lovely singing voice Rachel had ever heard. Music was the basis of Enchantment, for which the students of Dare Hall were famous. Most Enchantment spells required complicated melodies in order to repel evil, compel truth, cast crowds into enchanted sleep, and the many other things Enchanters could do.

At the beginning of the first class, those who had not brought their own instrument chose one from the available loaner instruments. Next, Miss Cyrene demonstrated a simple spell. She taught the class how to blow a single note that made a blast of wind push an object backward. To demonstrate, she put a hat on the table and played the note on her flute. With a whoosh of fresh-smelling air, like a garden on a spring morning, silver sparkles swept out of the flute, danced around the hat, and carrying it upward. The students gasped with delight.

Siggy, the princess, Wulfgang, and Joy O'Keefe turned out to be naturals at this, too. They could throw the target, a sewing dummy on wheels, all the way across the room to bang against the far wall. Quite a few of the other children could not budge it at all. Rachel, again, was in between. With a toot on her flute, she could push the dummy back a good six inches. She was pleased with her success, but it was humbling compared to her friends.

Siggy, who had never played an instrument, chose a trumpet from the classroom loaners. Immediately, he learned to produce truly horrible sounds. This pleased him to no end. The princess, on the other hand, could make beautiful music come from her clarinet. She could also play the harp, the violin and the cello. Nor was she the only student who was musically brilliant.

Rachel looked at her flute dubiously. It was a lovely silver instrument that had belonged to her grandmother. It had a beautiful sound, if played by someone who knew how. Rachel knew, in theory. She could read sheet music. She had been taking singing lessons since the age of eight. The lessons had paid off in that she could sing beautifully—she used to sing for her father when he came home from work.

Unlike schoolwork, which came to her easily, however, Rachel did not like playing the flute. Her parents had expected her to practice for an hour every day in preparation for coming to Roanoke and taking up residence in Dare Hall. The Griffin Family was known for great Enchanters. Peter, Laurel, and Sandra played beautifully, as did their parents. Only, Rachel had not practiced. She preferred to ride her pony or, later, her broom.

The truth was, Rachel had not wanted to live in Dare Hall. Her secret wish was to live in Dee Hall and study Gnosis, the Sorcerous Art of knowledge and augury. She had kept a framed picture of the handsome granite building—with its double staircase, its domed towers, and the many statues of famous sorcerers around the edges of its roof—under her bed. When no one was in her wing of the house, she took it out and gazed at it longingly.

She had not told anyone. Her family would have been outraged if they had known of her desire to break with family tradition, especially as tradition was ordinarily more important to Rachel than to her siblings. But she had concocted a plan. She had heard stories about the seven-sided room, where new students went to choose the object that determined which of the seven dormitories they would be assigned to. Picking an instrument would put her in Dare. Picking a book would put her in Dee. She had resolved to defy family tradition and chose an ancient tome.

Only she had never been given a chance. Upon arriving, the proctors had packed her off to Dare with the rest of her family without even letting her visit the seven-sided room.

She felt robbed.

After Music class, Rachel had a free period before True History. She slipped away and up the stairs to the higher floors of Roanoke Hall. Much as she liked Siggy and Nastasia, she was not used to spending so much time around other people. She felt overwhelmed.

There was another reason she wanted to be alone. Rachel knew she was not the best athlete, but she was a superb broom rider. This was because when she first received her broom, she put her whole mind into learning. She worked and worked and worked. Due to her perseverance, she could do things on a broom that much better athletes could not.

An example was the bottom of the servants' staircase. The first time she had taken that corner, she slammed into the grandfather clock—breaking both the clock and her front teeth. A visit to the dentimancer and the clockmaker later, she did it again, though this time it was her arm that she broke. Her parents had not been pleased.

Nowadays, Rachel noted with pride, she could round the turn at the servants' staircase at full speed, without harm to teeth, clock, or arm. Her perseverance had paid off. It was a lesson she would not soon forget.

As she had watched her classmates blast the practice dummy across the room in Music class, it occurred to her that maybe she could do the same thing with sorcery. She could not beat the students who had such massive natural talent. If she picked a few spells, however, and worked at them, over and over and over, perhaps she could become as good with them as she was with her broom.

But she did not want to do this in front of her new friends, both of whom took to the schoolwork so naturally. The very idea embarrassed her. She wanted to practice privately, so no one else knew what an effort it cost her.

Poking around the top floor of Roanoke Hall, she found a corridor between two turrets with little evidence of use. The air smelled dusty. The outside sounds were muted. A suit of armor stood beside a high round window. Across from it, someone had left a wooden doorstop lying on a small table.

Raising her flute, she blew the note that created a blast of wind. Sure enough, after two tries, a rush of silver sparkles swept the doorstop from the table. Rachel's lips parted in delight. Miss Cyrene's spell had smelled like fresh air. Hers smelled more like vanilla, which was still an improvement over the dusty hall.

Making the correct hand gestures, she tried to lift it back to the table using the cantrip for *up*. The triangle of wood wobbled left and right, floating slowly toward the table. Her whole body tingled. Twice she lost concentration, dropped it, and had to start over again. Eventually, the doorstop was back on the table. Then, she did it again.

Toot.

"*Ti.*"

Toot.

"*Ti.*"

Over and over, she repeated these two steps, until her limbs shook, and her lips grew tired. Picking up her flute, blowing on it, and putting it down to perform the cantrip became tedious. Rachel tried a trick her mother used. Instead of playing the blast of wind on her flute, she whistled it. Silver sparkles flew out of her mouth, tickling her lips. This made her laugh, ruining her spell.

She tried again and again and again. The sensation of magic rushing through her made her giddy. With no instrument to draw the power into its proper channels, it gathered in her mouth. Her lips twitched uncontrollably. She could not produce the proper sounds.

How did her mother do it?

Rachel's eyes widened. Taking a deep breath, she employed her mother's dissembling techniques, the trick she used to mask her emotions. Whistling, she kept her face still despite the internal rush of excitement. The dancing glints lifted the doorstop from the table and swept it down the hallway.

Rachel allowed herself a single whoop of delight. Then she returned to practicing, switching between the *up* cantrip and whistling. Somewhere around the fifteenth time, a pleasant masculine voice with an English accent caused her to jump.

"Try *tiathelu.*"

An older boy stood behind her—a very cute older boy. He had brown hair that was drawn back into a short ponytail and a slightly rangy look that made Rachel wonder if he was an outcast hiding from his persecutors. She could not imagine what else a boy would be doing up here. He looked about her brother's age. If so, he was short for sixteen, much shorter than Peter, though he was significantly taller than Rachel.

With an inward sigh, she noted that not only was her hair disheveled, but she was covered with dust.

"Rachel Griffin." She extended her hand cheerfully. "Who are you?"

"Gaius Valiant." He shook her hand. He spoke with a casual laid-back drawl, as if he were a spectator observing the drama of life and what he saw amused him.

"*Tiathelu*, you say?"

"*Ti athe lu.* 'up, place, go.'" He formed the hand gestures as he spoke. "It's a more advanced cantrip, works more smoothly."

"*Tiathelu.*" Rachel reproduced the hand gestures from memory, exactly how Gaius had just done them. They were the same gestures Mr. Tuck had performed for the cantrip he used to fly the book around the room and frighten Miss O'Keefe.

The doorstop rose into the air and followed her extended two fingers back to the table as quickly as she could move her hand. Rachel grinned with delight.

"Very good!" He sounded impressed. "You picked that up fast."

She tried it two times in rapid succession. It worked perfectly. She laughed with joy.

"Thank you!"

"No problem."

"That will make it much easier!"

"I like the whistling. I've never seen anyone do Enchantment that way before." He leaned casually against the wall, his arms crossed. "You're the daughter of Ambrose Griffin, right? The head of the Shadow Agency?"

Rachel nodded, very glad she could keep her face impassive. She could not, however, keep goose bumps from running along both her arms. *Shadow Agency*? Was that the name of the clandestine department of the Wisecraft for which her father worked? It was a department so secret that Rachel had not even known its name. Who was this boy?

Only then did she notice the Fulgurator's wand hanging at his side, a length of teak and brass tipped with a sapphire. A shiver went through her. He was a Thaumaturge student from Drake Hall. Thaumaturges used the lightning-wielding wands to hold the magical charges they wrangled from the supernatural entities they summoned. As Salome had pointed out, each Fulgurator wand required a very expensive gem.

Rachel looked him over carefully. His robes were neat but worn, even patched in places. The children who lived in Drake Hall were said to be either rich or conniving. He was certainly not rich. According to her sister Laurel, the less fortunate in

Drake Hall were worse than the well-to-do ones—manipulative, unscrupulous folk who got what they wanted by trickery.

She suddenly wished he would go away.

Rachel banished this thought as unworthy of her. He had been very helpful. She should not judge him based merely on reputation. Still, she could not help feeling nervous.

"Nice to meet you," he said, straightening.

"You, too." She smiled sincerely. "Thank you again."

He gave her a little bow and strode away. Rachel stared after him curiously. Then, she went back to work, knocking the doorstop off the table and lifting it up, over and over and over.

CHAPTER EIGHT:
THE RISE OF THE METAPLUTONS

TRUE HISTORY CONSISTED OF THE STUDY OF HISTORY AS IT HAD really happened, before the Parliament of the Wise tampered with it to befuddle the Unwary. Mr. Archimedes Gideon was the perfect tutor for this subject. He had been an Obscurer and had made changes to mundane records himself. He understood what the Parliament of the Wise wished to hide and how this practice was accomplished.

Mr. Gideon dressed in the black and gold robes of a Scholar. Rachel thought he was rather good-looking, though there was gray at his temples. His skin was the color of chocolate, and he sported a mustache. He spoke in a voice tinged with wry amusement. Leaning back in his armchair, his feet on the table, he gave a brief overview of the first month.

When he finished, Brunhilda Winters, a cheerleader from California with blond sun-streaks in her honey-colored hair and long limbs tanned from hours of playing volleyball at the beach, asked, "Can you give an example?"

Mr. Gideon rocked his chair backward, thinking. "Certainly. Mundane history reports that the English founded a colony on the island of Roanoke in North Carolina. When they returned later, the colonists had vanished. True History reveals this colony consisted of sorcerers evading persecution. They used their magic to uproot their new home. When the next ship arrived from England, the floating island of Roanoke had vanished.

"Virginia Dare, the first English child born in America, grew up to be a powerful Enchantress. She founded a school on Roanoke. For over three centuries, the island floated around the oceans of the world, visiting many nations, picking up additional teachers—which is why Roanoke is the only school where all seven of the Sorcerous Arts are taught. Roanoke continued to float until the early Twentieth Century, when it grounded in the Hudson River. It remains here today.

"Or, for another example, the Unwary know that during World War II, Hitler committed genocide against the Romani race, declaring the Gypsies to be the cause of Germany's ills and forcing them into concentration camps—in the travesty against humanity we call the Holocaust. The Wise know this was because the Gypsy sorcerers, such as Oppenheimer and Albert Einstein, refused to share their magic with Hitler."

"Einstein was a sorcerer?" Brunhilda asked incredulously.

"Of course," Mr. Gideon replied smoothly. "You don't think the mundane scientists would have been able to invent the nuclear bomb without the help of Gypsy sorcery, do you?"

Siggy put up his hand. "Sir? How do we know?"

Professor Gideon looked at him coolly. Evidently he had heard of the famous boy, but he had not taken a liking to him. "How do we know what, Mr. Smith? It has been found, by many repeated experiments, that speaking a complete idea is an aid to communication. Assuming that is your purpose?"

Siggy was undaunted. "How do we know this is true history?"

Professor Gideon's cool look hardened into coldness. "Some of what you will learn is based on the records of the Wise. For more recent history, some of your elders are old enough to recollect the events. We do keep track of what we have changed, young man."

"But the Unhairy have records and eyewitnesses too, right?" asked Sigfried. "We meddle with them, so they don't know the truth, and can't know it. Well...? How do we know someone is not doing that to us? People who stand to the Wise as the Wise stand to the Unscary? The Wiser-Than-Us? The Unfairy don't know about us. What do we not know?"

The professor snorted. "In your case, Mr. Smith, a very great deal." He waited for the snickering to die down, a small smile on his lips. "But it might be better to learn what the real history is, before we engage in denigrating it. The first semester will cover the antiquities, from the earliest roots of civilization in Egypt and

China and Atlantis, keeping in mind that our records of those days are more complete and stretch back considerably farther than what mundane archeologists have unearthed. Now, who can tell me at what point in prehistory the Wise diverge from the Unwary?"

"With the discovery that it actually rained if a shaman descended from immortals performed the rain dances?" asked Zoë Forrest, the tough-looking girl with a New Zealand accent and dark green hair. She wore it short, except for one long lock in front, into which she had braided a feather. A funny marsupial sat on her shoulder, eyeing everyone suspiciously. It had a nose like a squirrel only longer, a thick tail, and white spots all over its orangey fur. Rachel searched the encyclopedias in her memory and discovered it was a tiger quoll from Tasmania.

"Very good, Miss Forrest. That is, in fact, one of the divergence points."

Astrid raised her hand shyly. "Please, Sir, before we go on. That word you used in your overview...monotheism? What does it mean? I've never heard that word."

Very seldom did Rachel come upon a new word. She, too, had never heard this one. She checked her memory. It was not in any of the three dictionaries she had memorized. Was it another mystery word, like friar and steeple?

Mr. Gideon examined a roster of names. "Ah, Miss...Hollywell, right?"

Astrid ducked her head, embarrassed, and nodded.

"You grew up in the mundane world, did you not?" he continued, "The world of computers and cars. Had you heard of magic? Of the Wise?"

"N-no, Sir. I had no idea that sorcerers or dragons or anything of that kind was real. I guess you would call me...Unwary." Astrid frowned and asked shyly. "What exactly is the definition of Unwary?"

"Someone who does not know about the World of the Wise. About magic and sorcery," replied Mr. Gideon. "Usually, the Unwary are mundane. In other words, they cannot use magic. A few, such as yourself, were merely unaware of the existence of magic."

"A normal person, then." Astrid nodded. "I was Unwary."

Mr. Gideon's eyes danced with amusement. "That implies that we of the Wise are not normal, but I will let that slide. But, back to the topic at hand, you had heard of the gods?"

"Well, of course, I've heard of them," Astrid said slowly. "And my family gave offerings at temples occasionally. The way everyone does. You know, on big national holidays, such as Spring Equinox, Walpurgisnacht, and Yule, of course. But I thought the gods were symbolic—that Apollo was a personification of creativity and reason. That Isis represented fertility. That sort of thing. I didn't know they were real."

"How did you come to learn about us?" Mr. Gideon asked. "About magic?"

"I am interested in s-science," Astrid stuttered. Rachel felt so sorry for the shy girl who was being put on the spot. "I applied for a summer internship at Ouroborus Industries. They gave me an aptitude test. Apparently, I tested well for learning sorcery."

"I see. As to your question, monotheism means belief in a single god," Mr. Gideon replied. Laughter tittered though the classroom.

"That's absurd!" cried red-haired Ian MacDannan, grinning madly. "Nobody living on this planet—either of the Wise or mundane—believes in something like that."

"But..." Rachel squinted at the tutor, wondering if he was mocking the girl. "Nobody worships only one god. Do they? Wouldn't that offend the other gods?"

The tutor gave her a lazy smile. "You're the youngest Griffin, aren't you? Your sister Sandra was one of my best students. A sharper mind I have never met. Well, youngest Griffin, some people have believed so. Akhenaten tried to make the Ancient Egyptians worship the sun god alone. Other records from antiquity suggest there may once have been a tribe in the Middle East, called the Israelites, who held such beliefs. Have any of you heard of the Israelites?"

Most of the students, Wise and Unwary, shook their heads. Rachel reviewed the encyclopedias in her mental library. She raised her hand.

"Yes, Young Miss Griffin?"

"Don't some scholars think the Tribe of the Israelites may have been the ancestors of our modern Gypsies?"

Mr. Gideon nodded. "Some do hold that opinion, yes."

Wulfgang Starkadder raised his hand, his eyes dark and brooding. "They worshiped just one god? Or they believed in just one god?"

"The word covers both," said the tutor.

"How could it mean the second?" Joy O'Keefe spoke up, puzzled. "When there are obviously so many gods? Even the Unwary know there are many gods, right?" She looked at Astrid, who ducked her head, nodding awkwardly.

Mr. Gideon spread his arms. "A mystery. But it is mysteries that make pursuit of knowledge so fascinating."

Rachel nodded, her eyes sparkling. She was going to like this tutor.

"What you said in class about a Wiser than the Wise, do you believe that?" Rachel asked Siggy, as they spilled out of the school building into the sunny afternoon. They walked onto the bridge that led across the reflecting lake to the green lawns of the Commons. The air was alive with laughing and chatting. Three boys were having a boat race, each yelling to his self-propelling boat to go faster.

"You mean the idea that there are creatures who mess with us the way we mess with the Unburied?" Siggy asked. He jumped up onto the stone railing and spread his arms behind him as he ran, pretending to be dive bombing something. "Vvvvrrrrmmm! Pow! Yes. I do."

The princess strolled beside them, slipping her school book into her house-containing purse. She only ever carried one old gray book. Whenever she opened it, it contained exactly the text that was needed. Rachel longed to examine it but felt too shy to ask.

"That is a rather disturbing thought." Nastasia closed her purse. "Even more disturbing than some of my father's ideas about good uses for Vegemite. Do you have any proof?"

"Maybe." At the edge of the bridge, Siggy jumped to the ground and looked around suspiciously. Then he ducked his head down and looked thoughtful for a moment.

"Tell us! Tell us!" Rachel grabbed his arm.

Siggy lowered his voice. "Where does Lucky come from? And the scarab, and the piece of paper that ensorcelled the generously-endowed and abundantly overly-mammalian young lady from Drake Hall?" When Rachel gave him a sharp look, he shrugged, unconcerned. "The proctors said there were new types of magic. Where is it coming from, if not from something outside your World of the Wise?"

Rachel thought about this very hard. A piece of the puzzle suddenly clicked into another one in her head. "Maybe from the places the princess visits in her visions?"

"What places?" Siggy looked at Nastasia. "What visions?"

Nastasia solemnly repeated what she had told Rachel, including the part about Salome.

"Dead? Wow! That's ace! Can I do that? You say you go to these places? Does it happen when you touch me? Can you go to the same place over and over? What about Lucky?"

Rachel found herself grinning. It was so easy to think of amazing things when speaking with Sigfried. Already, the idea that there were other worlds—and that the people whom the princess was seeing visions about had come from these worlds, bringing their unfamiliar magic with them—was taking root in her thoughts.

The princess was not swept away by Siggy's enthusiasm, but her eyes crinkled kindly at his eagerness. "In no particular order, it only seems to happen the first time I touch somebody. It did not happen with you or Rachel. Also, it never happened at home. A lot of strange things happened at home—a great many of them involving my father, wombats, and bubble gum—but nothing like this." She added thoughtfully, "Next time, I am going to see if I can pick up an object and bring it back with me. I would like some kind of proof that I have not gone crazy."

"What a good idea!" Siggy chortled. "Pick up a gun or a repeating crossbow or an atomic bomb."

"I have not seen any of those things," The princess said primly.

Siggy shrugged, undeterred. "Something must be causing the devastation you keep seeing."

"Try touching Lucky," Rachel urged eagerly. "He's a new thing. Maybe he's from...Outside."

"Very well." The princess turned toward the dragon and curtsied. "If you don't mind, sir dragon?"

"Sure. S'okay with me, if it's okay with the Boss," Lucky said. "Will it hurt?"

"I don't think so. No one else seemed to notice," replied Nastasia. Reaching out, she stroked Lucky's soft fur. Rachel ached to pet him, but she felt too shy to ask about that, too.

The princess's expression went blank. Then, she gave a soft gasp. Water dripped from her hand. Small pink petals stuck to her fingers. She brushed the petals into her purse.

"Wh-what's that?" Rachel pointed at her hand.

Tiny, red lines—very regular lines, about an inch apart—covered her palms and left cheek. The lines began to drip. The princess was bleeding.

"Oh, my gods! She's been wounded! To the Infirmary!" Siggy lunged at the dainty princess to pick her up.

"Wait! Wait! I am not hurt!" Nastasia waved her hand in Sigfried's face. She brushed the blood off. Her hand was whole.

Siggy peered closely. The princess took a tissue from her purse and wiped the blood off her cheek, which was whole and fresh underneath.

"Are you sure you are okay? Good. It would have been horrible if you had been killed by touching Lucky." Sigfried wagged his finger at the dragon. "Lucky, why did you do that?"

"Wasn't my fault, Boss!" Lucky's shrug involved his whole body undulating like a wave. "I didn't do anything. Didn't see anything either."

"Where did the water come from?" Rachel asked.

"The river." Nastasia daintily brushed her fingers off on her robes.

"What river?" Siggy asked.

"I found myself on the bank of a river surrounded by willows and flowering cherry trees. Humanoid shapes drifted by wearing odd black and white masks. I leaned down and put my hand into the water to pick up some of the cherry blossoms. When I lifted my hands, it felt as if I had run into a net of spider webs or fishing line. As if I were pulling against a fabric of some kind. And where I pulled against it, the lines of blood appeared. Then I was back."

"That's...very strange." Rachel felt as if her whole body had turned into a goose bump. "So you are going another place."

"Where do you think you went? Chicago? Paris?" asked Siggy.

Nastasia considered for a bit, blinking her perfect corn silk lashes. Then, she said slowly, "This looked like Japan...but sometimes, it has been clear that I was not anywhere on the Earth. Once I saw two moons in the sky. One was big and blue."

"You *are* going to other worlds!" Rachel declared, awed.

"Aw! That is so unfair! I want to go to other worlds!" cried Sigfried. "I want to be the first man on Mars! Has anyone in the World of the Wise gotten to Mars?" Rachel shook her head. "I want to be the one to go!"

"It's got to be!" Rachel's mind leapt rapidly, analyzing what they knew so far. "That's where the new magic is coming from. Other worlds. Along with the people: Salome, Valerie, and Lucky!"

Thousands of topics interested Rachel Griffin, but none were as enthralling as the notion of other worlds. The idea called to her, whispering that she should awake. It was like a beam of light piercing an otherwise dark and gloomy chamber, illuminating wonders not previously beheld. Mentally, she added a wing to the library of her mind, with yards and yards of empty shelves, ready for the knowledge she hoped to collect. She wanted to know everything there was to know about these distant places. Even more, she wanted to *visit* them!

Siggy had picked up some rocks. He skipped one seven times across the water of the reflecting lake. Impressed, Rachel tried it, too. Her stone sunk like, well, a stone.

Siggy snickered, "You throw like a girl."

"I am a girl," Rachel objected.

"Oh. Good point." He looked faintly surprised, as if that taunt had never before failed to hit its mark.

As they skipped stones, a soft noise came from behind them. Tiny Magdalene Chase approached shyly. Losing her nerve, she backed away. Nastasia held out her hands, gently beckoning her forward. Despite her regal bearing, the princess regarded her with such gracious welcome that Magdalene overcame her fear.

She approached slowly, clutching her China doll close to her chest.

"Fear not," the princess assured her. "We do not bite...except maybe for Mr. Smith, who has been known to spit on a few palms."

The tiny girl blushed darkly. "Um...I wonder if I could..." She bit her lip.

"Pet the dragon?" asked the discerning princess. She arched a perfectly formed eyebrow of loveliness at Sigfried.

"Sure!" Siggy gave the girl his sky-sailor-blinding grin. "Lucky, let's give this young lady the royal treatment."

Lucky the Dragon zoomed forward and wrapped around the tiny girl. Magdalene made no noise, but she glowed as if an inner flame shone through her porcelain skin. She closed her eyes and rubbed her cheek against the dragon's soft fur. When the dragon finally unwrapped from around her, she gave a tiny curtsy and ran away.

Grinning, Siggy and the dragon bumped knuckles. In the distance, thunder rumbled from the direction of Stony Tor. Rachel noticed other freshmen searching the blue skies. The older students did not so much as twitch. Rachel wondered if this casual disregard of thunder led to them being taken by surprise when the noise heralded a real rainstorm.

"My question is," Sigfried turned back to the princess, "who is behind this? Who knows about these other worlds? There must be someone. People from beyond the edge of our world, beyond the moon. The Metaplutons!"

"Who?" Rachel asked.

"The Metaplutons!" Sigfried repeated. "The people beyond Pluto."

"That's a really stupid word," Rachel snorted.

Sigfried shrugged. "I got it from a film Lucky saw while peeking in someone's window. Only I don't think I remembered it right. That's how I watched all my TV, by the way. We did not have a telly at the orphanage."

"We do not have one either," Rachel replied. "Delicate electronics do not work well near magic. Gryphon Park is far too magical a place for mundane devices to work properly. I've never seen a moving picture." She paused. "But we can't use Meta-plutons. It's ridiculous."

"Metaplutons is a bit awkward." The princess considered the matter carefully. "But I cannot currently think of a better one. My father would no doubt suggest something significantly worse, like bumblesauruses, or wigglebockers. I recommend we stick with Metaplutons."

The princess was so stately and so proper. Yet her stories about the King of Magical Australia were so inane, that, if Rachel had not seen the solemn, almost pained, expression on Nastasia's face, she would believe the princess was inventing them.

How could the king of a country be so frivolous? How could such a frivolous monarch produce such a serious daughter? How could such a serious daughter be so fond of such a frivolous father? For Nastasia was clearly fond of her father. Rachel found herself mildly curious about the other Romanov children. There were two in Dare Hall and another in Dee. Were they like Nasta-sia? Like their father? Or something else entirely?

"No, no. You are right," Sigfried said solemnly. "Metapluton is much too ridiculous. We'll call them Metacroutons."

"What? That's much worse!" Rachel cried, grabbing at her head.

The princess sighed. "I warned you. Always best to accept the craziness and move on."

"Okay. Then Metaplutons it is. It honors Pluto. You know the adults are trying to take away his planet."

Siggy leaned over and whispered to Lucky, "Should we tell them…about last night?"

"Up to you, Boss," Lucky whispered back. "If they are part of your harem now, you might want to tell them."

"Harem?" Rachel stamped her foot in outrage.

"I should think not." The princess's voice had a steely edge.

"Lucky," Siggy grabbed his head, "I told you before. Humans don't have harems."

"Sure you do." The dragon insisted. "You just bite the female on the back of her neck, and she's yours."

"No one is biting the back of any part of me!" Rachel ex-claimed loudly. Fond as she was becoming of Siggy, it was definitely developing into a sisterly affection. "What happened last night?"

Siggy and Lucky exchanged glances.

The dragon spoke first. "Something bad came."

"Bad, how?" she asked cautiously.

"Bad as in it made Lucky not able to think any more." Siggy's voice shook slightly. "He turned into a dumb animal."

"It was…really horrid!" The dragon shivered from head to toe. His soft gold fur struck straight up like a frightened cat. He looked twice as wide as normal.

"That's terrib…" Rachel began and then froze. "Wait! When did this happen? Last night? In the middle of the night?"

They both nodded, the boy's head and the dragon's bobbing up and down together.

"The Raven!" Rachel stated. "I bet it was the Raven!"

"What raven?" Siggy asked.

"An enormous raven, bigger than an eagle. He came and talked to my roommate's lion. Tried to tell the lion that it had to go away."

"In our room?" The princess halted.

Rachel nodded.

"That is…very disturbing," Nastasia murmured softly.

"What did the lion do?" Siggy asked, intrigued.

"It refused to go."

"Did it talk?"

"Yes."

Rachel repeated the conversation exactly. She did not reproduce the voices like a ventriloquist, but she echoed the intonation of each speaker. Her lion's voice was calm and regal, and her raven's voice was hoarse and annoyed.

"Are you certain you did not dream this?" the princess asked.

"Yes. I heard it and saw it. When I asked Kitten if her lion could talk, she did not say no." Rachel paused, uncertain how to put into words the eeriness of the Raven or the sense of august majesty that miniature lion displayed, almost as if its tiny size were a trick of the eye, and it was a very massive creature indeed.

"That is hardly the same as saying 'yes,'" The princess pointed out graciously.

"You did not see her face," Rachel replied solemnly.

She considered telling them about the boy she had met in the upstairs hallway but held back for two reasons. The first was that if her father had not told her the name of the organization he worked for, he probably did not want other people knowing it. And if she did not tell them that part, then having met another student hardly seemed an event worth discussing.

The second was harder to put into words. Meeting someone in her private spot seemed oddly like a secret. She realized he was probably not a nice boy, being from Drake Hall. He may have had an ulterior motive for talking to her. Still, she felt reluctant to share him.

But something else occurred to her that she could tell her friends.

"You know, dragons don't speak in our world," she said slowly. "They are animals, like deer and zebras."

"And wallabies," the princess added automatically. "Wallabies never talk. No matter how much of the pink Monopoly dollars that Father calls money he offers for a talking one."

"So...what are you saying?" Siggy asked Rachel.

"The Raven. It was trying to stop the lion from being here. I wonder if it is trying to stop Lucky, too."

Siggy's eyes darkened dangerously. "It had better not..."

From the left, voices cried: "Look! It's Sigfried Smith! And his dragon!"

Girls swarmed everywhere, fawning over Siggy and squealing over Lucky. Rachel did not like being near the center of a crowd. Her chest seized up, as if she were wearing a garment that was too tight for her. She had to struggle to draw her next breath. As Siggy grinned and spoke boastfully to his adoring fans, she slipped quickly away.

Retrieving Vroomie from her room, she flew through the towers and spires atop Roanoke hall, slowly at first and then more quickly until she was whipping through them at lightning speed. The crowds, the campus, the disturbing visions, and the murder attempts all fell away. She was alone with the glory of flight.

She ate dinner with her new friends and retired early. Alone in her room, she lay with her head on her pillow and recalled the events of the day. More had happened in this one day than happened in a week or a month of her previous life. In fact, in her entire existence, she was not sure she had fit in so many extraordinary moments. In one day, she had started her new life, made friends, spied out an imposter, witnessed a murder attempt, bonded with her familiar, considered the possibility of a world beyond her world, met a helpful boy who might possibly be evil, learned the name of the clandestine organization for which her father worked, discovered that one of her new friends could visit other worlds in visions and bring back flower petals, and talked to a dragon.

Oh, and she had heard a raven talking to a lion.

Thinking back, she realized with a start that John Darling, her crush from afar, had been in the dining hall during dinner. She had not even noticed him. She replayed the few seconds of him laughing with her brother Peter that her memory had caught out of the corner of her vision. Freezing the image in her mind's eye, she concentrated on his smiling face and sighed.

As she thought back, she remembered something else that had happened that day. In the forest, she had found a statue of a beautiful woman with wings—a statue that made her want to cry when she thought about it, though she did not know why. A statue that...

Rachel sat upright in bed, her eyes flying wide open, though she could not see much of the darkened room.

When she had gone flying that morning, she had seen Bannerman Island. When she remembered back, the Obscuration failed to trick her perfect memory, and she had recalled the real Island of Roanoke.

In the same way, her memory of the glade with the statue did not match what she had seen at the time. Everything was the same, except that her eyes had shown her a tree bough above her head that had bounced despite the lack of wind.

In her memory, an enormous black raven sat upon that branch, staring down at her with blood red eyes.

CHAPTER NINE:
THE UNFORESEEN PERILS
OF BREAKFAST

RACHEL WOKE EARLY THE NEXT MORNING. AGAIN, THE DAWN WAS peeking over the horizon, and her roommates were asleep. Pulling out paper and ink, she filled her new fountain pen and wrote a long letter, detailing every aspect of the incident with Valerie and the fake Agent. Her father would see that the right people in the Wisecraft learned about these events.

Rachel tipped her chair back and thought about her father. He was a wise, kind, handsome man, beloved of his family and much admired by his peers and tenants. Over the last few years, with Grandfather gone and Sandra, Father's favorite, away at school, he and Rachel had become closer. Writing everything down and sending it to him made her feel as if her father were near, like she was one of his operatives gathering secrets for the Wisecraft. She imagined him reading her words and being so pleased that his littlest daughter was following in his footsteps.

Most of all, it made her feel hopeful. Father was an Agent of the Wisecraft; apparently he was the head of their super secret department. He must have answers as to what was going on—or at least know what the Wisecraft had learned about the new magic. If she reported everything to him, surely he would return the favor and share a little of what he knew.

She wanted so much to understand. The mysteries—a murder attempt, distant worlds, talking ravens and lions—were almost too intriguing to bear.

She had to know more!

She replayed her memory of the events again and again, writing down everything she had noticed. Then she dressed and

headed outside to take the letter to the mail room. A long wind-
ing staircase led down from the first floor to the cellars below
Roanoke Hall. Down here were the mail room, the Talking Glass
room—for calling home, and the Storm King Café—a shop that
sold sandwiches, drinks, and fancy desserts. Rachel slipped her
letter in the outgoing mail slot and checked her mailbox. Inside
was a note that read:

Dear Miss Griffin,

*Please report to the gymnasium at three-thirty on Wednesday
to assume your new position as my instructional assistant.*

Thank you,

Mr. Chanson.

Rachel smiled and tucked the note in her pocket. Her
parents had arranged for her to assist the P.E. teacher, who was
a friend of her mother's. She was to help teach beginners to fly.
It was not a paying position. Lady Rachel Griffin had no need of
monetary gain. She did, however, look forward to sharing what
she knew about flying with others and to learning more through
the process.

Her new friends were already seated when she arrived at
breakfast, so Rachel went through the line to get her food alone.
She was hungry, and the breakfast looked very tasty. She could
find no kippers and no kimchi, but her mother had warned her
not to expect them. She enjoyed picking out eggs and orange
juice and toast, as she listened to the bacon sizzling behind the
counter. It all smelled so appetizing.

As she moved to get her silverware, she saw Magdalene
Chase ahead of her, carefully choosing a piece of fruit from a
large bowl. The tiny girl's left eye was black and swollen. It
looked exactly the way her brother Peter's eye had the time he
came home from school after losing a particularly grueling
duel with some obnoxious boy with whom Peter had an on-
going rivalry.

A feeling of outrage far greater than could be contained by
her small stature began boiling inside Rachel. Somebody had hit
Magdalene. No matter who it was, it had not been a fair fight.
She was so distracted she did not pay attention to where she was

going until after she bumped into another student. Unfortunately, that student turned out to be Cydney Graves.

"Hey, look where you are going, Midget!" Cydney shoved her.

Rachel lost her balance. Her tray fell. Food flew everywhere. Orange juice drenched her robes, making her gasp as the cold liquid slid down her stomach. The delicious-looking eggs splattered across the floor. Her toast fell butter-side down and was stepped on by a bigger boy who lumbered past.

Cydney laughed loudly. Other students turned and looked. Some of them laughed, too. Rachel stood very still, her face showing no expression. Keeping her exterior calm was second nature, but she had no idea what to do next. What did one do when one was mocked? In stories, characters made amusing quips, but Rachel could think of nothing witty to say.

A group of bigger boys came around the edge of the serving counter. To her horror, Rachel realized that the tall athletic one with the unruly dark hair was John Darling. For a single instance, she imagined him coming to her aid, telling off Cydney, or even removing the orange juice stain with a cantrip, as her mother would have. He had always been so charming when she had seen him at Christmas parties and Wisecraft functions.

It did not happen. He just snickered at her with the other boys and walked past.

Rachel's world imploded.

Rachel ran. She did not want to pass through the crowded dining hall, so she darted down one of the long hallways. There were only two people in the corridor, an older boy, who stood looking at a painting on the wall, and a blond girl, who hung on his arm. The girl was very pretty, but it was a kind of pretty that reminded Rachel of Salome, only without Salome's sweetness. She was the kind of girl boys liked, a lot, but she was not the kind of girl Rachel would have wanted her brother to date.

They were going to laugh at her, too, no doubt. Rachel put her head down and ran, determined to plow by without stopping.

"Rachel?"

The boy turned around. It was the same boy with the chestnut ponytail she had met upstairs the previous day. He glanced at her, as did the blond, who smirked at the huge wet stain on Rachel's robes.

Rachel froze, mortified.

Casually, Gaius Valiant raised his right hand and pointed two fingers at her, his left hand gesturing with each word.

"Silu varenga. Taflu."

The orange juice rose off her garments, formed a ball, and sailed to the nearest trash can. Gaius winked at her and then turned back to the blond girl.

"Thank you!" Rachel cried, extremely grateful. But the boy did not turn around. Shrugging, she ran back to the dining hall.

The kitchens were already closed. Her stomach growled as she made her way to classes. Language was first again on Tuesdays, then Art, and a new class, Math. The classroom for Math had blue curtains. The sunlight shining through them dappled the table and books cerulean. The room would have been dim, but the tutor had added extra lights. As with the rest of the campus, domestic will-o-the-wisps provided the illumination. When they first opened the door, the tiny glowing flecks hung in the air like miniature stars. The moment a student entered a chamber, the will-o-the-wisps rushed together, forming shining balls.

Rachel loved this kind of lighting. She loved its gentle pearly glow. She loved the whispery sound the will-o-the-wisps made, almost like music. She loved the way they rushed together when she stepped into a room. As a child, she had spent many hours playing peek-a-boo with them, sneaking up on a room and flinging open the door, in hopes of catching a glimpse of the black expanse filled with teensy glittering stars before they swirled together.

The tutor was a cool, imposing woman named Dr. Mordeau. She was tall with dark hair streaked with silver that formed a formidable widow's peak above her brow. Her robes were the black and blue of a Thaumaturge. An ebony Fulgurator's wand with a ruby tip hung from a chain around her waist. Her familiar curled about her arms and shoulders. It was a large, black snake with strange feather-like ears.

Standing before them, she quieted the chatter with a forbidding frown. When they were silent, she began: "In this class, you will learn geometry, which you will need if you are to draw the circles and seven-pointed stars necessary for Warding and Thaumaturgy. This class is the gateway to both of those Arts. In later years, these two paths will diverge."

She went on to introduce geometry, which Rachel found fascinating. She loved the regularity of mathematics. She also loved anything to do with space and three dimensions. Geometry appealed to her exceedingly.

Rachel now knew her entire Core Group: the princess, Siggy, Joy O'Keefe—the seventh-daughter of a seventh daughter; the shy, scholarly Astrid—who was also her fourth roommate; Zoë Forrest, whose hair was a bright scarlet today; Wulfgang Starkadder—rumor had it that the nobility of Transylvania could all transform into wolves. With his dark, brooding, good looks, Wulfgang certainly seemed wolf-like—and a bass guitar-playing boy named Seth Peregrine.

Another group of freshmen from Dare were in Language, Music, and Math, but not in Art or True History. Rachel did not know about Science, as she would not have that class until the afternoon. This second Dare Core Group included the lion's owner, fierce little Kitten Fabian; the spirited cheerleader Brunhilda Winters; the lovely, gregarious Wendy Darling; tall somber Sakura Suzuki and three boys: Wendy's cousin, the loud and funny Irish Ian MacDannan; Enoch Smithwyck, an extremely British-looking boy with glasses and short sandy hair who spoke with a Japanese accent, having grown up in Japan; and a dark-haired boy from New York City named David Jordan, whose familiar was a mouse with the odd name of Electronic Pointing Device.

To Rachel's dismay, the other children in Math were from Drake Hall—the Thaumaturgy students. This meant they would most likely be very good at this class, since it was the gateway class to their Art. Given a choice, she would rather have had the class she shared with the snootiest kids not be the one they would excel at. Why couldn't she have had the kids from Drake in Language or Music?

Rachel did not mind Salome, who immediately shimmied up next to Siggy, batting her eyelashes at both him and poor David Jordan, or tiny Magdalene Chase, whose bruised cheek was now a faint green. She must have visited the nurse. Bruises were easy to heal. Cydney, Belladonna, and Charybdis, on the other hand, were another story.

Cydney and her friends sat down together next to their friend the sneering boy, whose name had turned out to be Arcturus Steele. They giggled at her from behind their hands whenever the tutor turned her head. The other students from Drake included Zenobia Jones, a dark-skinned girl from Chicago; Colin Row, a quiet, round-faced boy; a French boy named Coren D'Avern; and Spanish-speaking Napoleon Powers, whose father represented a section of South America on the Parliament of the Wise.

Toward the end of the class, Dr. Mordeau closed her textbook. "Before we end, today, I shall give you a brief tutorial on how to use your familiar to ward yourself. Wards made by familiars are not as powerful as those made with a proper athame, but they will protect you from some magical influences. Many types of Enchantment, for instance."

"Have you noted the change to your familiars? That their paws or feet or talons are now silver on the bottom?" Dr. Mordeau held out her hand.

Her snake had left her shoulders and curled up on a spot of sunny floor. It slithered over to her and up her arm. She held the serpent up, so that everyone could see the silvery scales on its stomach.

"Now. Stand up and instruct your familiar to circle you three times widdershins. Does everyone know what widdershins is? Counter-clockwise?"

Rachel giggled. As the owner of a pony named Widdershins, she certainly knew what the word meant. But it was a nervous, almost hiccuppy giggle. She was, again, the only one without a familiar. She stood still, her head slightly down, and hoped no one would notice. It did not help that her stomach growled loudly.

From across the table, she heard Cydney Graves tell Zenobia, Arcturus, Coren and Napoleon, "See that tiny Asian girl? She's so small she has to ride a training broom. It's got this huge, fat fan in the back, probably to keep it from falling out of the air when she wobbles."

The others laughed loudly.

"Training broom...to go with her training bra," snickered Zenobia, who was quite shapely, though she had nothing on Salome Iscariot.

Rachel's careful calm faltered. They were insulting Vroomie again. She felt the heat crawl into her cheeks.

Dr. Mordeau was erasing the chalkboard with a gesture of her wand. A ripple of breeze gathered the chalk back into the stick in her hand. As she turned, the blushing Rachel was directly in her sight. To Rachel's surprise, the imposing teacher spoke kindly to her.

"There is no shame in being a beginner, child," Dr. Mordeau stated. "I have never heard of a training broom. What is that?"

Rachel spoke in a small voice. "I am not a beginner, Ma'am. I ride a steeplechaser."

The tutor's eyebrows arched elegantly. "I did not know they still made those. Steeplechasers are said to be very difficult to master, having so many blades, and so many variations as to how the fan can be arranged. Can you control it?"

"Yes, Ma'am." Rachel drew herself up and lifted her chin. "I am Mr. Chanson's assistant. My job is to help the beginners learn to fly."

"Indeed?" If possible, her eyebrows went higher. "You must be very good."

Rachel blushed from pleasure and curtsied. "Thank you."

Across the table, Cydney's face had frozen in an awkward mask of surprise and dismay. Realizing this, she changed her expression to a sneer. However, she had lost the attention of the other children, who were now regarding Rachel with some interest. Much as their scrutiny made her uncomfortable, Rachel could not help feeling pleased. She did not smirk at the other girl—that would be too much like gloating, an unladylike behavior—but her heart glowed like warm coals. This was her best moment since coming to school.

Dr. Mordeau put her chalk down. "Who are you, child?"

"Rachel Griffin." It did not seem an appropriate time for her full title. The Drake kids would just use it to mock her.

"Griffin. Ambrose Griffin's daughter?"

Rachel nodded.

Something flashed through the tutor's eyes too quickly for Rachel to catch. The woman nodded and gave a wintry smile. "Welcome to my class, Rachel Griffin."

As they walked to lunch, Rachel contemplated the tutor's response to her father's name. What was it that had flickered through her eyes? Had it been admiration? Had Dr. Mordeau been impressed? Was the woman fond of her father? Rachel was extremely interested in her parents and their life before she knew them, especially her father. If this woman admired him, would she tell Rachel stories of his exploits? Anyone else would have to wonder, but Rachel Griffin was not anyone else.

She recalled her memory of the moment when she had confirmed her father's name, slowing it down. She had to replay it three times before she was sure. Once she identified the right moment, Dr. Mordeau's reaction was unmistakable.

The emotion that had burned in her Math tutor's eyes at the mention of her father's name was *hatred*.

CHAPTER TEN:

THE SIX MUSKETEERS

AND THE TERRIBLE FIVE

SCIENCE WAS THE FINAL OF THEIR SIX CLASSES. IT MET IN A LAB UP on the second floor. The students gathered at the central table, but the majority of the room was taken up by lab stations with sinks and Bunsen burners. Tinted windows kept the sunlight streaming through the courtyard from damaging the millions of fascinating objects stored on the shelves and in the glass cabinets.

Rachel chose a seat with her friends. Turning slowly in a circle, she let her gaze fall over the entire classroom, taking everything in: crystal vials, shiny copper crucibles, jars containing dried flowers and feathers and scraps of colored light that bounced around with a soft *zing*. A full-sized skeleton of a horse stood in the back corner. Someone had thrown a saddle blanket over it. Two stuffed bats and a tarantula hung from the ceiling.

Drinking in new information gave her a way to keep her mind from fixating on why Dr. Mordeau hated her father. Rachel was extremely curious, but no amount of speculation on her part was going to answer the question without more facts.

To the students' delight, the tutor was the famous Crispin Fisher. Mr. Fisher was a family friend of the Griffins and one of the Six Musketeers—the group of students, led by James Darling, who defeated Veltdammerung. Fisher himself had dueled one of the Terrible Five.

Mr. Fisher was a pleasant fellow with sandy hair and glasses who dressed in the black and orange of the Alchemists. He explained that Alchemy was the ancient Chinese art of putting magic into physical objects. All magical talismans—swords, grails, amulets of protection—were made by Alchemy. With the eager smile of an enthusiast, he assured them that when they were done with his fascinating class, they would all want to be Alchemists. It was his dream that someday Raleigh Hall would be full, and the other Halls empty.

He then launched into a rambling description of what his course would cover. His voice droned on in a pleasant monotone. Rachel listened carefully, but she noticed many students were no longer paying attention. Like in Math, the non-Dare students were the ones who were serious about Alchemy—the kids from Raleigh Hall. Even they seemed bored.

Siggy had begun to nod off, his mouth hanging open, when Yara Rahotep, a girl from Raleigh Hall interrupted Mr. Fisher.

"Tell us about fighting the Terrible Five!" she cried in her thick Egyptian accent. She had a sweet, dazed expression, as if she was never quite sure where she was.

"Yes! Tell us! Tell us!" clamored the rest of the students. Rachel clamored with them. She knew these stories. She had heard Mr. Fisher and Mr. and Mrs. Darling tell them at Yule parties. But she never tired of hearing them again.

Mr. Fisher glanced at the clock on the wall. "Well...I am not sure I should take the time..."

"There are students here who grew up in the mundane world," Zoë Forrest drawled. She sat with her chair leaning back and her feet resting on the table, chewing on the long scarlet braid that hung down from the side of her head. "They don't know about the Terrible Years."

"Oh...Good point." He crossed to a glass cabinet and removed some jars as he spoke. "When sorcerers go truly bad, people become afraid to kill them. This is because some sorcerers refuse to die. Either they have hidden their life outside their body, like Koschai the Deathless. Or they have made a deal with dark powers to bring them back when they perish, like Aleister Crowley. Or perhaps they have found a way to make their bodies repair themselves, after their spirit is driven forth, such as Simon Magus. Or they have separated their soul from their shadow because they know the secrets of *The Book of Going Forth By Day*, like Morgana Le Fay. Or, they are just plain scary like

Baba Yaga. Instead of killing them, the Parliament of the Wise turns them to stone.

"An archiomancer named Aaron Marley—who happened to be the great nephew of Scrooge's old partner, Jacob Marley—discovered the lost secret of turning people back from stone. He revived the five worst sorcerers of all history: The afore named Simon Magus, Morgana Le Fay, Baba Yaga, Koschai the Deathless, and Aleister Crowley. Hence the nickname the Terrible Five."

Mr. Fisher placed the jars on the counter beside the first lab station. By squinting, Rachel could make out bark, a blue butterfly, wool, and gold dust.

"Marley and the Terrible Five joined forces. They forged a cabal devoted to destroying the world, known as Veltdammerung—or, in English, the Twilight of the World. There were three prophesies about the Veltdammerung." Mr. Fisher sat on a stool beside the jars. "One predicted their rise to power, which came true; one foresaw their gaining control of some talisman called the Heart of Dreams, that never did happen; and one claimed that they would be undone by a boy named James Darling.

"They sent a smoky-winged creature to slay the Darling family. Only, somehow, the six-year-old James survived—which is how these things always work. Prophesies can be altered. Universally, however, committing an act of violence to change them seems merely to hasten their arrival. Look at Oedipus or Perseus or Paris.

"Some years later, Aaron found out about a meeting of the Agents. He had friends in the Wisecraft. The Veltdammerung took the gathering by surprise. In one fell swoop, they killed everyone who could have stopped them. Or so they thought.

"With the help of the Morth Brood—sorcerers who were tired of obeying the rules of the Parliament of the Wise and welcomed an excuse to practice black magic—the Terrible Five set about conquering the world—starting with the Wise. The Terrible Five had other servants, too. Supernatural servitors. The entire group of them—Marley, the Terrible Five, the Morth Brood, and their other servants—comprised the Veltdammerung."

Wulfgang Starkadder raised his hand. "Was the Terrible Five's Morthbrood the same organization that terrorized England in Morgana Le Fay's day?"

"Um..." The Science tutor blinked. "I...don't know. I think they were just named after the earlier Morth Brood. But there are secret covens of black magicians that have hidden from the authorities throughout the ages. These all rushed to the side of the Terrible Five."

"What happened?" Siggy asked, fascinated. "Did everyone die?"

"Obviously not, Bird Brain." Zoë Forrest rolled her eyes. "Some of us are still here."

"Hey, that's dragon brain to you," Sigfried shot back, grinning. Zoë's lips twitched with amusement.

Mr. Fisher gave them a gently remonstrative look. "They killed a great many, intimidating the World of the Wise. But we in the Young Sorcerers League did some research. We were able to discover how each of them had been captured the first time, except for Koschai the Deathless. A few of us older students joined together and vowed to stop them. People called us the Six Musketeers—because there were six of us to counter the six of them—the Terrible Five and Marley." He faltered and sadness overcame his features. "Or rather, we were five older students and one younger sister of two of our members."

"Wendy MacDannan," Rachel whispered softly.

Not softly enough to keep Mr. Fisher from hearing her. He swallowed and nodded. "Wendy MacDannan."

"Who was she?" Siggy finished folding his fourth paper airplane. Every time he completed one, he let it fly under the table, where Lucky burned it in mid-air. So far, they had managed this without singeing the other students.

"The MacDannans—there is one in your year—" Mr. Fisher looked around, but Ian was not in this class, "are descended from the Selkie. They are a strongly magical clan prone to the Second Sight. Wendy, the younger sister of Finn and Ellyllon, was blessed with this gift. Thanks to her visions, we discovered where Koschai hid his heart."

"Wasn't it in a duck?" called Arjuna Pandava, a boy from India with a faraway look in his keen eyes.

The tutor shook his head. "In a needle, in an egg, inside a duck, inside a hare, inside an iron chest on the disappearing island of Buyan."

"That's...pretty hidden," Sigfried snorted, amused.

Mr. Fisher nodded. "Ellyllon is friends with the mermaids. She talked them into taking her to Buyan, where she beguiled the three brothers who lived there—the Northern, Western, and Eastern winds—with her dancing. Once she destroyed the needle..." Mr. Fisher looked a bit sheepish, "I vanquished Koschai in a duel."

"But what happened to Wendy? I mean the one in your story. Not the one in our class." asked Ameka Okeke, the daughter of an Orkoiyot, a supreme chieftan of the Nandi people of Kenya. She had dark brown skin and beautiful slanted eyes much like Rachel's, courtesy of her Chinese mother. Rumor had it she was the Freshman class's best female soccer player.

Mr. Fisher's face faltered. "She...she tried to learn more by journeying into dreams, the realm from which conjured things come. The Terrible Five attacked her, trapping part of her in dreams forever. She...was never the same after that. The Wendy in your class, Wendy Darling, is her niece and namesake."

"Is she dead?" Siggy pressed. "The old one, I mean."

Mr. Fisher shook his head. "No. She is still with us. She is just..."

"Crazy," muttered Wulfgang Starkadder.

Mr. Fisher glared at him but did not contradict him. "She is...trapped at the age of fifteen, even though she is an adult now. She dreams even when she is awake."

There was an awkward silence. Mr. Fisher cleared his throat and returned to the subject of his class syllabus. Again, Rachel paid close attention. Again, the rest of the class, except for Astrid Hollywell, began to drift off. Siggy went back to folding airplanes. Ameka Okeke drew funny stick-figure pictures of her fellow students, making those to either side of her giggle. Joy O'Keefe slipped her day-glo pink photo album under the table and showed it to Nastasia. The princess clearly wished to pay attention, but she was too polite to stop Joy because that would have meant interrupting the tutor.

Ameka waved her hand. "Sir! Tell us about the Six Musketeers!"

"Well." Mr. Fisher paused in the act of placing more jars on the lab counter. "There was me, of course. I am the Alchemist in the group. You already know that. I made the shields we used to stop Morgana's deadly fire blast and the dagger that James used to kill Simon Magus. And I made our tarnhelm and tarnkappe. I used the stories about the original ones—the ones that came from the gods—as my models. Mine came out pretty well, if I don't say so myself. Though it was extraordinarily difficult work.

"Then, there's James. He's the most famous member of our team. You've probably heard of him—due to the *James Darling, Agent* pulp adventure comics, if nothing else. He was our Canticler. When he speaks, everything listens to him. He can make rocks talk, and rain sing.

"James came up with the idea of fighting back. Everyone else had given up, but James said: 'What do the adults have on us except a few more years of school. We have the resources of Roanoke Academy. Maybe a lot of children can do what a few adults can't.'"

"He must have been quite brave," the princess said approvingly.

Mr. Fisher nodded. "He was. Of course, the Darling family has a history of astonishing children. James's grandfather and his great aunt and uncle were the ones that put an end to the stealing of children by Pan's son, Peter. James had been raised hearing about their adventures in Neverland. It gave him faith that we could do what needed to be done."

"Is he really like the guy in the comics?" Arjuna asked eagerly.

Mr. Fisher smiled sheepishly. "Yes and no. He is smart and athletic. But he can't leap rushing rivers, cantrip fifty people at once, or fly a broom at 200 miles an hour through a snowstorm."

Arjuna looked disappointed. Wulfgang snickered.

Mr. Fisher tapped on the nearest jar, causing the gold dust within to dance. "Finn MacDannan is the cocky one. He was our Enchanter. There is nothing that man cannot do with music. When he plays, people can't keep from dancing, even when he doesn't use magic. But he had an obnoxious sense of humor.

"Scarlett Mallory, who later married Finn, is brilliant. In the entire four hundred years plus of Roanoke Academy, she is the only person who ever lived in all seven dormitories. Scarlett moved every year. She mastered all seven of the Sorcerous Arts. The only student I have seen come even close is Miss Griffin's older sister. Upon graduation, Sandra Griffin was presented with rings of mastery for five of the Arts taught here."

The other students looked at Rachel, who blushed, very pleased. She loved when people praised Sandra. Still, she could not help wondering, if Sandra was so good at everything, why was she, Rachel, not a better sorceress?

"Let's see," he counted on his fingers, "Wendy, myself, James, Finn, and Scarlett. Ah, right. The last Musketeer was Ellyllon MacDannan, our conjurer and a friend to mermaids. A strange young woman. She used to dance on the tables in the dining hall. Instead of shooing her off, the proctors would pull out their instruments and play for her. She was...quite provocative." He paused, as if caught up in the memory. "Nowadays, she is Mrs. James Darling."

"How could kids do all that?" Joy O'Keefe asked.

"They were college students," Rachel pointed out.

"Even college students?" Joy looked inquiringly toward Mr. Fisher. "Against such powerful sorcerers?"

"Who else was there?" Mr. Fisher shrugged. "We were the front line. We could give up and die, or we could go forward. We chose forward."

Yara asked dreamily, "So James married Ellyllon, and Finn married Scarlett. That's so romantic. Would you have married Wendy MacDannan, if she had not been injured?"

All the humor fled from Mr. Fisher's eyes. He spoke quietly. "I do not feel that I should answer that question."

There was a pause. Students squirmed. Mr. Fisher forced himself to smile, "Back to the Terrible Five. Each of us took on one of them. James fought Simon Magus. Scarlett Mallory defeated Morgana Le Fey. Finn MacDannan destroyed Crowley. Ellyllan and her mermaids overcame Baba Yaga, and I dueled Koschai and won." He looked amazed, as if his victory still surprised him.

Siggy leaned forward. "This Koschai the Deathless was bad news?"

"Oh, was he! A horrible, withered old man. He dressed in his own hair. Who does that, I ask you? He could kill people by pointing his bony finger at them." Mr. Fisher strode back and forth, pantomiming several cantrip gestures, as if recalling the fight. "It was an amazing duel. The best I have ever fought! Every spell coming from his wand was lethal! He could kill all living things in a ten foot radius. He could even kill the wind and make the air still for a week!"

"So you defeated the baddest of them all?" Siggy asked. "Ace!"

"Yeah." A grin spread slowly across the Alchemist's face. "Yes, I guess I did!"

"It's driving me crazy." Valerie rubbed her temples, as she sat on the bench in the walled garden. The scent of wisteria perfumed the air. The fountain, spilling from the cherub's trumpet, gurgled. Siggy, Nastasia, and Salome were with them. "I keep thinking I've seen a guy like you described...the guy who wanted to kill me." She shuddered. "Or whatever that scarab thing would have done to me. But I can't remember where."

Rachel shuddered, too, but for a different reason. The idea of not remembering disturbed her. She knew other people could not do what she did, but knowing in the abstract and watching someone suffer from forgetfulness were entirely different.

"No matter what, though!" Valerie pounded her fist on her thigh, looking both fierce and impishly cute. Rachel noted that Siggy noticed this, too. "I am going to get to the bottom of this. My father was the best detective on the Kennebunkport police force. He taught me quite a bit before he... I am going to figure out who this guy was, why he attacked me, and why this man said the 'gift' was from my father.

"Can't get to the Internet on this island. Drives me crazy. Though the World of the Wise isn't on the web. So if he is a Wise guy, I couldn't trace him that way."

"Wise guy, oh that's funny." Salome was buffing her nails to make them shine. "Not that I haven't heard it before...but with you, it takes on an additional Mobbish meaning."

Valerie's nose crinkled with amusement. "I've written my friend Charlie back home with a list of searches I want performed. If the information is out there, Charlie will find it. Also, I asked him to send me a copy of my father's list—names related to the case he was working on when he disappeared. Maybe there's a clue there. Meanwhile, I plan to talk to people here. Someone might know something—who that guy was, if nothing else." She leaned forward conspiratorially. "If anyone asks, I'm interviewing people in an effort to find the perfect article—so I can get onto the staff of the *Roanoke Glass*, the school newspaper."

"Great idea!" Rachel grinned. Her grin faded slowly. Sitting down beside the little pool, she asked gently. "Your father died?"

"No. He...disappeared." Valerie looked down. Her golden hair fell over her eyes.

"Oh! I am so sorry!" Rachel clutched her books, horrified.

Valerie peeked through her golden locks. "Thank you. People say he ran out on us, but it's not true. I don't know where he went. Or where he is now. Or if he is dead. But he would *never* have run out on Mom and me."

Rachel looked into Valerie's face and believed her. She stated with calm determination, "I am positive he did not." Valerie gave her a tiny, grateful smile.

The princess had been sitting reading her uber-textbook. Shutting it, she asked, "Do you think the scarab sent to Miss Foxx could have come from a remaining member of the Morth Brood? Even in Magical Australia, we hear rumors of them rising again. Weren't they known for killing people by sending jinxes?"

Despite the warmth of the day, Rachel shivered. "I...hope not. They were...not nice. After the Terrible Years, my father helped hunt them down. I was not born yet, but from what I have gleaned from my mother and my grandparents, it was very dangerous work. The Morthbrood used the worst kind of magic."

"Really?" Salome looped her hand in the air twice. "What would Valerie have done to come to the attention of real baddies, like the Morth Brood? Her father was a mundane policeman. He dealt with gangs and mob violence and the like."

"None of those people could have followed her here," Rachel replied slowly. "She must have come to the attention of someone in the World of the Wise. Someone...not good."

Sigfried had been lazily tossing pieces of a ham sandwich he brought out of his pocket into the air for Lucky to catch. Hearing Valerie, he straightened and knelt before her on the pebbly mosaics, solemn and sincere, like a statue of some ancient knight.

"Milady! My heart burns with wrath against those who have offended you!" His eyes blazing with an uncharacteristic seriousness, he looked even more handsome than usual. All the girls sighed. "No maiden so fair should walk beneath the sun in fear of craven murderers! If by my life, or by my death, I can maim or slay or annoy your foe, I need but your favor to put in me the heart of a hero, that I shall not fail to accomplish all that I have said."

"Technically," the princess stated, "It is incorrect to call a commoner milady."

"Um...if I said yes, I would be aiding and abetting a crime before the fact. But I am grateful for your offer." Valerie's eyes seemed unnaturally bright, as if she was fighting back tears. Flippantly, she added, "If you actually make yourself useful, I may just keep you around."

Siggy grinned and gave Lucky a thumbs-up. The dragon flew in a loop.

Salome asked, "So do you really have a fortune, Sigfried Smith? Did you get it from the dragon you killed? Where do you keep it? Is it in a bank somewhere?"

"Bank!" Siggy exclaimed, appalled. "Let someone else touch it? Certainly not! I keep it under my bed, except for the part on top of the bed that Lucky and I sleep on."

"You...sleep on a bed of gold?" Valerie sounded both disbelieving and amused. "Aren't you afraid someone will take some of it?"

"Lucky knows every coin. The first day, I showed my roommates what happened to a book Lucky breathed on. They won't touch it."

"You...destroyed a book?" Rachel gasped and Valerie together, horrified.

Before Sigfried could answer, three older students walked into the walled gardens. The foremost was a young woman with flaxen hair. She was so lovely and glided with such stately grace that Rachel would have thought her the most beautiful creature alive, if she had not been sitting next to the even more beautiful Nastasia Romanov. Everyone was beautiful and blond here; everyone but her.

Except the next girl, who had red hair. And what hair! It cascaded in waves to her hips. She had a mischievous, pixy-like smile that matched that of her younger brother Ian. She was Oonagh MacDannan, the daughter of Scarlett Mallory and Finn MacDannan. She winked at Rachel, whom she knew from Wisecraft events. Rachel smiled back shyly.

The last was a familiar-looking young man with intense gray eyes. He was dressed in the subfusc style with a silver tie clip that looked like a wolf. An athame, a ceremonial knife used for drawing protective wards, was tucked into his boot.

The statuesque beauty spoke first. "Hello...You're Sigfried Smith, aren't you? I've heard very good things about you, Mr. Smith. We have come to invite you to a meeting of the YSL, the Young Sorcerer's League."

Rachel had been splashing her fingers in the fountain that spilled from the trumpet in the hands of the little marble, fish-tailed cherub. Upon hearing this, her hand dropped into the pool, forgotten. Oh, she wanted to join, too!

She knew a great deal about the YSL. The organization was hundreds of years old. All the best sorcerers had been members, including her grandfather and her parents. As Mr. Fisher had just related in Science class, during the Terrible Years, after Simon Magus and his dark allies had slain all the Wisecraft Agents and taken over the school, it had been the YSL who had stopped them. James Darling had been the League's president that year, and the other members of the Six Musketeers had belonged as well. The entire organization had provided support for the Musketeers and, ultimately, faced the Veltdammerung. Rachel's uncle, Lord Emrys Griffin, had been a member. He had died in that confrontation. He had been seventeen years old.

Rachel gazed longingly at the older students, but they were all looking at Sigfried now.

Siggy rose to his feet and eyed the newcomers suspiciously. Then he got a good look at the tall blond. His eyes locked on her chest, as if it was magnetized, and stayed there. He could not seem to tear them away, no matter how hard he tried. His mouth hung open, and he made a gurgling sound. Rachel feared he would drool.

"Excuse me," Nastasia asked primly, "Who are you?"

The stately blond was clearly amused at Sigfried's misfortune. "I am Rory Wednesday."

Oh. No wonder! The Wednesdays were descended from the Rhinemaiden Loralei and the god Odin. That certainly explained Rory's extraordinary loveliness. The original Loralei had been a siren who led men to their deaths with her beauty and singing.

Valerie kicked Sigfried in the shin. Blinking, he hopped on his other foot and bit his own arm, hard. He stayed that way, eyes bulging, murmuring under his breath. "Ouch. Ouch. Ouch."

Oonagh stepped forward and flashed her pixy smile, undaunted. She spoke with a charming Irish accent. "I am Oonagh MacDannan. I believe me little brother is your roommate, Mr. Smith. Rory and I are classmates. We are both Seniors in the Upper School. We live in Dare Hall with you. You may hear me practicing in the dorm. I play the tuba."

The thought of someone playing enchantments, casting listeners into sleep or causing them to dance without ceasing, with a tuba was so ridiculous Rachel could not help giggling.

Sigfried evidently thought biting his arm was insufficient, so he screwed his eyes shut, but nodded his head up and down, making polite gestures with his other hand. Valerie rolled her eyes. Salome giggled, but she looked slightly petulant at not being the center of attention.

The young man put his foot on the bench next to Nastasia and leaned his elbow on his knee, the knife in his boot jingled. He gazed down at her with piercing gray eyes. "Your prowess at your studies has also preceded you, your highness. We would be honored to have your company as well." He stepped back and bowed. "I believe our fathers are friends. My name is Joshua March."

A shiver of anticipation ran through her. She glanced sidelong at Nastasia. A tiny spark of rebellion gleamed in the princess's eyes. She looked at Rachel and arched one eyebrow. Rachel gave her a tiny encouraging nod.

The princess rose gracefully to her feet, a vision of loveliness. She extended her arm. "I am pleased to make your acquaintance, Joshua March. As you know, I am Nastasia Romanov. I am well acquainted with your father, an admirable man."

Joshua casually took her outstretched hand in his larger grip and shook. All the blood rushed out of Nastasia's face. Her eyes rolled up in her head, and she fainted.

CHAPTER ELEVEN:
LOPSIDED ENCOUNTERS

JOSHUA SHOUTED AND CAUGHT THE PRINCESS. RORY AND OONAGH rushed to her side, as did Siggy. Rachel hovered nearby, uncertain how to help. Guilt gnawed at her. Why had she encouraged Nastasia to disobey Xandra Black's prophecy?

A young man with brown hair ran into the walled garden and slugged Joshua in the face. Joshua looked extraordinarily surprised. He fell backward, dropping Nastasia. Siggy caught her, slinging her into his arms.

"What did you do to my sister!" shouted the newcomer.

"Whoa, Alex! Whoa!" Joshua cried, throwing his arms in front of his face. He lay on the pebbly stones, his head suspended over the pool. "I didn't do anything. I swear. Stop now. I won't tell my father."

Alex kept his fists up, but he took a nervous step back.

"Infirmary," Siggy ran off, carrying Nastasia, Alex Romanov close on his heels.

Rachel hurried after them, but Nastasia did not wake up. Her sister Alexis and her older brother, Ivan, the Crown Prince of Magical Australia, soon arrived. Alex and Alexis were twins, though he had dark brown hair, and she was blond. Rachel guessed them to be about Peter's age. Ivan was older, definitely a college student. He was tall and lanky with a handsome chin and spiky brown hair. With so many siblings hovering around, the nurse sent the other children away.

Rachel crept up to her private hallway and sat down against the wall, next to the suit of armor. She sat for about a minute in absolute silence, her limbs trembling. Then, shakily, she rose to her feet and began practicing with the door stop, knocking it off and floating it up again. It was easier to practice than to think about what had happened.

She had encouraged the princess to disobey Xandra Black's prediction, and something terrible had occurred. She felt so bad for her friend, so worried, so guilty. On top of the attack on Valerie, the princess's visions, and the teacher who hated her father, this was hard to take.

That was before she considered the smaller things: having her breakfast knocked from her hands, or having her broom mocked, or not being invited to join the YSL. Any of those might have ruined her day on their own. Next to the bigger things, however, they seemed inconsequential.

Finally the class bell rang. Reluctantly, she returned downstairs and found Siggy and Joy. Joy's eyes were red, and she kept blowing her nose. She reported that Nastasia had been moved to the Halls of Healing run by the Order of Asclepius, in New York City. Rachel was touched by how upset Miss O'Keefe was on Nastasia's behalf.

Dinner was a quiet affair, except for Siggy, who vowed loudly to avenge the princess, if he could just identify the offending party. He repeated his offer to Valerie to avenge her, and asked Rachel if she needed avenging. Should they wish his help to burn off anyone's face, he assured them, they need only say the word.

After dinner, Rachel practiced in the empty hallway again. Being by herself and concentrating on something concrete brought a sense of peace. Also, the work was paying off. She could now whistle the doorstop off the table and float it up again with ease. She searched around the unused tower rooms until she found a dusty tome much larger and heavier than the doorstop and began practicing with that.

On her way back to her dormitory, Rachel ran across Gaius Valiant. He stood in the hallway, studying the same painting he had been gazing at that morning. When he heard her footsteps, he turned and smiled at her.

"Ah, Miss Griffin. How are you this evening?"

"Just fine," she spoke cheerfully, "and you?"

Rachel stopped beside him and examined the painting, too. It was a picture of a windblown field. In the distance were windmills and a farm house. A crest had been painted above the barn door. She peered at the pastoral scene, wondering what he saw in it.

Gaius said, "I am well. Did you have a good second day?"

Rachel answered flippantly. It was easier than sharing what she felt with a stranger. "Very eventful. I've only been here two days and already my friends have been targeted for murder, fainted in the walled garden, and all sorts of stuff."

"Yes, it has been an eventful couple of days," he said. "We must remain vigilant in times such as these and be sure that we watch out for our own."

"Yeah. It would be a bummer if we accidentally watched out for someone else's," she replied with an intense seriousness only available to thirteen-year-old girls.

He smiled at her comment. Rachel found herself smiling, too, but she shifted her weight nervously. His phrasing struck her as mildly sinister. And yet, something about this young man brought out a frivolity in her that she ordinarily kept contained.

His face became serious. "Tell me, do you know what a geas is?"

Rachel nodded. "Sure. A compulsion that makes you do something, like go on a quest. Or buy margarine instead of butter."

Stepping a bit closer, he lowered his voice. "A geas is a type of ensorcelment that causes someone to lose their free will for a time. It's very dangerous, but one of the good things is that people *know* they are under a spell. If the geas breaks, they remember they were being controlled. They can tell someone."

He glanced cautiously to either side, but there was no one in the hallway. "I have heard, from a reliable source, that a certain group has improved upon that spell. They have a new geas that doesn't even leave you aware that you were controlled. I am not sure how exactly it works, but, if it's true, it's very dangerous. Extremely dangerous. There are geas-breakers among the Agents. They can release someone from a geas relatively quickly. If this new geas exists, they might not be able to break it. Or, if they do, the person won't even know what happened."

"That's terrible!" Rachel blurted out.

"It might behoove you to warn your father," Gaius drawled. "There are whispers that forces thought long vanquished are growing in power. If they can control the Parliament of the Wise with almost no trace, those of us who support law and order are at a severe disadvantage."

Rachel's eyes got bigger as he spoke, though she kept them trained on the painting. Who was this boy? Why was he telling this to her, the youngest child at the school? Was he part of some very bad crowd from which he wanted to escape? From the look of him, she guessed he was a poor student, struggling with his classes like Remington Blake and Zachary Duff. Had this got him into some kind of trouble? Either way, she was certainly going to tell her Father!

When he finished, she nodded decisively, like a soldier receiving orders. "I will!"

Gaius added, "I would have told your brother Peter, but he doesn't like me very much. I am not sure if it's because I'm in Drake, or, more likely, because he's jealous that I am so damn handsome." He winked at her and turned to leave.

The boy was rather good-looking, though not nearly as handsome as Peter, who, Rachel had it on good authority from girls who lived in Gryphon-on-Dart, was spectacularly attractive, almost as much as their father. Still, the sheer arrogance of Gaius's response amused Rachel.

Keeping her voice deadpan, despite the mockery behind her words, she tapped her finger against her cheek, as if thinking. "Yeah, I can see how that might daunt him," she intoned sadly, "Poor Peter."

Skipping away as the older boy snorted with amusement, she headed downstairs to the mail room. She managed not to start giggling until she was in the cellar with her paper out, starting to write. Then, she giggled a lot.

When she eventually recovered from her giggle-fit, she composed a letter to her father repeating what Gaius had told her. She included a report about Nastasia, complete with a description of her visions and Xandra Black's prediction. She told her father everything. With all the strange and disorienting things going on, it made her feel sane and secure to have someone to report to. Some of this information might be crucial to the security of the World of the Wise, and there was no one her Father could get it from except her. Smiling, she prepared an envelope and slipped the letter into the outgoing mail slot.

On her way up the stairs again, the wavering note of a flute sounded. Blue sparkles danced over Rachel's body accompanied by the scent of pine. Rachel's limbs locked up. She could neither move nor speak. Cydney Graves, Charybdis Nott, and a young girl with dark skin who looked a great deal like a toad stood on the staircase, gazing down at her.

Cydney put her hand over her mouth, as if very concerned. "Oh my! I am so sorry! We were just practicing dueling. I am such a horrible shot. I completely missed Lola and hit you." The girls behind her snickered. "I will run and get Nurse Moth right away."

Lola, the toad girl, said, "No need. I know the counter spell." She raised her hands, forming cantrip gestures. "*Gos-el lu siathe.*"

Rachel felt her nose swell, a frightening and unpleasant sensation. It doubled in size. The extra mass in her line of vision disconcerted her. She felt ill. The girls snickered more loudly.

Lola said, "Oh, I must have gotten the hand motion wrong. Let me try again." She repeated the gesture and the words. This time, the Rachel's chest suddenly felt unbalanced.

The girls laughed cruelly. Cydney stepped close to Rachel, leaning toward her in mock dismay. "Oh, I'm ever so sorry. We'll get Nurse Moth."

They ran up the stairs. Rachel could hear them giggling well into the distance. A strange feeling of calm settled over her, as if there was no point in becoming upset when she was incapable of acting. However, she did think: *Hasn't Siggy been waiting for someone to call on him to revenge them?* She imagined Cydney and her friends with their hair on fire, screaming.

These girls would rue the day they attacked her! Rue the day!

Time went by. A lock of hair fell across her face. It tickled but she could not scratch. She wondered morosely if motion, when it returned, would be accompanied by body-wide pins-and-needles. A little dark-haired head poked around the top of the staircase. It was Magdalene Chase. She no longer had a black eye—but she had a red handprint on one cheek. She peered around and then scuttled closer to Rachel.

Magdalene whispered, "I'm sorry I couldn't help you with them. I...just couldn't. But I can help you now, if you promise not to tell them who released you. Promise?" She waited a moment. "I will take your silence as a yes."

Stepping back, she raised her right hand in a fist with only her index finger sticking up and moved it before her in a straight horizontal line. "*Obé.*"

The muscles in Rachel's jaw and arms and legs relaxed. She realized that the whole time she had been stuck, it had been her own muscles holding her in place. There was no pins and needles, but she felt sore all over, as if she had been running for an hour straight.

Magdalene looked at Rachel's nose and chest. Her cheeks grew redder. "Um, I don't know how to fix that."

Looking down, Rachel saw her right breast and shoulder were enormously swollen. The sight terrified her. Her stomach twisted. She felt nauseous.

"Thank you so much! You have my undying gratitude." She managed to give Magdalene a sincere smile. "Of course, I'll never tell anyone. But I owe you. So just ask if you need something, any time...especially from Siggy, the boy with the dragon? He's dying to avenge someone. He'll kick the bum of anyone whose bum you want kicked—you just let him know."

Magdalene's eyes lit up at the mention of Sigfried. Rachel made a note of this. She was sensitive to the least hint of who liked whom. Her father used to tease her that she sensed these things with her mystic girl powers.

Rachel looked down at herself again and shuddered. "Do you know if they really went to get the nurse? If so, I can hide in a corner and wait for her. I wonder if there's a tarp or a blanket in the cellar somewhere."

"I was following them, but I stopped to help you. I don't know if they went or not. I...wouldn't bet on it. Maybe if you just cross your arms?" Magdalene patted Rachel's good shoulder sadly, adding, "But it's pretty late. I doubt you'd run into anyone on the way there. Or, at least, only a few people..."

Rachel slipped her arms under her robe and crossed them in front of her, hiding the distortion to her chest; however, her enormous shoulder still stood out in an obvious fashion. Quietly vowing to herself that she would find a way to protect Magdalene from whomever was abusing her, she began running for the Infirmary.

CHAPTER TWELVE:
SECRETS IN THE HALLWAY

RACHEL RAN OUT OF ROANOKE HALL AND DOWN THE WALK TOWARD the forest. Once among the trees that surrounded Drake, Raleigh, and Dee Halls, she darted south toward the Infirmary, which was beside the gymnasium. In the dark, she had trouble seeing the path. She nearly lost her balance, lurching dangerously due her lopsidedness.

She paused to get her bearings. It was hard to see because her hair kept blowing in her eyes. Above her, she heard a soft sound, like the beat of the wings of death. An eerie shiver ran up her spine, as if the feathers of those wings had brushed her. She turned and looked, but there was nothing there.

Rachel stood still and thought back. In her mind's eye, the great raven with its scarlet eyes flew through the night sky toward Roanoke Hall. She gasped. The Raven turned its head and looked at her. Rachel met its gaze. A horripilation of dread passed across her entire body. She tried to swallow but could not.

Then the Raven was gone.

But it had seen her watching it.

Ahead, she heard cruel girlish laughter. Cydney Graves and her friends stood in front of the Infirmary. Rachel froze. The idea of walking out in front of them, deliberately exposing herself to mockery, was too horrible. She hesitated.

Hiding in the shadows, she plotted the doom of those who had humiliated her. Vivid pictures of Siggy's delight as Lucky breathed on the three girls, and they erupted into geysers of flame played through her imagination. She smiled with spiteful glee.

Two of them moved in her direction. Rachel bolted. She ran the other way, smack into the chest of someone coming down the path. Looking up, she found herself staring into the cheerful face of a tall young man of Spanish descent in his early twenties. He was dressed in a black turtleneck and trousers. It was the proctor, Mr. Fuentes.

"Whoa! Whoa! Careful, Miss. Oh, my! What happened to you?" Fuentes squinted at her in the dark. He made a gesture and said a word. The air lit up around them, glowing softly. Rachel still had her arms crossed in front of her, so he could not see the travesty that was her right breast. Her enormous shoulder and nose were obvious to the eye.

The words burst from Rachel's lips. "Girls. Over there. Cast a spell on me. I want to go to the Infirmary, but they are in the way."

Fuentes gazed at the other young women, his eyes narrowing. "Is that so?" He patted her good shoulder. "Wait here."

Rachel grabbed his arm. "Please...don't make it worse for me."

"No problem." He gave her a big grin and a thumbs-up.

He strode to where the girls waited, laughing, and stood with his hands on his hips. Despite being generally good-natured, he looked rather formidable when he frowned. "Do you girls know the penalty for using magic on your fellow students outside of approved dueling situations? You can get expelled. You should be ashamed of yourselves."

The girls' smirks dried up. They looked embarrassed and frightened. Fuentes made a "go away" gesture. They quickly departed. Grinning, Fuentes gestured to Rachel. She came timidly forward until she stood in front of him, her head down. He put his arm around her shoulders. His body blocking her deformities, he led her to the Infirmary.

"A patient for you, Nurse Moth!" he called good-naturedly.

The nurse arrived and bustled Rachel into a bed. The flame-colored curtains were only half closed. Rachel glimpsed another girl, a pale redhead with braided pigtails, on the first cot. An otter curled around her sleeping body.

"Again, you!" The nurse threw up her hands. "Between you and your two friends, you have been here more than not. And school has only just begun! For you, though, I have the good news. Your friend, the Princess of the Magical Australia, has awoken. She appears to be fine. They keep her in New York for the night, for observation. Tomorrow, she return for the classes."

Relief rushed through Rachel, leaving her giddy. Like someone removing a soaking wool blanket from her shoulders, guilt and fear lifted. Thank goodness. In addition to her happiness on her friend's behalf, Rachel was pleased for the other students. Other children were already looking to the princess for leadership. They seemed lost and disconsolate without her.

The nurse bustled off to get her flute, setting chimes jangling. Overhead, the orrery clicked as its planets rotated. Fuentes sat down on a chair beside Rachel's bed. "You're the littlest Griffin girl, aren't you? Ambrose's daughter?"

Rachel nodded. "I am Rachel."

"Welcome to Roanoke," he grinned.

The door opened, and another man came into the Infirmary. He was older, short with broad shoulders and steely gray hair. He crossed over to where Rachel lay and looked her over.

Fuentes saluted him. "Boss, this is Rachel Griffin. She was…disaccommodated by some fellow freshmen. Rachel, this is the head of security here at Roanoke: Maverick Badger."

Rachel gaped. She had heard of Maverick Badger. When the Terrible Five took over Roanoke twenty five years ago, only Mr. Badger and an Art tutor named Miss Jacinda Moth had stood their ground to protect the students. Nowadays, Miss Jacinda was known as Dean Moth.

"Did you really capture the Heer of Dunderberg after Simon Magus released him from his prison in Stony Tor?" she asked, wide-eyed.

He chuckled and gave her a grim smile. "Sure did. And I have the burn marks to prove it. So, you are Sandra Griffin's little sister, are you? We miss Sandra around here. She's an excellent sorceress and, on top of that, one classy lady. What's she up to now?"

"She's working for the Wisecraft at their Scotland Yard location…doing paperwork." Rachel grinned. "She says it is very boring. I think she's in the accounting department."

"Doubt she'll stay there long," Badger replied gruffly. "She's meant for better things. So...what happened to you?" He glanced at Fuentes.

"A little run in with some expanding cantrips," he said mildly, gesturing at Rachel's nose. The rest of her was covered by a blanket.

"Humph. Well, if it keeps up, let me know. I love crushing the spirit of unruly students." Maverick Badger slammed his fist into his palm with a satisfying *whack*.

Rachel giggled. Then she leaned forward, which was much harder than usual as she listed heavily to one side. "Mr. Badger, you've been at Roanoke a long time...have you ever seen a raven. A very big raven?"

Fuentes shook his head, but Mr. Badger ran his hand across his stubbly cheek.

"You mean a raven with blood red eyes?" he asked gruffly.

"Yes!"

"Did someone you know see this raven?" he asked carefully.

"Um...someone did. Y-yes." Rachel leaned back against the pillows the nurse had propped behind her and pulled her legs against her chest. "W-what is it?"

"Don't know." Mr. Badger shook his head, scowling. "But it's never a good sign, that raven. Ill omen. Something bad's sure to follow."

"Oh," Rachel whispered softly, shivering.

Glancing over, he saw the nurse was returning with her flute and rolled his shoulders. "Must keep going. Got rounds to do. Hope you're back on your feet soon, Miss Griffin."

"Thank you, sir." Rachel shivered as she watched him go.

The nurse's enchanted healing music restored Rachel to her proper shape. The process was not painful, but the twinkling green sparkles tickled and stung. Exhausted, she fell into a dreamless sleep. She spent the night in the Infirmary.

In the morning, Peter and Laurel came by to check on her. Peter was quite disturbed by what had happened. He kept asking her who had attacked her, whether it was an older boy, one his age, and urging her not to walk around alone at night.

Laurel, on the other hand, seemed quite amused. She regaled Rachel with tales of similar fates that had befallen other students, including one about a Junior at the Upper School who had been turned into a fish. When her siblings finally departed, Rachel ran back to her room, changed, and headed to breakfast.

She arrived to find Siggy tossing pieces of blueberry muffins into the air for Lucky to burn, to the delight of an entranced audience. Each time he threw, Siggy shouted, "Pull!"

Rachel got her food and waited patiently for a chance to speak to her friend. When the crowd dispersed, she let those around her, including Valerie and Joy O'Keefe, know that Nastasia was on the mend. Then, she scooted her chair beside Sigfried's and spoke to him privately. "So, you know how you wanted to be a knight and avenge wrongs done to us?"

"Yes! Do you have an enemy? Point me at them! Lucky and I will reduce them to ash...or burn their breakfast, whichever you prefer."

"Last night, some other students cast a spell on me, made me..." she could feel her cheeks getting hot. "They paralyzed me and did some other mean stuff."

"Just point them out!" he cried. Then he leaned toward her conspiratorially. "Or better yet, point with your elbow, that way they won't see and won't notice us coming."

"Those girls there, at that blue table."

Siggy's face froze. His normally mobile expression remained still for so long that Rachel began to fear someone had paralyzed him. Then, he drooped, as if his entire spirit were crushed. "I...can't attack girls!"

"Oh... W-what do I do?"

"I-I don't know!" He scowled. "It's not fair!"

"I can help." Zoë Forrest put her tray down next to Rachel. Her hair was lilac today. She flipped the chair around and straddled it backwards.

"How?" Rachel eyed her warily.

Zoë gave Rachel a lazy grin. "Can't tell. But I can humiliate them. Won't hurt them. Won't get anyone expelled, but...'humiliation galore.'" She spoke the last phrase as if it were a quote. Rachel did not recognize the reference. "What do you say?"

"Um...." Rachel said hesitantly. She glanced at Sigfried, but he was too busy struggling with the conundrum of how to avenge her without attacking a girl. "Okay."

"Great!" Zoë dug into her French toast. "You'll see my handiwork tomorrow morning."

A trip to the mailroom found two letters in her mailbox. The first was a short chatty letter from her mother asking about school and giving her the latest news from the estate. That made Rachel smile. The second was from her father. She opened it eagerly.

Her father's letter read:

Dear Rachel,

If you encounter anyone using the new geas, report it immediately to Ivan Romanov, Yolanda Debussy, Agravaine Stormhenge, Marta Fisher, or John Darling. Hope school is going well.

Love,

Father

Rachel frowned, slightly disappointed. She had expected some mention of how clever she had been to learn this information, of how thorough her reports were, or of what a good team they made. Even better, she had hoped that his letter might contain clues—reports on strange happenings, news about the new magic, information about the scarab or Nastasia's visions or the Raven. But of course, she had only written her letter the night before, so he must have had only seconds, after it came through the Post Glass, to jot off an answer and post it back to her. And she did appreciate the possible opportunity to speak to dreamy John Darling.

Still, she wished her father had taken a moment to let her know that he appreciated her effort. She wanted so much to be of use to him.

Wednesday had two free study periods. One between Language and Math and another in the afternoon between Music and True History. Rachel had already read all her assignments for the first week, but she did not mind reading ahead. She loved learning about the history of early sorcery and the discovery of the Original Language.

She tried to study in her dorm, but next door, Wendy was playing the trombone and a few floors down, Oonagh was booming away on her tuba. Rachel retreated to Roanoke Hall and headed upstairs to the abandoned hallway to practice.

She was quite surprised, and yet somehow not surprised at all, when she looked up from wafting the large tome back to the table and found Gaius Valiant leaning casually against the wall. What was he doing here again, hanging out in the hallway with a thirteen-year-old girl?

Didn't this boy ever go to class?

"Here again, eh?" He gave her a big grin.

"It's as good a place as any." She flashed him a wry smile.

"I suppose." He glanced at the dusty hallway. "Most people practice in their dorms or in the gym."

"My dorm is a very crowded place." She sighed. "People play instruments very loudly. It's hard to hear oneself think, much less read."

He thought about this and then nodded slowly. "I can picture that."

"Where are you from?" she asked, suddenly curious about him.

"Cornwall. My father owns..." he hesitated briefly, "...a farm there."

"Really?" she asked with great interest. There were several tenant farmers on the Gryphon Park estate grounds. Rachel had visited them often during the last several years, and she had read a great deal on farming in her grandfather's library. A good duke made a point of knowing all about how to manage his estate. "A magical farm or a mundane one?"

"Mundane," he drawled with a smile. "I only learned there was magic the summer before I came here. Before that, I wanted to be a scientist."

"I don't know very much about scientists," Rachel admitted. She leaned toward him and confided, "I want to be a librarian."

"Read books and do research all day." Gaius nodded pleasantly. "I could see that could be enjoyable."

Rachel rolled her eyes, "Not a mundane librarian! A Librarian of the Wise, like the great Darius Northwest."

"Sorry. Never heard of him."

"You've never heard of 'Daring' Northwest?" Rachel was outraged on her hero's behalf. "He was the first librarian adventurer! When a patron came into his library looking for a work on the waldgeist, and he did not have any, he went into the wilds of Germany and hunted one down. Not only did he go on to write the definitive work on Teutonic and Slavic forest spirits, he also brought back the only waldgeist ever known to live in captivity. I want to be like him!"

"What an interesting guy." Gaius looked intrigued. "Are all sorcerous librarians like him?"

"Not all, but many follow in his footsteps. I want to be one who does. I want to go places no one has gone before and see things never seen before." Rachel pushed her hair out of her eyes and tried in vain to get it to stay in her barrettes. "In my opinion, it is the perfect profession for a bookish person afflicted by wanderlust." Which she was, in a terrible way.

When reading, Rachel often suffered from a nagging fear that the author might have missed some detail that would have been crucial to her. She longed to go see for herself, just in case. Besides, how else was she going to learn the amazing things no one else knew, if she did not poke into places no one else went?

Turning her attention back to Gaius, Rachel asked, "So you grew up among the Unwary? How long ago was that? What year are you?"

"I'm a senior at the Upper School. So this is the beginning of my..." he paused, mentally counting, "fourth year here."

"So you are...seventeen." Her heart fell. That was very old, as old as her brother Peter.

"Sixteen. I was invited to come a year early."

"Really! Me, too!" she burst out. A shiver of intense delight shot through her. Only a really bright child would be invited to Roanoke early. He must be just like her.

Rachel narrowed her eyes and regarded him thoughtfully. He had shared the secret about the geas with her. She found that she wanted to share something important with him, something private. She did have the one secret she had never told anyone.

It was a tiny thing that meant nothing in the grand scheme of things, but it meant everything to her.

She leaned forward. "Can I tell you a secret? Promise not to tell?" Even after he nodded, she had trouble getting herself to speak the word, after having kept this to herself for so long. She whispered, "I really wanted to live in Dee. I want to be a Scholar and read books all day." Louder, she continued, "Isn't that a terrible thing for someone with the last name of Griffin? All Griffins go to Dare. It's been that way since before the dawn of time."

He laughed and said, "Honestly? After I got here and learned about the dorms and the different Sorcerous Arts, I wanted to join Dee, too. The folks in Drake are a bit pompous for me. But there are good people in the mix."

She felt as if she had met the other half of her soul. The feeling was so intense that she could not bear to look directly at him. She turned her back on him and whistled. Her blast of wind knocked the book from the table. It fluttered in mid–air and hit the ground with a loud *thump.*

"Very good!" He sounded sincerely impressed. "You've improved a lot in two days."

Rachel went pink with delight. Over her shoulder, she asked teasingly, "So, why are you in Drake rather than Dee? Because of your devil-may-care, rebel-who-plays-by-his-own-rules attitude?"

He shrugged. "I'm not sure. Maybe because I don't care about the pursuit of knowledge as much as other things: family, friends, me... The list is rather long."

She looked again at the patches on his robes. Why did he stay in Drake if he found his dormmates pompous? Was it because of the few good people?

"Glad to hear your friend the princess is better," he said. "What happened to her?"

"She..." Rachel hesitated, biting her lip.

This also was a secret, but not her secret. And yet, he had told her something truly important, at least that was the impression she had received from her father's letter. The secret about Dee Hall mattered to her but to no one else. Maybe she owed him more.

"If I tell you, will you keep it to yourself?" she asked seriously.

He considered for a bit and then nodded. Rachel moved to stand right beside him and spoke very softly. He leaned toward her until their heads were very close. He smelled good.

"Sometimes, when the princess touches people," Rachel whispered, "she finds herself in a different landscape. A real landscape, because she brought something back once. Each time it's different, and she doesn't know what it means. Anyway, a girl named Xandra…"

"Cassandra Black? The seeress?"

"I guess. Xandra Black came and told her in this eerie voice not to touch Joshua March. But Nastasia did not trust the voice, so she touched Mr. March anyway. And she fell over."

"I…see." He straightened and stood with his head titled back slightly, his hands clasped behind him. Rocking on the balls of his feet, he contemplated what she had told him. "By March, you mean the Grand Inquisitor's son?"

"Oh!" Rachel's eyes went big. "Yes. That was who it was."

"I see," he said again. "These landscapes she sees, can you tell me anything about them?"

Rachel shook her head. She did not yet know what was important and what was not. She felt she should not say too much. "Only that they were mostly bad places."

"Hmm." He murmured more to himself than to her, "I wonder what would happen if she touched me." He thought a while longer. Rachel went back to lifting and dropping the book.

After a time, Gaius said, "You're friends with that Valerie Foxx girl, aren't you? The one who was attacked?"

Rachel was in the midst of carefully lifting the book. She nodded without turning around.

He said, "I saw her yesterday talking to Jonah Strega. He's…he's a rather scary person—even to guys like me. You might want to warn her to stay away from him."

"She's interviewing people to write a piece for the paper," Rachel repeated Valerie's cover story. She decided not to mention Valerie was investigating her own attempted murder.

He shrugged. "Just figured you might want to know."

"Thanks." She smiled.

When he spoke again, Gaius's voice had more of a lilt to it, a familiar lilt. "Well, that's all the time I have, my love. I'm off."

Rachel stood there, the heat slowly rising in her cheeks. Her eyes bore into the back of the older boy as he sauntered away.

My love?

Oh. She knew she had recognized that lilt. He was from England's West Country. In Cornwall, everyone—men, women, and children—called everyone else "my love." Still, it almost sounded as if he had meant it in a completely different way.

It was a long time before her cheeks were no longer hot enough to fry an egg.

CHAPTER THIRTEEN:
COMIC BOOKS AND FLYING CLASSES

RACHEL ARRIVED AT THE TABLE WITH HER LUNCH TRAY. SIGGY AND Valerie were sitting close together, poring over Valerie's findings. The intrepid reporter girl had clipped photos of the people she had interviewed to the brightly-colored folders in which she kept her research. Rachel recognized several students—all children whose parents worked for the Parliament of the Wise.

As Rachel approached, she noticed that Sigfried's arm was slowly sneaking around the back of Valerie's chair. Her mystic girl powers tingled. Siggy *liked* Valerie. She approved of his taste. Grinning, she sat down, but not so near as to distract them.

Zoë joined them, as did Kitten, Brunhilda, Wendy, Zoë's friend Seth Peregrine, and Siggy's roommates—Ian MacDannan and Enoch Smithwyck, the British boy with the Japanese accent. Zoë launched into a description of what the Science tutor had told them about the Terrible Five and the Six Musketeers. The others listened with interest.

Siggy leaned forward. "Did you tell them how Mr. Fisher defeated that guy who could kill people. Kobe the Deathless?"

"Koschei," Zoë murmured dryly. "Koschei the Deathless. He was Russian."

"Coat-tie...whatever." Siggy waved his hand. "That's not the point. The point is that this James Darling guy gets all the credit, because there are comics about him, when Mr. Fisher actually did all the work. He's the real hero."

"That's not true!" Wendy Darling cried, defending her father. Her cloud of chestnut hair floated around her, emphasizing her piercing blue eyes.

"Sure it is!" Siggy cried. "He dueled the Deathless guy. That was cool! What did Darling do? Stab some guy with a knife Mr. Fisher made. Mr. Fisher should be the star of the comic! Darling's a glory hound, taking credit for another man's accomplishments. He should be ashamed!"

Wendy did not answer, but her face had turned rather splotchy. She stabbed at her baked potato with her fork.

"Hi, guys." Joy O'Keefe tentatively approached the table with her tray. She looked rather sweet in her subfusc outfit, except one of her twin velvet ribbons had fallen into her food and left a ketchup stain on her white shirt. "Whatcha talking about? Can I join in?"

"Sure." Siggy flashed her his blinding grin. He moved over to make room for her, stuffing two sausages and some cookies into his pocket. "The more the merrier."

Joy pulled out her chair and put her tray on the table, but she remained standing, captivated by his cuteness. Reaching up, Zoë pushed on her shoulder. Joy dropped into her chair. Rachel's mystic girl powers tingled again. Joy *liked* Sigfried.

Looking up from where he was drumming on his upside-down salad bowl with twin knives, Seth Peregrine said, "As the resident comic geek, I feel compelled to point out that comics aren't about fighting the Veltdammerung. It's about Darling's life as an Agent, after he graduated—fighting rogue sorcerers and banshee gone bad. That kind of thing."

Rachel rested her cheek upon her palm. "My father appears in *James Darling, Agent.* The character Merlin Phoenix is based on him. You know: Ambrose Griffin—Merlin Phoenix?"

"No, really?" Zoë had been toying with her long braided forelock. She pointed the feather at Rachel. "The guy who sneaks up on people, appearing and vanishing like Batman?"

Rachel was not certain who Batman was, but appearing and disappearing sounded like Merlin Phoenix. She nodded.

"Cool!" Zoë and Seth grinned and high-fived each other. Apparently, they had been friends before coming to school.

Rachel turned to Joy, who still stared at Sigfried. "So, you have six older sisters. Do you have any brothers?"

"Huh?" Joy started, breaking free of the spell cast by Sigfried's cuteness. "No, just sisters."

"I'm the youngest, too," Rachel confided. "I've two older sisters and a brother."

"It's really hard being part of a big family." Joy picked up her sandwich. "Everyone has heard of you. Yet no one knows you. I'm always Hope's little sister or Temperance's little sister. Sometimes I wonder if these people realize I have my own name.

"And if they happen to be acquainted with some talent of one of my sisters, it is even worse. They aren't ever satisfied unless I have that talent, too. As if I could be as good a singer as Patience and as good a dancer as Faith, while also being as good a scholar as Mercy. Well...no one compares my singing to Patience, because she's too shy to sing in public. But she's really good."

Rachel counted the names. "What's your other sister's name?"

"What?"

"Joy, Hope, Temperance, Faith, Patience, and Mercy. What is the name of your other sister?"

"Oh. Charity. She's the one who is just a year older than me. She has it even worse. She follows in everyone's footsteps, and she doesn't even get the distinction of being the youngest."

"Or the seventh daughter of a seventh daughter."

"Or that." Joy nodded. "Though so far, that hasn't made much of a difference."

"Except that you are one of the best sorceresses in our entire Freshman class."

"I am, aren't I?" Joy looked surprised, as if she had only just noticed how much better she had done in the hands-on portions of their classes than most of the other students.

Suddenly, Joy squealed and jumped to her feet, pointing with her sandwich. "Look. It's the Princess!"

Nastasia glided toward them, accompanied by her oldest brother, Ivan. Her beneficent smile lit her lovely face. Pale gold hair surrounded her like a brilliant cloud. Leaping up, Rachel rushed to her. The princess looked a bit pale but otherwise well. Rachel would have hugged her, but she remembered Nastasia did not care for familiarity. Rachel respected that.

Joy, on the other hand, did not hold back. She threw herself at the princess and hugged her tightly. Nastasia looked terribly uncomfortable, but she took it graciously. Rachel felt for her. The two of them exchanged sympathetic glances.

"You're alive!" Joy shouted, squeezing her tightly.

Nastasia endured the familiarity with a kindly, long suffering smile. When Joy released her, she straightened her robes, looking resigned.

"What happened?" Rachel whispered.

"I will tell you all after lunch." Nastasia whispered back. "The dining hall is hardly an appropriate place for such tidings." Rachel nodded.

They returned to the table. Joy clung to the princess's arm, pestering her with questions. Nastasia did her best to respond graciously, but Rachel could tell she was uncomfortable. Eager to rescue her friend by changing the topic, she wracked her brain for a suitable subject.

Leaning forward, she confided, "I have something to tell you, too. An older student—we'll call him Evil Rumor Monger #1— told me that someone's developed a new kind of geas." At Siggy's look of confusion, she explained. "A spell that compels a person to obey."

"Like hypnotism?" Valerie pulled out her notebook and jotted this down.

"Yes, very much so." Rachel cut another piece of her battered fish. "Normally, geases force you to act, but the person is aware they are being forced. With this new spell, you don't know you've been geased—which is much worse."

Siggy scratched Lucky behind his immensely long whiskers. "Did a sorcerer develop this? Or is it another kind of new magic, like Lucky and the ensorcelling paper?"

Rachel's eyebrows shot up. "I didn't think of that. Could be."

"That paper was like what you just described, wasn't it?" Sigfried continued, "It made Salome think something. When we described what actually happened, she immediately forgot."

"That's rather creepy!" Joy frowned down at her plate. One of her ribbons rested in her ketchup again. She pulled it out and wiped it off, sighing.

"Very creepy," Rachel murmured softly.

"Where did you meet this older student?" the princess sniffed disapprovingly.

"Upstairs, when I was practicing the cantrips we learned in Language." It was out of her mouth before she could stop herself.

"Practicing our spells!" Nastasia's face lit up. "What a superb idea. I believe I will practice, too. Any of you who wish are welcome to join me. Perhaps it would be useful to form a practice club. Back in Magical Australia, we had clubs for everything: gardening, shopping, de-wombatting the castle."

Rachel felt as if a large weight had dropped onto her heart. There was no way to explain that she had been practicing solely for the purpose of catching up with those who were already better than her, such as Nastasia, Sigfried, and Joy. If Nastasia took up practicing regularly, Rachel would never catch up. She berated herself for spilling her secret.

"As to the matter of the geas—" The princess brought her neatly-folded napkin to her mouth. "We should bring this up at the meeting of the Young Sorcerer's League tonight."

"I would kind of rather you didn't," Rachel winced. She regretted that she had mentioned the subject. "It was told to me in confidence—for me to tell my Father. I do not know if Father would want it bandied about."

"Ah." The princess nodded sagely. "We will say no more of it."

Rachel smiled, and the anvil squashing her heart lifted a little. The matter of practicing aside, she decided she really liked the princess. Nastasia reminded her of Rachel's paternal grandmother. Born during the reign of Queen Victoria, Grandmother Griffin had been a true Victorian *grande dame*. She had been concerned with matters of rank and prestige—with preserving the virtues of the past and keeping them from vanishing in the modern world—but she had also loved horses and galloping. She could clear all the hedges on the estate while fox hunting, even in her two hundredth year. She had been a stern woman but a loving one. She would have approved of Princess Nastasia Romanov as a friend for Rachel.

"Besides," Rachel added, "I was not invited to the YSL meeting." She did not add that the two freshmen she had seen invited were absurdly cute and the best in their class at magic.

"Ah, it can't be anything big." Sigfried shrugged. "Probably just a social gathering...Bet they asked me so they could have a famous boy and a dragon to spice up the party."

"You must come with us," Nastasia insisted firmly, her eyes crinkling warmly. "I am sure they would not mind if we brought you."

"We'll all go together," Siggy assured her with a big grin.

Rachel smiled, very grateful. It was good to have friends.

"Hi, everyone!" Salome stood behind Valerie and Siggy, her hand on her hip in her favorite provocative pose. She gave them all a huge smile, showing her perfect teeth. "I just dropped by to say hello to Valerie."

As Valerie smiled up at her friend, Rachel glanced over at the table where Salome had been sitting with her dormmates, Belladonna Marley and that crowd. Magdalene Chase sat by herself at the far end of their table. There was a new bruise on the tiny girl's chin. Pain shot through Rachel's heart. Magdalene had risked the wrath of the other Drake girls to save her. Rachel wanted to return the favor, but she had no idea how.

Leaning toward Salome, she asked softly, "That little girl. Her face is bruised. What happened to her?"

"What, you mean Eunice's little torture poppet? She 'ran into a door.'" Salome made air quotes, smirking and speaking with the glee girls used when sharing rumors. "Or at least that's the way Eunice tells it."

"Eunice?"

"Eunice Chase, Magdalene's older sister." Salome shrugged. "Magdalene really doesn't belong in Drake. She should move."

During the afternoon break, the princess had a meeting with Dean Moth. Rachel returned to the abandoned hallway, hoping to get a jump on practicing before the princess formed her club. Also, she hoped she might see her mysterious visitor.

Thinking of the boy from the hallway left a warm feeling inside her. There was something pleasant about having a secret friend—even if he was a bit unsavory. She was very grateful for his help getting the orange juice off her robes and for the information she had passed onto her father. Every time she recalled that he, too, had wanted to live in Dee, their shared secret glowed inside her like an ember. She wished she could do something for him, bake him cookies or bring him a muffin. But this was not like home, where she could ask Cook to help her make a treat for somebody. Anything she could get from the dining hall, he could take on his own.

He did not show up. Apparently, he did go to class occasionally.

After class, Rachel grabbed Vroomie and headed for the gymnasium. The day was perfect for flying, a deep blue sky and very little wind. Clusters of purple wisteria spilled over the gym. Their perfume filled the air. Rachel breathed in, smiling.

Professor Chanson waited for her with a broom of an unfamiliar design. She examined the custom-made broom with great interest. It had eight blades, wider than hers, and the fan was a strange shape. Mr. Chanson was an extraordinarily handsome man with hair so black it almost appeared a steely blue. He would have been intimidating except that his glasses gave him a mild-mannered appearance.

"Miss Griffin! A pleasure to see you again." He smiled at her, flashing very white teeth. "How did your first three days of classes go?"

"Well." Rachel rested her broom on its nose and leaned on it. "My new friend ended up at the Halls of Asclepius...but I guess it was pretty good, other than that."

He nodded. "Yes, that was unfortunate. I am so glad to hear she has recovered. But, we did not come out here to discuss such dreary matters. We are here to fly. Hop on."

He climbed onto his broom and lifted up off the ground very slowly. Rachel knew instantly that he must be an excellent flyer. It took great control to produce slow, steady flight. Rachel herself was particularly good at this. As he watched intently, she calmly put down her bookbag, mounted her broom, and rose slowly with smooth precision.

When she had risen to his level, he gave her a warm smile and said, "You are a talented young woman. How long have you been flying? Four years? Seven?"

Rachel shook her head. "I only got Vroomie, here, about a year and a half ago. But I used to spend hours watching the fliers from the Pinswallow Broom Ballet. And I've read every book on flying in our library." She did not explain that she had seen the Pinswallow Broom Ballet once, at the age of six, but she had re-played the memory every night before she went to bed for the next seven years, watching how the brooms moved, picturing the maneuvers from different angles, and imagining new routines they could have performed.

His keen blue eyes widened, impressed. "Well, you're years ahead for your age. Come, let's fly around a bit."

They flew over the Commons and southward, soaring above the charming red, arched bridges of the Oriental gardens. They whizzed across the lily pond, skirting so low that she could see eyes of the sea fairies reflecting up from below the surface. Circling around, he took her back via the Monument Garden, with its statues and fountains, and the Menagerie, where the larger familiars could be housed. She caught a glimpse of a greyhound and what looked like a three-headed chimera, though maybe it was three familiars standing close together.

Continuing their circuit northward, they flew over the west-ern dormitories. The pale chimneys and pyramidal towers of Marlowe Hall came first. Students loitered around the tree-speckled lawn, conjuring hoops and columns that shimmered and then vanished with a sensation like waking from a dream. Next was Spenser Hall with its multiple gables, which reminded Rachel of the architecture back home along the Avon. Then the paper birches with their carpet of ferns that surrounded Dare Hall and its many spires. The sparkles of Enchantment floated out some of the windows. Dare had been built by the same ar-chitect who had designed the North Wing of Gryphon Park. It looked a great deal like her home.

As she passed her room, Rachel felt the warm presence of her familiar. Glancing at her window, she saw Mistletoe gazing back at her. Sitting next to her cat, gazing out the window, was the miniature lion.

The pale birches with their curling bark opened up behind Roanoke Hall, revealing a grassy area with tree stumps from which saplings grew, as if the area used to be forested and was recovering from some recent disaster. Flying over the back wall, he led her over the courtyard in the middle of Roanoke Hall. A scrimmage game of flying polo and a soccer match were under way. Students sat watching the games. Some looked up and pointed as the two of them whizzed by. Rachel grinned and waved.

On the far side were the eastern dormitories. De Vere, a somber building with arrow-slit windows, was nestled in among hemlocks. Directly east of Roanoke was Drake Hall, an imposing granite structure complete with its own moat. After that came the yellow stone of Raleigh and then, finally, Dee Hall—a noble granite structure with four domed towers and statues of famous Scholars decorating the top. As they passed by the real-life version of the photograph she had kept hidden under her bed, Rachel could not help gazing at it longingly.

South of that came the Infirmary and an ivy-covered out-building that the proctors used for storing gear, next to which lay the path to the cottages where the staff lived. Then, they were back at the gymnasium.

Mr. Chanson landed. When Rachel landed beside him, he nodded in approval. Leaning his broom against the brick wall of the gym, he gazed at her warmly. "Well, Rachel, you are definitely a natural at flying. I have seen, maybe, one or two students who can fly as well you in the past five years, and none of them your age. Do you play flying polo or race? If so, you should definitely support your team. Every student is assigned to a sports team for their freshman year. Sophomore year, there is a draft. Once you get drafted, you are on that team forever. You can come and play, any day, any activity, for the rest of your life.

"Whatever team gets you will be extraordinarily delighted. The last four years Laura Diggle had been dominating Track and Broom for the *Maenads*. This is her last year, though. She is most likely going on to fly professionally. We would all like to see someone keep her humble before she goes." He flashed Rachel a ridiculously bright smile.

"Um..." Rachel stammered, blushing slightly. "I don't play polo or race. I don't like...that kind of thing. Not on brooms, anyway. I did play polocrosse on my pony occasionally, but...I wasn't very good. Mainly, I fly through hallways, around corners, and up spiral staircases. Steeplechase stuff."

"Really? That is quite unusual flying indeed."

Rachel replied simply. "I came from a very big house."

He nodded. "I know. I have visited Gryphon Park. An amazing place. Okay, I am going to give you a flight path around the campus. Please follow it safely but as quickly as you can. Try and keep it fluid."

Mr. Chanson pointed out several landmarks to which he wanted her to fly. It was a complex path, including a few tricks he wanted her to perform. None of it was difficult, however, especially as she would have no trouble remembering his exact instructions. Rachel stood still, head cocked as if listening hard. She visualized every part of the route in her head. Then, she leapt on her broom and flew the course with elegant grace.

When she came back and landed, he declared, "Wow. That was extremely impressive." He studied her for a bit. "How many children were studying on the Commons?"

Rachel tilted her head, recalling. She counted quickly, "Fifty-seven."

His eyebrows leapt up. "You have an amazing memory. It's quite remarkable."

"Thank you." She made a very small curtsey, pleased.

"Now. Down to business." He led her into the gym to the closet where the brooms were kept. "Let me tell you what I need from my assistant. First off, I need you to keep an eye on the new students, especially when they lift off for the first time. I may need to chase down floaters. I'd like you to keep an eye on the rest whenever I am gone. Make sure we don't have kids heading off to the four corners of the universe. Finally, I would like you to demonstrate basic techniques while I am explaining them. Does that sound like something you can handle?"

"Oh, yes!" Rachel saluted. "I did something similar for my neighborhood Junior Broomsticks class back in Gryphon-on-Dart. I'm good at keeping an eye on stragglers."

"Excellent. During the warm weather, we fly outside. During the winter, we fly in the gym. The gym changes shape to produce any gym equipment we need, including a flying track. The chambers can get bigger and smaller as needed. Ah, here come our students. Look sharp!"

The students arrived, mainly freshman who were new to broom riding, including some of her dormmates. Most of those attending this class had grown up in the mundane world. A few

were from the World of the Wise but had not owned a
broom. There were a couple of older students, too. Rachel was
introduced to Merry Vesper, a lovely girl with a long golden braid,
and Mylene Price, the pale redhead she had seen asleep in
the Infirmary. Both were Juniors in the Upper School who had
been too ill during their earlier years to participate in sports.

They moved out to the track, which was to the south, between
the gymnasium and the Oriental gardens. As the new students
donned their floating vests, Rachel jumped on her broom and
demonstrated the basics of leaning and maneuvering as Mr.
Chanson described them. Some of the students picked it up
quickly. Others had trouble. She watched with amusement as
Siggy and cheerleader Brunhilda Winters flew for the first time.
Brunhilda took to her bristleless like a fish who had been raised
on land coming home to a river. Siggy also did well for a beginner, though he kept trying to do tricks far beyond his ability.
Once Rachel had to save him before he fell off from where he was
hanging upside down from the bottom of the red Flycycle.

Of the two older students, Merry took to the broom immediately. Her familiar, a reindeer, watched her dubiously from the
ground. Mylene did well for about twenty minutes. Then, she
grew lightheaded, her face pale, and had to go lie down in the
Infirmary.

The only real surprise was Sakura Suzuki. Rachel's dorm-
mate came from an ancient line of sorcerers, who traced their
lineage to the Japanese sun goddess. She was an orphan, raised
by her aunt and uncle. A tall girl with glasses, she had tied bells
into her long pig tails that tinkled as she attempted to fly. Rachel
would have expected someone from an ancient sorcery family to
be a natural, but Sakura could not get a broom to work properly,
even though Mr. Chanson switched her bristleless twice.

Sakura had trouble in other classes, too, Rachel realized. She
failed to accomplish tasks other students did with ease or, even
stranger, produced unlikely results. Failing to perform a cantrip
or enchantment suggested a lack of magical talent. But not being
able to get a broom to fly? That did not even make sense. The
bristleless did not rely on Sakura's talent any more than a
mundane car depended upon the endurance of the driver.

As Rachel contemplated this, the broom Sakura was struggling with bucked and dumped her. With a *whoosh*, it shot forward, rocketing away at an extremely high speed. Rachel darted after it, but it outstripped her. Rachel gaped. No simple Flycycle should have been able to fly faster than her steeple-chaser. Ever.

"*Varenga!*" Mr. Chanson stretched out his hand. The racing broom swerved and returned to his grasp.

"Wow!" Rachel murmured, impressed. She had seen her father use that cantrip. Grinning, she determined that she would master it, too.

Chapter Fourteen:
The Alarming Report
of Nastasia Romanou

THAT EVENING, THEY GATHERED DOWNSTAIRS IN THE DARE HALL music room to hear the princess's news. Rachel and Nastasia were joined by Siggy, Joy, Valerie, and Kitten. Joy and Kitten had been with them in the dorm, so Nastasia invited them along. They had invited their other roommate, Astrid as well, but she had declined. Siggy had invited Valerie.

The music room was downstairs, below ground level. It was a vast area designed for concerts, with a raised dais that could be hidden behind red velvet curtains. A grand piano sat next to a drum set and some music stands. The walls were of wood paneling, shaped around the stage area to increase the acoustics. The middle of the chamber was open space. To the right were racks of folding chairs and a door leading to a workshop for repairing instruments. To the left, a fire burned merrily in a large fireplace. Comfy armchairs had been placed in a semi-circle around a blue and purple braided rug. The air smelled of pine smoke and saw dust.

The children gathered by the fireplace. The princess's Tasmanian tiger padded around the room sniffing things and rubbing his cheek against them. Lucky the Dragon flickered in and out among the chairs, occasionally pausing to let one of the girls pet him. Joy's huge fluffy white cat played with a piece of string that she dangled for him. Kitten's tiny lion rested on the warm slates before the hearth. Valerie stretched out on a thick shag rug, her head resting on Payback's stomach. Only Rachel's familiar was not present.

The princess sat very straight, her back not touching the chair. She looked like a young queen enthroned among her subjects, her golden hair spread out around her like a royal mantle. Joy sat on the floor between her and Sigfried. In one hand, she held the string for her cat. In the other, she clutched a pink and blue Witch Baby—a bobble-headed rag doll that was a popular collectable item among the children of the Wise. Rachel had glimpsed at least six of the multi-colored Witch Babies on Joy's bed and three on Wendy's bed. Kitten had one, too.

Rachel did not own any herself, but Laurel had received two as gifts. Dolls were not Laurel's thing. Her sister had shorn their hair, painted their faces like Goths, and attached strings to them, so she could fly around on her broom at night and dangle the ghastly toys in front of the windows of Unwary children—much to the dismay of Rachel's parents.

Folding her hands neatly in her lap, the princess cleared her throat. "You may all be curious as to what happened to me."

"That's the understatement of the century!" murmured Valerie. She sat up and opened her notebook, pencil poised.

"I will go directly to the meat of the matter. When I touched Joshua March, I found myself standing on a glacier. It was extraordinarily cold." She chaffed her arms as if even the memory of it chilled her. "The scene was horrific. An older version of Mr. March was undergoing an ancient Roman form of torture. He hung from outstretched arms with his stomach slashed open. His internal organs had spilled onto the ice." The princess seemed perturbed but did not shiver at this, though several of the others did, including Rachel. "There was a creature with him, a very tall man. Beautiful but in a painful way. He had wings of smoke and fire. He tried to keep me there, but something pulled on me, and I came back."

Outrage contorted Siggy's features. He socked his fist into his palm with a satisfying clap. "Did you happen to get the rotter's name and address and preference of armaments?"

The princess held up her hand, as if requesting patience. "There is more. I came back quickly, but they kept me in the Halls of Healing for observation. Agents came by to guard me. I spent the night being protected by Agent Standish Dorian and..."—a sweet smile flickered across her face, as if she anticipated the effect her words would cause and wished to apologize before hand—"Agent James Darling."

The other girls cried out in delight. Joy actually squealed and insisted on high-fiving Nastasia. Rachel grinned appreciatively. A soft sound behind her made her turn around. Kitten had fallen asleep in the rocking chair near the fire, her head nodding against her starched white shirt. Leander sat purring on her lap. Rachel had not realized that lions could purr.

"You mean the bloke we were just talking about? The one who stole the glory from Mr. Fisher?" Siggy had crossed over to the dais and was examining a music stand. He seemed to be trying to determine whether it could be turned into a weapon. "The one with the comics, who helped him destroy the Terrible Five? Ace!"

"That's just amazing! You are the first of us to meet him!" Joy cried. She squeezed her pink and blue Witch Baby, hugging it to her. "My sister Mercy is a huge fan of the *James Darling, Agent* comics. And Faith has a huge poster of him on her wall."

"Nastasia isn't the first." Rachel tucked an escaped strand of hair behind her ear. "Mr. Darling is a friend of my parents. He used to be my father's partner, years ago. Together, they hunted down the remnants of the Morth Brood. They captured some of the big names: the necromancer Claudius Stark and Eliaures Charles, the Serpent Master." She did not add that she had a crush on his son.

Or, she had, before he snickered at her in the kitchen. Now, she was not so sure. "Mr. Darling gave me a broom ride once, when I was little. He's an even better flier than me."

The princess nodded graciously, as if acknowledging the honor that had been paid to her. Then her expression grew grimmer. "But, alas, Agent Darling was unable to help, because that night, the creature with the wings of flame came into my dreams—where the Agents could not protect me."

The girls gasped. Rachel leaned forward eager and intrigued. "Can you tell us more about this flame-winged thing? Where is it from?"

The princess spoke gravely. "He called himself the Light-bringer. Only he said it was easier for him to go to places without light. Maybe one does not bring light to places that have it?

"Either way," Nastasia concluded, "he did not have much chance to say a great deal, because a raven came and told him his time was up."

"Was it the very large raven with red eyes?" Rachel recalled the moment, the night before, when the bird saw her watching it, as well as Mr. Badger's warning. She shivered again.

"Yes! Exactly," the princess continued. "So far as I could tell, they were working together. The raven seemed to be in charge of keeping things out of our world. But he had let the Lightbringer in." A frown appeared on her perfect brow. "Also, this raven was somewhat...uppity."

Rachel recalled the gruffness with which the bird had spoken to the lion and smiled in spite of her trepidation.

Valerie looked up from her notebook. "So now that..."

Whatever Valerie might have intended to say was lost, because Zoë Forrest stepped out of the sleeping Kitten. One moment Kitten snored quietly in the armchair by the fireplace. The next, Zoë had stepped out from the space her body occupied. Landing hard on the slate before the hearth, she looked up into the faces present and winced. On her shoulder, her tiger-striped quoll—which really had spots rather than stripes—blinked its bead-like black eyes.

"Oops." Zoë murmured.

"Wha...how did you do that?" Rachel stared at Zoë, amazed. Not only had she appeared from nowhere, but her hair was blue and green plaid. One could not do that with hair dye!

Kitten stretched and stifled a yawn. "How peculiar. I just had the oddest dream about you, Zoë."

Nastasia sat with her hand covering her eyes, overcome with some emotion. When she recovered, she said simply, "I did not tell anyone about you, Zoë....as we had agreed."

"Um...yeah. Thanks for that." Zoë crossed the room and threw herself down into an armchair. The feather in her long braid of hair swung back and forth like a plumb bob. The quoll sniffed at it. "Not that it does me a lot of good now...but that's not your fault. The last few days, when someone was asleep down here, it was Sarpy—Umberto Sarpento, the school custodian. Usually, when he is asleep, no one is nearby. Sarpy snores something mean."

"How did you do that?" Valerie echoed Rachel's question.

Zoë stuck one leg in the air, waving her leather sandals. The soles were the same silver as a familiar's paws. "These were made for me by Aperahama Whetu, a Maori shaman. They let me walk into the Long Ago Dreamtime."

"The what?" Joy put her doll down.

"That's what the folks Down Under call the place where dreams take place. You know how a familiar can grab stuff from the world of dreams and pull it into the physical world? I can do something like that, only I can cross physically and walk through dreams. But someone has to be asleep for me to move in and out."

"Wow!" Rachel whispered.

"She came into my dream last night," the princess stated softly.

"She was in my dream, too. Just now." Kitten brushed hair from her face and petted Leander. "I was dreaming about our fabulous magic carpet—the one that my brother Squirrel's phoenix used to take us on wonderful trips. My siblings say I'm daft. That this never happened. Only I remember it quite clearly. We went to the beach once, and to a tower filled with treasure."

"Treasure?" Sigfried's eyes gleamed. "Where exactly was this?"

"What do you need more treasure for?" Valerie scoffed, her eyes dancing with mischief. "You already have an entire dragon's hoard."

"You can never have too much treasure," said Siggy, who was firing the music stand. Something about his voice reminded Rachel of Lucky, who was nodding emphatically.

"Let's talk about treasure later." Rachel leaned forward. "I want to understand what happened."

Zoë shrugged. "I came through Kitten's dream just now. I should have known it wasn't Sarpy. He would never dream about well-dressed children. You were wearing really odd clothing in your dream, Kitten."

"Not odd. Just...old fashioned." Kitten scrunched up her face, striving to remember. "I could swear we used to dress that way. Maybe Squirrel and Bobcat are right, and I am bonkers."

"Whatever." Zoë shrugged. "But I did walk through your dream, and I was there last night, in the princess's. I wanted to help, but there wasn't much I could do against that...what was that thing? I was going to hit him with my magic Maori war club, but he left." She turned to the princess. "You were so impressive. He kept threatening you, and you just defied him. You didn't even lose your temper or anything."

"I behaved as became my station," Nastasia replied with quiet dignity. She frowned, dissatisfied with herself. "Alas, I was ineffective. I need to grow stronger."

"You were amazing!" Zoë flipped the braid containing the feather over her shoulder, to the consternation of the quoll. She grinned. "That guy was freaking scary. I would have been bawling like a baby."

Curled up in one of the comfortable leather armchairs, Rachel played back the memory of Zoë's arrival. It was hard to pinpoint. It was as if she woke from a dream, and there Zoë was—very much like it felt when Jemima Puddleduck appeared in their Art class.

Siggy put down the music stand and crossed to where the princess sat. He sank down on one knee. From his robes, he pulled a dining hall steak knife and laid it at the princess's feet. "Ma'am, into your service, I offer my life, my strength, my fealty. I have already vowed to defeat your sworn enemy, the rabbit. Grant me the honor to bear my blade in your service! In life or death if I may serve you, I will. I have no sword to offer, but when I get one, I shall! Meanwhile, this knife will have to do."

Something crossed the princess's face very quickly. Rachel played the moment back and saw sadness and something else she could not quite place. Pain, as if her feelings were hurt perhaps? Either way, Nastasia hid it quickly. As gracious as the Lady of the Lake, she rose and took up the knife, tapping him with the blade on either shoulder and the top of his head. "You do me great honor. Rise, Sir Sigfried."

"Now you have a knight, like a real princess," Joy giggled, gazing admiringly at Siggy and Nastasia. A look of eagerness came over her face, lighting it up. "I want to serve, too! We girls can be ladies-in-waiting."

"I'm not waiting on anyone." Zoë waved a hand in objection. "I've waited enough tables, thank you!"

"Waited tables? Have you really?" Kitten looked up from where she was petting her tiny lion. "But you're only fourteen, aren't you? Is anyone here older than fourteen?"

Everyone shook their head.

Rachel murmured. "I'm thirteen."

"One of my great uncles made me help out in his restaurant," shrugged Zoë, who could easily have been mistaken for fifteen or sixteen. "Besides, things are different in rural Moldova."

"Moldova? I thought you were from New Zealand," Rachel asked, surprised.

Zoë rolled her eyes, which she did with great enthusiasm. Her whole face looked lively. "I'm from everywhere. My grandmother was a Moth, from the far flung Moth clan. So I have relatives in every corner of the earth. More relatives than you could count in your worst nightmare. After my mom died, I got to live with them all. Or at least, it seemed like it. Nothing helps a little motherless girl discover her place in life like sleeping on the couch of relatives who talk in front of her about how much she doesn't matter to them.

"Eventually, though, I ended up with a distant cousin in New Zealand who was a Maori tribesman. He had left his tribe and was living in town, working as a barber. But part of the family still lived the old way. One of them, the shaman, took me under his wing—he was a bit crazy, but he cared about my opinions. He made my sandals and gave me my enchanted *patu*, which is Maori for war club." Reaching into her backpack, she pulled out a short paddle made of shiny greenstone. Intricate spiral designs had been carved up and down its length.

"The Moth family...You mean like the nurse and the dean?" Valerie flipped through her notes to a list of names. Zoë nodded.

"One of my aunts married a Moth," said Joy.

"Wish I'd been sent to live with her."

"She married a cowboy."

Zoë nodded. "I've got pretty colorful relatives. At least a third of them are cowboys. They live on some huge ranch in Uncanny Valley, Nevada, where everyone is welcome. Only my father never saw fit to send me there. No. He went for the really eccentric ones. The mountain climbing couple in the Swiss Alps who were never home because they competed in yodeling contests. The wacky billionaire who gave all his money to a charity that did pot-bellied pig rescues and went to live in a grass hut in Bangladesh. That was a fun three months. Have you seen the size of the insects in Bangladesh? Imagine finding them inside your unmentionables.

"Then there was the French family where everyone was impeccably dressed. If you committed a fashion faux pas—like, say, wearing sneakers with a skirt, or socks with sandals— you were locked in the attic without dinner. I'd like to see them deal with huge bugs in their unmentionables!

"Then, there was a Russian great aunt who only ate oatmeal and pickles, which would not have been so bad, had she not insisted that I eat only oatmeal and pickles, too. I won't even tell you what she did the time she caught me eating a ham and black bread sandwich. It was bad enough that my father yanked me out of there. Then came the old Japanese guy in his nineties who made me dress like Alice, from *Alice In Wonderland*, and wear bunny ears...all the time. Otherwise, he wasn't so bad, though, really. Oh, and the coupon-cutting fanatic who forced me to climb into dumpsters to retrieve sales fliers. Let me tell you, after them, the Maori barber seemed positively normal."

"How did you meet Seth Peregrine?" Kitten petted the purring lion. "You knew each other before coming here, right?"

"My dad lives in the same town in Michigan as Seth and Misty Lark—in the U between the thumb and the finger." Everyone else stared at her blankly. Zoë chuckled and pet her quoll, "Sorry. A little Michigan humor. Two years ago, Dad decided I was old enough that I could live with him during the school year. I met Seth at the dojo. I wanted to win a fight for a change."

"Seth does martial arts?" Sigfried made a karate gesture with his hands. "You mean, like Ju Kwan Do and Tae Jitsu?"

Kitten asked, "Are those real martial arts? Or did you make them up?"

Valerie rolled her eyes. "He is mispronouncing Tae Kwan Do and Ju Jitsu."

Zoë shrugged. "Seth's a hockey player. Hockey players need to know how to fight."

Rachel rested her chin on her knees, watching Sigfried and Lucky mock jab at each other. She felt terrible for Zoë. Her situation was almost as bad as Sigfried's. How horrid not to have a proper loving family.

"Misty Lark. Does she have short straw-colored hair?" Nastasia glanced at Zoë, who was chewing on a lock of her plaid hair. Zoë nodded. "I saw her with you and Seth in the vision I had when I touched you. You were standing on a busy street corner, facing some other young people. From your demeanor, I believe it was a brawl—only you were all playing instruments. Between you there was a shower of jagged dancing lights—like a multi-colored Aurora Borealis. Oh, and in the background there were two children playing on the sidewalk. They were wearing bells on their shoes and hats...and floating in the air."

Zoë shrugged. "Sounds cool, but it means nothing to me. I'm glad to know that Seth and Misty were my friends, even before I came to this world."

The princess's brow drew together in thought. "I wonder why some students from the same landscape know each other, such as you and Seth, and some do not. When I touched Sakura Suzuki, I saw her with Enoch Smithwyck in what I took to be ancient Japan. But they do not know each other now."

"Sakura Suzuki?" Valerie asked. "Is she the Japanese girl whose spells go horribly astray?"

Joy nodded. "She is my roommate." Leaning toward them, she lowered her voice respectably, though a note of excitement crept in. "She's an orphan. When she was five, her mother and father were killed right in front of her. She watched them die."

"How tragic." The princess's voice broke slightly.

The others were quiet for a time. Siggy seemed particularly dismayed. He frowned, his face a sullen mask. Rachel looked down, tracing a triangle on the thigh of her robe. Not having a family was bad enough. But having one and losing it? The idea was so horrid, she did not even know how to feel about it.

Eager to think about something else, she turned to Valerie. "You had a question earlier that got interrupted?"

"Oh, right!" Valerie said brightly. Payback's ears perked up. "So, Princess, is it no longer safe for you to touch people?"

Nastasia shook her head. "No. I have only been warned not to touch two people. I do not seem to be in danger otherwise."

"*Two* people?" Rachel leaned forward. Valerie lean forward as well, her notebook ready.

Nastasia nodded. "Xandra Black—or the voices that possess her—warned me not to touch Mr. March. Last night, my father came to visit me at the Halls of Healing. He told me that under no circumstance should I touch Vladimir Von Dread."

"Is that so?" Rachel recalled watching the prince of Bavaria stride across the lawn, students scurrying out of his way like leaves before a storm. "I wonder why. Do you think he is being tortured, too?"

"More likely, he himself is evil." Valerie chewed on a stray blond lock as she wrote furiously in her notebook. "I bet Salome is right about him."

The princess stated, "My father confirmed that the Von Dread family is wicked. The King of Bavaria refuses to uphold the rules of the Parliament of the Wise. He lets people practice forbidden magic without facing prosecution."

Joy leaned forward eagerly. "Everyone knows that Bavaria is where the last of the Morthbrood are hiding. My sister told me that the King of Bavaria offered money to any Morthbrood member who wanted to come and live in his country—as long as they shared their secrets."

Valerie's comment about her friend reminded Rachel of one of the puzzles she was still mulling over. "In the princess's vision of Salome Iscariot, she had been dead for twenty years. What does that mean?"

"Wait, Salome? My Salome?" Valerie jumped to her feet. "You are talking about my best friend, here. H-how could she be dead?"

"Maybe she's a ghost," Joy whispered, spooked. She sat down with her knees pulled up against her chest and hugged her Witch Baby. "I remember when you touched me, you said nothing happened. What about everyone else? Have you touched us all?"

Valerie opened her mouth as if she was going object to the change of subject and then shut it again. She crossed to the far side of the music room and began pacing. As she walked back and forth, she snapped her lens cap on and off, chewed worriedly on her lip.

Sigfried crossed to where she stood and patted her awkwardly on the shoulder. "There, there." Valerie snorted in ironic amusement, but her cheeks went slightly pink.

"Is there anyone here you haven't touched yet, Princess?" Zoë asked.

The princess glanced around. "I believe I have touched everyone but Miss Fabian."

"Kitten!" Joy bounced up and down. "Now, do Kitten!"

"I bet I know what Nastasia will see," Rachel said softly.

"Really?" Joy looked skeptical. "How could you know? Are you psychic?"

"We're all psychic," Sigfried quipped from where he stood with Valerie. "We're sorcerers."

"I bet she'll see the things Kitten remembers," Rachel said. "The world with the magic carpet and the old-fashion garments."

The princess crossed over to the fireplace and extended her hand to Kitten, who gave her a dimpled smile and reached toward her. The tiny lion growled. Kitten began to pull away, but the princess grasped her outstretched hand anyway. Nastasia stood very still. Then, her eyes rolled back until they were entirely white. Slowly, she began to sink.

Dashing across the room, the newly knighted Sigfried caught her and lay her on the rug in front of the hearth, patting her face in an attempt to rouse her. The tiny lion leapt onto her lap. Putting its paws on her chest, it breathed on her face. Her eyes fluttered open.

"Princess! Are you all right? What happened? What happened?" Joy hovered over her, peering into her face with concern. Kitten and Rachel knelt beside her, too.

Nastasia rubbed her temples. "There was light everywhere. It was too bright to see, and I was in horrible pain, as if my very self were on fire. Then, a deep voice spoke. It said, '*Child, you should not be here. Not yet.*' A moment later, I found myself standing on a beach. It was pleasant, though it was still very bright. I did not see any sign of Miss Fabian." A furrow appeared in her perfect forehead. More to herself, she murmured, "Maybe that was the kind of light the Lightbringer meant."

CHAPTER FIFTEEN:
OVERLOOKED AND INVITED

AT PRECISELY SEVEN FORTY-FIVE, IVAN ROMANOV AND AGRAVAINE Stormhenge, the male college resident for Dare Hall and the head of the fencing team, came to collect Nastasia and escort her to the meeting of the Young Sorcerers League. With his athletic build and curly blond hair, Agravaine reminded Rachel of a grown-up Sigfried, if Siggy were more calm and collected than currently conceivable. Rachel looked after them hopefully, but they were talking about Nastasia's time at the Halls of Healing and paid Rachel no heed.

Then, Kitten's older sister, Panther, came to get her. Panther took Astrid with her, too, though Astrid did not particularly want to be included. The tiny lion accompanied them, as did Astrid's red-winged blackbird. Rachel, who burned to be invited, stared after Astrid's retreating back. She wanted to offer to take her place but failed to summon up the courage to voice the words.

From the window, she saw her brother Peter going off with his friends, including John Darling and some of Darling's red-headed cousins, all in their red and blue YSL cloaks. Their familiars, mainly cats, darting in and out around their feet. Laurel, too, for all her wildness, was a member. Her sister ran down the path with several friends, laughing and tossing their YSL medallions.

Rachel sat down on her bed, waiting for Siggy, but he did not come by. She looked for Mistletoe, but he would not come out of the hole in the wall. She read for a bit, but she felt so filled up with sadness—from being left out of the meeting of such a historic organization, from being forgotten by her friend, from not being invited to begin with—that she could not concentrate. She got up and wandered the halls, looking for someone to talk to.

Every room was empty.

Rachel checked the lower floors. She checked the common room. She pulled opened the massive doors at the back of the front foyer and peered into the massive, empty theatre in the center of Dare Hall. She even gathered her courage and checked the boys' side. Sigfried was not there. The entire dormitory was empty. Everyone in Dare Hall had been invited to the YSL meeting...except for her.

Rachel went to the library, which took up three stories in the eastern leg of the hollow square that was Roanoke Hall. It was a wondrous place filled with enormous stacks and tiny spiral staircases. The moment she walked in and smelled the familiar musky odor of old tomes, she felt much better. Maybe she had not been invited to the meeting, but the sheer amount of knowledge available to her was enough to lift anyone's spirits. She could not be unhappy among her old friends, books.

Yet, even with all this knowledge calling to her, the pain of having been overlooked continued to burn in her chest like a smoldering ember she could not douse.

She browsed through the school's selection of "Daring" Northwest books and found two she had not read before, one on *Kelpie, Each-Uisge, and Nixies*, and one on *Kallikantzaroi and Their Cousins*, which she promptly checked out. The school also had his work on griffins, a copy of which was prominently displayed in the main library at Gryphon Park. There was a whole chapter on the Arimaspians, Rachel's ancestors.

After that, she looked up ravens. She found a great many references, references to Odin's Hugin and Munin; to the Native American trickster god; and to the places in which ravens were considered birds of ill omens or portents of death. Ravens deserting their nests were said to be terribly bad omens, and it was believed that if the ravens ever deserted the Tower of London, the English monarchy would fall. Ravens could even be taught to talk, the way parrots and magpies talked.

But nowhere did she find anything about a giant raven with blood red eyes.

After a time, she could not concentrate. Her mind kept picturing a future where she was a great sorceress, and the kids from the YSL were sorry they had not invited her. After that, it wandered to images of Cydney Graves and her friends with their heads on fire and other spiteful pictures of their suffering and humiliation. She wondered what Zoë had in store for them.

Pulling out her fountain pen, she practiced writing Rachel Chanson in her notebook, surrounded by little hearts. The P.E. instructor was so very handsome. She knew from her mother that he was not married. He had such keen blue eyes that seemed to look right through her. Then she tried out Rachel Darling, which made her both blush and giggle—until she remembered how John had snickered at her in the breakfast line. Then she blushed for a different reason. After that, she wrote Rachel Valiant—Evil Rumor Monger #1 was cute in his own way, and then Rachel MacDannan—while she had not picked out a particular MacDannan, Ian had two older brothers in Dare Hall who were quite entertaining. Rachel Dread? Or would it be Rachel Von Dread? No. He was evil. She crossed that out. Then, she surrounded the remaining names with flowers and stars and tiny, smiling hearts.

Finally, she gave up and wandered back to her favorite hallway. Something about practicing magic brought a sense of calmness. Or it kept her troubles at bay. Also, it was very satisfying to see herself improve. She could now whistle and blast the huge book all the way to the far wall, some forty feet away.

She left at one point to use the loo. When she returned, she found Gaius Valiant waiting for her. Or at least, she thought he had been waiting. Maybe he had not, because he looked surprised when she arrived.

Giving her a big smile, he drawled, "So, how's the practice going? And, I must ask, why aren't you at the YSL meeting? I thought everyone was invited, except those of us from Drake Hall."

Rachel's initial delight upon seeing him turned into sadness. "Nobody invited me. I thought we were all going to go—my friends and I. But people came and got them, and nobody told me where it was. Apparently, it's only for people who are really good at magic…who don't have to practice as much as I do. Or maybe it's only for very cute people."

"Well, I think you have already disproved your second theory." Gaius waved his hand casually. "As to the first, I don't think that is the case. I think, perhaps, your friends overlooked you. It is a new school year and such. I am pretty sure that there are people in the YSL who are not very skillful. I could be wrong, though, as I have never been to a meeting. You could ask Miss Fisher or Miss Debussy. They are in the club."

Rachel blinked. She had already disproved her second theory? Had he just called her *very cute*?

Gaius continued, "And if they are too snooty to have you, you can join the Knights of Walpurgis. We're mostly Thaumaturges from Drake, but there are a few from the other Arts in the mix, some Conjurers, some Canticlers, some Alchemists. You'd be the first from Dare."

She asked, "The Knights of Walpurgis? I've never heard of them."

Gaius leaned back against the wall. "They're an old group. Been around for years, though not as old as the YSL. The Knights meet on Thursday nights. Tomorrow is our first meeting for the new school year. Would you like to come?"

"I'll have to think about it." Rachel frowned doubtfully. She was not unwilling, but the YSL was famous. She had wanted to be a member as long as she could remember. She had never heard of this other group. "Can you tell me more about them? What do they do?"

"The Knights are dedicated to the practice of magic. Mostly for self defense, but we also share new spells we have learned or discovered. And we work to increase our skills. It's a rather elite group. I was surprised when they asked me to join. But I can invite someone, and I know the Griffins are a rather well-known and respected family. You should come."

Rachel's eyes sparkled. "Should I come in disguise the first time? Hidden under a robe or something so they don't know I'm from Dare?" She laughed. "Okay, I'll come."

"Great!" Gaius's face lit up. He looked extremely pleased. "I'll come collect you after supper tomorrow. We hold our meetings in the gym. We try to schedule our meetings so they don't interfere with other clubs, like the YSL or the crazy Enchanter boys from Dare Hall who are obsessed with hunting vampires. I am sure that we'll have a wonderful time."

"Okay. I'll look forward to it. Now, um...I guess I should get back to practicing."

"Would you like to practice on an animate person?"

Rachel's eyes glittered with delight. "Sure!"

"Do you know the Word of Ending?" Gaius pulled off his robe and stood before her in a dark gray tee-shirt and sweat pants. He looked rather good that way. Not wanting to be caught staring, she averted her eyes. "It stops the effects of many cantrips and a bunch of other things, some hexes and jinxes. It's best to know how to undo effects which may be caused in practice. Like, if you wanted to cast the paralyzing hex that I hear my dormmates used on you. In fact, why don't we try that?"

Rachel's face scrunched up. She eyed him hesitantly. "Is there something else that Word of Ending is useful for that doesn't require me to hex someone? What if I messed up the ending part, and you got stuck that way? That would be really embarrassing."

He shrugged. "Well, I'd rather just be stuck here, in an out of the way place, until it wore off, than have you unable to turn me back from being a duck. Or unable to get the broccoli to stop growing from my ears. And you should practice the paralyzing hex anyway. It's an enchantment, and it's very useful."

"Well...um...." She whistled the notes she had heard Cydney play the night before. Nothing happened.

Gaius smiled encouragingly. "You have to concentrate. Hold firmly in mind what you wish to accomplish."

"Okay! Okay!" She shut her eyes tightly, as if bracing for a blow, and tried it again. She caught a whiff of pine. When she eventually opened her eyes, he was standing before her, straight as an arrow, with his arms at his sides.

"Oh!" Rachel clapped her hands to her face.

She stood there looking petrified herself. Finally, she started to raise her hand to perform the Word of Ending. Then, she paused and giggled a bit. A mischievous look crept over her face. Walking forward, she stood on tiptoes and gave the frozen young man a very little kiss.

Running back, she formed a fist with a single finger up, and moved it horizontally in front of her, shouting, *"Obé!"* imitating the hand gesture motion and voice tone Magdalene had used when setting her free. Then, she turned all red, because, of course, now he could move and speak.

"Shall we do it again?" Before he could answer, she whistled the same notes. Blue sparkles swirled around him, sweeping his hair upward. He froze again.

Then, she freed him and froze him yet again. She did this fifteen times in a row, until the whole hallway smelled like evergreen. Finally, she let him stay unfrozen. Surely, by now, enough time had passed that he would have forgotten that she had kissed him.

He picked up his robe and crossed to where she stood. "Well, one more time is appropriate I think." And he leaned in and kissed her.

A shiver of energy rippled though her body and out her hair, like a cat on a Halloween decoration. She blushed entirely red from scalp to sole, but she felt tremendously happy.

Gaius smiled, but it was not the big, super confident smile he usually gave her. It was a bit toothier, and his cheeks were sort of red.

He said, "Well, distractions aside, I will come by your table to get you tomorrow after dinner. I should get back to my room and actually study a bit."

He turned and walked away at a slightly faster pace than a stroll.

CHAPTER SIXTEEN:

WRAITHS IN THE DARK

WHEN RACHEL RETURNED TO HER ROOM, THE DORM WAS STILL empty. She lay on her back, aglow with delight, and played over and over again her memory of Gaius's kiss. It had been her first kiss. She wondered, though, which one counted as the first, hers to him while he was paralyzed? Or his to her? Or had she not had a proper first kiss yet, because they had not kissed each other?

Contemplating these important questions, she reviewed the rest of her eventful day: her letter from her father, her conversation with Gaius in the morning, the reappearance of the princess and her intriguing adventures, Zoë's extraordinary power to walk through dreams, her first day of her new job as Mr. Chanson's assistant—showing off her flying and watching the new stude...

Rachel sat up straight. It had happened again. She had remembered something that had not been visible to her eyes. Just before Mylene Price turned pale and left the broom lesson for the Infirmary, a black shadow had appeared. The shadow had been shaped roughly like a person but taller. It appeared next to Miss Price and sunk one of its arms wrist deep into the girl's chest.

Rachel shuddered and thought back. She recalled seeing Mylene in the Infirmary the night before and in the dining hall a couple of times. Each time, when Rachel checked her memory, the shadow was with Mylene. In the dining hall, it just looked as if Mylene's own shadow was dark and misshapen. In the Infirmary, it lay half inside her sleeping body.

The will-o-wisps, which had been sleeping in their nighthoods, rushed together and formed a glowing ball of light. Her roommates came in, laughing and talking.

"...keep working on the new spell they taught us tonight." The princess glided in. "I am disappointed in how inadequate my spellcasting is compared to the older students."

"But you can't expect to be as good as the older students. They have been here for years." Kitten held her tiny lion around the middle. She plopped him on her bed. Calm and dignified, he turned three times and curled up into a ball.

"That is no excuse," the princess replied primly, placing her bag on the vanity her brothers had carried out from the house in her purse.

Kitten bounced on her bunk. The lion opened one golden eye. Kitty cried, "That was great fun, Rachel. You should have come."

"No one invited me," said Rachel softly.

Astrid and Kitten looked stricken. Nastasia clapped her hand to her forehead, horrified. "Rachel, I must apologize. I had intended to take you with me. Ivan was so busy asking questions, I forgot. A princess should never go back on her word. I will make it up to you."

"It's okay. I got invited somewhere for tomorrow night." Rachel stood up. "Listen, I have discovered something important. There's a girl in the Infirmary who has a wraith eating her. I think she's there now. Or she was earlier. We have to go save her!"

The princess straightened. "We must help this poor unfortunate soul! Let us..." Glancing out the window at the darkness, she frowned in disappointment. "We cannot go out. It is after curfew. A special exception was made for returning from the YSL."

"But...she's in trouble."

The princess looked compassionate but stern. "We cannot break a rule. Rules are what hold life together. Without them, there is only chaos."

"But...she's being eaten by a wraith!" Rachel insisted.

"Did this just start?"

"No," Rachel admitted reluctantly. "It's been going on for some days. Maybe longer."

"We shall tell someone first thing in the morning," Nastasia assured her gently.

"I could tell the college resident?" Kitten offered. "Her name is Yolanda Debussy. She lives in the tower. She's a junior. She is also student delegate for our dorm. She represents the girls' side of Dare Hall on the student council. Oh, and she's president of the YSL this year."

Yolanda Debussy. Gaius had mentioned her as a YSL member Rachel might approach.

"That is an excellent idea." Nastasia nodded approvingly.

"Where does she live?" Rachel asked.

"In the main tower on our side. College upperclassmen normally live on the lower floors. They get the privilege of not having to climb as many stairs. The college resident lives up here, so we freshman can have access to her," Kitten explained. "Shall I go get her?"

"It's okay. I'll do it myself." Rachel ran out of the room. She ran up the tower stairs and knocked on the door at the top. A tall slender young woman with pale orangey hair came to the door in her nightgown. "Yes?"

"Are you Miss Debussy?"

"I am." She nodded graciously. "Can I help you?"

"There is a wraith eating Mylene Price!"

"Excuse me." Yolanda stepped into the hallway, her face filled with concern. She looked back and forth as if expecting to see the events Rachel described. "Wha...where? Miss Price isn't in our dorm. What makes you think she is being eaten by a wraith?"

"I saw the wraith. It had its arm inside her."

"When did you see this?"

"A couple of times. Yesterday. Today. I only just put together what I saw."

"And you saw this, and no one else did?"

Rachel nodded.

"How?"

Rachel opened her mouth and closed it, unwilling to tell a stranger about her memory.

Yolanda Debussy ran a hand through her short coppery hair, which was wet. She must have just stepped out of the shower. "Miss...Griffin, right? Laurel and Sandra's little sister? Listen. It is late. If this is not urgent, why don't we discuss it in the morning, okay? If you are still worried about it tomorrow, tell me, and I'll help you find a tutor."

"But..."

"Good night, Miss Griffin." Miss Debussy closed her door.

Rachel clomped back down the staircase. She paused on her floor. Should she go back to bed? After all, it was possible that Miss Price had been wraith chow for years. Was one more night going to make a big difference?

Rachel recalled how the young woman's face had shone with joy as she tried her broom for the first time and how pale she had turned when the wraith came back. With calm determination, Rachel stomped down the stairs. It was dark outside, though the stars shone brightly. Rachel headed for the Commons. The gravel of the pathway crunched loudly under her feet. Ahead, she saw Mr. Fisher speaking with Mr. Tuck and another tutor. She ran up to them.

"Mr. Tuck! Mr. Fisher! There is a wraith eating Miss Price!"

"Where?"

The tutors all turned, ready for action. Mr. Fisher drew an ornate athame.

"Er...I'm not sure," Rachel replied. "But there is this wraith. It sticks its hand in her chest, and she turns pale."

Mr. Tuck ran a hand over his beard. "Miss Griffin. Did you attend the YSL meeting?"

"No."

"So you were upstairs, sleeping?"

"I was in bed. I was not asleep."

He nodded knowingly. "Of course, you weren't...and yet, I believe you have woken from a nightmare, Child. If there were a wraith following Miss Price, we would know. It would set off the alarms. Creatures like that are not allowed to wander school grounds."

"But..."

He put his arm firmly around her shoulder. "Now, let us get you back to bed. You live where? Dare Hall? Of course. You are a Griffin."

"Yes. Dare." Rachel murmured dejectedly. She let Mr. Tuck escort her back to the door of her dorm. "Thank you, Sir."

"Good night, Miss Griffin. Sleep tight. May the night bring no more nightmares."

Rachel slouched into her dorm. Ahead of her rose the stairs.

She stopped and stared up the sweep of marble heading toward her room. A spark came in her eye. The resident and the tutors may not have believed her, but she knew someone who would!

Extending her right hand toward the staircase, she gestured. *"Varenga, Vroomie!"*

With a *swish*, the broom whistled down the stairway and flew to her hand. It had worked! She whooped with delight. Leaping on it, she swept across the foyer, up the far staircase, landing on the fourth floor of the boys side. Voices came from inside one door. Hopping off her broom, she knocked. The door, which had not been entirely closed, opened

"Excuse me, can you tell me where...Siggy! There you are!"

The door had swung open to reveal Siggy, Ian MacDannan, and Enoch Smithwyck. From the look of it, they, too, had just returned from the YSL. They were pantomiming exchanging cantrips using random made-up gestures. Enoch straightened up sheepishly when he saw her, but the other two kept right at it.

Rachel burst into their room and froze. Gold coins covered one of the bunks, cascading from the bed to form a large pile around and under it. Necklaces, figurines, jeweled chalices stuck out amidst the shining coins.

"You really do sleep on gold!" she blurted out, her jaw gaping. Then, recalling why she was there, she cried, "Boys! There's a girl in the Infirmary who is being eaten by a wraith."

"Let's go!" Siggy grabbed his robe and threw it over his pajamas.

"You can't go out," Enoch objected. "It's after curfew."

Siggy grinned maniacally. "I can go to the Infirmary if I am wounded. Here, slug me!"

Rachel crouched in one of the magical chambers of the gym, her head pressed against the hot rocks of the sauna. As soon as her forehead felt sufficiently hot, she bolted across the short gap of lawn from the gymnasium to the Infirmary. Within, Mylene rested on a bed. Her otter familiar snuggled against her, one of her pale red braids flopped over its dark fur. Siggy, sporting a huge bruise on the side of his jaw, sat on another. A disappointed Ian MacDannan was being turned away by the nurse, who rolled her eyes at his fake purple spots. She groaned when she saw Rachel. After putting the back of her hand against Rachel's hot forehead, however, Nurse Moth led her to a bed.

Rachel padded across the green marble and settled down on the firm mattress, watching the nurse examine Siggy's bruises. Nurse Moth had given her the same bed she had slept in the previous night. So far, Siggy and Rachel had both been here once, twice counting now, and Nastasia had been here once. That made five visits between three students in three days. She wondered if the school reported to her parents when she visited the Infirmary.

As she sat there, recalling the previous evening, she thought again about her brief conversation with Maverick Badger. He had said seeing the raven was a bad omen. But did it count if the raven thought it was invisible? Or only if it deliberately manifested itself? On the subject of invisibility, Rachel glanced over at Mylene for ten seconds. Then she recalled five seconds back. A shiver traveled up her body. The shadowy entity was still there, its arm stuck deep into the redhead's body.

Rachel called loudly, "Nurse! There is a spirit creature there. A shadowy thing. It's hurting Miss Price!"

"What?" Nurse Moth turned. "Where?"

"Right there!" She pointed with her whole arm. "It's invisible. But it's hurting her. When it puts its hand in her, she turns pale. It's been hanging around her for days."

"Let's go, Lucky!" Siggy leapt up and sprinted toward Mylene's bedside. The dragon swept after him. Spooked, her otter darted under the bed. Its whiskered nose poked out from beneath the sheets and hissed at them.

"Where is it?" Sigfried looked around. "Even I cannot burn something I can't see!"

Mylene glanced around her, frightened. She spoke with a French Canadian accent. "You mean a wraith? There is no wraith here. My father is a professional wraith hunter. I know all the signs. There is no tell-tale extra shadow. Or the feeling of biting cold."

Rachel jumped to her feet on the bed, still pointing. "It's right there. I can see it."

The creature angled its shadow-like head in her direction. Slowly, it began to glide toward Rachel. She glared at it. Similar to breaking an Obscuration, she soon found she could see it without having to think back. It resembled a dark floating cloak.

It came closer and closer and closer. Then, it was upon her. Immediately, she began to feel weak. She pushed at it, but her hands went right through its substance. Two points darker than shadow regarded her from where its face might be. She stared back fiercely, undaunted.

"Okay. Now it's eating me," she announced. She felt strangely calm, not frightened at all. Her thoughts had become entirely clear, as they did when she flew at high speed. "It's right here."

She whistled sharply. A blast of wind blew away from her. The silver sparkles did not so much as ruffle the wraith.

"Boy, you don't scare easy, do you?" Siggy ran toward her, impressed. His eyes seemed to be tracking the wraith. "Lucky, Griffin's being eaten by a wraith. Yet, she's sitting there, cool as a cucumber, and reporting what is going on!"

"She's one brave cookie," said the dragon. "I'm going in, Boss."

Lucky sped through the air, mouth open to breath fire. Outside the window of the Infirmary, there was a flapping of wings. Lucky's eyes dulled. He began chasing his tail like a cat. Then, he zipped away through an open window, off across the campus.

"Lucky! No!" Siggy cried. "Lucky! Talk to me? I can't hear him in my head! He's turned into a dumb animal again! I think he's heading for the menagerie to eat people's familiars! That's what he tried to do last night!"

Hear him in his head? Rachel did not have time to wonder about this.

"It's the Raven." Her mouth went dry. "He's here."

The wraith loomed over her. Rachel felt lightheaded, but she refused to give in to fear. She stubbornly glared back at the specter. The more life it drew from her, the more substantial it became. Its cloaked form solidified, becoming visible even to Mylene. Siggy charged toward it, shouting. Mylene cowered backward. Her familiar clambered up on her bed, hissing at the wraith. It rubbed its damp nose against the side of Mylene's face, comforting her.

"What is that?" Mylene murmured. Her otter's whiskers tickled her, causing her to giggle slightly in spite of her fear. "It doesn't look like a wraith."

Music filled the room, lovely music. The nurse, her eyes wild, stood in the center of the Infirmary, playing her flute. White sparkles spun in the air, weaving their way toward the intruder. It grabbed at its head and howled, a high eerie sound that made hairs stand up all over Rachel's body.

Mylene covered her ears. "There *is* a wraith here! Their cries are unmistakable!"

The music grew louder, more glorious and insistent. White sparkles swirled throughout the chamber, accompanied by the scent of roses. The fragrance reminded Rachel of summer days at Gryphon Park, walking among the flowering trellises in the warmth of the sun. She recognized this as the kind of Enchantment used to bind evil. The creature howled again and dashed through the wall, out toward the Commons.

Drawing his steak knife from his robes, Siggy ran from the Infirmary and sprinted after it. Rachel wanted to go, too, but her legs gave out. She sat down hard on the bed, feeling woozy. A minute passed before she felt well enough to stand. The nurse hovered over her, passing her scrutiny sticks up and down Rachel's body. Nurse Moth announced that she had an elixir that would help and retreated into the back room. The moment she was out of sight, Rachel ran.

She burst from the Infirmary and onto the lawn. Her legs felt shaky, but she did not slow down. She did extend her hand. "*Varenga*, Vroomie!"

A *whoosh*, and her broom, which she had left by the gym when she heated her forehead, came swooping across the lawn. Oh, she dearly loved the *varenga* cantrip! Leaping on Vroomie, she swept off after Sigfried.

The wind rushed by her ears. She flew toward the center of the lawn. Ahead, Siggy faced the wraith. His knife did nothing to the insubstantial creature. That did not stop him from acts of insane courage. He stabbed his hand into the wraith's life-stealing substance again and again. She shot up beside him, hovering.

"Have at thee, varlet!" Siggy shouted, stabbing the thing yet again. The wraith plunged its hand into his chest. Siggy went pale, but this did not stop the frenzy of his attack.

Rachel wanted to help him. She tried *tiathelu*, but the insubstantial creature did not lift. Nor could she paralyze it or blow it away. Rapidly, she looked around. If she could not affect it directly, could she help another way? She flew off in search of aid. Maybe she could find a proctor. As she approached Dare Hall, she heard music. She flew toward the sound, shouting, "Help! Help! Wraith!"

Down the path pelted four older boys, followed by a panting Ian, whose face was rosy with exertion beneath his painted purple spots. The older boys carried violins, flutes and pan pipes. They wore baldrics from which hung wooden stakes and garlic. What had Gaius said about "crazy Enchanter boys from Dare Hall obsessed with hunting vampires?" These must be the boys he meant. How clever of Ian to go get them!

"Wraith!" Rachel waved her arms again, relying on balance to keep her on the steeplechaser. "This way."

The boys did not hesitate. It was as if they had lived their whole lives for this moment. Rushing across the lawns, they formed a rough circle around the wraith and began to play. They were classmates of her brother Peter, Rachel saw, seniors in the Upper School. The leader was Abraham Van Helsing, a tall young man with soft brown hair, a distant descendent of the Van Helsing who vanquished the vampire that used to rule part of the Starkadder territory. Abraham blew into a set of pan-pipes he wore on a brace around his neck. He carried a crossbow that shot sharpened wooden stakes.

Next to him was one of Ian's older brothers, Conan. He had red hair and a rascally grin. As he played his fiddle, Conan danced an Irish jig. The white sparks issuing from his instrument danced to his tune. To either side of him were Max Weatherby, a rangy dark-haired boy with a big chin, who played a flute, and Alex Romanov, the princess's brother who had slugged Joshua March. He also played a violin.

Max put a crystal vase on the ground. Rachel recognized it as a spirit-catching vessel. Two cats, presumably the boys' familiars, came forward and sat warily to either side of it. The four boys continued to play. Their music was similar to the nurse's, only wilder, leaping and rising until Rachel could hardly stay still. The urge to jump and twirl and throw herself about grew so strong, she could not resist. She flew rapidly in a circle, chasing the shining twinkles of white light that issued from the boys' instruments, circling the wraith. So quickly did she fly that it was as if the air itself glowed with a pale sparkling fire. Dancing white glitter lodged in her hair causing her to laugh out loud. The more the boys played, the brighter and thicker the bands of sparkles grew. The air smelled like roses and honeysuckle.

Rachel knew what was supposed to occur. She had seen her father and mother do this once to capture a ghoul that had been troubling their farmer tenants. The glittering strands of sparkles should constrict around the wicked creature, bind it up, and suck it into the vase. However, nothing happened. The strands seemed unable to grasp the shadowy cloaked form. One of the cats got bored and left the jar to bat at the twinkling lights.

"That's not a normal wraith!" Abraham Van Helsing cried. "It is resisting our binding."

"It is warded," Conan MacDannan called in his rich Irish brogue.

"Warded?" Max Weatherby shouted, lifting his mouth from his flute for an instant. "Are you out of your tiny Irish mind? How can a wraith be warded? That makes no sense!"

"Nonetheless," Conan called back lightly, "we've got to break the ward, if we want to capture the nasty beastie."

"What breaks that kind of ward?" Alex Romanov asked, his Australian accent carrying across the lawn. Rachel tried to picture his gracious princess of a sister out here shouting and wearing garlic. She failed. Perhaps this slugging and vampire-hunting brother took after their wombat and Vegemite-loving father. "Mold? Bells? Will its ward go down if it attacks us? Most wards do?"

"Don't know. Try firing something at it," Conan suggested. "Maybe it will strike back."

Abraham lifted his head from his pipes. "A stake won't do jack. Look at the crazy kid with the knife. And none of us have wands."

The more the wraith drained Sigfried, the more substantial it grew. Sigfried's knife actually caused slight ripples in its form now, as he stabbed it. *That's it*, Rachel thought as she flew among the sparkles, circling the wraith, *I'm getting a wand.* She never wanted to be stuck like this again, watching someone suffer and be unable to help. The desire to protect others burned in her chest like a star.

Siggy dropped to his knees. His face was paper white. The wraith had both hands stuck inside her friend. As she watched, it pushed its head into Sigfried's face.

Sigfried made a horrible noise and fell over. He lay curled up on the ground. But even that did not stop him. Despite all this, his knife hand rose up and continued to stab at the substance of the wraith, which was so close to solid now that his knife actually tore it. Rachel flew toward him, not certain how to help, but determined not to let her friend die.

"Boss! Boss! I'm back. Get out of the way! I got this!"

Lucky the Dragon jetted across the lawn like a furry river. Darting to Siggy's side, he breathed. Fire erupted from his mouth, striking the strange, dark entity.

From where he lay on the ground, a pale and shaky Siggy threw his head back and laughed maniacally. "Burn, Baby, burn!"

The cloak-like shape popped like a bubble. Underneath was a real wraith, gaunt eyes, skull-like face, narrow bony hands.

"Now!" cried Abraham Van Helsing.

The music crescendoed. The swaths of glittering sparkles swirled around the wraith and yanked it toward the crystal container. With a horrible yowling scream, the terrible creature was dragged into the vase.

CHAPTER SEVENTEEN:
A THOUSAND, THOUSAND SHARDS

RACHEL SAT ON HER BED IN THE INFIRMARY, WRAPPED IN A BLANKET and shivering. A mug of hot chocolate warmed her cold, trembling hands. She sipped it gingerly. Siggy sat in the next bed, drinking his own cup of cocoa and skillfully high-fiving Lucky's softly padded palm without snagging his razor-sharp talons. Across the way, Mylene Price sat propped up against some pillows, her bright-eyed otter curled in her lap. There was a little bit of color in her face. She had not said much, but her eyes shone with shock and gratitude.

The door to the Infirmary opened, and two of the proctors: Mr. Fuentes and Mr. Harvey Stone, a dark-skinned man of medium height with tight curly hair, came in, followed by their boss, Maverick Badger. Mr. Fuentes came over immediately and shone a big smile in Rachel's direction.

"Hey! I shouldn't be seeing you back here so soon, Squirt! What is this about you offering yourself to a wraith as a snack? Don't you know that's bad juju?"

Rachel grinned back at him. "Better me than her." She pointed across the way at Mylene. "That wraith has been living off her for three years. Now it is gone, and she can get healthy."

Fuentes eyebrows arched, impressed. "Good for you. Only next time,"—he squatted down in front of her and took one of her hands; his grasp seemed so large and warm.— "come to us and tell us, rather than taking on the wraith yourself. Okay?"

"I told the tutors. They didn't believe me," Rachel said. She felt a strange empty sensation as she said this, as if Miss

Debussy, Mr. Tuck, and Mr. Fisher had personally betrayed her. "I told the nurse, too. But she couldn't see it."

"I don't get it. How could *you* see it? How did you know it was there?"

She gave him her biggest grin. "Magic."

He laughed out loud and stood, releasing her hand. Disappointed to have him let go, Rachel put it back on the warm cup.

"Okay, don't tell me," he drawled. "I know many people here have unusual talents. But remember what I said. Next time. Tell us."

Fuentes headed off to speak to the nurse. As Rachel continued to sip her cocoa, Mr. Badger came over and sat on the bed next to hers.

"You all right, Miss Griffin?" he asked gruffly.

"I'm okay."

"Listen." He leaned toward her and lowered his voice. "I asked around for you...about the Raven. Most of the staff here have never even heard of him, but I spoke to Nighthawk, the Amerindian fellow who is the head Warder on campus. He said something..." Badger's eyes narrowed, "...peculiar."

"Really?" Rachel wanted to hear what so badly that she could hardly breathe to form words. "Wha-what did he say?"

"He said that in his culture the Raven is a trickster, a clever guy. But in some cultures, the raven is an omen of death, an omen of doom." Badger paused, leaning even closer. Rachel caught a whiff of wood smoke and musk. "Nighthawk said the Raven with the red eyes is something bigger. It's an omen of the doom of worlds."

Cold icy fingers, far worse than the touch of a wraith, passed across the back of Rachel's neck.

"Doom of worlds?" Her voice came out a hoarse whisper. "Whose world? Ours or...others?"

Badger gave her an odd look. He stood up. "Don't know. That's all he said." He pinned her with his fierce gray eyes. "You hear about anyone seeing that Raven, you'll tell me, right, Miss Griffin?" Rachel stared up at him, but she did not move, did not nod. He grunted. "Right. Have a good night, Miss Griffin."

Rachel sat on the bed, shaken. Mr. Badger's words had disturbed her more than the other events of late, more than the murder attempt on Valerie, more than seeing the princess faint after she touched Mr. March, more than being eaten by a wraith. All those things were personal, affecting only a few.

But the doom of the whole world?

She thought of the princess's visions of desolated and destroyed landscapes. Was the Raven causing this? Or did his appearance indicate that a doom was coming, the way thunder indicated the presence of distant lightning? And what did it mean that the Raven was here?

Closing her eyes, she thought about the Earth: the cool rushing rivers, the leaping waterfalls, the tall majestic mountains, the golden fields and stark stone mansion of her home, the thick dark forests of Roanoke Island—not to mention art and science and magic, and libraries, all the good things of human civilization.

Were those things at risk?

She felt lost, alone, not certain whom to tell or how to proceed. She knew only that she wanted, with all her being, to protect those who were threatened. And then, she remembered what to do, and suddenly she felt snug and safe. She could report to her father. Taking paper and pen from her robes, she wrote down everything.

When Rachel woke next, moonlight streamed into the Infirmary, casting odd shadows and bathing the floor in silvery light. The green balls of healing light had dimmed until they were nothing but a near indistinguishable flicker. The dancing will-o-wisps were snug in their nighthoods. It was so quiet that she could hear the tick of the grandfather clock across the chamber and the whirr of the orrery motors. In the distance, thunder rumbled.

Overhead, constellations twinkled: the Big Dipper, the Lyre, Orion. She stared up, scrunching up her face in her effort to make sense of this. Then, she understood. The domed ceiling, a cloudy blue by day, had tiny glow-in-the-dark crystals set into it, forming an image of the night sky. The phosphorescent planets on the orrery, Venus and the rings of Saturn, shone pale green against this backdrop of stars.

Nearby, something moved.

"Sigfried?" she whispered hoarsely.

"Yeah."

"You're awake, too, eh?" Rachel grinned. "What's wrong? Can't sleep without all that lumpy gold?"

"Our gold?" Siggy sat straight up. "Lucky! You better go check on it."

The dragon uncurled from where he had been wrapped around his master. "Right, Boss, I'm on it. Only...what if you need me?"

"Then, I'll call you back. You can get back here quick, right?"

"Right. Got it." Lucky zipped off, slipping out an open window.

Rachel sat up and propped her pillow against the headrest behind her. "So, who finally slugged you? Ian or Enoch?"

"Are you kidding?" Siggy snorted. "They are both soggy wimps. Don't get me wrong. I like 'em, but they would not have lasted a week at the orphanage. Or even a day. Especially Enoch the Wuss. Nay, it was Seth Peregrine. Good upper cut!"

"The bass guitarist who plays hockey? Zoë's friend?"

"Yeah, he's from a tough part of town. Used to be in a gang. He can actually fight. He's offered to teach me."

"You can't fight?" Rachel asked, confused.

"I can fight. I just can't box. Or wrestle. Guts I got. What I lack is technique."

"What does it mean to fight without technique?"

"Mostly I flail around wildly until the other guy goes down."

"How did you kill the dragon? The one in the sewers with all the gold?"

Siggy fell silent. A breeze blew through the Infirmary. The chimes rang softly.

"Siggy?"

His voice, when it came, was low and hesitant. "Promise you won't tell anyone?"

"I promise."

"I didn't. Lucky talked to it, and it blew itself up."

"Wha-what?" Rachel shook her head in confusion.

"Lucky talked it into blowing itself up. Lucky did it."

"Weird..." Rachel was not sure what to make of that. "Lucky

can talk to you in your head, can't he?"

"What makes you say that?" Siggy asked defensively.

"Oh...just a hunch."

"Yeah. Yes, he can. We talk to each other in our heads, and I can see through his eyes."

"So that is how you knew that the man who was after Valerie had come back!"

"Exactly," Siggy said. "Lucky can see a lot of things others can't see. He can also make himself invisible. He does stuff like turn invisible and drink the coffee tutors leave on their desk. Only he has to be careful, a few tutors can see through his invisibility, as can myself, the princess, and Dread."

"Von Dread?" her eyebrows shot up.

Siggy nodded. "And Wulfgang...sometimes. He and Joy are not as good at it as the princess and me, but they can catch him sometimes."

"Hmm."

Rachel felt sad that she could not do this. Then mirth bubbled up inside her. She, of all people, should not be envious of people's ability to see things that normally could not be seen.

"I have a secret power, too," she whispered.

"What is it?" Siggy's eyes grew large. "You must tell me! We are friends. Friends hold nothing back! They tell each other everything!"

"I have a perfect memory. I can remember everything," she confessed. "When I remember back, I can recall things my eyes didn't pick up....when did Lucky drink the coffee?"

"Mr. Tuck's coffee, this morning."

Rachel tipped her head back and recalled Language class. Sure enough, she recalled Lucky sitting on the table, his long tongue flickering into the tutor's mug.

"Okay...I can see Lucky when I remember back," she said, "Which is a warning. I'm not the only person who can do this. My mother can do it, too. There maybe others...people who won't see Lucky at the time, but who will know what he was up to later on."

"Good to know," mused Siggy.

They both settled back. Rachel gazed at the constellations glowing overhead.

"By the way," Siggy said suddenly, "Lucky's not the only familiar who can turn invisible. He and I caught Dr. Mordeau's familiar sneaking around when nobody but us could see it. You know, the creepy, eared snake?"

"Really?" Rachel leaned forward. "Siggy, do you remember when Dr. Mordeau asked about my father?"

Siggy blinked. "No."

"At the end of class, when kids from Drake were teasing me about my broom?"

Siggy blinked again. "Sorry. What day was this?"

Rachel rolled her eyes and sighed in exasperation. "You missed other children picking on me and humiliating me?"

"Were there explosions? Descriptions of other planets? No? Then why would I care?" Siggy asked. "I was watching what Lucky was doing. He's been investigating the tor to see if there is a way into where the Heer of Dunderberg is imprisoned. We want to see a storm imp."

"Good grief!" Rachel sighed. "Well, she mentioned my father, and when she said his name…" Rachel paused.

"When she said his name…what?" Siggy asked impatiently.

"Her eyes were filled with hatred." Rachel paused. "Dr. Mordeau hates my father."

"Why?"

"I don't know. But…" she paused, thinking hard. "She is too old to be a schoolmate of my father's, which means it is unlikely that she hates him for personal reasons. And she's not English or Scottish or something, so it's unlikely that it has to do with him being a duke."

"What does that leave?"

"The Wisecraft. It leaves hating him because he is an Agent."

"Who hates the Agents?"

"Evil people." Rachel's mouth seemed unexpectedly dry. "People with wicked intent."

"Huh." Siggy thought about this. "We'd better keep an eye on her then. I'll have Lucky go investigate her. But he'll have to be stealthy. She can see him."

"Definitely send him, but tell him to be careful."

"Don't worry!" Siggy snorted with pride. "He's smarter than the average dragon. He can talk the Queen's English."

Rachel settled back against her pillows. "How...how did you meet Lucky?"

"Found him as an egg."

"Where?"

Siggy spoke haltingly, as if he was reluctant to tell the story. "I had run away and was hiding in the sewer. The rozzers were coming. One of the other boys had ratted me out. I remember wishing with all my heart that someone was on my side, and something rolled against my foot. It was this egg. Lucky hatched out of it, and we've been together ever since. We're brothers!"

"That's really cool!" Rachel whispered, her heart so filled with emotion that it was hard to speak.

What would it be like to have no one, no safe haven to return to in a storm? Her family was so loving, so supportive. She could not even imagine life without them. Deep in her heart, she silently whispered: *Fear not, Sigfried. You never need to be alone again. I will be there.*

At that moment, Rachel resolved that, no matter what came, it would be so. She would be his family. She felt too shy to speak these words aloud.

"I am so glad you and Lucky found each other," she said softly. "I wonder what it means that he came from another world? Was that before he was an egg?"

"I don't know. But I'd like to find out more. What if Lucky has some home that belongs to him?" Siggy spoke with great seriousness. "A family that actually wants him? Not one that throws their children away."

Did Sigfried believe he was in an orphanage because someone had thrown him away? How horrid.

"Siggy, I haven't had a chance to tell you..." She leaned forward, eager to share with him her few secrets, so there would be no distance between them. "Remember the Raven I told you about? I have seen it more than once. It knows I can see it." She shivered. "Mr. Badger, the head of the proctors, the security guys here at school, he just came and told me that the Raven is an omen of the doom of worlds."

"Does that mean our world is doomed?" Siggy asked.

"I don't know. Maybe. But omens do not necessarily cause the thing they foretell. Maybe it appears on worlds, before the catastrophes that the princess keeps seeing, and rescues a few people. Maybe our world is a refuge for the survivors," Rachel said thoughtfully. "The princess did say that the Raven seemed to be in charge of people entering and leaving our world."

"Leaving and going where?" Siggy's voice overflowed with eagerness. "And how does one do this? And when can I go?"

At the thought of visiting other worlds—of seeing these distant places, the ones the princess was visiting—a wanderlust gripped Rachel so powerful that it felt like a physical tug. She wondered if this was how the tide felt when the moon pulled on it.

"Me, too," she whispered, her mouth dry. "I want to go, too."

"Hello, Rachel." A wonderfully familiar voice roused her from dreams about rowing uphill on a river of hot chocolate. Rachel stirred and fought for consciousness. A tall man stood over her, smiling—an extraordinarily handsome tall man. He had dark hair and very steady hazel eyes. A black Inverness cloak draped from his shoulders to his ankles. There was an air of implacable calmness about him but also a sense of wry amusement, as if his keen intelligence allowed him to discover the humor where others could not.

"Father!" Rachel leapt up and threw her arms around him, hugging him and holding on tightly when she was assailed by a sudden lightheadedness.

He lifted her up and held her against him, his cheek pressed against her cheek. "Are you all right, Dear?"

"I am! I am fine!" Rachel cried, delighted.

"I brought you some sweets...from home."

"Smarties! And Aeros!" she cried. She held out her hands and watched the brightly colored boxes and bars fill them. "And Cadbury's Flake! And toffees!"

"Your favorites."

"I wrote you another letter, but I haven't had time to send it yet. It's here!" She fumbled with her pocket, trying to draw out the letter she had written the night before without dropping the chocolates. This only partially worked.

"It is all right. I..."

"No! Read it! It will tell you everything." She shoved the letter into his hands and stood up on her bed, her body tense with excitement. She watched his face carefully while he read it, waiting for his surprise, waiting for his praise, waiting for the moment when he read about the doom of worlds. Most of all, she waited to hear what he had to tell her—the answers to her burning questions.

Ambrose Griffin read the letter and folded it neatly. He spoke very gently in his rich, soothing Father voice that she so loved. "Rachel, I sent you here to Roanoke to learn sorcery and become a young lady, not to work for the Wisecraft. I have operatives for that. What I want is for you to go to school, to make friends, and to learn. I want you to enjoy being a little girl."

"But...Father..." Her voice broke. Even with the secret skills she had learned from her mother, she could not mask her desperation. "Wh-what about this new magic? What about the attempt on Valerie's life? Do the Agents have any suspects? What about the Raven? Surely you know something? Surely, you can tell me..."

"No buts," he said. "I have to go. I am needed at a very important meeting. Attend school and have fun. And forget all about this Raven."

"B-but...I can't do that! I...can't! He knows I can see him!"

"No buts," he repeated. He leaned over and gently kissed her forehead.

If the universe had been painted on glass—and someone struck it with a cricket bat, shattering it into a thousand, thousand sharp shards—it might have felt like this. Her father's words snapped the rudder off the ship of her soul. There was no longer a safe harbor against the storm of events around her.

She had been expecting so much. Instead, he had taken her secrets and given her nothing in return. And now he had given her an impossible order. How could she forget the Raven? She could see it. Worse, the Raven knew that she could. She could not forget the Raven.

She could not forget anything.

She wanted so much to cry out, to explain how wrong her father was, how this was not what she needed, how she could not possibly obey him. But she could not force her leaden tongue to move. She stared at him mutely, as he kissed her gently on the forehead again and departed, leaving her standing, hopeless, her hands overflowing with candy.

CHAPTER EIGHTEEN:
THE MARVELOUS AMULET
OF SIGFRIED SMITH

RACHEL ARRIVED AT THE DINING HALL, HER POCKETS STUFFED WITH Smarties and Aeros. The smells of breakfast filled the air, but she did not feel hungry, neither for omelets nor for candy. She sat with her friends and stared blankly at her tray.

Salome arrived with an air of excitement and took a chair next to Valerie. She leaned forward, gleefully imparting her juicy gossip. "I don't know what you all did, but high marks! Take a look at Cydney and her friends. Word is that they woke up covered with urine and blood and all sorts of gross stuff. The dorm stank this morning. I can tell you that!"

Rachel glanced over at the table Salome indicated. Magdalene sat by herself, a new bruise on her cheek. Her little porcelain doll stood near her feet under the table, looking oddly alert. A little farther down the same table, Cydney and the other two girls who had attacked Rachel sat with towels wrapped around their heads like turbans. Rachel stared at them with a rising feeling of curiosity and delight. So, Zoë had succeeded. What had she done?

"Huh?" Valerie put down her glass of milk, leaving a mustache. "They're wearing turbans. Is that the in-look in the World of the Wise? If so, you guys need a new fashion."

"You should see what's underneath," murmured Zoë, twirling one finger through her electric blue hair. Even her eyebrows and eyelashes were blue today.

"Yes. What is under the towels? I am so curious," Salome mused, tapping her fingers on the table. "Wonder how we could get them to take the towels off."

"I could send Lucky over there to pull on them," Sigfried offered. He had three plates in front of him, each piled with food he was wolfing down hungrily. Occasionally, a piece of toast or an apple disappeared into the pockets of his robe.

"Could you?" Salome leaned way forward in such a way as to reveal her remarkable cleavage. Sigfried glanced away, scowling. He reached out and took Valerie's hand. Her cheeks went pink with delight.

Over by the other table, Cydney Graves gave a shriek as her towel dropped from her head. Rachel remembered back a few seconds. Sure enough, she could recall Lucky yanking on it with his teeth. He had pulled hard and the swath of pale pink terry cloth had come away from her head. Underneath, Cydney's hair was puke green. The other two towels also came off. The unpleasant color particularly stood out against Lola's dark skin.

Valerie snapped a photo, her flash temporarily blinding Cydney and her friends. Their resulting shrieks attracted attention. Soon, everyone in the dining hall was pointing and laughing. Cydney and the other two quickly left the dining hall, surrounded by Belladonna and several other girls. Their retreat was accompanied by hooting and cat calls.

Rachel tipped her chair back and crossed her arms behind her head. Her expression slowly transformed from thoughtful to amused to delighted. Bringing her chair legs forward with a *bang*, she leaned against the table and pulled her elbows around her head, so that her arms hid her face. Then, she giggled and giggled and giggled.

"Thank you, Zoë," she whispered when she could speak again, wiping away tears of laughter. "That was...very satisfying."

"My pleasure," Zoë mouthed back. "Anything else? More enemies you need humiliated? People you want whacked with a magic *patu*? Relatives who need someone to sleep on their sofa? You would be amazed what people let slip into the cracks in their couches."

"No." Rachel's eyes sparkled. "I'm good."

Zoë winked. "Mission complete."

"That was quite amazing," Salome was still staring after her departing dormmates. "How did you do it, Rachel?"

Smirking, Rachel began cramming her eggs into her mouth. "Magic!"

Tempted by the lovely morning, Rachel took her broom and flew through the towers and spires at high speed. Her mind grew quiet and alert, entirely occupied with the clarity needed for high-speed precision flying. Finally, panting, she sailed gently back toward her dorm.

As she went, she mulled over the problem of not having anyone to report to. When she was little, her highest loyalty had been to her grandfather—he had been the captain of the ship of her soul. His hand had guided the tiller of her heart. Grandfather had been wise and canny. He had become duke as a young man, back when having a title meant something, when dukes still ruled. He had been a British general, commanding men and changing the fates of nations. His fierceness and his imposing presence intimidated people of every rank.

But Rachel had never been daunted. She had recognized him for the brave and noble man that he was. No matter how he bristled, she treated him with unrestrained love. He was often brusque, but she learned the secret to how to approach him, how to not be frightened by his public aspect, how to speak to him in his own metaphors. He had loved hearing her recite things: books she had read, sights she had seen, conversations she had overheard. He had encouraged her to make the most of her perfect memory, and Rachel had loved memorizing things and reporting them to him.

After he died, there had been a period of emptiness accompanied by darkness and a terrible buzzing noise. It was as if her soul had been wounded and would not heal. Slowly, over the next year, her father moved into the void. Father was thoroughly competent yet relaxed, assured and amused. Rachel loved him dearly, but she did not understand him as she had understood Grandfather. She could not guess his moods the way Sandra could. Yet, Father listened carefully to her, and Rachel had loved him for it.

Only, Father had failed her.

She could not to be angry with him. She understood. Who could blame a father for wanting his daughter to be safe and pay attention to her classes? And yet, the position of the captain of the ship of her soul was once again vacant.

Rachel had no idea how to fill it.

On Thursdays, first period was free for her Core Group. Rachel showed Siggy and Nastasia the library. She was a bit disappointed that they were not as entranced as she had been. Apparently, not everybody was in love with the very concept of miles of books. She wondered how Gaius felt about libraries.

Seated in an out-of-the-way corner, the three of them bent their heads together. Whispering, Rachel filled the princess in on the happenings of the previous night, both the matter of the wraith and what Maverick Badger had told her.

"I am very pleased to hear of your bravery and that of Mr. Smith. And certainly helping Miss Price is commendable," Nastasia said gravely. With her pale golden hair pulled back by a light blue ribbon, she looked both regal and as lovely as a summer's day. "But you should not have broken curfew, and you certainly should not have lied to the nurse."

Rachel blinked at her in surprise. "But...Mylene Price was being *eaten* by a *wraith*! Besides, I did not lie. The nurse drew her own conclusion from my forehead being hot."

Nastasia gave her a thoughtful, disapproving look. "We must always do what is right. Even when aiding others."

Rachel goggled at her. Then she sat back and crossed her arms, frowning. The princess had a stronger understanding of right and wrong than she did. But was Nastasia right about this? Should Mylene have suffered another night because the adults would not believe Rachel? In her heart, she did not think so.

Siggy was not the least daunted by Nastasia. "Right by who? No one told me not to leave the dorms at night."

"There is a curfew at ten pm—" the princess began.

Siggy cut her off. "No adult has mentioned that to me. And if they haven't told me, it doesn't count. Besides, grown-ups only invent rules in order to have a reason to punish children. The key is not to get caught."

"That is hardly the standard by which virtue should be measured." Nastasia gazed at him as if he had disappointed her.

"What do I care about measuring virtue, whatever that is? Is it a liquid or a solid? Do you measure it in grams or in yards?" Siggy spit out the paper he had been chewing, adding to his arsenal of spitballs, which formed a small pyramid on the table.

"A knight should be concerned about virtue." Nastasia pushed her pencil back and forth on the table, frowning uncomfortably.

Rachel did not care for the mulish expressions on her friends' faces. It was time to change the subject. "Enough about last night. Let's talk about what we know. The horrid Raven is the doom of worlds. There are many people here from other places. We do not know if the Raven is destroying those worlds or just heralding their doom…but he wanted to send Kitten's lion away, and he seems to be friends with the lightbringing torture-creature. Am I missing anything?"

"No. I believe that is what we know so far," Nastasia said. "This vision power is rather frustrating. It keeps showing me things, but the information I receive is worthless. There is no way for me to act or fix anything based on what I've seen."

"No, Nastasia, no!" Rachel drew back, horrified. "Information is never worthless."

She could not even imagine having the princess's visions and not loving them with all her heart. Of course, if she had been the one to have the visions, she could have replayed them over and over and might have discovered additional clues the princess was overlooking. Rachel sighed. So far, she was doing a pretty decent job of not coveting her friends' amazing gifts, but it became much harder if they did not appreciate what they had.

"It is meaningless if it has no bearing on our current lives." Nastasia turned the page of her ubiquitous text book.

"You have to love information for itself," Rachel insisted, her eyes afire. "Only then can you find its usefulness, its true worth. Sometimes, I have known a bit of information for years before I found a use for it. Suddenly, it's the very bit I need. Like the fact that Beatrix Potter became Mrs. Heelis. I knew that for ages before I needed it.

"Sometimes, I think I have such a good memory because I love knowledge so much," Rachel mused. "I love information, and it loves me. It seeks me out."

"Why?" Siggy asked curiously.

It touched Rachel that he did not disbelieve her. Usually, when she said such things, people just gawked at her.

"I don't know." She considered his question. "Maybe so it can sit in my perfect memory and be remembered."

"I'd forgotten you had a super power," Siggy said.

Rachel shivered. The very notion of forgetting disturbed her.

"I've also got a magic power." Siggy turned to Nastasia. Leaning forward, he filled the princess in on his link with Lucky.

"And that's how you overheard the proctors talking, isn't it?" Nastasia asked, smiling with delight. "Lucky overheard them."

"Yeah, of course," Sigfried said casually. "That's it."

Rachel leaned back, frowning. Her eyes rested on the patterned tiles of the ceiling while she recalled the event in question. Slowly, she said, "No. It could not have been Lucky. He was still over by your bed, with us."

Siggy was silent for a long time. Twice, he stabbed his pencil against his notebook, drawing thick dark lines that left an indent in the paper. "No. It wasn't Lucky."

"How did you do it?" Nastasia asked.

"You promise to tell no one?"

"I give you my solemn word," Nastasia said.

"Not even my father," Rachel swore, which was easier today than it would have been yesterday. Rachel felt the compass needle of her loyalty sway ever-so-slightly from her beloved family toward her two new friends.

"I found something in the dragon's horde, an amulet. It lets me see around me in three hundred and sixty degrees. I can look through walls, see invisible things, things even Lucky can't normally see."

"Wow." Rachel gasped in astonished joy. "You mean you can spy on everyone around you, all the time?"

"That's right." Siggy nodded.

"Amazing!" Rachel gaped, her mouth hanging open at such a marvel. "Can you look through anything?"

"Almost anything. I can't look into the girl's dorm, or locker rooms, or bathroom."

The princess passed a hand over her golden hair. "The amulet cannot see into the girl's bathroom? Do you know how it came upon this limitation?"

"No. The *amulet* can see into the girls' bathroom. *I* can't look into the girl's bathroom. What would King Arthur say when he wakes up? He'd never knight me." Siggy spoke in complete seriousness.

"Oh..." Rachel blinked. That sounded like something her brother Peter would say. "That is very decent of you."

"It's tough," Siggy admitted. "But so far, I've managed to hold out."

Nastasia pursed her lips. She seemed both disapproving and amused at the same time. "So, you can overhear what is going on around us? How fascinating. My father would love something like that. He's forever complaining about the poor quality of his spies, most of whom never report in. Of course, it is impossible to tell if he is serious. The spies that never report back are probably fruit bats and kookaburra. For all I know, his real spies might be perfectly suitable."

"Yes. I can hear everything around us." Siggy wadded a piece of paper into yet another spit ball and tossed it over a banister into the hair of a red-headed student a floor beneath them. Rachel pressed her hand against her mouth to contain her mirth. The princess tsked in mild disapproval.

Pointing at a nearby table, Nastasia asked, "What are they saying?"

Siggy glanced over at the three sophomore girls and rolled his eyes. "They are talking about which tutors are attractive." Rachel giggled. She had strong opinions on that subject.

Nastasia wrinkled her nose, uninterested. She pointed at some older students. "And over there?"

Siggy tilted his head, listening. "They are discussing the arrival of the Transylvania royalty early Sunday morning. The girl with the green dangly earrings, the one who is waving her hands, is saying: *'The Starkadders sailed up in a flying clipper ship. It's enormous. It landed on the common, huge sails billowing everywhere. The princes and princesses came out in age order:*

First Romulus—the crown prince, then Remus, Freka, Fenris, Beowulf, Luperca, and Wulfgang. Two little ones stayed inside and waved, a boy and girl." Siggy paused. "That's all she said. Now, the girl next to her is talking about something called Witch Babies."

"Quite impressive," Nastasia acknowledged with a regal nod.

Rachel tapped Sigfried on the shoulder, pointing. "Siggy! Over there. What about them?"

Below, on a lower level of the library, Cydney Graves and her friends sat studying, their hair stuck up under their square scholar's caps. Siggy tilted his head. He spoke as the girls spoke. Rachel watched over the banister, tracking who was speaking.

Cydney: "Once we find the spy, that person is going to be so sorry. We'll make sure they're never welcome in Drake again!"

Lola: "Could be Salome. She talks to that girl."

Belladonna: "Nah, Salome's too cool. Also too smart. She wouldn't offend her dormmates right off. She knows she has to live with us for the next eight years."

Lola: "I bet it's Magdalene. She's such a little twit."

Cydney: "But how could Magdalene do it? How come we didn't wake up?"

Charybdis Nott walked up to the others, put her books on the table, and pulled out a chair.

Belladonna: "Charyb, there you are. So....what were you talking to Jonah about?"

Charybdis: "Jonah? I didn't talk to him."

Belladonna: "Yeah...riiiight."

Cydney: "Boy, he's cute...though a little creepy. Can you introduce me?"

Charybdis: "I didn't talk to him!"

Cydney: "Okay, be that way. Keep it to yourself."

Charybdis: "I didn't...argh! Enough about that. What about our hair? How long will it last? How do we turn it back?"

Cydney: "Don't know, but I'm going to find out! My brother'll figure it out. He'll find a way to take care of everything."

Lola: "You and your brother! You would think Randall Graves was Adonis born again. Okay, so about this Science assignment...?"

Siggy stopped talking and leaned back. "They're just talking about school work now."

Rachel giggled. "It hasn't occurred to them that it wasn't an inside job. It's nice to have a secret weapon."

"It is indeed." Nastasia pressed her lips together to contain her mirth. Her eyes sparkled. "We are quite fortunate to have Miss Forrest among us. And Mr. Smith's amulet."

"I wish we could do something for Magdalene." Rachel said softly. "I think she looks up to you, Siggy. I don't suppose you could have Lucky burn her sister? If her sister's the person hurting her. Could you spy on her and find out?"

"Sister!" Siggy threw up his arms and groaned in frustration. "Arrgghh! Why couldn't it be a brother! Then, Seth and I could go introduce him to our right upper cuts! See if the rotter would beat a girl after that!"

"Hurting her?" the princess asked.

"She has these huge bruises on her face, as if someone has been hitting her. Salome hinted that it might be her sister."

The princess's brow creased, concerned yet cautious. "If she is indeed being abused, we should tell a tutor. Or perhaps Dean Moth. But are you certain? It is unwise to make accusations like that without solid facts."

Rachel frowned, petulant. "The tutors'll probably just tell us we had a nightmare."

Siggy scowled. "Why did you and Magdalene have to be attacked by girls? If only it had been boys. Lucky and I would have had such a grand time scalding them!"

Chapter Nineteen:
Pay No Heed to
The Howling of the Wind

Art was followed by Math. Rachel watched Dr. Mordeau but could not catch her doing a single insidious thing during their Introduction to Euclid lesson. Nor did the tutor betray any hint as to why she hated Rachel's father.

After class, they gathered at lunch, still riding the high of Zoë's successful humiliation of Rachel's nemeses. Nastasia arrived with her entourage in tow, girls who followed her adoringly—some had even put aside their subfusc in favor of full-academic robes such as the princess wore—and boys who were awed by her beauty. The young men vied for her attention, doing silly things to show off, most of which she studiously ignored.

The princess graciously addressed those pressed around her. "Barbie, I will speak to the Dean about your concern. She is a family friend. Esteri, I am very sorry about your sister. Perhaps you should try speaking with her one more time."

Several of the boys pressed forward, inviting the princess on a broom outing or to the café for a sarsaparilla. The princess lowered her lashes, flustered. She did not answer any of them but, instead, addressed the entire gathering. "Thank you for escorting me. I release you to go sit with your friends for lunch. Anyone who wishes may join me after dinner for a practice session. We will meet here in the dining hall and find a quiet place to review what we have learned in class so far."

Rachel's grilled cheese suddenly seemed rubbery. She had so hoped that the princess would forget about practicing. Her only consolation was that, if a whole group was working together, they would probably get in each other's way.

Turning away from the others, Nastasia sat down between Rachel and Joy. Was that relief that flickered across her face? Rachel played back her expression. Yes, it was definitely relief. How odd. Nastasia seemed so poised and regally gracious, as if the tremendous adoration she received was but her royal due. Could it be that she did not enjoy the attention of the other children? Perhaps so, because when she saw Rachel glancing her way, she gave her a tiny grateful smile, as if to say that she was glad to be back in the shelter of real friends.

Ashamed, Rachel chided herself for her less than gracious attitude toward the princess's practice club. This was a school of sorcery, after all. She should hardly be upset with her friends for wanting to improve their skills.

Vladimir Von Dread strode through the dining hall, stopping nearby to speak with a pretty young woman who hailed him. Rachel watched his cool, precise motions and the implacable way he spoke. His regal bearing reminded her of Nastasia.

"You should marry Von Dread," Rachel whispered conspiratorially to the princess, who was carefully arranging her napkin on her lap. "You are both royalty, and you show great concern for propriety."

"Yes! You two would be perfect for each other!" Joy cried, eager to join in. Rachel noticed that Joy no longer wore the headband she had sported the first couple of days. Her hair now flowed around her shoulders the way Nastasia's usually did. "Then you would be Queen of Bavaria!"

"You two could be stiff and proper together." Valerie looked up from her BLT. "You know, stirring your tea with the correct spoon and all that. It would be hilarious."

Zoë paused in the midst of wolfing down her hamburger and glanced at Von Dread. "Sure. The princess's the most beautiful girl in the school. He's the handsomest guy, except maybe for Sigfried here." She jerked her thumb at Siggy. "But Sig's an orphan and fourteen. Von Dread is a twenty-year-old godling."

"I shall marry whomever my father chooses." Nastasia cut her hamburger and bun into small bite-sized pieces and ate them with a fork. "If it will benefit my family for me to marry him, so be it. If not, then not."

"Which would you prefer?" Rachel asked, watching Von

Dread as he listened impassively to the young woman, his arms crossed. Zoë was right that he was pleasing to the eye, but there was something cold, almost scary about him. "If it helped your family, and you had to marry him? Or if it did not?"

"Whichever benefited my family." Nastasia nibbled a bite off her fork.

Joy's jaw dropped gradually, as if in slow motion. "You're going to let your father pick your husband? I love my father a lot. Don't get me wrong! He might be the best dad ever! But...that doesn't mean I trust him to pick the boy who is right for me." Her eyes darted sideways, toward Sigfried, and veered away again. Pink spots appeared above her cheek bones.

"A father's idea of a good son-in-law is not always..." Zoë pursed her lips.

"I can sum our objections up," Valerie interrupted. "What if he picks someone odious?"

"He would do no such thing, unless it were important for the realm. And if it were, then I would hope that I might have the wherewithal to bear it," Nastasia replied. She patted her lips with a second napkin, not the one covering her lap.

"B-But..." Joy cried. Her eyes, a honey brown that matched her hair, were wide and distraught. "What if you didn't love each other?"

"If we are devoted to the purposes of our marriage, we shall come to love each other in time," Nastasia replied patiently.

Rachel was again reminded of her grandmother. Grandmother Griffin had possessed a wonderful knack for explaining the reason behind the traditions of her youth. She made it clear why aristocrats were required to act as they did. Rachel tried to put into words what she had learned from her.

"I am of two minds on the subject of marriage." She dipped her grilled cheese sandwich into her soup, something she was not allowed to do at home. "I am sure love is wonderful—though I've never been in love. But, strange as it seems, love matches often aren't any more successful than arranged ones. Look how often they end in divorce. In an arranged marriage, at least the families are benefited, and often the couple do come to love each other."

"Precisely," Nastasia gave Rachel a grateful look.

Rachel smiled back, aware of how small their oasis of respect for traditions was in the vast desert of modern sentiment. Joy, Zoë, and Valerie gawked at them as if they had sprouted new noses.

"Nastasia." Zoë tipped her chair back and swung her bright blue braid around in a circle. The feather fluttered with a thw*p-thwp*. "Not to poke a sore spot, but...isn't your father the one who puts emus on Olympic teams and uses pink monopoly money with kangaroos on it that no one else will accept for your national currency? Aren't you afraid, if you leave your choice of future husband to him, he'll marry you to a mop or something?"

"There is a danger of that," Nastasia acknowledged with a sigh. "Luckily, my mother, the Queen, is quite a serious person. She has made Father promise that he will not engage any of us to a wallaby or an emu." Her face remained solemn, but her eyes crinkled merrily. "As my sister Alexis pointed out, though, dingoes are still an option."

Lunch was followed by Music and a long Science lab. After class, Rachel ran to the gym to help with broom practice. Thursdays were for intermediate students who wanted to learn tricks. Here, Rachel was a great help to Mr. Chanson, since she could demonstrate everything he wished to teach.

When the flying class ended, she headed back to her dorm, floating low to the ground on her broom, with her feet resting on the handlebars. Halfway across campus, she heard unpleasant giggling. Cydney Graves and her friends swooped around her on their long Flycycles.

"Look, it's the baby on her training broom," Cydney mocked, bumping Vroomie. A beginner would have fallen off. Rachel was not even discomforted.

"Steeplechaser," Rachel replied coldly. She stroked Vroomie's polished walnut handle, as if to soothe the broom's hurt feelings. "I mentioned that before. Some people learn slowly."

"Speaking of learning. Aren't you too young for Roanoke?" Cydney looked her over cynically. "How old are you? Ten? Go home, Preschooler."

"You should thank me. I gave you half a figure," Lola Spong laughed. Rachel was again struck by how much the girl looked like a toad. Perhaps the Spong family was descended from trolls. Some families were. "I don't think they make bras like that, though—big on one side? Would you like me to do the other side, too, so you can have a matching pair?"

"How's your balance now?" Belladonna Marley purred with false sympathy, flying so close that her tail fan knocked against Vroomie. "Listing a little too much to the right?"

The memory of her humiliation, of stumbling across campus with her engorged nose, shoulder, and chest, came rushing back. Rachel's cheeks heated up until they felt as if they had been left too long on the skillet. She considered putting on a burst of speed and racing ahead. If she wove through the trees, she could lose them. They would discover first hand how much better she and Vroomie were.

That smacked of showing off, however, a low to which she did not care to descend. Also, much as they irritated her, if any of them tried to follow her and got hurt when their clunky, awkward travelers smashed into a tree, it would be her fault. Not that she could really bring herself to mind.

Ahead of her, Princess Nastasia of Magical Australia came walking up the path from the Dare Hall. "There you are, Miss Griffin," she spoke cheerfully, her gaze resting only on Rachel. She did not so much as glance at the girls from Drake. "It is a pleasant afternoon, isn't it?"

"Nastasia." Rachel was certain her cheeks were glowing red hot, but she managed a cheerfully smile.

"Ooo." Lola cried eagerly. "It's the princess of No Place Anyone Has Ever Heard Of!"

The princess walked with extreme nobility and grace, gliding toward them like a swan crossing the reflecting pool. Reaching Rachel, she pivoted and slipped her arm through Rachel's. Knowing how much the princess disliked familiarity, Rachel's heart beat with astonished gratitude. She flew a little lower, so that they could move forward side by side.

"How did your class go?" the princess asked, as if no one else were present. "Mr. Chanson seems like an upstanding gentleman. Is he a good instructor?"

"Yes. Very!" Rachel's eyes sparkled at the opportunity to discuss her favorite instructor. Before she could say more, she was interrupted.

"Why does she have a job? She's a freshman?" Charybdis asked the other girls.

"Obviously, she needs the money to buy a new porcupine to comb her hair," drawled Cydney. "Look what a bad job the old one is doing."

Rachel resisted her desire to smooth her fly-away locks.

Lola snickered, "Maybe she should lend some of her salary to her friend, so the 'princess' can buy a map and pick a real country to be royalty of."

Rachel turned on Lola and started to retort, but Nastasia lay a soothing hand on her arm.

"Pay no heed to the howling of the wind," the princess instructed with calm fortitude.

"Hey, everybody! Let's touch the princess," Charybdis shouted, excited. "Maybe she will faint."

"Leave her alone," Rachel cried, moving her broom between Nastasia and Charybdis.

"Do you hear the caterwauling of felines?" The princess cupped her free hand around her ear, her manner as gentle and ladylike as ever. "Their yowling means nothing."

"She called us catty!" Charybdis cried. "She did, didn't she?"

"Well, you are," Rachel replied tartly. She was impressed that Charybdis had caught that. Charybdis struck her as a bit dim.

"Cats are never worth shouting at. Again, just pay them no heed." Nastasia covered her mouth with her hand and leaned toward Rachel. From behind her palm, she whispered conspiratorially. "They hate that."

Rachel began to giggle. The princess launched into a discussion of their classes so far. Catching on, Rachel followed her lead, ignoring the other girls.

Cydney scowled. "This is getting boring. Let's go do something else."

"Let's go follow boys around!" Charybdis exclaimed, pointing. "There's a cute one!" The girls from Drake turned their brooms and sped off toward the Commons.

"Thank you," Rachel said gratefully. To her embarrassment, her voice shook slightly.

"Think nothing of it," replied the princess, mirth dancing in her eyes. "It was a pleasure."

"It wasn't nothing to me," Rachel replied under her breath.

The princess heard her. Squeezing Rachel's hand, Nastasia gave her a very kind smile. "Then, you are welcome." Arm in arm, they walked down the path to Dare Hall.

At the dorm, they found Zoë sitting on the front steps, playing with her tiger quoll. She was reading their True History assignment and throwing pieces of beef jerky to her familiar. It caught them out of the air.

"Hey, Ladies," Zoë gave them a lazy smile. "Beautiful day, isn't it?"

"Indeed," Nastasia inclined her head, a little smile playing over her lips. "Overhead, the clouds stream by. Yet, below, we find ourselves untroubled by the breeze."

"Quite poetic." Zoë threw another piece of beef jerky to the quoll. "But then, a princess should be poetic, I believe. Don't you think so, Griffin?"

Before Rachel could answer, there was a *whoosh* behind them, followed by unpleasantly familiar laughter. Rachel spun around to find Cydney Graves and her friends hovering over the gravel path at the bottom of the stairs. All four grinned victoriously.

"So, you have visions, do you, Princess Nastasia?" Cydney asked snidely. "Are they real? Or are you just crazy as a June bug?"

Rachel recoiled as if struck. How had they found out? The princess's expression never changed, but she lay a steadying hand on Rachel's shoulder.

"Bug off, debutants." Zoë made a flicking gesture, as if flicking away a fly. "Don't you nasty rich girls have better things to do than pester innocent princesses?"

"And you!" Belladonna turned on Zoë, narrowing her eyes menacingly. "We know all about your sandals and your dream walking! You come into our dorm again. It will be the last mistake you make."

Chapter Twenty:
Of Skunk and Snitches

THE PRINCESS INVITED RACHEL TO STUDY WITH HER AND JOY, BUT Rachel did not need to study. She grasped everything the first time, so she never reviewed, and she had read ahead for all her classes. She sat with the other girls for a few minutes. They chatted about classes and boys, but Rachel could barely pay attention. Her mind was too caught up in worrying about how Cydney and her friends found out about the princess's visions and Zoë's sandals.

Taking her leave, she headed outside, her broom in her hand. Who could have told them? Who had they spoken to in the short time between when they left and when they returned? Charybdis had led them off to go talk to a cute boy.

A shiver of terror jolted her body as powerfully as if she had brushed against a live wire. *Please,* she begged silently, *please, let it not have been Gaius.*

She had not told Gaius about Zoë, but he could have told about the princess. Either way, someone she liked had betrayed them. If it was not him, it was one of her other friends. But who could be the snitch? Who could she trust for sure?

Best to work backwards—to figure out first who it could not have been. It was not Zoë or Nastasia. They had both looked shocked when they discovered that their secrets had been spilled. It was not Siggy. Of that she was certain. For all his boasting and lying, she had never met anyone more sincere or more devoted to those he had determined to be his comrades. Valerie struck her as the type who kept things quiet, though she was good friends with Salome. Had Salome told her dormmates to keep from being a suspect in the matter of the hair? Did any of Rachel's friends have siblings or friends in Drake?

The whole matter distressed her tremendously. Zoë's ability to walk through dreams had given them such an enormous advantage. If the world itself was in danger, they needed all the advantages they could get! It galled her that others now knew. Someone might tell the tutors, and the adults might make Zoë stop.

Rachel had always trusted adults implicitly. Since she arrived at school, however, they had been letting her down. First the tutors did not believe her about Mylene and the wraith, and then her father... Her bottom lip quivered. Life at Roanoke was not what she had expected.

"Are you going to study?" Rachel asked Sigfried, whom she found romping with Lucky in the ferns behind Dare Hall.

"Study? What's that?" Sigfried snorted. "Certainly not. I'm going exploring."

"Oh! Me, too!" Rachel cried, delighted. She pulled a Cadbury's bar from her pocket and split it in half. "Chocolate?"

Sigfried's eyes became very round. "Ace! I had one of these once. One of the other boys nicked some from a corner shop. Boy, was it good." He shoved the half a chocolate bar into his mouth. He tried to keep talking, but Rachel could not make out what he was saying.

She giggled. "Do you want to explore on foot or by broom?"

"Whets go wy woom."

Rachel and Sigfried climbed on Vroomie, and the two of them were off. They swooped over walled gardens and glided above the sun-speckled ferns growing beneath the paper birches. Then they sped across the Commons and beyond, to the hemlocks. Soaring upward, they burst above the branches into the brilliant fall sky. Small birds flocked together, calling to each other as they gathered to head south. Rachel watched their freedom with a sense of joy. Recalling the statue of the young woman with the bird wings, she wondered what it would be like, to fly as they did—probably a great deal like flying on a broom only more wonderful.

The first orange leaf of autumn drifted down to land in the creek that ran through the hemlocks. Lucky dived in and snaked through the water, a red and gold flicker beneath the surface.

Looking down at his friend, Sigfried asked suddenly, "Hey, when do we learn to run so fast we leave a sonic boom?"

Rachel laughed. "No one can do that."

"Mr. Chanson, the gym teacher, can."

"That's impossible. People have tried such things, but they get ripped apart. You'd have to be invulnerable."

"Chanson can do it. I want to do it, too."

"No, he can't!"

"Yes, he can. Lucky saw him. I watched through Lucky's eyes. Chanson crossed the campus so quickly, he looked like a blur."

"That's...impossible." Rachel frowned. She sighed blissfully as she thought about the handsome physical education teacher. Then, her eyes widened. "Unless... Hey! I bet you he's from Outside!"

"You mean he was born in the woods?"

"No...like Lucky. Lucky has magic from outside that turns off near the Raven. I bet you Mr. Chanson is from another world, too. We should ask the princess to shake his hand."

"Hey, you may be right!" Siggy's face fell. He scowled. "But that would mean that I couldn't learn to run that fast, wouldn't it? And the princess says it's impossible to turn into a dragon. Life is so unfair!"

They flew up the river to where it emerged from underground on the inner side of the wall of trees that marked the wards of the school. Circling back, they came at Roanoke Hall from the back side.

Leaning forward, Sigfried pointed at the central bell tower. "Hey, can we stop there?"

"Sure." Rachel flew to the spot that Sigfried had indicated. Part-way up the bell tower, buttresses arched out from around a central cylindrical core. There was just enough room for them to land. Siggy peered in the window at the spiral staircase within. Then, he lay on his stomach and, pulling some grubby sandwiches from his pocket, began stuffing them into the gargoyle-tipped drain pipes.

Rachel watched him. Finally, her brows drew together. "Siggy, why do you stick sandwiches in your robes? Aren't you afraid your clothes will end up smelling like food?"

Stretched out on his stomach, Siggy answered absently, "I like the smell of food. But you are right: keeping it in my pockets is too obvious. I have been finding hiding holes and nooks about campus where it can be kept safe, and squirrels and grown-ups won't find it."

Rachel leaned against one of the arched buttresses, frowning down at him. "You are hiding food from grown-ups?"

Siggy threw her an odd look. Climbing back to his feet, he lowered his voice conspiratorially. "That's how they control you, you know. Grown-ups control kids by controlling the food supply. But they can't keep you from running away if they can't keep you hungry."

Bewildered, Rachel asked, "Why would grown-ups take away our food?"

Siggy looked left and right, as if he feared being overheard. "Listen. You're young yet. This world is going to chew you up like bubble gum and blow you up until you pop and get stuck in someone's hair. And I mean chew you with its back teeth!

"You just don't get it," he continued. "Grown-ups take things away. Food. Lights. Your mattress. That's what they do. Grown-ups take things. You've got to be ready."

"What?"

"Listen, I wouldn't normally do this, but you're pathetic. You'll never survive on your own, so—here. It is half a sausage and a handful of scrambled eggs I managed to sneak out of the cafeteria, when no one was looking. You hide it. When you are put on short rations for something you've done, you go to where it is hidden and eat it. You'll feel better. A mouthful of food makes you stop crying. You can't let them see you cry. They sense weakness."

Siggy pulled a wiggling lump of yellowish substance out of one of his pockets and offered it to Rachel. Moisture dripped from between his fingers. In his other hand he had a cylinder of meat with a bite out of one end, covered in lint. A pungent odor assailed her nostrils.

"It will go bad." Rachel stared at it in mesmerized horror, trying to keep her stomach from roiling. She wanted to take it from him, the way she had accepted his goopy handshake, but she could not get her hand to jerk toward him.

Siggy looked surprised. He put the offering down on the ledge of the nearest window. "Go bad? You can stay out of trouble long enough for your food stores to go bad? Wow! What's your secret? How do you not get caught?"

"I don't have any food stores!" Rachel held onto the buttress with one arm and waved her other one around emphatically.

"What about that stuff you gave me? The chocolate?"

"That was a present from my father. He gave it to me this morning. But I don't have anything else," Rachel insisted, "just what's in my pocket."

Siggy looked stricken. "That's—that's the saddest thing I've ever heard! Come on, you can have some of mine. Otherwise you have nothing to fall back on when the bad times come."

"But—"

Siggy's expression darkened. "The bad times always come."

"Siggy! It doesn't work that way here at school. The kitchens will have food every day. If they stopped for some reason, my parents would feed us."

"I can see I am going to have to take you under my wing. Parents make you weak. You cannot rely on them."

"Um..." Rachel's whole body ached with sorrow, but she could not think of anything to say that would help. Her heart swelled with gratitude for her parents. Her problems with her father were nothing compared to this. It seemed so unfair that her family was not something she could share with Sigfried. "I'll keep that in mind. Thanks."

Siggy stuffed the unaccepted food back into his pockets. Standing so close, Rachel noted a huge mud stain covered the front of his black robe. They climbed back onto Vroomie and set off circling the campus slowly. Rachel mused quietly, wondering if the matter of Siggy's robes were any of her business. Finally, she resolved that she should say something. After all, in stories, friends looked after one another.

"Um...Siggy..." Rachel tugged on his sleeve, where his arm

encircled her waist. "I can't help noticing that you've been wearing this same robe for four days. It's getting kind of dirty. You do know that if you put it in the bin in the corner, the *bean-tighe* will come do the laundry, right?"

"The what? The Band-aids?"

"The *bean-tighe*. The fairy housekeepers. They look like tiny old women in old-fashioned peasants' clothing."

She could feel Sigfried shrug behind her. He said, "It's the only one I have. If I washed it, what would I wear in the meantime?"

"You only have one robe?"

"Yep."

"But..." Rachel blinked. She looked down at where his bare feet hung beneath them. "Don't you have any shoes?"

"Nope. Outgrew my last pair. They pinched my toes. Hurt a lot. The nuns never got around to getting me new ones."

Rachel's heart filled to the brink with pity and overflowed. "Siggy, you can't go to school here with just one robe and no shoes! This is New York. It is going to get very cold. You need boots and a hat and sweaters to wear under your robes and many other things."

"I suppose I could use some of my gold to buy clothing." Siggy winced as he said this, as if parting with a single piece of his treasure caused him physical pain. "But I don't know how to go about it. There are no shops in my dorm."

"Would you like me to do it for you? Buy you a proper wardrobe?" she asked hopefully. "Some things can be bought at the supply shop under Raleigh Hall. It's similar to the bookshop under Dee, only it sells alchemical supplies, robes and gear. Other things can be ordered. I have all the catalogs."

"Catalogs of what?"

Rachel craned her head back over her shoulder, trying to discover from his expression if he were kidding. His eyes were squinting against the wind.

"Clothing catalogs," she said. "For buying shoes and things through the post."

"Is that allowed? That would be a great relief!" he cried, his voice quite sincere. "Girls are supposed to be good at that kind of thing, aren't you? You order for me, and I'll give you the money. But I can only spare coins I don't like as much. Some are scuffed or melted around the edges. The former owner exploded when he died."

Rachel blinked. "Oh! You mean the dragon!"

"Yep. So, yeah. I can pay."

"Fine. Wait just a second." Rachel shot back to Dare Hall and dropped Siggy off in the feathery ferns behind the dormitory.

Bending low over the handlebars, she dart into the air and through the open window into her room. Once there, she quickly gathered some of the catalogs stored in her trunk. As she did so, she noticed the tiny lion sitting in a splash of sunlight in the center of the room, washing.

Rachel looked left and right. No one was around. Squatting down, she smiled at the little tawny creature. "Hello. Your name is Leander, right?"

It cocked its head and looked up at her.

Rachel leaned forward and whispered, "Can you tell me what is going on?"

The tiny feline stared at her with its wide golden eyes.

Undaunted, Rachel continued, "What does it mean that one of your children was brought here and you're in her heart? Who is the Raven? Why does he want you to leave?"

With supreme dignity, the lion began to lick its paw. Rachel sighed. Jumping on her broom, she hurried back to Siggy.

She found Sigfried and Lucky with their heads bowed together, concentrating. Sigfried had his right hand up, his fingers together, the gesture Mrs. Heelis had used when she conjured Jemima Puddleduck.

"So, what was the word that nun...er, I mean tutor...used to conjure stuff?"

"*Muria*, but don't..." Rachel began.

"No. Lucky and I can do this! Watch!" Sigfried lowered his hand, just as the teacher had. "*Muria!*"

Rachel felt as if she were waking from a dream. An animal

now waddled among the ferns—a black animal with a long white stripe that ran from its forehead to its back before splitting into two strips that continued to its black bushy tail. An unpleasant stink struck her nostrils.

"Look, it worked!" Sigfried shouted gleefully. "I conjured something! I think it's American! Here, Kitty, Kitty!"

"Siggy...that's a..."

Lucky shouted, "Skunk!"

The frightened creature lifted its tail. Something horrid shot out, spraying all over Sigfried and his only robe. The stuff stank dreadfully. Rachel's eyes watered painfully.

"Lucky, get it!" Siggy threw up his arms to protect his face. Bringing his hands down again and gesturing, he shouted, "*Til!*"

The still-spraying skunk wobbled into the air. Rachel was duly impressed that Sigfried could lift something so heavy with just the *up* cantrip. She could only lift heavier things with the more advanced *Tiathelu,* and the skunk looked much heavier than her old tome. Siggy held up two fingers and gestured as if to fling the skunk away. To Rachel's surprise, it went flying. Lucky breathed on it.

The putrid spray coming from the skunk caught fire. Stinking and flaming, the skunk flew end over end into a crowd of students, who were walking down the gravel path leading to Dare Hall. They screamed and ducked. This did not protect them. The free-flying spray flew everywhere. Students grabbed their eyes, shrieking. Two girls were struck with flaming skunk-fluid, and their garments caught fire. The first one stopped, dropped, and rolled. The other pointed at her burning skirt and performed a cantrip. The flames sputtered and died.

As everyone else ran away, Siggy charged toward the skunk. First he pulled the trumpet he had borrowed from the Music tutor from one of the large inner pockets of his robe and blew. A blast of air slammed the skunk into a tree. Then he shouted for Lucky, who sped forward and breathed again. This time, there was a brief *whoosh,* and a ball of fire. The conjured creature popped like a dream.

The crowd cheered. With not a single trace of shame, Siggy grinned and bowed. Then he clasped his hands overhead like a prizefighter, basking in his victory adulations. Pinching her nose against the stench, Rachel watched, amused and embarrassed. When Sigfried glanced back at her warily, she winked at him. Today, Sigfried was a hero for saving the school from a flying, flaming skunk. No one would ever learn otherwise from her.

CHAPTER TWENTY-ONE:

VALERIE FOXX,

FEARLESS REPORTER GIRL

THE STUDENTS WHO HAD BEEN SPRAYED, INCLUDING SIGFRIED, headed for the Infirmary. Rachel returned to her room and changed her clothes, leaving the vaguely skunky ones for the laundry *bean-tighe*. While she was at it, she carefully filled the bowl by the door with milk that she had carried up from the dining hall in a pewter pitcher intended for that purpose. That way, the *bwbachs*—who were rather like brownies, except that they wore turbans and fur loin cloths—would clean the room. Then she visited the Raleigh Alchemical Shoppe, purchased some robes for Sigfried, wrote out the orders for the garments she could not find there, both over and under-garments, and ran down to the mail room to post them.

On the way down, she passed Gaius Valiant coming up the spiral staircase. Anger and shame coursed through her as she recalled her suspicions that he might be the "cute boy" who betrayed them to Charybdis. Turning her face away, she gave him the *cut direct*, and hurried down the stairs.

She put the order into the post and returned to her secret upstairs spot to practice before dinner. She could now waft the tome around with ease and could slam it against the wall. She needed something bigger. She would have to look around for a larger object that she could carry up here. For the time being, she continued to practice with the book, which was now looking rather beaten up. That made her feel guilty. She did not approve of abusing books.

As she was finishing, footsteps echoed around the corner. Glancing down the hall, Rachel was both delighted and annoyed to see Gaius Valiant walking toward her. He looked so adorable, she nearly forgot her anger toward him, but the idea that he might have betrayed her stung. She turned her back and quickly took off in the other direction.

"Rachel. What's wrong?" Gaius quickened his step until he fell in beside her. His stride was much longer than hers.

She turned on him. "You told, didn't you? After you promised not to. You told them about the princess's visions!"

"No!"

"But Cydney and the others. They knew all about them!"

"They didn't hear it from me," he insisted hotly. "I did not even tell... I didn't tell anybody." Returning to his normal calm, he held up his hands and drawled, "I said nothing. Not a word, not so much as a single syllable."

Rachel looked at him long and hard. He endured her scrutiny.

"So? What's your decision?" He searched her face. "Are we still on for tonight?"

Rachel sighed and nodded. "I believe you."

Very pleased, he gave her a mock bow. "I will not disappoint, milady."

Rachel laughed, suddenly aware that her hair was, as always, flying every which way. She ran her hands over it, trying to push some of the escaping locks back into the twist at the back of her head, but to no avail.

"So they found out?" Gaius leaned against the wall and crossed his arms.

"Yes, and about Zoë, too...something I really, really wish had stayed a secret." She sighed. "I had had such plans for her."

"That she can walk through dreams? Yeah, that's big. I've never even heard of such a thing. Even familiars can only reach into the shallows of dreams. Any other big news? I heard you fought a wraith!" He looked impressed.

Rachel grinned. "Got sipped on by one is more like it. The boys you told me about—the vampire hunters?—They fought it. Siggy and Lucky—Sigfried's dragon. Lucky would have got it right off, had the Raven not come and turned him into a dumb beast."

"Raven?"

Rachel looked around and then spoke in a hushed voice. "There is a giant Raven that flies around on campus invisibly. When he comes near Lucky...it's like he becomes a local dragon, a creature who cannot talk." Oddly, she thought suddenly, that had not happened to the little lion when the Raven spoke to him. "Nighthawk says the Raven is an omen of the Death of Worlds."

"That's...scary." Gaius's eyebrows drew together.

"Yes, it is."

"We've got to find out more," he said.

Rachel liked his attitude. "Yes, we do!"

"Must go study." He saluted. "See you after dinner?"

"Sure thing." Rachel stepped over and kissed him on the cheek. "See you then!"

She ran off without looking back.

There was still fifteen minutes until the dining room opened for dinner. Rachel wandered into the walled garden and found Valerie Foxx threading film into her camera. Payback lay near her feet, panting. As she leaned over to pet the Norwegian Elk Hound's thick fur, it occurred to Rachel that she and Valerie were much alike, both brainy and inquisitive. It would be nice to be better friends with the girl Siggy liked. Rachel sat down next to Valerie and gave her a hopeful smile. For a second, nothing happened. Rachel remembered her attempt to befriend Cydney Graves and wished that she had not smiled. Then, to her relief, Valerie smiled back.

"It's so weird to be doing this." Valerie snapped the back of her camera shut and turned the crank twice. "I feel like I'm in an old movie. It's a good thing our Photography Club had access to a darkroom. I considered it a historical oddity at the time. But now I'm really glad I took the class on using film."

Rachel blinked. "What else would you use?"

Valerie looked up in surprise. Then, a quirky smile caught her lip. "You Wiseborn are so cute. Most cameras are digital now."

Rachel frowned. "You mean...like a computer."

"Basically. Yeah."

"Oh." Rachel had trouble caring about mundane things. It was the only part of *everything* she did not find interesting. "So, you've been here at school a few days. How do you like it?"

Valerie crinkled her nose and gave Rachel a tiny, sad smile. "I feel...humbled."

"Humbled?" Rachel leaned against the wall, batting at the purple wisteria blossoms that had snagged her hair. "Why is that?"

"Back at home, I was street savvy." Valerie smiled sheepishly. "I was Miss Connected. My mother's a reporter, and my dad's a cop. I knew everyone, and everyone knew me. Plus, I knew how to do research. I was the Girl on the Street. I knew how stuff worked.

"Here at Roanoke, I know nothing. Outside the Iscariots, I have no connections in the World of the Wise. I don't even know what's physically possible and what's not. I feel like one of those tuna that has just been flipped out of the water and is now wriggling around on the deck. I might have been a master in the ocean. But up here, I'm just cat food."

"I guess that would be disconcerting." Rachel sat down on the bench.

"Oh it is!" Valerie brushed her hair from her eyes and held up her camera. "Say cheese!"

Rachel gave her a big smile, holding two fingers up in a V beside her face.

Valerie snapped a picture and laughed. "Oh, that's so cute! You look like an anime girl."

"A what?"

"A Japanese cartoon girl. They do that finger thing when they have their pictures taken."

"I got that from my mother and my sisters. They always do it."

"Must be an Asian thing."

"Could be." Rachel shrugged. "I'm one-eighth Korean."

Valerie hooked her camera back onto the red strap she wore over her shoulder. It hung above her hip. "Sad about the snitch, isn't it? Joy told me."

Rachel smoothed the pleats of her robe, frowning. "I love telling people secrets. I can't do that if the stuff we know has already been spilled—to people who might use it against us."

"I've been making a list of suspects," Valerie held up her notebook, "but so far, I haven't found anything conclusive. This is assuming, of course, that a person told the students in Drake—rather than that they spied on us with magic or discerned it with augury," her face twitched oddly, "which is possible in the magical world, isn't it? Remember what I said about not knowing the laws of nature?"

Rachel shivered. If one of Cydney's friends or acquaintances had a device like Sigfried's amulet, how could they discuss anything safely?

"What you said about not having enough information…" Rachel pulled her legs up on the bench beside her and hugged her knees. "It is the same with the other matters we're investigating. We have all these pieces of information, but no leads. Nothing we can act on. You're the reporter genius. Any ideas?"

"Honestly? I haven't found out very much. There is no Internet here. No computers upon which to practice my Google Fu. Did I mention I have a black belt in that esteemed art?"

Rachel giggled. "I have no idea what that means, but…I'm sorry?"

"Why is it that technology doesn't work here?" Valerie grabbed her head. "The very concept doesn't make sense to me."

"Because the inanimate world is more awake," Rachel explained. "It works the other way, too. In areas of heavy technology, magic is more difficult. Sometimes, cantrips stop working altogether. The world believes it is mechanical and just won't listen to sorcerers."

"Can anything be done?" Valerie asked. "More insulation? Ablative shielding?"

"That is what Ouroborus Industries is working on."

"It's so weird that they are part of the World of the Wise." Valerie did a sort of a shivery dance at the creepiness of it. "At home, our dishwasher is an O.I."

Rachel nodded. "They're trying to find ways to get the two worlds to work together."

"I hope they succeed. Quickly!" Valerie declared. She sighed and put her journal down on the bench. "I don't have any idea how to proceed. I didn't even know about magic till Salome told me over the summer. I am still trying to learn what is *normal* magic, and what is *weird*. So far, Nastasia's visions are under "weird," as is Sigfried's dragon, and this Raven."

They spoke for a time, discussing the princess's encounter with the Lightbringer entity, the Raven's effect on Lucky, and how nice it would be to have their own furry dragon. Payback lifted her head and whined. Valerie petted her fondly.

"What's next?" she asked.

"Oh! And someone's trying to kill you," Rachel said. "Do we have any leads on that?"

Valerie got a strange look on her face, as if she were trying to control her expression the way Rachel and her mother did, but was unable to do so. Her eyes shone with unshed tears. Her lip quivered a bit. Rachel felt terrible. She wished she had not brought the topic up.

Valerie's voice was mostly under control. It only wobbled a little. "My contacts among the Agents have assured me that Roanoke Academy is the safest place for me—other than sitting in the Wisecraft office, which might be interesting at first, but would probably get boring once I realized that keeping me safe did not include letting me in on Agent business. I have no idea if any of our fellow students are in the know—but if so, I haven't ferreted them out."

"So you haven't found anything useful?" Rachel asked, disappointed. She had not known what could be learned by talking to their fellow students. But since Valerie had been bothering to try, Rachel had imagined she was a super sleuth who could put a mystery together from the tiniest of clues. She was chagrinned to discover that the girl reporter had detected nothing.

"I didn't find anything I was looking for. All I learned was a bit of gossip."

"Oh, what was that?"

"This is old news, but it may be new to you, since you're new here. There was a big stir when Colleen MacDannan picked Drake Hall. The MacDannans have always been in Dare. The kids from Dare and Drake Halls were all in an uproar when it happened, four years ago."

"The MacDannans are famous Irish Enchanters. Three of the Six Musketeers were MacDannans," Rachel said. She wondered glumly if it would have caused the same kind of fuss had she moved into Dee. Probably not, because there was a direct rivalry between Dare and Drake, the same as between Marlowe and De Vere and between Raleigh and Dee. Moving from Dare to Drake would make a much bigger stir than Dare to Dee.

Valerie continued, "I also found out that the Starkadder family—the royal family of Transylvania—is notorious for back-stabbing and in-fighting. Many among the Wise are amazed the children have been so well-behaved here at the school."

Rachel nodded. She had heard such stories.

Valerie blushed and added, "You found out things that affect the whole world, and I found out old rumors. Great. You should have asked Penny Royal to be your friend. She's a girl in my dorm who's an amateur Detective." She sighed.

"What about that Strega guy?" Rachel asked suddenly. "What did you learn from him?"

"Who?" Valerie frowned.

"A guy who Gai...who Evil Rumor Monger Number One reported having seen you talk to. His name was Jonah Strega."

"I never talked to a guy with a name like that. I don't know who your Evil Rumor Monger is talking about."

"Maybe you didn't get the guy's name. He is supposed to be kind of creepy."

"I would have remembered talking to someone who was creepy. And I wrote down everyone's name." Valerie pulled out her notebook and flipped through it. "Strega. Strega. Nope. I never talked to this guy."

"Huh..." Rachel's brow furrowed. "Why would ERM #1 claim you did? What could he possibly gain from that?"

"Don't know. Maybe he wants you not to trust me?"

"But..." Rachel scrunched up her face, puzzled. "It doesn't make any sense." Something tugged at her memory. She reeled it backwards. Pieces snapped into place. "You know what's weird? Earlier, in the library, someone asked Charybdis Nutt about her conversation with a guy named Jonah. She claimed she had not talked to him, either. I thought at the time that she was just being coy, but..."

"That is weird." Valerie looked disturbed. Her hound lifted its head, alert. "You know...what if there is no spy? What if..." A frightened look came over Valerie's face. "Okay, I'll watch out for anything odd. Er, I have to go, I'll talk to you later." She gathered her things, whistled to her dog, and hurried off, her eyes unnaturally shiny.

Rachel watched her glumly. She had great sympathy for someone who did not want to cry in front of other people, but she felt bad about having unintentionally upset Valerie.

CHAPTER TWENTY-TWO:
THE KNIGHTS OF WALPURGIS

GAIUS APPEARED BESIDE HER AS DINNER CAME TO AN END, LOOKING quite handsome despite his patched robes. He bowed and offered his arm. Rising, Rachel accepted, inwardly delighted at the surprised looks on her friends' faces. He took her out of Roanoke Hall and across the bridge over the reflecting lake toward the gymnasium. The sun was setting. Brilliant fiery colors painted the western sky. Rachel walked along beside him, very aware of the place where his arm touched hers. She felt slightly breathless.

There was something nice about having a friend that belonged only to her. Being a friend to a boy who needed a friend made her feel good, too. She did not mind if he was ignored by others. From his demeanor and the fact that he bothered to hang around with underclass girls, she guessed he was both unpopular and a poor sorcerer, brilliant when it came to theory but struggling with the spell work. She was proud of herself for being the kind of girl who would befriend someone no one else cared for. It gave her a kind of secret, glowy feeling.

Gaius strolled casually beside her, pausing to kick a piece of gravel so that it bounced down the pathway. He spoke cheerfully, "I hope you understand just how fantastic this evening is going to be. No one from Dare has ever been to a Knights meeting. I am so happy you've agreed to be the first."

"I am honored to be asked." Rachel gave a tiny curtsey.

She gave him a sideways speculative glance. She was dying to know more about the Shadow Agency where her father worked, but if she let on how little she knew, he would clam up. People always spoke more openly with those whom they thought were already in the know. How to approach the topic without spooking him?

Inclining her head toward him, she murmured, "It is so nice to meet someone else who knows about the Shadow Agency. It's difficult having no one to confide in."

Gaius winced. Gesturing expansively with his free hand, he drawled regretfully, "Alas, I fear you know a great deal more than I. All that I know is that they are responsible for tracking and investigating the new magic that keeps appearing. I do not know any specifics."

Rachel assumed her calm mask. Underneath, her emotions churned. Her father was the person *responsible* for hunting down the new magic? *Her father?* The thing she wished most to know was his *area of expertise?* Could it be that he really had not valued her reports—because he already knew the information she had sent him?

The thought made her want to weep.

"Hmm. In that case, we had better say nothing else," she said aloud, which saved her from having to reveal that she had nothing more to say.

They entered the gym and went through the second door on the right. The chamber beyond was much larger than should have fitted into the gymnasium. This did not disturb Rachel. She was used to things being bigger on the inside, such as the princess's bag and many rooms back home at Gryphon Park. The room where the Knights met was warm and brightly lit. It had a clean smell, like freshly-laundered sheets. One side had been divided into dueling strips, like at a sorcery tournament. The other held a massive table, long enough to seat forty. The benches around this table were more than half full, and students continued to arrive.

At the head of the table sat Vladimir Von Dread. He regarded the room as an emperor surveys his domain, his folded hands clad in their black, gauntlet-like, dueling gloves. It seemed to Rachel as if an aura of authority and power crackled around

him, as he waited patiently for the other members to take their places.

A shiver ran down her spine. If Von Dread ran this group, there might be a good reason why none of the cheerful Enchanters of Dare Hall had joined the Knights of Walpurgis. The unpleasant things Salome and the princess had said about Dread came back to her, as did her father's bad opinion of his father, the King of Bavaria. She glanced furtively at the door. Maybe she should leave.

Only then did it occur to her to wonder why Gaius had invited her. She swallowed uncertainly, her palms sweaty. Could this be some kind of a cruel trick, intended to humiliate her and perhaps Dare Hall by association? Why did he hang out in empty hallways with thirteen-year-olds anyway?

At the other end of the table sat another tall older student. He had dark hair and dark brooding eyes. His robes also bore a royal golden crest. While he lacked Von Dread's palpable aura, he maintained an air of somber dignity. Examining him, Rachel realized that this must be Wulfgang's oldest brother, Romulus Starkadder, the crown prince of Transylvania. Rachel would have nodded at him, but he did not so much as glance her way. If Von Dread surveyed the chamber as if he owned it, Romulus gave the impression that the events around him were beneath his dignity. He spoke with the person seated beside him, a young man whose brown hair fell in his eyes, but the Transylvanian prince paid little attention to anything else.

As Romulus gestured in conversation, Rachel caught the glitter of a deep purple jewel on his right hand. A jolt passed through her body. Could that be the Kadder Star, Transylvania's greatest treasure? If so, it was one of the most powerful sorcerous talismans known to the World of the Wise. She was astonished the prince would wear it openly at school.

Coming farther in, Rachel scanned the room. She recognized Salome Iscariot, who smiled and waved, Bernie Mulford, a cheerful prankster who was the son of her parents' friends, and her second cousin, Beryl Moth, a college junior whom she knew only in passing. She also recognized Cydney Graves, who did not look happy to see her. Cydney's hair was still an unpleasant shade of green. Most of the other faces present were unknown to her.

The tension in Rachel's chest eased. Salome seemed pleased to see her, so maybe this was not a practical joke. Also, there were no familiars in the room, which made this the first place Rachel had gone since the Familiar Bonding Ceremony where she did not feel instantly out of place. Besides, if her being invited had been part of a prank, Cydney would have looked excited, instead of scowling as if she had taken a bite of an apple and found a worm.

Salome beckoned Rachel over. She was sitting with two very handsome boys, who must be her brothers, and a third boy, who was holding her hand. The hand-holder had sandy blond hair and was good-looking in a roguish, bad boy way. Rachel gathered this must be the boyfriend Salome had mentioned: Ethan Warhol, son of some flamboyant American Senator. Rachel slipped in on the bench next to Salome. Gaius stepped up beside her and made a scoot over motion with his hand, gesturing for the older Iscariot brother, who was a college student, to make room for him. To Rachel's surprise, the young man gave up his seat, sauntering off to sit with some other upperclassmen farther down the table.

As she sat waiting for the rest of the club to arrive, Rachel wondered what the evening would hold. Based on what she had overheard from her dormmates, the Young Sorcerer's League meeting had sounded delightful. It had begun with a series of flowery welcome speeches, which had bored Sigfried. There had been a fascinating discussion about the nature of sorcery. This had been followed by a break, during which members had been given a chance to get to know each other. They had concluded by teaching some real spells. Everyone had lined up and practiced together. Siggy and Nastasia had learned two new cantrips, one that formed a shield in the air and one that deflected flying objects.

Rachel sighed. She would have loved participating in the discussions and learning new spells. Wistfully, she wondered if the Knights bothered teaching their members magic, or if they were more of a malevolent social club, where members sat around grumbling and boasting. Looking up and down the table, she could imagine this crowd wasting time once a week whining and vaunting. On the other hand, Gaius had mentioned sharing spells, so the evening might not be a total waste.

An older student strode into the room and sat down next to Romulus Starkadder. There was an exchange of looks between that side of the table and those seated around Von Dread, except for Dread himself, who sat with his fingers steepled, looking straight forward.

Salome leaned over and whispered gleefully, "Oh, the drama! At the beginning of last year, Simon Komarek challenged

Vladimir for leadership of the Knights, and Vladimir won. According to the rules of the club, if there is a challenge and a duel, the loser is kicked out for the rest of the year. This is Simon's first day back."

"Wow!" Rachel murmured, glancing back and forth between the two camps. She was impressed with Vladimir Von Dread's absolute imperturbability. He might be evil, but he made evil look so very good.

She examined Simon. Her brother's best friend was a boy named Peter Komarek. Everyone called the two of them Peter Squared. Could Simon be Peter K.'s older brother?

"I'm hoping for a little excitement today. I've already finished my nails." Salome spread out her fingers for Rachel to see. She had painted the nails several layered shades of pink, from light to dark giving them a flame-like appearance.

Before Rachel could reply, Von Dread rose and addressed the gathered company. She had forgotten how tall he was. He stood over six feet with the well-muscled body of an athlete. At nineteen, he was still slender, not as broad-shouldered as his build promised, but he already showed the makings of a truly impressive man.

"Greetings and welcome to the Knights of Walpurgis. I hope that everyone's summer was pleasant and productive." His voice resonated through the chamber, deep and steady. "Secretary?"

A stern young woman with dark auburn hair sitting two chairs to Von Dread's right rose to her feet. "Since this is the first meeting of the new school year, in keeping with our charter, there are no previous minutes and no Old Business. We can proceed directly to New Business."

"Thank you, Naomi." Von Dread turned back to the gathered company. "As there are new members present, let us begin with introductions. I am Vladimir Von Dread, leader of the Knights of Walpurgis and of Drake Hall. I am a junior in the college." He inclined his head to his right. "William?"

Next to Von Dread sat a tall, rather good-looking young man who examined the world around him with an expression of cool scientific curiosity. He stood up and introduced himself as William Locke. Rachel straightened up and gazed at him with tremendous interest. William Locke was the only son of Leonard

Locke, one of the partners who owned the massive, multi-national corporation, Ouroborus Industries. O.I. made the Flycycle—the bristleless broom Cydney and her friends had been flying—as well as hundreds of other new and interesting products, some of which mixed technology and magic. They apparently hired both sorcerers and scientists. William Locke was even richer than Salome Iscariot.

The other partner in Ouroborus Industries was Rachel's father's cousin, Iron Moth. Iron Moth was the father of Rachel's second cousin Beryl, who sat next to the redheaded Secretary. The redhead introduced herself as Naomi Coils. Rachel recognized the name. The Coils were a prominent wealthy family among the Wise.

Rachel recalled overhearing her father tell her mother he was concerned about American Anfarin families in general, and the Lockes and his cousin in particular, because they were involved in bad magic. This conversation stood out to her because he did not say black magic. She had never heard the term 'bad magic' any other place.

The introductions circled around the table. The majority of those present were from Drake Hall, though all seven dormitories were represented—Rachel being the only person from Dare. There were about forty members in all, though only four freshmen. The other member of her class—beside herself, Salome, and Cydney—was an elegant red-head with a long graceful neck named Wanda Zukov from Dee Hall. Her father, Maugris Zukov, was serving time in jail for aiding the Terrible Five. He had been a high lieutenant in the Morth Brood.

As the introductions continued, Rachel recognized many names. Most of the students were from established families, though not everything she had heard about these families was good. Toward the middle of the table sat Eve and Joshua March, the children of the Grand Inquisitor—the head of the Wisecraft and Rachel's father's boss. The other students gave them a wide berth, as though frightened of drawing the attention of their terrifying father. Rachel shuddered as she recalled the princess's description of the tortures the older version of Joshua had suffered in her vision. Rachel glanced sidelong at him, but he was smiling and talking to his pretty, dark-haired sister.

And then, there was Samantha Strega. The Stregas were infamous because in every generation for the past ten or so, there had been a murder in the family. Usually a son went insane and killed his parents. It had not happened yet this generation, but Rachel remembered an old news article about an intruder who had attacked and seriously injured Samantha. The article had not mentioned specifically that the assailant had slit the girl's throat, but when Samantha stood up to introduce herself, the scar on her neck was plainly visible. She was a pretty girl, but her voice sounded hoarse and raspy.

Had Samantha really been attacked by an intruder? Or had she been attacked by a member of her family? And was she the sister of Jonah Strega, the creepy young man to whom no one seemed to remember speaking?

Rachel scanned everyone's faces, memorizing them together with their names. She quickly organized her memory, putting siblings together, noting who seemed to *like* whom. A number of Starkadder princes and one of the princesses were present. Rachel recalled Valerie's comments about them but spotted no sign of secret tension. The easy-going young man with his hair in his eyes, seated next to Romulus Starkadder, turned out to be Randall Graves, the older brother of the obnoxious Cydney Graves. Rachel recalled from the library that Cydney's friends accused her of having a big brother fixation.

She noted Penny Royal, whom Valerie had claimed was an amateur detective. She also recognized Tess Dauntless, the blond she had seen hanging on Gaius's arm in the hallway, the time her robes had been covered with orange juice. Rachel could not help noticing how Tess's eyes kept drifting to Gaius's face. The other girl frowned whenever he smiled at Rachel.

Salome's turn came to introduce herself. She bounced to her feet. "I am Salome Iscariot, Carl and Devon's little sister. I'm a freshman in Drake. And this," she gestured at Rachel with both hands, as if presenting her on a platter, "is my best friend Valerie's friend, Rachel Griffin. She is an amazing sorceress and, I am told, our very first member from Dare Hall! I am very happy that she decided to join us. Thank you, Gaius, for inviting her."

The other students examined Rachel with some curiosity. William Locke and Randall Graves both smiled. Randall even winked. Remus Starkadder, a shaggy blond-haired Adonis who was the second-oldest of the Transylvanian princes, looked her over with a leering smirk that made Rachel uncomfortable, but at least it seemed affable. Only Cydney Graves scowled. Rachel let out a breath she had not realized she had been holding, relieved of her unreasonable fear that Gaius had invited her here as some kind of cruel joke. She did not acknowledge Cydney with even so much as a glance, but she did shoot Salome an appreciative smile.

Rising, she curtseyed to the gathered assembly. "Thank you for having me. I hope that I will prove a credit and not a burden."

From the head of the table, Vladimir Von Dread nodded graciously. "Welcome, Miss Griffin. We are honored to have you join us."

Gaius introduced himself next, drawling casually in a proper, upper class English accent, without the slightest hint of his West Country lilt. Then it was on to Colleen MacDannan, the coppery-tressed Irish girl on his other side, who, like Gaius, was an Upper School senior from Drake. She, too, kept darting little sideways glances at Gaius. Apparently, Rachel and Tess were not the only girls who had noticed how attractive young Mr. Valiant was.

When the introductions were complete, Von Dread stood and addressed the gathered company. "Welcome, members new and old, to this school year's first meeting of the Knights of Walpurgis. We meet because knowledge is *power*. We must have power to defend the security of our lands and uphold order. We are the enemies of chaos and disunity. We share our knowledge because this act makes us all stronger." He glared at the gathered assembly, as if daring them to gainsay him.

Rachel listened carefully, trying to discern what kind of person the crown prince of Bavaria was. He spoke of power like a tyrant, but he also spoke of order and unity and fighting chaos. Ideas that resonated with her. Somehow, this was not what she had expected him to say.

"Later this year, we will hold an election to decide who will replace Urd Odinson as my lieutenant," Vladimir gestured at Urd, an elegant dark-haired young woman from De Vere Hall who was seated to his left. "Urd will be graduating in May. Any Upper School senior or higher can be nominated or nominate themselves. Is there anyone who would like to make a nomination at this point?"

Natalie Armstrong, whose thick blond hair hung almost to her waist, raised her hand. "I nominate Freka Starkadder. It is my hope that she will go on the following year to take over as leader. I think we all can agree that Vladimir has done an excellent job of leading since his senior year at the Upper School. I believe we should continue to have a younger leader who can hold the office for multiple years in a row. I have heard that before most of us were here, the Knights used to have one college Senior for a year at a time." She flashed her dimples. "How can we get anything done like that?"

Tess Dauntless, who was seated next to Natalie, seconded the nomination. Freka Starkadder rose and nodded to the gathered company, smiling. She had an intense, almost feral beauty and straight hair the color of oak that fell over her eyes in long bangs. Looking at her, Rachel could well believe the rumor that the Starkadders could transform into wolves.

As Freka sat down again, Salome glared at Carl, the younger of her two brothers, elbowing him across her boyfriend's lap. Carl grunted and stood up.

"I nominate Gaius Valiant," Carl Iscariot announced, "I think he's shown good judgment in finally getting someone in here from Dare. We need leaders who can get along well with all the Sorcerous Arts. New blood will only make us that much stronger."

Gaius rose, his hands in the pockets of his patched robes. "Uhhh, I am not sure..."

"I second that nomination." An awkward boy with a large Adam's apple and glasses interrupted him. According to his introduction, he was Topher Evans from Dee Hall. "Valiant's a stand-up guy, and everyone knows he gets along with everybody. Plus, he's pretty smart, for a guy from Drake." The boy smirked at this last bit. Gaius shrugged and sat back down.

Rachel gazed at Carl's face. She thought he was mocking Gaius, and her cheeks had grown quite hot. But people were smiling, as if they actually liked Gaius. No, Carl seemed entirely serious.

Huh.

No one else was nominated. Rachel considered suggesting someone, just for the fun of it. Maybe the girl sitting next to Gaius. Colleen MacDannan was the cousin of Siggy's roommate Ian, and if Valerie's information was correct, the only member of the extended MacDannan family ever to live in Drake Hall. It might seem like a Dare plot, to support the one person who might be thought to be friendly to her dorm. The Knights seemed to be organized so rigidly. Causing chaos for chaos's sake took on a certain appeal.

"We will table any discussion about leadership until next meeting." Vladimir Von Dread rose to his feet again, instantly dominating the room. "With that done, I know that many of us have heard of the wraith attack on Miss Price of Canada. The wraith used a magical protection which rendered it invisible to normal means of detection. Further, it was feeding on Miss Price by direct contact, rather than draining her strength from a distance. All this is quite unusual. Does anyone have any other information on the attack?"

William Locke raised his hand. He spoke with dry, scientific precision. "Wraiths have natural magic and somewhat limited intelligence. They are smarter than animals, but we do not have any records showing them to be smarter than an intelligent child. I have found no previous history of them using defenses such as this one did. I have conflicting reports of who destroyed it. I have heard Miss Griffin was there. Can you tell us how the defense was broken?"

Everyone looked at Rachel.

Terror shot through her like darts. She hated being the center of attention. To keep from panicking, she turned to her memory. Rising to her feet, she gave a complete report, running through what happened step by step and mentioning any detail she thought pertinent. She started with her arrival at the Infirmary. She did not explain she had already known about the wraith or how she could see it.

When she finished, William Locke and the secretary, Naomi Coils, both looked at Von Dread. He kept his gaze trained on Rachel, however, without acknowledging them. Topher Evans had an odd look on his face. Romulus Starkadder raised an eyebrow but did not look around. Salome was the only one not paying attention at all. She sat examining the flame design on her fingernails, looking bored.

As Rachel sat down, Topher Evans leaned forward as if to ask a question. He glanced at Von Dread, who gazed steadily back at him, his expression cold and disapproving. Evans sat back and did not speak. Others chimed in, however, discussing the issue. Several conversations sprang up simultaneously.

"Enough chatter." Von Dread did not shout, yet his voice cut through the chamber. "It is important to note that it should have been one of us who detected and destroyed that creature. Not a gaggle of crazy Dare students with delusions of grandeur." He leaned forward, his gloved fists resting on the tabletop. "That creature was obviously sent here to sow destruction among the students. We must find out who sent it and deal with him accordingly. Does anyone here know who was responsible?"

There was a silence.

Rachel gazed at her lap. Inside she was seething. She had been the one who detected the creature, and the good boys from her dormitory had defeated it. Vladimir Von Dread was an arrogant blighter who thought the universe revolved around him. It did not. Moistening her lips, she found the courage to speak up. She rose to her feet again.

"Mylene's father is the chief wraith hunter of Canada." Rachel spoke calmly. "She's been sick for years. Now she's better. The wraith may have been an attack on her father and his family." She did not add: and not on this school or its students.

Vladimir Von Dread smiled slightly. He did not seem dismayed. "Very interesting, Miss Griffin. Evans, you're from up north. Have you heard of anything like this?"

Topher Evans shrugged. "I am from Alaska, not Canada."

Von Dread nodded impassively and turned back to Rachel. "If you find out anything else, Miss Griffin, we would all be interested in hearing about it."

"Yes, Sir!" Rachel replied cheerfully, her hands clasped behind her back.

Beside her, Salome giggled, "Gods, you remind me of Valerie."

As she sat down, Rachel thought glumly that Von Dread was probably the one who had sent the wraith. He exuded wicked intent. He was far too smug to be one of the good guys.

"Besides the wraith attack," Von Dread continued in his deep, penetrating voice, "there have been other disturbing occurrences. A new freshman in Raleigh named Yara Rahotep was found wandering around outside the grounds. She was apparently out there all night. She claims she has no idea how she got there."

Salome languidly waved her flame-colored nails back and forth. When acknowledged, she said, "I share a class with Miss Rahotep. She's rather...mmm...unfocused. Are we certain she didn't walk out there and forget?"

"Miss Rahotep is known to be absentminded. However, her brother assures the proctors that she has never previously forgotten her actions so completely." Von Dread rested his black gloves on the table and leaned forward. "The unscrupulous often target those who are less able, precisely because such victims are less likely to be believed. It is our job to protect such people from depredation.

"Second, there was a murder attempted on a Dee student named Valerie Foxx. Someone tried to give her a hexed talisman but was thwarted by two students from Dare Hall, Sigfried Smith and Princess Nastasia Romanov. The authorities have not yet caught this man. If anyone hears anything, you will report it to me. Immediately."

Rachel raised her hand.

Von Dread inclined his head toward her. "Yes, Miss Griffin?"

"The man was disguised as an Agent."

"Excuse me? Which man was that?"

"The one who tried to kill Valerie," Rachel said, speaking calmly and simply. "He was disguised as an Agent. He had a piece of paper that made people think it was an Agent's badge. But it wasn't. Sigfried Smith was able to resist it."

"Interesting. No one mentioned that."

"Yes," Rachel frowned, suddenly angry at the adults again. "You'd think that would be the first thing the tutors would tell us. 'Look out for rogue Agents.'"

"Indeed." Von Dread looked thoughtful. "Thank you, Miss Griffin. Next, there is a new student in Marlowe Hall named Misty Lark. Her family was murdered recently. She was the only witness and has, as of yet, not recovered enough to explain to authorities what she saw. Some people from my house took it upon themselves to harass her. I have ended that behavior."

He leaned forward and struck the table with his black-gloved fist. The noise reverberated throughout the chamber. His voice was fierce yet calm. "You will not bother the young woman, or you will answer to me. If you hear anything about the murder of her parents, you will report to me immediately. I have it directly from Dean Moth herself: Miss Lark is to be protected."

Rachel's heart ached on behalf of Misty Lark, Zoë and Seth's friend. She remembered her from the Familiar Bonding Ceremony, a straw-haired girl with a tiny unicorn for a familiar. No wonder the poor girl's expression had been so blank.

An eerie shiver slid down her spine. First Sakura Suzuki, then Misty Lark. Wasn't it odd to have two girls in the same freshman class who had both witnessed the death of their parents?

"Does anyone else have anything to share?" Von Dread asked. "Strange occurrences? Matters of interest to the Knights?"

Rachel considered telling them about the Raven; however, her father had told her to forget about it. She decided to keep that to herself. Then, she waited nervously to see if Cydney Graves mentioned the princess's visions or Zoë's shoes.

Bernie Mulford, the son of the friends of Rachel's parents, casually raised his hand. When acknowledged by Von Dread, he gave the gathered company a jaunty grin. "Did anyone ever find out who was behind the Rain of Fish incident last year? Not that I mind rainbow trout falling on my head." He changed his voice to a thick hick accent. "Them critters is good eatin'." In his normal voice, he added, "Still, it would be nice to know if we need to be prepared to protect ourselves from falling sea creatures on a regular basis."

Von Dread arched an eyebrow at Urd Odinson, the stately upperclassman with wavy chestnut hair who was seated to his left. She spoke calmly without rising. "That turned out to be an unfortunate mishap involving a botched attempt to feed a familiar."

Several people snickered. Bernie looked faintly disappointed, as if perhaps he had already designed his anti-rain-of-fish protective gear.

"Any other business?" Vladimir looked up and down the table, examining each face. "No? Very well. Let us take a short break. I will speak with our newest guests. We will reconvene in fifteen minutes."

CHAPTER TWENTY-THREE:
THE ANCIENT AND HONORABLE
ART OF DUELING

VLADIMIR VON DREAD STRODE TO THE PRACTICE AREA, AWAY FROM the rest of the group, and stood, waiting. Cydney Graves and Wanda Zukov immediately joined him. Salome took her time. She walked over and whispered in Ethan's ear, causing him to snicker. Rachel briefly waited for her and then went to join the others. To her relief, Gaius accompanied her. He stayed close, smiling down at her side, his hand gallantly supporting her elbow.

The three girls and Gaius waited quietly, while Vladimir Von Dread stood, arms crossed, awaiting Salome. When she finally arrived, Dread glared at her, which he did extraordinarily well. Salome hardly acknowledged the admonishment, except to look a little more bored.

Von Dread flexed his black gloves. "Ladies, I wanted to share our rules here in the Knights. First of all, we are expected to conduct ourselves according to the rules of the school. If a member is repeatedly disciplined for any reason, the leader can put your expulsion from the group to a vote."

Rachel's face remained calm, but inside she could not help being amused. *Yeah,* she thought wickedly, *better not break the school rules because being expelled from school isn't so bad, but one wouldn't want to risk getting thrown out of a club!*

"Second," he continued impassively, "while we are not a secret society, we do expect a certain level of decorum. I would be disappointed to hear of a member going around repeating everything she heard here to her friends. Such behavior would most likely get you challenged and possibly expelled."

Rachel instantly rebelled. Her loyalty was to Sigfried and Nastasia. Of course, she would share everything with them. After all, she had only agreed to attend this meeting, not to join the Knights and become a mindless minion of Von Dread. She resolved to repeat everything to her friends the instant she got back to her dorm.

"Third," Von Dread continued, "we expect our members to be civil with each other. If you are violently opposed to another's membership, you may challenge them to a duel. If you win, they will be expelled for the remainder of the year. If the other party wins, you will be expelled for the same period. If you feel the need to challenge someone, let me know, and I will explain our dueling rules."

Rachel did not glance toward Cydney Graves, but she could feel the other girl glowering. A tingle of excitement crawled across her limbs. Cydney was going to challenge her. She was certain of it. A smile tugged at the corner of her mouth. Last time, on the stairs, she had been taken by surprise. This time, thanks to Gaius, she would be ready.

"Fourth," he continued, "you have to have been a member for at least two years before you can invite a new member. And then you may only bring in one per year. If your member makes a fool of him or herself, it will reflect badly upon you."

Vladimir seemed to be speaking directly to Salome. Salome still looked bored, but her cheeks were a shade redder than normal.

Poor Gaius, Rachel thought suddenly, *my behavior is going to reflect upon him.* Sighing, she resolved to give up any plans to cause chaos for chaos's sake.

"Are there any questions?" Von Dread asked, searching each of their faces.

The girls shook their heads. Von Dread nodded once and departed, returning to the table. Wanda followed him. Cydney gave Rachel one last dirty look and headed back to her seat. This left Rachel standing with Salome and Gaius.

"So." Rachel flashed them a big smile. "How do I prepare for my duel with Cydney?"

Salome turned her back to the table and spoke in an exaggerated whisper. "I am more than willing to act as a double agent here. I can convince her to challenge you right away. Or you could challenge her. We should decide soon though, so she doesn't have any time to plan."

Rachel glanced at Gaius, expecting him to object. She felt strangely confident, as if her training session with him the night before had prepared her for anything. She girded herself, ready to argue, to insist she could do this. To her surprise, Gaius grinned encouragingly.

"If you challenge her," he drawled with a wave of his hand, "it will catch her off guard. Also, we'll know exactly when it will happen. However, there are a number of benefits to waiting for her challenge."

"Indeed?" Rachel liked the approval she saw in his eyes. "Like what?"

"If she challenges, you get to be the first one to pick your second," Gaius explained expansively. "She cannot pick a second who is of a higher year than yours. Also—and this is important— you can call for your second to champion you and duel in your place. If you do so, she can do the same. Or she can choose to fight your champion. She cannot challenge you and then decide to have her second champion her. You have to call for that first."

"Then, I definitely don't want to challenge," Rachel decided. "Why give up an advantage like that?" Though frankly, she had no idea whom to choose for her second.

"Good. Good." Gaius nodded. "If the contestants do not choose to have their seconds fight, then both seconds get to cast one protective spell on their primary before the duel starts. What I would highly recommend you do," he leaned toward Rachel conspiratorially, "is wait for her challenge. Then pick me as your second. I can beat any of us in my year, and I can crush any of the younger members. Of this, I am rather sure."

Rachel stared at Gaius starry-eyed. Tingles of excitement ran up and down her arms. *He could beat anyone his age or younger? He was rather sure?*

Slowly, she reviewed everything she had learned about him tonight—his comment just now, his nomination, the respectful way other students here acted toward him, the looks girls kept sending his way.

Gaius was not the outcast she had taken him to be. He was not friendless. He was not trying to escape a bad crowd. He was not even a bad magician. If his recent statements were to be believed, he might actually be an excellent sorcerer.

More than that, he was *popular.*

She had been *completely wrong* about him.

What else might she have been wrong about? Rachel glanced surreptitiously toward Von Dread.

"But I wouldn't even need to fight," Gaius laughed confidently. "I have a spell I can cast on you that I am ninety-eight percent sure none of the other people my age know. It will pretty much instantly win the duel for you."

Salome danced with excitement. "So, what do you want to do? Shall I go do my stuff? I guarantee she will challenge you when I am through!"

Rachel glanced at Gaius. He grinned encouragingly. "Okay. Go do whatever it is you do, Salome. I am sure you are a natural."

"Oh, I am!" Salome gave Rachel a thumbs-up. Then, she giggled, "I love doing this sort of thing!" With a wink, she sauntered off towards Cydney.

Rachel turned to Gaius, who was watching her with amusement. "What else do I need to know?"

Gaius rocked backward on his heels, thinking. "Well, there are rules against any spell that could cause permanent damage. No exploding her or turning her permanently into a toaster."

Rachel pressed her hand over her mouth, giggling.

"I've only seen two official duels," he continued, "In both, relatively light spells were cast. Vlad beat Simon with the petrifying spell you used on me. Before that, Naomi Coils beat Samantha's psycho brother with Glepnir bonds. You know, those bands of golden light that constrict people? If you can't continue casting, you lose."

"Samantha's psycho brother...that would be Jonah Strega?"

Gaius nodded.

Huh, Rachel thought, *him again.*

"So. Think you are ready?" Gaius had not tied back his hair. His silky chestnut locks fell around his face. Rachel longed to reach up and run her fingers through them. This impulse took her by surprise. She had never felt a desire like it before.

"I don't know many spells." Rachel forcibly drew her attention away from the boy, who was standing too close to her. "The only useful spell I know is the petrifying one we practiced." Recalling what had followed, Rachel tried hard not to blush. "I can use that one. It would be nice, though, to have something classy."

"I can teach you something good," Gaius promised, his eyes dancing. "If she challenges you next week, we will have seven days to practice it. Also, as I said, I can place a reflection spell on you. It will make it so, if you wish, you can just stand there and win. That would be slightly amusing."

Rachel pictured this and giggled.

Over by the table, Salome sat down next to Cydney. Rachel watched Cydney go from mistrustful, to curious, to serious, to seriously angry. This took Salome approximately thirty seconds. It was almost as if Salome had a skill in annoying people. Or a magic power. Or both.

Cydney stomped over to another section of the table and sat down. She glared at Rachel angrily, very angrily.

"Wow," Rachel murmured, taken aback. "Salome is scary. Cool...but scary."

Only, Rachel was not sure what Salome had done was cool. An uncomfortable tightness gripped her chest, as if she had just participated in something unsavory.

Shaking off the feeling, she turned back to Gaius. "Standing and doing nothing and winning would be funny...but I don't think that is the right approach for me." She glanced back at the table to find Cydney glowering at her. Her eyes were red and shiny, as if she was holding back tears. She was not just glaring at Rachel. She was also glaring down the table at Randall Graves.

As Rachel regarded the other girl's hot anger, a strange thing happened inside her. As long as Cydney had been cold and disdainful, Rachel had despised her. But the moment she saw pain and uncertainty on the other girl's face, her hatred evaporated. Cydney no longer loomed in her mind like a despicable bugaboo. Instead, she seemed like an unhappy little girl—a little girl just like Rachel.

"Um..." Rachel's voice faltered. Her lips suddenly seemed uncomfortably dry. "I wonder if Salome went too far. It looks like Cydney's feelings are hurt. That's her brother, right? I wonder what Salome told her?"

"Uh, didn't she assault and disfigure you?" Gaius murmured. "She did it, and then she bragged about it. I think it's acceptable for her feelings to be hurt."

"Maybe..." Rachel moistened her lips, "but I wish I knew what Salome said to her. Well...shall we join the others and learn stuff? I love learning stuff!"

"Indeed, we should get back." Gaius took her elbow again and escorted her to the table.

Cydney's cheeks were now poinsettia red. Her eyes bulged. The more annoyed Cydney grew, the more amused Salome became.

Cydney leaned over and whispered something in the ear of an older girl who had introduced herself as Eunice Chase. Rachel had heard the name before. Oh, of course! Eunice was the older sister of little Magdalene and possibly her abuser. Rachel's stomach clenched with frustration. If only she could do something to help the tiny girl who had risked herself to rescue her! She thought of challenging Eunice to a duel but discarded the idea. Eunice was a junior, while Rachel had been at school for less than a full week. She had more chance of finding an aardvark under her bed than she did of winning that confrontation.

Rachel glared at Eunice, who glanced briefly in her direction. Eunice turned back to Cydney and mouthed the word: "No."

Vladimir Von Dread stepped up to the table. The other students fell silent. He opened his mouth to speak, but Cydney stood up, interrupting him. Pointing at Rachel, she stated loudly, "That girl should not be here. I'll duel her for her right to membership!"

Eunice Chase whispered but not low enough to keep her voice from carrying, "I said *NO*. Damn you!"

Rachel kept her face calm, but inside she was startled. So, Cydney was not even going to wait until next week, as Gaius and Salome had predicted? Glancing around the table, Rachel gauged people's reactions. Most of the other students looked surprised. Cydney's brother Randall seemed confused. Salome looked like she might explode from sheer glee. Her brother Carl had an expression of exasperation that only repeated irritation can create. It was directed at his sister. Vladimir Von Dread also looked annoyed.

Von Dread hid his expression and nodded impassively. "Very well. Do you accept, Miss Griffin?"

Randall Graves started to stand up. "Wait, this isn't..." but Von Dread glared at him. He stopped mid-sentence and sat back down.

Rachel turned to Cydney. "I will duel you, if you like...but, afterward, one of us will have to leave the club. If you win, that means that the Knights of Walpurgis will lose any information I might bring in—including its only contact in Dare Hall, which is the home of Sigfried the Dragonslayer and Princess Nastasia Romanov, who seem to be in the midst of a number of the recent happenings."

Cydney shouted back. "Your stupid, crazy friends can't keep their dumb mouths shut! We don't need an in with them!" Cydney's brother Randall covered his face with his hand, embarrassed. Eunice leaned away from Cydney, as if she wished she were sitting elsewhere.

"And it's not like I can't ask-OW!!" Cydney turned on Eunice, who had pinched her under the table, and shouted, "I wasn't going to say who. And it doesn't matter if she knows."

Cydney turned back toward Rachel. "One of your dear little friends is a snitch. Good luck figuring out who." She looked tremendously smug. "So are you accepting my challenge or are you leaving?"

Relief broke like a wave over Rachel. She let out a deep breath. No matter what happened next, she had just gained very valuable information. The leak was another student—and not something supernatural, such as Siggy's amulet. She replayed Cydney's comment, hoping for a clue as to the name of the culprit, but Eunice had pinched her before Cydney's lips could start to form the name.

"Very well, then." Rachel bowed slightly. "Mr. Valiant, would you do me the honor of being my second?"

Gaius sat calmly with one leg crossed over the other. "Of course."

As he spoke, he looked across the table at Cydney. A strange thing happened to her face, as if she were tremendously angry but suddenly became concerned. Only she could not let go of the anger, so both emotions played tug-of-war for control of her features.

"I choose Eunice," Cydney stated.

Eunice did not look up. "I decline."

Anxiety gained the upper hand in the war for Cydney's features. She glared at Eunice, but Eunice would not glance her way. Cydney then looked around the table, but around that moment everyone else found other things that were immensely interesting to look at. She started to say her brother's name, but Randall was much older than Gaius, and therefore, according to the dueling rules of the Knights, she could not pick him.

Gaius rubbed his upper lip and spoke quietly beneath his hand. "Do not let her off the hook." He gazed directly at Rachel, his eyes very intent.

He thought she could do it! A great sense of confidence bubbled up inside of Rachel. So her presence here reflected on Mr. Valiant did it? She suddenly burned with the desire to make a good impression. She glanced around at all the averted gazes and felt so sorry for Cydney. She wished she could just back out, but she did not wish to let Gaius down.

Rachel shrugged. "I could offer to be your second, but that would be just silly."

Cydney stuck out her chin. "I don't need a second. I'll face yours, if you are too scared to fight me yourself."

"I will fight you," Rachel replied.

A boy with spiky hair who had been sitting alone, not speaking to anyone, stood up. He had introduced himself earlier as Michael Cameron, an Upper School junior from Marlowe Hall. "Well, if I don't have to duel, I'll second for you."

A number of people snorted or laughed outright. Rachel felt great sense of relief. She was proud of this young man for volunteering. She thought all the worse of the others, who would not stand up for one of their fellow members, even if she were making a cake of herself. Michael Cameron was the kind of young man Rachel would like for a friend.

Cydney straightened up, but her face had flushed all crimson again.

Vladimir Von Dread held up his hand. "Silence. This is a not a light matter. Seconds, please take your young ladies to a dueling strip."

Michael walked to one of the dueling strips, a length of bare oak floor surrounded by mats. Cydney followed him. The closer she came to her side of the floor, the more her courage diminished. Her shoulders hunched, and her face grew paler and paler. Rachel, on the other hand, felt inexplicably confident. It was not an arrogant feeling, just a quiet certainty. She knew without doubt she could do this.

When they arrived at their designated spot, Gaius lifted his sapphire-tipped wand and tapped her lightly on the chest. A mirror-like shimmer spread across her body and then faded from view.

He leaned over, whispering in her ear, "This spell acts like a mirror. It will bounce back any spell she has the skill to throw—once. Michael will protect her with a *bey-athe* shield. It will be weak. I am not saying this because I am plotting with him. I just know he's a lousy sorcerer. Anything you cast will wipe out his shield. It might even break through and hit her.

"Remember, she's going to be hit with whatever she casts at you first. I doubt that Michael knows that I can do this, so she'll expect a shield as well. If you paralyze her, which I am sure you will, you can get off one last shot before Vlad ends the duel. Just keep that in mind."

Gaius winked at her and stepped back. Trills of delight traveled up and down Rachel's body. She smiled a little mysterious smile and took her place. Across from her, Michael raised his hands and performed a cantrip. A translucent shield glittered in mid-air and then faded. If she squinted, Rachel could see it—a large shield-shaped heat shimmer hanging in front of Cydney.

The crown princes of Bavaria and Transylvania walked to either side of the mid-point. They both raised their weapons. Vladimir held the same sapphire-tipped ebony and gold wand he had used to destroy the scarab. Romulus favored a dueling ring, in this case, the ring set with the Kadder Star. There was something mesmerizing about the Star. Once she glanced at it, Rachel found it hard to drag her eyes away. She averted her eyes just as both princes gestured with their casting weapons. Translucent walls of the same heat shimmer-like substance sprang up to either side of the dueling strip, separating the spectators from the contestants.

Everyone gathered around to watch. Von Dread stepped forward and spoke to Rachel and Cydney. "When I give the signal, you may start casting. If you cast before that, you will be disqualified. You are not allowed to use spells that cause permanent wounds. Do not break this rule, or you will answer to me." As he said this, he looked directly at Cydney. Her face had gone ashen. She held her flute with trembling fingers.

"Aren't you going to take out your instrument?" Cydney taunted, her voice thin. Around them, others nodded, as if they had been asking themselves the same question. Rachel just shook her head, her lips quirking up into a slight half-smile.

Von Dread stood like a statue for what seemed to Rachel to be half a millennium. Then he dropped his wand arm and shouted, "Begin!"

Rachel let her face go still as a mask. Then, she whistled. Twice. Blue sparkles swirled toward Cydney. Then, she gestured and shouted, "*Tiathelu!*" while spinning her two pointing fingers in a circle. Simultaneously, Cydney tried to play her flute with her shaking fingers. She managed a few notes, theoretically enough to paralyze Rachel. The thin stream of blue glitter bounced off Gaius's mirror spell and swooshed back toward her.

Rachel's first swirl of blue sparkles struck the shimmering shield protecting Cydney. The shield popped like a soap bubble. Rachel's second spell hit her, even before Cydney's own spell could rebound. Blue sparks danced up and down Cydney's body. Her limbs froze.

Rachel's *tiathelu* cantrip did lift the paralyzed Cydney from the ground—but only a few inches. Not enough to rotate her in a circle, as Rachel had hoped. Apparently, there was quite a difference between floating a large book and lifting a person.

"Match!" Von Dread's voice echoed in the vast chamber. "Miss Griffin wins."

CHAPTER TWENTY-FOUR:
THE SINGULAR ADVANTAGE
OF EMPLOYING A WAND

APPLAUSE BROKE OUT AS STUDENTS GATHERED TO CONGRATULATE Rachel. Gaius and Salome cheered excitedly. A huge grin split Gaius's face, and Salome jumped up and down, clapping with glee. Charmed, and still in the grip of the confidence that had carried her through the duel, Rachel bowed to the gathered company. This brought on a second wave of applause.

Randall Graves shuffled over to Cydney, his cheeks pink with embarrassment. Standing before her, he moved his index finger in a horizontal line and murmured the Word of Ending: "*Obé.*"

Cydney stumbled. Then she glared at him, pushing on his chest to shove him away. His face went blank with surprise. Then, he shrugged and backed away.

"Congratulations, Miss Griffin," Von Dread stated gravely, and he winked at her.

It happened so quickly that Rachel had to play back her memory of the moment several times before she was certain. But, sure enough, he had actually winked.

Whoa, Rachel thought, stunned, *Now, I'm in danger of thinking he's cool.*

Von Dread turned to Cydney. "Miss Graves, please collect your belongings and depart. If someone wishes it, you can be re-invited to the Knights next school year. Farewell."

Cydney did not look at anyone. She just grabbed her things from the table and rushed out of the room. Rachel watched her, torn between feeling triumphant and sorrowful.

"Congratulations, Miss Griffin," Gaius announced loudly, stepping in front of her and bowing, extremely pleased. Rachel did not say anything, but her eyes shone.

For an instant, she thought: *Hey, I'm good!* Not wanting to walk down the primrose path of vanity, she stuffed that notion into her mental Trunk of Dangerous Ideas, right next to *Gaius Valiant is soooooooo cute!* Then, she imagined slamming the lid, determined to make sure that such hazardous thoughts did not get out again.

Vladimir Von Dread called them all back to the table. Rachel returned to her seat. As she sat down, Salome leaned over and whispered to her.

"That was fantastic. Please, please tell me you have more enemies."

"Um...not at the moment. Sorry."

Out of the corner of her eye, Rachel noted that Gaius had sat down beside her again. He still grinned, tremendously amused. She also noticed that Randall Graves was examining Gaius and her curiously. He did not look angry but he studied them both closely. This sent an unexpected thrill through her. He clearly regarded the two of them as a team.

Rachel gave Randall a little sad smile, as if to say, "Sorry about your sister." She felt for him; he clearly had no idea why it had happened. Whatever had Salome said to make Cydney so mad at him? Rachel would have assumed that it had something to do with dating—being a girl, she assumed everything had to do with dating—except that no one would believe a college junior would date a thirteen-year-old freshman.

Randall Graves noted her sorrowful acknowledgement and shrugged, smiling back.

Next to Salome, Ethan Warhol called rather loudly, "Hey, Mike!"

Michael Cameron looked up from where he was again sitting by himself. "Yeah?"

Ethan sneered. "So, did you mean to help Griffin? Or did a freshman really blow your shield away and hit the person behind it?"

Around the table, people sniggered. Rachel blushed and looked down at her lap. She found his comment a bit insulting. Thinking about it, she realized that while she knew she had been practicing hard, no one else did. To everyone else, it looked like a new student with no training at all had more skill than Mr. Cameron, an Upper School junior.

Michael responded with a quirky half-smile. "Hey, I never said I was any good. Maybe she should get some friends who have enough backbone to stand up for her." He stared directly at Eunice as he said this. Eunice blushed and looked away.

"Wait, I think I'm catching on here." Rachel whispered to Salome, "Eunice invited Cydney, the same way Gaius invited me, right? Only Cydney just made Eunice look bad, the same way I made Gaius look good?"

Salome whispered back, "Exactly. You've really helped out Gaius by beating her. Eunice won't be able to bring her back until next year. If she bothers. No one likes Cydney much, but she does have 'friends.'" Salome made air quotes. "Just not how you and I think of them. More like people who grub up and have an agreement to not annoy each other as much as they annoy everyone else. Bitches." Salome's analysis of Cydney's friends made Rachel snicker. Inwardly, however, she felt quite sad for Cydney.

"Well then," Von Dread addressed the gathering, "shall we spend some time practicing?"

The students broke into small groups to practice spells. Many squared off in pairs and began dueling. When they practiced, the Knights did not hold back. They fought until one of them asked to stop or could not continue. The other person automatically won. All the spells seemed to be of the kind that could be undone with the Word of Ending. Still, the force and vigor of their attacks amazed Rachel. No one was badly hurt, but there were some sprains, bloody noses, and Michael Cameron's shoulder became dislocated. He left to go to the nurse.

Rachel watched the flurry of spells shoot back and forth: sparkling blasts of wind, golden glowing Glepnir bonds, hexes that paralyzed or caused sleep or uncontrollable dancing, cantrips that threw the opponent hither and yon, spells that made the victim babble like a madman, or muted them so that they could not speak, or coated the ground with ice.

No wonder no one had brought their familiars. Who would want to risk them with all the dangerous spells flying through the air.

Toward the other side of the chamber, Vladimir Von Dread dueled Romulus Starkadder. They both knew how to catch their opponent's spell and throw it back at the caster. They volleyed a single sparkling enchantment back and forth a number of times before Romulus finally deflected it. Most of the contenders stood straight on, shooting and deflecting spells with their wands or rings. Von Dread and Romulus, however, stood sideways, like fencers. They deflected incoming spells with their free hand, leaving them free to concentrate on attacking.

Suddenly, what she was seeing rearranged itself in Rachel's head. Realization dawned.

Oh!

That was why none of the Enchanters of Dare Hall came. The Knights of Walpurgis was a *dueling* club.

Dueling required a Fulgurator's wand or a dueling ring. Enchanters, who normally played long intricate pieces of music to accomplish the more complicated of their spells, seldom bothered with casting talisman. Rachel glanced at the people around her and felt disdain growing within her.

Then, she paused, watching.

The advantage of a casting device was that you could shoot off a great deal of magic very quickly. The gems could hold what was known as charges—spells, cantrips, even powers from supernatural creatures—that could be stored in the gem for later use. For serious duelists, Fulgurator's wands were preferable to dueling rings because they kept the more dangerous magic, such as lightning, farther from the caster's body. Casting talisman took a great deal of time to maintain; her father often spent hours refilling his gem.

Once prepared, however, the spells could be used instantly. No time was wasted speaking words or pulling out an instrument. Also, Thaumaturgy allowed for the layering of spells and cantrips, resulting in more complicated effects than could be produced if performing the sorcery on the spot. As she watched, Naomi Coils turned Simon Komarek into a toad. That could not be done with cantrips and Enchantment!

Suddenly, Rachel felt torn. It was as if she were poised upon a pivot, teetering between two options. On one side was generations of devotion to Dare Hall and Enchantment, her brother and sisters, her parents, the weight and force of tradition, all of which were tremendously important to her. On the other? She watched the spells zing back and forth. If the world were actually in danger, it would be very useful to be able to act quickly. Also, it was nice not to feel so out of place for not having her familiar with her.

And then, there was Gaius…

And she did want a wand. Maybe it would be wise to learn how to use one.

Her dream was to grow up to be like the great librarian Daring Northwest. Because of this, it was her secret ambition to take the same course of studies as Agents—a rather grueling regime that required mastery of a great deal more of the Sorcerous Arts than the average student undertook. Unlike her father and her sister Sandra, Rachel did not want to work for the Wisecraft. The idea of an organization telling her where to go did not appeal to her. But if she wished to head off into the wilds on her own, facing angry *sidhe*, fending off tricky *vadatajs,* and distinguishing ponies from phooka, she would need to know how to handle herself.

Undergoing Agent training was a great way to prepare, and Agents stored up their spells like Thaumaturges. They needed to be able to draw on their magic instantly.

Slowly, she felt the needle of her compass of allegiances shift again. Siggy and Nastasia still came first, of course. But after that? Why should she feel loyalty to some building where she had not wanted to live anyway, rather than to this group who had invited her and welcomed her? Suddenly, she now felt surprisingly loyal to the evil Von Dread and his Knights of Walpurgis. Her desire to blab the evening's events to her friends diminished to nothing.

First thing tomorrow, she would write home and ask her parents to buy her a wand. While she was at it, she would order one for Siggy, too. Watching the duelists fire off their fantastical array of spells, she had no doubt he would want one.

Gaius gathered Rachel, Wanda, and Salome together and taught them the bey-athe shield cantrip. He was an excellent instructor, patient and insightful. All three of the girls picked up the gestures and pronunciation for the shield very quickly. Then, they practiced dueling.

Wanda was a good partner. She was very nice and did not seem to have an ounce of negativity to her. Her spells were powerful but chaotic. She did not always get an effect when she cast. When she did, however, her spells held a powerful punch. Salome seemed distracted most of the time. She was rather good at dueling, though, when she paid attention. Rachel had to work very hard to keep up.

But work hard she did. She had made a good impression for Gaius tonight. She did not want anything else she did to take away from that.

The longer the night went on, the more something quite different began to absorb her attention. Gaius was going to walk her home, and he was going to kiss her. She knew this, as inexorably as she knew that the sun would rise the following morning. She felt as if she and Gaius were being drawn toward each other. It was almost as if they were already boyfriend and girlfriend and just had not acknowledged it yet.

Only, Rachel was not sure that was what she wanted.

The sensation was very strange. It was not as if she had decided that she wanted to be his girlfriend and was hoping he would like her, too. But rather, it was as if fate had decreed it, and Rachel had the choice of complying or resisting. Each time the thought surfaced, she pushed it away, firmly turning her attention back to practicing. But the top of her mental Trunk of Dangerous Ideas kept popping open, and she found herself thinking about this all over again.

As the evening continued, Von Dread and a few other older students walked around the room offering advice, watching and critiquing. At one point, when Rachel and Wanda were dueling, the Bavarian prince stood with his arms crossed and watched the entire match. When Rachel eventually "won" the duel, Dread nodded and moved on.

Rachel watched him speculatively. Salome, the princess, and her father all agreed that he was evil. Was he? She recalled how he had championed poor Misty Lark, hearing again the fierce conviction in his otherwise-calm voice. Was that how evil boys acted? An idea occurred to her. Salome had called him the unofficial head of Drake Hall, claiming the students there listened to and obeyed him. Impulsively, Rachel ran after him.

"Mr. Von Dread, may I speak with you for a moment?"

He paused and nodded again. "Yes, Miss Griffin?"

Rachel spoke quietly, making sure that no one overheard her. "I cannot help but notice that you seem devoted to law and order. I want to ask you a favor. There is a girl in Drake Hall, a freshman, who seems to be..." Rachel paused to moistened her dry lips and then forged ahead. "She often has bruises, as if someone is hitting her. There isn't anything I can do, because I cannot protect her in her dorm. But you can. Maybe...do you think you could look out for her, try to keep people from abusing her? Her name is Magdalene Chase."

He listened closely. When she finished, he said, "I will speak to the college resident and to her sister, Eunice. As you might have noticed, bruises quite often accompany dueling practice. You, whom I have heard are quite a flyer, probably also realize they accompany broom sports. I will not make assumptions but, if I find she is being mistreated, I will see to her protection and punishing those responsible. Is there anything else I can assist you with?"

"Just..." Rachel bit her lip. Her heart beat so loudly that she had trouble hearing herself speak. Had speaking to him been a huge mistake? "Someone thought her sister might be the person who... Please be careful whom you talk to. And please don't mention I was the one who expressed concern. Her dormmates don't like me. If they knew, they might be meaner to her."

He waved his hand dismissively. "It doesn't matter whom they like or dislike. If they are hurting the young woman, they will stop. I am not a tutor or a fool. I will notice if they continue to heap abuse upon her after I have told them not to."

Not a tutor or a fool. Rachel liked that. It meant that he would not ignore her the way Mr. Fisher and Mr. Tuck had about the wraith. A wave of gratitude assailed her.

She put her hand on his arm and gave it a tiny squeeze. "Thank you."

Von Dread lay his fingers over hers and nodded one more time. Rachel ran off. Behind her, she saw him standing and looking at Magdalene's sister. Eunice was busy doing something and did not notice. Then she saw him glaring at her and flinched noticeably.

When Rachel arrived back where the other freshman stood, they were watching a match between two college students, Taka Ishizuka from Japan and Seymour Almeida, a young man with a scar across his cheek. When Almeida won, he vaunted loudly, strutting back and forth and congratulating himself. Gaius rolled his eyes.

Gaius continued to instruct them, introducing a new cantrip called *nothor* which caused airborne objects to swerve away from whatever it was cast upon. It was useful for deflecting arrows and weapons, such as firearms, and also for certain kinds of spells. As the girls began practicing, they were interrupted again by Almeida vaunting. He had beaten a cheerful young woman by the name of Jenny Dare. Rachel recognized her as the pretty young woman she had seen Von Dread speaking with in the dining hall. She was descended from the school's founder Virginia Dare, for whom Dare Hall was named, though Jenny herself lived in Marlowe. She lay dazed on the mats while Almeida laughed and taunted.

"Excuse me a moment," Gaius murmured to the girls.

Gaius walked across the room and bowed to Almeida, who shrugged and grinned. "Sure, Valiant. You want to go down, too? My pleasure."

The two of them squared off and the duel began. Seymour stood face on. He held his wand in one hand, shooting and parrying incoming spells as best he could. Gaius, on the other hand, stood sideways like a fencer. He used his wand to attack, while gesturing over his head with his left arm to deflect a spell. He used the same horned gesture that he had used to send the orange juice he pulled off her robes into the trash can.

He was lithe and quick on his feet, dancing and weaving to avoid gouts of orangey sparkles and glowing golden bands. While Almeida shouted, his face growing red as the match grew harder,

Gaius remained calm, his slight smile never leaving his lips.

Eventually, Almeida hung upside down in mid-air, his wand on the other side of the chamber. Glowering, he conceded. Gaius lowered him to the ground and bowed. Without a comment, he returned to instructing the girls.

The meeting ended at midnight. Many people left well before that. Rachel continued practicing diligently to the end, despite the fact that she was starting to weave on her feet. She could not remember the last time she had been up so late.

Gaius left when the last group shuffled out. A number of people paused to say goodbye to Rachel. She smiled cheerfully at each of them. While everyone was leaving, Von Dread called to Eunice, referring to her as Miss Chase, asking her to please stay so he could speak to her. She went slightly pale but agreed. Rachel was careful not to look their direction or do anything that might indicate this had anything to do with this. She did wish that Von Dread had not looked over at Eunice right after she had spoken with him. She sighed. Clearly, he was a law and order type but lacked a sense of delicate feminine diplomacy.

The rest of them left the gym. Gaius escorted Rachel out into the darkness.

"Thank you, Mr. Valiant," she said softly, once they were on the lawn. "I believe we made a good team."

"Miss Griffin, it was an honor and a privilege to be your sponsor." Gaius replied gallantly. "Thanks for not losing. I'll walk you back to the Dare Hall, if you don't mind?"

"That would be very kind of you, sir." She leaned toward him and confided. "I must admit that it's way past my bedtime, and I'm feeling a bit woozy."

Gaius took her arm, squeezing it once. He walked her back, all the way to the front steps. Once there, he smiled, leaned in, and kissed her lightly on the lips.

Rachel gazed up at him, her lips slightly parted. Beneath her calm and happy exterior, she felt frightened. He seemed very big, and she did not know what he wanted from her. She feared her fear showed in her eyes.

He whispered, "Have a good evening, Rachel."

Rachel nodded once. Then, she turned and ran into the dorm, pausing briefly to wave cheerfully over her shoulder.

CHAPTER TWENTY-FIVE:
WITHOUT A TRACE

RACHEL WOKE UP EARLY YET AGAIN, TOO EXCITED AND TROUBLED TO sleep. Mistletoe lay curled beside her, his warm body cuddled against hers. It felt so strange to be able to tell exactly where he was with her eyes closed—even the parts of him that were not touching her. She ran a hand over his silky fur. He purred sleepily as she gently pushed him aside.

She rose and pinned back her hair. Then, grabbing her broom, she slipped out through the window and soared upward. She glided through the pre-dawn twilight, a hint of peach glowing along the horizon. All around her, birds sang their joyous morning songs. Rachel was aware of the loveliness of it all, but her mind dwelt on other things. The feeling that had gripped her last night—that she and Gaius were being drawn toward becoming boyfriend and girlfriend—was even stronger this morning, and she was not at all sure how she felt about this.

The idea of being admired by a dashing and competent older boy was intoxicating. She had liked Mr. Valiant even when she thought he was a mediocre student and a loner. Now that she knew him to be a brilliant scholar and popular, talented sorcerer, his attention to her was even more exhilarating. Plus there was their shared secret about both wishing they had ended up in Dee, which still made her glow inside when she recalled it.

And he had paid attention to her. Rachel played back her memory of the previous evening, carefully noting the interactions between the girls and boys. Ethan Warhol was definitely interested in his girlfriend, Salome, but she seemed interested in everyone. Bernie Mulford, the son of her parents' friends, was a male Salome, flirting with all the girls. William Locke and Naomi Coils were almost certainly an item, and Samantha Strega, the girl whose neck had been slashed, had a thing for Seymour Almeida, the braggart with the scar on his cheek.

Most of the other girls vied for the attentions of the two crown princes, but neither Von Dread nor Romulus showed interest in any of the young ladies batting their eyelashes at them. Gaius was nice to everyone. Even so, it was hard to ignore the fact that he had spent more time with her than anyone else. Her natural humility balked at this conclusion, but her memory confirmed it. She could recall perfectly all the times he had blown off other girls to pay attention to her.

Could it be that he *liked* her?

And he had kissed her. Twice now. Though, they had yet to kiss each other. Rachel had been too frightened last night to return his kiss. The memory of his lips brushing hers warmed her. She felt like melting right off her broom.

But...

First of all, she was thirteen, a year younger even than Valerie and Sigfried. While there were a few students in her year who had boyfriends, such as Salome, most freshman girls did not. Many girls were not allowed to date until they were sixteen or older. As far as she knew, at eighteen and twenty respectively, her sisters Laurel and Sandra still did not have steady boyfriends.

Second, Gaius was an older boy. Older boys were scary. They expected things. Things no thirteen-year-old girl wanted to do. Rachel knew she was not ready for those things yet. Even the idea of snogging terrified her.

Third, he was a Thaumaturge from Drake Hall. They were reputed to be unscrupulous. The reputation might be unwarranted in this case, but what would her family think?

Fourth, he was a commoner. That might not matter to most people, but, again, Rachel was not certain how her family would respond.

Fifth, there was the brother factor. She did not want to date a boy of whom her brother had not approved, and she could not imagine Peter wanting to see his baby sister in the company of an older commoner from Drake. Still, if Gaius really liked her, he could petition Peter for his permission. The thought of him doing so delighted her.

Finally, much as she liked Gaius, Rachel was not entirely sure this was the boy she wanted. She still felt giddy when she thought about John Darling, and there were a great many other interesting boys at school. What if she started dating this one and discovered she preferred someone else? That could be painful.

Rachel sighed and dipped downward, skimming so close to the hemlocks that she could breathe in their pungent evergreen scent. Diving lower, she shot between the trees, maneuvering around the trunks at breakneck speed. Her hair tugged free of its barrettes. She laughed joyfully, racing her broom against the wind.

Eventually, she slowed down and hovered among the hemlocks. The sky was aglow with dawn light now, all golden and fiery red. Watching the sunrise through the branches, it occurred to her that the statue with the wings must be nearby. She sped off to look at it again.

It took her much longer to find than she expected. She went too far, skirting near the line of trees that made up the wards of the school. Beyond, the tor rumbled, as if the imprisoned Heer of Dunderberg and his storm imps were playing at a giant game of nine pins. After searching vainly, she flew above the trees and used her memory to retrace her path from that first morning. Even so, she did not see it until she tried searching while remembering back. Apparently, this area was veiled by its own Obscuration. She wondered why. The place was in the deepest part of the forest, surrounded by the creek and steep rocks. It would be nearly inaccessible by foot.

Spotting it, she wove through the trunks, landing where she had landed the first day. Only, this was not the right statue. Hopping on her broom again, she circled the area three times, but she could not find any others. Slowly, she returned to where she had started.

She gazed around her, comparing this wingless statue and its surroundings with what she had seen last time, an eerie tingle spreading across her body. The glade looked the same. There was still a split pine growing to the left, a rounded granite boulder to the right, and above, the bough upon which the Raven had perched. Nervous, she thought back a moment, but no great black bird sat brooding on the branch.

She drew closer to the statue. It was the same feminine form, draped in stone robes. The moss on the cheek still reminded Rachel of tears.

But...

Where were the wings?

Had someone broken them off? Her stomach lurched. She hurried around behind the statue. No. The back of the cloak was as weathered and lichen-covered as the rest, as if it had been thus for decades. She ran her fingers over the cold stone but could find no rough or broken spot.

Rachel stared at the statue, blinking. Had she imagined wings? Had she dreamt wings? Had there ever been wings? Carefully, she recollected her previous visit. The winged statue gazed back at her from her perfect memory, sorrowful and wise.

The hairs stood up along the back of her neck. There had been wings. They had been here. *She remembered.*

How could they be gone, leaving no trace?

By the time Rachel arrived back in her room, Kitten and Astrid had left for breakfast. The princess sat on a chair in front of her vanity. She tugged on her tortoise-shell hairbrush, which was tangled in her long, pale golden locks. It looked quite painful. Rachel winced, but the princess did not whimper or cry. Her perfect lips merely arranged themselves into a slightly dissatisfied moue.

"May...I help?" Rachel approached her tentatively.

Nastasia gave her a grateful look. She said apologetically, "At home, there were many servants. I...have never had to brush my own hair before."

Rachel's eyebrows flew up, but she pressed her lips shut so as to squelch any comment. She, too, lived in a household maintained by *bwca, bean-tighe,* and servants. Her mother had not allowed her daughters to rely too heavily on their lady's maids. It had been one of the few battles her mother had won in the days when Grandmother Griffin ruled Gryphon Park. There had been a time when Rachel had resented this, wishing that she could have been waited on like a lady of old. Now she had occasion to feel grateful for her mother's foresight.

She disentangled the brush from the princess's silken locks and gave her golden hair a few gentle strokes, smoothing out the mess. She started to continue brushing it but paused. If she did it for her today, Nastasia would be in the same predicament tomorrow.

Rachel handed the princess her brush back and then fetched her own. Pulling out what barrettes the wind had not already stolen, she let down her hair. It formed a dark fringe across her upper back.

"Okay. You hold the brush like this." She held up her hand, demonstrating. "And you put your head like this." She tilted her neck this way and that, showing the other girl how to reach the various portions of her hair. "With longer hair, you can put it over your shoulder, like this."

Nastasia tried it, moving her brush very cautiously. When it did not get snared, her hand sped up. She brushed her hair with long, firm strokes.

"I believe I have it!" The princess's face broke into a sunny smile, pleasure chasing away the clouds of dismay.

Rachel grinned. "Oh! And if you want to comb it, you comb it from the bottom up."

"Excuse me?" Nastasia looked baffled. "How...I am not sure what you mean."

"Like this." Rachel ran and got her comb. "See. If I start at the top of my head, the comb gets stuck in the first tangles. If I try to just push through, I tighten the tangles. If I keep yanking on it, I'll probably pull out some hair by mistake. Ouch!

"Instead, you start at the bottom—the first couple of inches—and comb downward, untangling one knot at a time. They come out more easily when you pull from below than when you push from above. Then, you move your comb up to the next knot. By the time you reach your scalp, you've removed the knots, and you can comb it freely. Like this..."

It took Rachel several minutes to get her hair tangle-free. Her hair was straight and black but lacked the thickness of her Korean ancestors. Each individual strand was thin and wispy, like her paternal grandmother's. Her hair was always escaping from whatever she used to restrain it. In the winter, when the static electricity increased, it became nearly impossible to manage.

The princess watched her at first. Then, she caught on and followed suit, carefully teasing out the knots in her pale golden tresses. Soon, both girls could freely comb their hair.

"See...not so hard." Rachel grinned happily. "It just takes a little getting used to. You'll be a pro in no time."

"I thank you." The princess ran her brush through her hair again and again, until it shone like silk. She beamed with pleasure. "You have been of great help to me this day."

"You are most welcome," Rachel replied gallantly.

The princess put her brush and comb away. As she did, Rachel caught a glimpse of herself in the mirror above the vanity. Her newly-brushed hair, clipped back with a large black and white polka dotted bow, looked neat and orderly for a change. She wondered shyly if Gaius would think she looked cute.

"Breakfast next." The princess picked up her ubiquitous textbook.

The two of them headed outside and down the gravel path toward Roanoke Hall. The leaves on the white birches were beginning to fall. Splashes of bright yellow dotted the path. Clouds were moving in, forming castles in the blustery sky.

"How are you enjoying school?" Rachel asked as the stones crunched beneath their feet.

Nastasia petted her Tasmanian tiger and sighed. "I find it enjoyable but wearying. I had not realized there would be so many people. Or rather, I knew the number of the student body, but I did not realize so many of them would expect things from me. No matter where I go, there seems to be someone who wants something from me. Frankly, most of the time, I can't figure out what it is. Occasionally, I wish I could go somewhere a bit more private."

Rachel listened with interest. It *had* been relief she had caught on the princess's face when she dismissed the gaggle of students following her in the dining hall. She marveled how graciously her friend bore the impositions she was suffering, not revealing by so much as a hint to those clamoring for her attention that they were a burden. A warmth spread through Rachel, a secret, quiet happiness born from the knowledge that, in Nastasia's mind, she, Rachel, was a real friend and not part of the demanding crowd.

"There are a lot of people," agreed crowd-shy Rachel with great sympathy.

She considered telling the princess about her empty hallway, with the suit of armor and the doorstop, but balked. She knew from experience the advantage of having a place no one else knew about, where she could retreat if she wished time to herself. If she told Nastasia, someone would know to look for her there. Besides, Nastasia had a whole house in her purse into which to retreat if she wished privacy.

A slight, happy smile touched Rachel's lips. One person knew about her hallway, but she did not count him.

"Then there is all this free time." The princess frowned, spreading her hands as if to indicate extra time. "I don't know what to do with it."

Rachel, who found her day quite crowded between classes, helping Mr. Chanson, and after-class activities, frowned at her, puzzled. "What do you mean?"

"At home, everything is scheduled for me."

"Everything?" Rachel asked, utterly aghast. "All your time?"

"How else is one to learn the things required of one's royal role?" Nastasia asked. "In addition to my scholastic studies, there was dancing, music—several different instruments, art, strategy, penmanship, tennis, diplomacy, protocol, and law. The things princesses must know to prepare us for what our futures might require of us.

"When I was not with a tutor, I was studying, or appearing at formal court functions. I never had to decide about how to spend my time because something was always expected of me. I never had to make decisions about anything.

"Now, I am not sure how to fill my time, except to copy the kind of thing we did at home: organize some social gatherings. At home, it would have been a charity tea or a meeting with diplomats' wives. Here I am considering a study group and a practice club."

The idea of having someone tell her how to spend all her time made Rachel's chest constrict. She jumped up and down on the gravel path, trying to shake off the feeling of breathlessness.

"Wow," Rachel murmured. "I was exactly the opposite. At home, all my time was my own."

"Did you not have studies?" Nastasia watched her antics with a mixture of puzzlement and amusement.

"Oh, I learned the things aristocratic girls must know, which was a rather similar list to yours." Rachel waved her hand. "You know: dancing, singing, needlework, riding, farming, accounting. The things you need to know to run an estate. But with the exception of a few dance and music classes—oh, and I took gymnastics—I was left to myself."

"What about your studies?" Nastasia asked again.

"My parents realized that I learned much faster on my own. So they turned me free in the libraries—between Gryphon Park and Gryphon-on-Dart we had a number of very nice ones.

"My life was exactly the opposite of what you describe," Rachel mused. "It was a constant series of decisions: should I study grammar or mathematics? Should I study now or ride my pony? Should I ride my pony or fly my broom? Should I trust in the levers to avoid the upcoming pillar, or throw my weight to the right? The hardest thing about school, for me—other than the enormous numbers of people—is not being able to choose what to do when."

"But..." Nastasia shook her head as if she could dispel the madness that was Rachel's life. "How could your parents tell if you were progressing? What was to keep you from spending all your time on frivolous pursuits?"

"Every Friday, I met with Mother and told her what I had learned during the week," Rachel assured her. She did not explain she could recite back what she learned in complete detail, or that her mother, who shared the same gift, could listen to her recitation at high speed.

"Oh. Well. I guess that was all right then. Your mother would have noticed if you had shirked your studies."

Rachel replied primly, "If I had been the sort of person who shirked my studies, my parents would not have dismissed my tutors."

They walked along in silence. Rachel wondered if she should tell the princess about the statue and the disappearing wings. It sounded so crazy. Before she could decide, the princess laid a hand on her arm.

"Rachel, you have done me a kindness, so let me do you one in return."

Rachel looked at her hopefully. "Yes?"

"Let me pass on a warning," the princess spoke solemnly, leaning closer. "That young man you left the dining hall with last night? You should not associate with him. He does not have a nice reputation and is known to belong to a bad crowd."

"Really?" Rachel's voice quivered slightly. "What h-has he done?"

"Among other things, he has a very bad reputation when it comes to dealings with young women. Also, he is a Thaumaturge. There are reasons why that kind of magic is not practiced by decent folk."

"O-oh." To her tremendous embarrassment, her voice hiccupped.

"You should not associate with a wicked boy, Rachel. It is wise to avoid those who behave immorally. We must not compromise with evil, not in any way."

"Um...right. Thanks for telling me." Rachel bit her lip. She kept her face calm, but a huge lump had formed in her throat. It did not go away, no matter how many times she swallowed.

Chapter Twenty-Six:
The Tricky Process
of Acquiring a Boyfriend

As Rachel approached the table with her breakfast tray, Joy waved to her. The buzz of breakfast conversation was as loud as ever. Rachel had to get close before she could hear her.

"Did your brother Peter find you?" Joy bounced up and down in her seat. Without her headband, her very straight hair fell into her eyes. Rachel wondered if she was wearing it down to be more like the princess.

"No." Rachel glanced around the dining hall, but Peter had already departed. "Did he say what he wanted?

"Nope. Just to tell you that he was looking for you."

"Huh." She sat down beside Joy, wondering what he might have wanted. Had someone seen Gaius kiss her? She very much hoped not. That would have certainly enraged her brother. Peter still thought she was eight years old.

The kiss, which had brought her such joy earlier, now tasted like dust in her mouth. Had she allowed herself to be taken in by a cad, like the heroines of all those Gothics she had found in the east library at home? Oh, she had so hoped that would never happen to her! Gaius did not seem like a cad. But then, what would she, a thirteen-year old girl, know about the conniving ways of men? Surely, Nastasia, a wise princess, knew more about these matters than she did.

Her breakfast included eggs and English muffins with butter and marmalade. The marmalade smelled particularly sweet and tangy today. She breathed in the delicious aroma before taking a bite. Buttery, marmalady goodness filled her mouth, dancing on her taste buds, lifting a few of her fears about having been kissed by a cad, and dispelling all concern about the wrath of Peter.

Valerie arrived, her camera bumping against her hip. She had a big smile on her face and was carrying a thin box. She plopped down next to Rachel. "Where's Siggy?"

"Still in the kitchen filling his tray."

Valerie leaned closer, grinning. "So. I hear Gaius Valiant is your boyfriend."

"What?" Rachel jerked so violently that her bite of egg flew off her fork, nearly hitting Wulfgang Starkadder sitting farther down the table. The temperature of her cheeks rose at least a hundred degrees. "No! No, he's not!"

It was one thing to think such thoughts in the privacy of her own head. It was another to hear someone say it, all the more so after the princess's recent revelation. Her heart thumped like a runaway horse. Had Peter heard this rumor? She certainly hoped not!

Still, Valerie's words brought an odd rush of pleasure. If someone else thought she and Gaius were an item, maybe her feeling that they were being drawn together was not mere insanity; maybe something really was happening between them.

"If you say so," Valerie grinned, snapping a picture of her.

Rachel opened her mouth to ask Valerie where she had heard this, but Sigfried arrived. He carried a tray so full that sausages and hashbrowns spilled off it. None of it hit the floor, though. Lucky saw to that. Putting the tray on the table, Sigfried began shoveling the food into his mouth even before he finished sitting down.

"Sigfried!" Joy moved her tray to sit beside him. "I hear you saved a whole group of children from a skunk! One that was on fire no less! That was very brave!"

Siggy nodded, accepting his due praise. He tried to reply, but his mouth was too full.

Valerie stood up and slid her thin box next to Siggy's tray. She walked around the table and stood grinning beside him. "Stand up, Siggy. I have something for you."

Sigfried paused to cram more food in his mouth. He stood, warily. Valerie opened the box and held it out for him to see. Inside was a brand-new bowie knife atop a leather sheath. Its steely blade gleamed.

"Is that...for me?" Sigfried gawked in wonder, his mouth nearly full.

"You said you wanted me to give you a favor, so you could be my champion. I thought this would be even better." She tried to speak casually. However, her cheeks had turned all pink, and her words tumbled out in a rush.

"Wow! This is the next best thing to a real sword. Ace!" Siggy swallowed rapidly, hardly chewing. He picked up the knife. Holding it aloft, he turned it this way and that, appreciating the way the light shimmered along the steel blade. He started to strap the sheath on, frowning as he fumbled with the straps and buckle.

Valerie rolled her eyes. "Siggy, allow me. Here."

Taking it from him, she unzipped his robe, revealing his naked chest. Putting her arms around him, she passed the leather under his garment and strapped the sheath to his bare skin. He flushed.

"There. That's how you wear a knife. You want it at chest height so you can draw it and go directly for the heart in one motion." She pantomimed the stabbing motion. Then, she waved an admonishing finger at him. "But don't stab anyone, unless they are actually trying to kill you. And no more stabbing wraiths that can't be hurt by knives and letting them eat you, okay?"

Siggy's cheeks continued to grow pinker. He gazed at Valerie and the knife as if, together, they were the most beautiful things in the world. Valerie had begun to recover her aplomb. Now she blushed even more deeply. She caught her breath and lowered her golden lashes, gazing downward, suddenly shy.

"Cool! A girl who knows how to wear a knife!" Siggy beamed. "Can't beat that!"

"We should stick together." Valerie stepped back, grinning. Pulling off her lens cap, she snapped a picture of Siggy and his new knife.

His hand in front of his face as he blinked after the bright flash, Sigfried declared, "I've decided I'll be your boyfriend."

"What?" Valerie's eyes blazed with indignant fire. "Y—you don't get to just decide things like that! You have to ask."

"No." He shook his head emphatically. "All I ask is whether you want to be my girlfriend. Because it will be really awkward for you—if you were my girlfriend, but you did not want to be. Here." He draped his silky red and gold dragon around her shoulders like a feather boa. "Hold Lucky and pet him while you're thinking it over." Sigfried stood as close to Valerie as a dance partner, as if he were about to lead her around the dining hall in a wild waltz. He gazed steadily down at her. "Now. Do you want to be my girlfriend?"

Valerie turned entirely pink. She stroked Lucky's soft fur, as the dragon nuzzled her cheek. "Why yes! Yes, I do!"

"Kiss! Kiss!" Zoë chanted.

Joy joined the chant, too, but her heart did not seem to be in it. She looked pinched and sad. Rachel did not chant, but she watched all this with delight, a warm joyful feeling filling her at Siggy's happiness.

Siggy kissed Valerie.

As Rachel finished her French toast, a shadow fell across her shoulder. Looking up, she was startled to find Vladimir Von Dread looming beside the table. He bowed before the princess.

"Miss Romanov." He towered over her. "I have heard tell that you see visions—glimpses into the pasts of those you touch. I would be curious to know about my own past." Von Dread pulled off his black dueling glove and extended his bare hand toward Nastasia.

"I am sorry, Mr. Von Dread." Nastasia lifted her chin proudly. "I have been instructed never to touch you."

"But you.... Wait. Never to touch me, personally?"

The princess nodded. She regarded him with quiet dignity, as if she had said all there was to say on the subject. The prince of Bavaria frowned in annoyance.

Rachel stepped up beside Nastasia. The princess had stood with her against the girls of Drake Hall. She would return that favor by supporting the princess against the Drake boys—even if it meant facing down the most intimidating, and most handsome, of them all. Nastasia moved slightly closer to her, as if grateful for the support. The two girls linked elbows.

"Mr. Von Dread," Rachel met his gaze evenly, "Miss Romanov was instructed not to touch another student. She touched him anyway, and something very bad happened. She ended up in a place where he was being tortured. The creature doing the torturing could see her. Not only that, it tried to keep her there. Then, it tried to attack her later in her dreams. There may be something dangerous in your past," Rachel concluded. "Something that could hurt Nastasia."

"Ah." He nodded thoughtfully. "But you are willing to touch others than myself? I would be quite interested to see how the process works."

"There is little to see," Nastasia replied graciously. Her pale gold lashes brushed her cheeks. She was as lovely as he was handsome. Rachel could not help noting what a pretty couple they would make. "But yes, I am willing to touch others."

Von Dread glanced across the dining room. His gestured imperiously at a table of younger students from Drake Hall. "Almeida, MacDannan, Valiant. Attend me."

The braggart with the scar, the pretty, copper-tressed Irish girl, and Gaius came obediently to his side. Gaius winked at Rachel. She smiled back, warmth kindling within her. Her pleasure was quickly dampened, however, by the concerns the princess had raised. Was Gaius really wicked? The thought made her heart beat at an odd, uneven rate.

"Please allow Miss Romanov to touch you," Von Dread instructed. "She will then report to us as to whether doing so has caused a vision."

Colleen MacDannan put out her hand first. The princess touched her and shook her head. "Nothing."

"What does that mean?" Von Dread asked.

"I do not know, but I did not receive visions when I touched any of the other MacDannans here at the school, either. As well as quite a few other people," Nastasia replied. "Miss Griffin, Miss O'Keefe, and Mr. Smith, for instance." She nodded at Sigfried, who was sitting with Valerie, demonstrating the fine art of balancing a spoon on one's nose.

"I wonder if it means that we are from this world," Rachel mused. "It is unlikely that everyone came from somewhere else."

With a start, Rachel realized that if her theory was true, she herself was local. An initial pang of disappointment at not hailing from some distant place was swept away by a sudden swell of pride and something stronger: fierce, unassailable love.

This was her world. She *belonged* here.

Closing her eyes, she solemnly vowed to do everything in her power to keep it safe.

"Interesting." Von Dread nodded, replacing his glove. "We should have brought William. He would have found this fascinating. Mr. Almeida?"

The young blond man with the scar on his face strutted forward, grinning. The princess did not respond to his swagger. She merely put out her hand, her expression gentle. She was so beautiful that he halted, flustered, his outstretched hand forgotten. She took it anyway.

Watching Nastasia, Rachel thought again about how sad it was that the princess did not seem more pleased with her lot. How much fun it would be to have such visions. Rachel would so have enjoyed being able to pull them up and examine them again and again.

The strength of her yearning curled her hands into fists. She longed to know everything—and that included every detail the visions might show about each student in the school. She was certain that she could have found something useful in each one.

Information was like that. It had to be loved.

The same held true for Siggy's amulet. If Rachel owned such a talisman, she would be glancing around her at all times, so that, if nothing else, she could pull up the memory later of what she had seen and check for details she might have missed. Of course, if it were hers, she would never do anything else—like attend to her studies. So, it was for the best that it was not.

And it was not as if she did not appreciate her own gifts, her perfect memory, her ability to use that memory to break Obscurations, and her skill on a broom. When she thought about these things, a happy warmth grew inside her. All sense of envy faded.

Nastasia withdrew her hand. "Mr. Almeida, I saw you in a magical duel with another man. You were grown up and fighting in a forest made of glass. The other man was dressed in blue and silver armor. Spells flew back and forth very quickly. Jagged black fire struck your face, leaving a wound exactly where your scar is now."

Seymour ran a finger along the scar on his face. "That's

weird. I got this in a broom accident when I was a kid." He frowned at Von Dread, as if expecting an explanation.

Von Dread showed no reaction. "And Gaius?"

Well, that was interesting. The prince of Bavaria had called all the other students by their last name. But Gaius, he called by his first name. Now that she thought about it, Gaius had called him by a nickname, Vlad. Rachel wondered what this signified.

Gaius came forward. He looked so good-natured with his huge, congenial smile. Her heart rebelled against the bad things she had heard about him. But that did not mean that they were untrue. More likely, she, a thirteen-year-old girl, was not very discerning when it came to matters of character. The thought caused a painful tightening in her chest.

Rachel swallowed. Gathering her courage, she gestured from him to the table and back, introducing those present.

"People, this is Gaius Valiant. Gaius, these are my friends: Nastasia, Joy, Sigfried, Valerie, and Zoë."

Gaius's eyebrows leapt up. "Sigfried the Dragonslayer? The boy who saved the campus from the flying, flaming skunk?"

"The very same," Rachel beamed proudly. "Oh, and this is Lucky."

Lucky stuck his head out from under the table and peered at Gaius. Then he snaked over to whisper in Sigfried's ear. "Just a boy. Nothing to see. Unless you want me to take him?"

Siggy was busy stuffing food into the pockets of his robe. He whispered back. "Not yet."

"Very well, Mr. Valiant," the princess said sternly, "put out your hand."

Gaius did. The princess touched him. Rachel leaned forward watching intently. Time seemed to slow down to such a degree that she grew sure she would starve before the next event. Would the princess never speak? Did it seem to everyone as if two ice ages had passed? Or was it just her? Wistfully, she wished she were the one with an excuse to touch Gaius's hand.

"You were surrounded by stars in outer space," Nastasia said finally. "You piloted a ship shaped like a crystal teardrop. You flew toward something that looked like a giant cloud of glitter, maybe a nebula? As you approached, it rearranged itself to form a huge reflective surface. You called it the Mirror Nebula.

"You flew toward this surface. For some strange reason, the image reflected was of your body, even though you were in your ship. Your reflection had flares of multi-colored light coming from its shoulders. Also visible in the mirror was an object in the far distance—a huge metallic moon surrounded by many thousands of these graceful teardrop ships and, something else? Jump gates? Worm holes? Then, the artificial moon exploded."

A shadow passed across Gaius's face. "Was it...my fault?"

"Why would it have been your fault, Mr. Valiant?" The princess asked, puzzled.

"I..." He shook his head, setting his pony-tail wagging. "No reason."

Rachel watched this with interest. Was Gaius from a world of starships and explosions? Was that why he had wanted to be a scientist? And why did he think he was responsible for the destruction of the artificial moon?

"Thank you, Miss Romanov." Von Dread inclined his head once more and departed. Seymour and Colleen followed him. Gaius hung back.

"Thank you, yet again, Princess." He bowed gallantly to the princess. "That was eerie and a bit disturbing, but I appreciate your efforts. I'm sure Vlad will want to perform experiments on us now, to make sure we have not been mutated into alien monstrosities or the like. Hopefully, it will not be too torturous."

"Is there normally a danger of that?" Zoë asked from the table. Her hair was pink today, though the feather tied into her forelock braid was still electric blue. "Mutating into alien monsters, I mean."

"Not so far as I know," Gaius drawled back, amused, "but there is always a first time."

"Does he normally torture you?" Sigfried asked, intrigued. "Or is it only now that he knows you are a Metacrouton?"

"Only when the pursuit of knowledge requires it," Gaius replied cheerfully. Rachel could not tell whether or not he was kidding. "Though I had not realized that I was a Metacrouton. Is that a giant bread product for very large salads? Or perhaps a very large bread product that appears in salads meant for giants?"

"It's Siggy's term for people from outside our world," Rachel explained. "Actually, Metapluton is his word for people from outside our world, but he has trouble remembering it correctly."

Gaius turned to her and bowed deeply. "Let me congratulate you again on your duel last night, Miss Griffin."

"Duel?" the others asked with interest. The whole table was looking at her now.

Rachel lowered her lashes, shy before the attention. "I fought Cydney Graves."

"And Miss Griffin won, I might add. Very nicely done." Gaius patted her on the shoulder. "Well, I mustn't keep Vlad and his torture implements waiting. Have a good day, Rachel."

As she watched him go, Rachel noticed that Vladimir Von Dread had stopped to speak with Magdalene Chase. The tiny girl's normally pale cheeks were tinged pink from embarrassment, but she stared up at him, her eyes aglow with hero worship.

So he really was not a tutor or a fool. Good for him.

CHAPTER TWENTY-SEVEN:
UNSATISFACTORY ALTERNATIVES
TO SAVING THE WORLD

AS THEY WALKED TO CLASS, SIGFRIED FELL IN NEXT TO RACHEL. HE moved until his head was close to hers and whispered, "How did you learn to paralyze people? That sounds totally ace! I want to learn that!"

"How did you hear about that?" Rachel asked, surprised. She was wearing new leather boots today, a gift Sandra had sent from London. The heels made a satisfying *click-clack* against the marble floor. "That boy you just met, Gaius Valiant? He taught me."

"The one who is about to be tortured by Von Dread." Sigfried nodded solemnly, as if commending the fellow to his fate.

"I don't think Dread's actually planning to torture him...at least, I don't think."

"As to how I heard about it," Sigfried glanced around them and whispered again. "Last night, I was really bored. You were busy, and Sean Peregrine was practicing with his band—he plays bass guitar and some girl who never talks plays the drums—so he wasn't available for brawling. Anyway, rather than gouge my eyes out from sheer ennui, I sent Lucky to spy on Dr. Mordeau."

"Really?"

"Yeah. After you beat her, that Skinned-Knee girl..."

"Skinned-Knee?"

"Yeah, isn't that her name?"

"You mean Cyd-ney?"

"Whatever. Isn't that a boy's name? Or a town in the Princess's kingdom? Anyway, after she lost to you, she went to Dr. Mordeau, who questioned her about the duel and about you."

"About me? Wha-what did she want to know?"

Siggy shrugged. "Mordeau seemed very surprised to hear you were at the club. She wanted to know who had invited you. When Squidkey told her..."

"Cydney."

"Again with the Whatever." Siggy formed a W with his fingers and shoved it at Rachel's face. She batted it away. "When she told her, Mordeau looked even more annoyed and said something about not trusting Von Dread."

"Von Dread?" Rachel's voice rose. "What does he have to do with it? Does that mean that Dr. Mordeau disapproves of the Knights? If so, does that mean she is looking out for me?"

"No idea. Mordeau's snake spotted Lucky at that point, and he had to skidoo."

"Oh no! If the snake saw him, Mordeau knows he was there."

"Yeah, so what?" Siggy shrugs. "Most people don't know he's intelligent—much less that I can see out of his eyes. If anyone asks, I'll say he was off wandering around on his own."

"Oh...good point." Rachel pursed her lips. "Did you learn anything else?"

"She had another student with her. A blond kid. Older than us."

"What was he doing?"

"Helping her sort papers, mostly."

"Must be her student helper—the way I help Mr. Chanson."

"Student helper, then...but when Squidknee was there, he...did something weird."

"Weird...how."

"Well, Lucky said he started petting her."

"Mordeau let a student pet her? Yuck!"

"Not Mordeau! The girl with the boy's name."

"He pet Cydney....pet how?"

"Running his hands over her hair and stuff."

"And...stuff." Rachel blinked. "You mean like...*boyfriend* petting?"

"I don't really know. I wasn't paying attention during that part. I was counting my coins. But Lucky said that Mordeau stopped him. She said, '*Not this one. I'll call you another for that.*' And he replied, '*How about the one from last time? I liked that one. She was much more satisfactory than the first one.*'"

Chills raced each other up and down Rachel's arms. "That's...creepy!"

"Yes. It is creepy."

"What...could it mean?" Rachel asked, trying to think of less disturbing interpretations than those that first came to mind.

"No idea."

The morning brought Language, Art, and Math. Again, Rachel kept a sharp eye on Dr. Mordeau, but did not catch her showing any dismay toward either Sigfried or herself. As class let out, the tutor even said with gracious coolness, "Congratulations, Miss Griffin. I hear you are turning out to be quite a duelist."

Rachel flushed. "I do my best, Ma'am."

"I am sure you do. Your family has a reputation for producing strong sorcerers. Still, true dueling requires a wand, and that requires Thaumaturgy." Dr. Mordeau gave her a thin-lipped wintry smile. "Perhaps you should consider transferring to Drake Hall."

In the excitement of last night's kiss, Rachel had been distracted from her resolution to get herself and Sigfried a wand. After thanking the Math tutor, she rushed back to her room and ordered a wand for Siggy with the money left from what he had given her to buy him clothing. A length of gold with a ruby tip, which would be good for fire magic, seemed perfect for him. Then, she wrote a letter to her father, requesting a wand for herself, silver with a diamond tip. According to the books she had read, diamonds were best for all-around magic. They were also good for casting lightning bolts, though not as good as amber. Then, she dropped by the mail room and mailed both missives.

As she walked up the stairs, her steps lost their bounce. Only a day ago, she would have included a report for her father, telling him about the meeting of the Knights of Walpurgis. She would have enjoyed writing it up, commenting on the members, the information she had learned, and the duels. Now she wrote nothing.

If he would not listen to the things she needed to report, she could not bring herself to tell him anything. But whom could she trust with her secrets? In novels, clever characters trusted nobody entirely. Rachel could not survive like that. She was too young, her heart too vulnerable. Left alone, her many obligations—to family, tutors, friends, and more—threatened to draw her in twenty different directions, tearing her apart. She needed one person to whom she was loyal above all others—one person to whom she could tell everything.

But whom could she trust? Who would listen carefully? Who would put her secrets to good use? Her father was so competent and wise, but he had recused himself. Mr. Tuck was erudite and profound, but he had not believed her when she told him about the wraith. Fuentes had saved her from the Drake girls, but he had not yet let Valerie know anything about the scarab or who attacked her. Mr. Badger had told her about the Raven, but he was taciturn and a bit intimidating.

Peter and Laurel? Rachel loved her brother and sister, but they thought of her as a little child, unable to take care of herself. If she told them any secrets, they would just try to stop her from learning more—as Father had. That was hardly going to help her right now.

Her friends? The princess had stood up for her. But she could not bring herself to swear fealty to Nastasia as Sigfried had done. She was gracious and kind. But occasionally, she struck Rachel as too rigid in her thinking, unable to bend when bending was required. Beside, Rachel was British. She already had a monarch.

What of Sigfried himself? Rachel adored him, but he was so careless, so outrageous in his behavior. He seemed more like a brother who needed guidance than a mentor. Valerie? She investigated things. She might love listening to observations. But she had arrived at school with a best friend, Salome, and did not seem to be looking for a new one. Zoë? She took revenge upon the girls from Drake for her. She was amusing, but Rachel could not imagine confiding everything to her.

Then there was Gaius.

Rachel sighed. Even at the tender age of thirteen, she understood that making a sixteen-year-old boy the center of her private universe—even if he shared the secret of wishing he lived in Dee Hall—was a bad idea.

After lunch, Rachel took a walk by herself, wandering down along the boardwalk that ran through the hemlocks, beside the creek. Heading south, away from where she had explored before, she came to a stone arch. Through it, lily-of-the-valley carpeted the forest floor, stretching between the great oaks. There were no flowers, but their distinctive leaves rose into points that stretched as far as her eye could see.

Rachel walked through the archway and strolled under the oaks, singing softly:

"White coral bells upon a slender stalk,
Lilies of the valley deck my garden walk.
Oh, don't you wish that you could hear them ring.
That will happen only when the fairies sing."

Rachel had only twice had the pleasure of hearing the lilies-of-the-valley at Gryphon Park ring. A person had to be up at just the right hour on just the right day, or the flowers bloomed and faded without one ever catching them while the fairies were singing. Her sisters had even worse luck than she did, but Peter, who was more patient, had heard them several times. He camped out one year, so that he would be sure to be there at the right hour. He did hear them, but he came back with his hair tied in so many elf knots that Mother had to shave it off.

Rachel loved hearing the lilies ring—but not so much that she wanted to risk having her head shaved. Besides, she had the advantage that she could play back her memory, and they sounded as sweet as the first time. She did so now as she passed among their bloomless leaves.

As she walked, her feet swishing through the greenery, she mulled over the problem of the snitch. How to discover who it was? The best solution would be to divide up the information at their disposal and give only a little bit to each person—and then wait to see what made its way to Drake Hall. They could wait to do this until they had more secrets, or they could dole out made-up information.

She knew which option Sigfried and Nastasia would pick. Sigfried would be all for lying; the princess would insist on the truth. The question was how to get them to agree on a plan.

So much was at stake. Thinking about it made her heart thump against her ribs. The Earth could be in danger, some terrible future awaiting them—like the fates Nastasia saw in her visions: icy plains, horrendous fires, metallic moons exploding. Rachel knelt on the damp earth and ran her fingers over a smooth-veined Lily-of-the-Valley leaf. She breathed in the pleasant scent. Everything was so idyllic, so peaceful. Yet this glade, this very leaf, would be destroyed if the world froze or burned.

She had no idea what to do to stop such an impending fate. All she knew was that if the world was in danger, she had to help.

Her world.

It might seem ridiculous to think a thirteen-year-old girl and her fourteen-year-old friends could save the world. But there was a precedent. Wendy MacDannan had not been much older than Rachel when she helped defeat the Terrible Five. True, Wendy had not fared well, but she had done terribly brave and wondrous things before she lost her sanity.

During that fight, she and James Darling had been the front line. That was what Mr. Fisher had called them: the front line. They might have been young, but where they were—that was where the war was fought. Now, the front line was here: Valerie and the man who was trying to kill her; Nastasia and her visions; and maybe even Rachel herself. No one else could see the Raven who was the omen of the World's End.

It was frightening to find oneself on the front line, and yet...

When danger came, a person had a choice. Run away, or step forward and confront it. Rachel refused to run.

If death was inevitable, she wanted to stare it in the face before it took her.

It took forever for her to corral Sigfried and Nastasia and get them away from the other students. Finally, Valerie hurried off to get her books, and Joy detached herself from the princess's side to speak to the second of her six sisters. Rachel pulled the two of them into the outdoor courtyard inside the walls of Roanoke Hall.

The weather was especially nice. Thunder rumbled from the north of the island, but there was not a cloud in the sky. The sunlight beat down warmly on the children's faces. A breeze caught the hair that had escaped Rachel's black and white bow. A long lock tickled her face.

The princess tilted her head back and admired the perfect heavens. "What a lovely day!"

"It is," Rachel agreed, then she sighed, "which makes it all the more odious that we need to discuss snitches."

Sigfried stared up at the towers and spires of Roanoke Hall. Lucky snaked through them, dodging in and out, a red and gold ribbon against the brilliant blue. "You mean Sneetches? The kinds on beaches with 'stars upon thars?'"

Nastasia actually giggled. She pressed her fingers against her lips, as if she hoped to stop the noise from escaping.

"No." Rachel sighed. "The kind who betrayed us to the kids in Drake Hall." She told them what Cydney had said.

"So...there really is a spy?" The princess had been watching her Tasmanian tiger chase its tail, a happy smile on her face. Now, her face fell. "I thought maybe they had a magical device, like Sigfried's."

"I am bloody glad they don't!" Sigfried shot back. "It would be very hard to hide. Just standing here, with my hands in my pockets, doing nothing, I can see the smudge of mud on the shirt of that football player over there. I can see the two kids hiding in the alcove by the far edge of the wall, smoking. Don't they know smoking is bad for them? Lucky, demonstrate!" Up above the towers, Lucky let out a long plume of flame. Below, some of the kids playing soccer stopped and gawked. "And I can see the leaves that have collected in that flat area on the roof that is lower than everything else around it. It would make a good hide-out. But, if someone were up there talking, they would never have any idea that I could see and hear them."

"We have to decide who we are going to tell things to in the future," Rachel confided seriously. "And who we should not share them with."

"We need an Inner Circle!" Siggy declared. "Lucky, you decide. Who's in? Who's out?"

The dragon came diving down to join them. "You should include the members of your harem," Lucky said in his deep gravely voice. "Who's in the harem?"

"Good grief! Enough with the harem!" Rachel sputtered. She kicked her feet, her heels making an indentation in the soft earth. The princess's face had drawn into a moue of distaste.

"Only Valerie is in the harem," Siggy replied stoutly. "I am a one woman man. My philosophy is you remain utterly loyal, until the other person betrays you—then you kill them."

"That could be a bit severe under certain circumstances," the princess stated thoughtfully.

Rachel rolled her eyes. "Can we please stop talking about Siggy and his murderous rages and discuss the matter at hand?"

"I will point out that it is Lucky who brought up harems, not me." Siggy tackled the dragon. The two of them rolled back and forth across the grass, wrestling.

"Lucky!" Rachel glared at him. The dragon broke free and then ducked behind Sigfried, his long scarlet whiskers and serpentine body protruding on either side. Rachel shook her head, amused in spite of her impatience. Sigfried took advantage of the distraction to pin Lucky to the ground.

They debated the topic for fifteen minutes, finally coming to the conclusion that the Inner Circle would consist of the four of them—Rachel, Nastasia, Sigfried, and Lucky—plus Valerie. Rachel would have liked to limit it to those present. For one thing, it was easy for them to get together, as they lived in the same dormitory. For another, she was not sure whether Valerie was repeating everything to Salome, and Salome had not yet been vetted. Sigfried refused to keep information from his girlfriend, however, which Rachel had to admit was admirable. Nastasia pointed out that it was unlikely that Miss Foxx would have arranged her own murder. So, reluctantly, Rachel agreed.

"Okay, we have an Inner Circle. How do we discover the identity of the snitch?" she said.

"Do we need to?" asked Siggy.

"Certainly. Otherwise, we may be excluding people who could otherwise be valuable members," Rachel explained. "The best way would be to give different information to different friends and see what ends up at Drake Hall. Maybe Salome will help us...if she is not the Sneetch...er, I mean snitch...herself." Out of the corner of her eye, she eyed both of them warily. Then, gazing up at the sky, she asked casually, "Do you think we should make up stories and pass them out to different friends? That way we don't have to put any real secrets at risk."

"Great idea!" Siggy grinned. "Can I be in charge of concocting lies? I'll make up some doozies."

The princess's brow furrowed. "That would not be honest."

"True, but if we tell the truth, the enemy will learn our secrets." Siggy countered. "If we lie, the bad guys will get their comeuppance, and we can apologize to our friends later."

"Lying is wrong," The princess spoke firmly. She smoothed out the skirt of her robes. "We must do the right thing at all costs."

"You may be willing to do it at all costs." Siggy lounged against a tree. "Me, I'm only willing to spend forty-nine ninety-five on honesty. After that, I'd rather save my money for something more interesting. Like crossbows. Or frogurt."

"You should not be so frivolous," the princess lectured him, a furrow of concern marring her perfect brow. "Are you not my knight? Did you not swear to serve me? Doesn't that mean you must obey my will?"

"It means I will take orders. Are you ordering me to spill our few remaining secrets to the enemy? If so, can we use your secrets? I'm not keen to have people know mine. Oh wait! Yours already got spilled. So, is it my secrets you are ordering me to spill now?"

They talked on, going in circles. Exasperated, Sigfried said, "If we are going to accomplish anything, we need to agree on our purpose."

"Purpose?" Rachel cried, amazed anyone could even ask such a question. "That's obvious! We're trying to save the world!"

"Of course," Sigfried nodded, "but how? And at what price?"

"Save the world?" The princess arched a lovely eyebrow of her own in obvious surprise. "I thought we were forming a social club."

If the sun had dropped out of the sky, and the princess had punted it across the lawn like an American football, Rachel could not have been more surprised. She would have squawked an objection, but shock paralyzed her vocal cords. Sigfried, too, goggled in astonishment. His jaw flopped open.

Had Nastasia not heard the part about the death of worlds?

Before Rachel could recover, Alexis Romanov came running across the grass toward them, her blond ponytail bobbing. She looked a good deal like her younger sister, only she was just a pleasant-looking young woman, not mind-blastingly, astonishingly gorgeous. Her eyes were so wide with distress that the whites were very prominent. Her face was unusually pale.

"Nastasia! It's Father!" she cried. "He won't wake up! Mother says he was trying to protect you from the being that attacked you. The winged one. He's captured Father! Come quickly, Ivan wants to talk to us, and then we are to go downstairs and call Mother on the Talking Glass!"

Alexis grabbed her sister's hand, and the two princesses ran off. Rachel was left staring after them, sympathy for their plight inhibiting her from giving voice to her outrage at the princess's blindness to their current danger.

CHAPTER TWENTY-EIGHT:
THE UNFORESEEN DANGERS
OF REMEMBERING

LUNCH WAS FOLLOWED BY MUSIC AND FRIDAY'S ONLY FREE PERIOD. Searching the grounds, Rachel found a hunk of granite, too big for her to lift easily, and an unused trash can. Using the *Tiathelu* cantrip, she maneuvered the rock into the garbage can. Slowly, with many breaks, she used the cantrip to waft the can, stone and all, up to her favorite hallway.

She practiced blowing the rock off the table. This proved difficult. She only succeeded once. The wind she could whistle up was not powerful enough. Yet, the fact that she succeeded at all gave her hope. She refused to be daunted, trying again and again and again.

She also practiced lifting and twirling the trash can. It was not as big or as heavy as Cydney Graves, but it was awkward and bulky enough to give her trouble, which was exactly what she wanted. She worked at this diligently, lifting the can and slowly turning it end over end. She had been at this for nearly thirty-five minutes, sweat pouring down her forehead, when something warm brushed against her ankle. Looking down, she was surprised to see the tiny lion.

"Hello, Leander."

The lion rubbed against her leg again. It walked a short distance. Then, it turned and looked over its shoulder at her, gazing up with its large golden eyes.

"You want me to follow you?" Rachel wiped her forehead on her sleeve. "Look, I know you can talk. Can't you just tell me what you want?"

"Come," said the lion in a voice that was much deeper than Rachel expected from such a small frame. "Your friend needs you."

"Which friend? Never mind!" she cried. "Whoever it is, I want to help!"

"Then, come." The lion loped off.

Rachel followed at a run.

The tiny lion darted downstairs, stopping before the Ladies Room. Rachel charged through the door. She ran to a stall from which she could hear crying. The door was ajar.

Inside, Valerie Foxx sat on the floor next to the toilet, sobbing, a paper towel pressed against her nose. Bright red blood dripped over her fingers. A pile of blood-soaked towels lay beside her. The water in the toilet was reddish. Her eyes were bloodshot, and her tears were slightly pink.

Looking up in shock and fear, Valerie started crying even harder.

Rachel's first urge was to drop to her knees and hug her. Before she let herself do this, she looked around the bathroom and thought back a few seconds, searching for a wraith, or the Raven, or anything else not visible to her ordinary sight. She checked the other toilets and the rectangular shower-stall-like area filled with litter for familiars but saw nothing unusual.

Running to the dispenser, she grabbed a handful of toweling paper. Then, she ran back and knelt beside Valerie. Handing her the fresh paper towels, she laid a hand on her shoulder.

"What's wrong? Are you all right? Can I help?"

In between choking and sobbing, Valerie whispered, "I'm the snitch."

"Wha-what? Did someone find out and beat you up?"

"I know it's me." Valerie trembled. "I can't remember doing it, but I did it."

"Wh-what?"

"Someone cast a spell on me, but I don't remember who or how. I went to the Wisecraft Offices in New York City. Mr. Iscariot had arranged for me to meet some Agents—I had a lot of questions about the World of the Wise, and I really admire spies and cops. When I arrived at their office, one of them mentioned I was late. But I wasn't late. I got there early."

"I don't understand," Rachel's heart was pounding in her ears. The smell of blood was making her lightheaded. She pushed her squeamishness aside, concentrating on her friend.

"I remember I got there early on purpose. But I can't..." Blood spurted from Valerie's nose more profusely. "Can't remember what happened between arriving there, and when I met the Agents. I never thought about it afterward, but I should have. Even now, I can tell something is trying to keep me from thinking about it. I feel it pushing in my head. It hurts!" Valerie had been trembling since Rachel arrived. She began shaking harder.

Terror gripped Rachel. Blackness crowded around the edges of her vision. The very idea of something blocking her memory made her chest tighten, and her stomach twist with nausea. But she could not panic now. Valerie needed her. Swallowing with effort, she invoked the outward calm of the girls of the Family Griffin, and forced herself to think clearly. A calmness came over her thoughts, as if she were riding her broom.

"First of all, don't worry about snitching," Rachel instructed her with gentle firmness. "If it was you, and it was because of a spell, it's not your fault. We all love you, and we'll stand with you through this! Second, if trying to remember hurts, don't try to remember!" Those last words nearly stuck in her throat, but she forced them out. "Now we know about the spell. We can figure out how to break it—then you will be able to remember without... pain."

"I... I can't..." Valerie murmured, trembling.

"Okay," Rachel forced herself to keep calm, though her legs were shaking. "We've got to get you to the Infirmary. Can you stand up?"

Valerie did not seem to hear her. Rachel knelt and hugged her. Valerie slumped against her shoulder.

"I think...I...want my mom..." Valerie's eyes rolled up, and she passed out.

Rachel shook her, but the other young woman did not wake. Blood continued to run down her upper lip. She was extremely pale. Her breathing had become raspy and shallow. Valerie's body was pressed against Rachel, nearly pinning her down.

Rachel could feel the other girl's heart racing unnaturally quickly. She gently pushed until Valerie flopped backward, resting against the wall.

Leaping to her feet, she pointed two fingers at her slumped friend. "*Tiathelu!*"

Valerie's unconscious body wobbled into the air. Rachel maneuvered her out of the stall and through the outer door into the hallway. She shouted so loudly her throat hurt, "Help! Someone, help!"

By the time she reached the hall, she was panting. Keeping something so heavy in the air took effort, and she was already tired from her strenuous practice. The blond proctor, Mr. Scott, was coming the other way. When he saw the blood, his face went slack with surprise. He rushed toward Valerie.

"I can help you, Miss Griffin. Sorry, I heard the crying, but I saw you go in and thought it was, well—girls cry in that bathroom a lot."

He pulled the floating Valerie into his arms with ease. Kneeling, he rested her weight on his leg and held her with one arm. With the other, he took her pulse and checked her temperature, placing the back of his hand against her forehead. Concern had driven away any other expression.

He whistled. A tan terrier came tearing around the corner and ran up to him, panting eagerly. Its little pink tongue lolled from its black mouth.

"Spike! Go for help!"

The dog turned and raced away.

Talking mostly to himself, he murmured, "Shock. Low blood pressure, I think. And she's very cold. Did you see what hit her? How long has she been bleeding?"

"I don't think anything hit her, Sir." Rachel spoke rapidly but with great precision. "Someone messed with her memory. What can I do to help? Should I get Nurse Moth?"

"I've already sent my familiar for the nurse. She should be here soon," he said. "Was this young woman awake when you found her? Was she laying on the ground or upright or standing?"

"She was sitting up, and she talked to me. But she had lost a lot of blood. Blood was gushing out of her nose. Like it is now.

And there were lots of bloody paper towels. I don't know how long she had been in there."

"Do you know what caused the bleeding?"

"Trying to remember." A shiver went through Rachel as those words sank in. She tightened her grip on herself. "Someone at the Wisecraft Offices in New York City cast a spell on her last week...I think it might have been the new geas—the one you can't remember being under. She can recall the time to either side of the event. She was trying to make herself remember what happened in between. Trying to fight the geas spell. That started her nose bleeding. But she didn't give up. She kept trying." Rachel's voice broke, full of admiration.

Nurse Moth came flying around the corner on an orange and white Flycycle, carrying a small bag. She leapt off and knelt beside Valerie, clucking with concern. The noise sounded decidedly French when she made it. Pulling her flute from the bag, she knelt beside her patient and began to play. The music was eerie and yet comforting, reminding Rachel of flying her broom through newly-budded leaves with the smell of crabapple blossoms in the air. Green sparkles swirled out of her instrument and passed over Valerie's face. The blood flowing from her nose slowed noticeably.

Lowering the instrument, she murmured, "Miss Griffin, reach into my bag and find the clean cloth. Then dampen it and wipe off Miss Foxx's face for me? Please be gentle, *cherie*."

Eager to help, Rachel found the cloth right away and ran back to the Ladies Room. Turning on the warm water, she thrust it under the faucet. Then, she ran back. Kneeling beside her friend, she wiped the blood from the other girl's face.

Nurse Moth lowered her flute and drew a small crystal vial out of her bag. Unstopping it, she asked Mr. Scott to hold Valerie firmly. An odor both pungent and sweet filled the air, reminding Rachel of currant preserves. Opening her patient's mouth and lifting her tongue, the nurse let a drop of the healing elixir fall from the glass rod attached to the stopper. Valerie's breathing became less raspy. With the nurse's approval, Mr. Scott picked her up and carried her to the Infirmary.

Rachel had remained calm during the emergency. Now that it was over, her whole body trembled. Her legs wobbled. Her hands trembled. She felt like a sapling in gale-strength winds, every leaf and branch shaking. She followed Mr. Scott and Nurse Moth into the brick and columned building that was the Infirmary. Inside, her boots clicked against the green marble. Chimes jingled. The air held the mingled sweetness of sandalwood and the sharp tang of disinfectant. The bright flame-colored curtains swayed in the breeze. While the proctor put Valerie in a bed, Nurse Moth sat Rachel down in a wicker chair near the fountain. She filled a glass with the gurgling fountain water and handed it to Rachel.

Rachel sipped from her glass. It tasted unusually good: crisp, cool, and refreshing. The liquid inside rippled from the unsteadiness of her fingers.

"Um…if you think she is going to wake up soon, I'd like to stay." She looked up plaintively. "Otherwise…could I have a pass to get out of True History. I…think I am too upset to go to class."

"Thank you for your assistance, *cherie.*" The nurse smoothed Rachel's hair, much of which had escaped again and floated wispishly about her face and shoulders. "Why don't you relax here and finish your water. The Proctors may have some questions for you."

A short time later Mr. Fuentes showed up, along with Mr. Gideon, whom the dean had apparently sent for. So much for True History; even her tutor was not in class. The handsome Fuentes winked at Rachel as the two of them crossed to Valerie's bed. She managed a shaky smile back.

The door swung open again, and Jacinda Moth, the Dean of Roanoke Academy, entered the Infirmary. The dean was short and stocky with a shock of ear-length white hair. She moved with purpose and an air of brisk command. Rachel had never met her, but she instantly recognized her. The dean joined the others, and they spoke together in hushed tones.

Rachel sipped her water slowly. She wished Siggy were here with his amulet. Leaning back, she opened the books in her mental library and took out the puzzle piece-shaped clues she kept inside. A few snapped together: Valerie had been geased. That much was clear. If she were really the snitch, then whoever had done this to her knew children in Drake Hall. Was that how Gaius had come to hear about the new geas spell? Was the princess right about him? Did he know who was behind abusing Valerie? Did he know that it had been happening?

The thought made her water slosh.

Breaking away from the group, the dean walked over and squatted down in front of Rachel. "Hello, Miss Griffin. I am Dean Moth. We have not met before, but I know your family. I am sorry to see you in the Infirmary again so soon. The school year is only five days old, and this is your third visit." Her white bushy eyebrows arched upward, giving her blunt, round face an expression of wise inquiry that communicated both kindness and suspicion born of decades of dealing with conniving students. "I cannot help wondering if you are trying to beat the old record set by James Darling for number of visits to the Infirmary in one week."

Rachel giggled slightly. Then, she said haltingly, "Valerie…she wanted her mom. Is there any way to send for her?"

"I will send for her." The dean patted Rachel's arm. "Miss Griffin, we have a few questions for you. Please wait here for now. I can send someone to get your books if you wish."

"O-Okay. I'd rather go…but if you need me, I'll stay."

"I will send for your friends, Mr. Smith and Princess Nastasia, right? Do you know if Miss Foxx spent time with any other students besides the younger Mister Iscariot, Miss Iscariot, and Mister Warhol?"

Rachel's lips parted in surprise. The dean, who had the Upper School and the college to run, had taken the time to discover who her friends and Valerie's were? No wonder Dean Moth was known as the greatest dean alive. A lump formed in Rachel's throat. She struggled very hard not to cry.

"Mr. Smith is her…her particular friend," she said in a very small voice. She hoped she was not getting Valerie into trouble. She was uncertain whether freshmen were allowed to have boyfriends. "Also, she might want her familiar. It's an Elkhound named Payback."

The dean nodded. "Is there anything else I can do for you, Miss Griffin?"

Rachel slid her foot along the floor, her toe tracing a black vein running through the green marble. It took some time to coax her voice to form the words she wanted. Then, she blurted out, "Dean...Ma'am...could you possibly...Could you ask Gaius Valiant to come by? When he's done with class and being tortured by Mr. Von Dread, I mean. I...I have a question I need to ask him."

"Yes, I will ask him to come." The dean looked as if she was going to ask Rachel a follow-up question. Perhaps what a freshman girl from Dare wanted with a senior boy from Drake Hall. Or maybe why Vladimir Von Dread would be torturing a fellow student. Though from the dean's expression, maybe such conduct on Von Dread's part was not particularly new. Whatever it was, the dean thought better of it.

Nodding to Rachel, she left to join the nurse and the proctors. They spoke for a short time. Then, Mr. Scott departed, followed soon after by Mr. Fuentes and Mr. Gideon.

The nurse fretted over Valerie, playing first one song and then another. The music was restful to the ears, the gleaming twinkles beautiful to behold, and the accompanying scent of warm fortifying chicken soup. Sparkles of light the color of sunshine through leaves swirled out of the nurse's flute and surrounded her patient. Rachel associated that particular shade of green with songs her mother had played for her when she had been ill as a child. It brought back comforting memories of being snug in her pink canopy bed surrounded by her stuffed animals, with a cup of warm milk steaming beside her.

She wished she were back in that bed now. Nothing bad ever happened there. Murderers did not stalk young girls. Blood did not spurt all over friends' faces. Bullies did not deform her with magic. Fathers did not let their daughters down. Never. Ever.

Who was she going to tell about all this? What was the use of having a perfect memory to record all the facts, if no one wanted to hear about them? The last thought seemed petty compared to Valerie's troubles, but the wound it left on her heart was deeper than the rest.

A familiar warmth rubbed against her leg. Looking down, Rachel found the tiny lion looking up at her expectantly. Its golden eyes were full of warmth and wisdom. Rachel knelt and hugged the little beast. Comfort radiated off it like heat from a fireplace. Rachel began to cry. Silent tears ran down her cheeks. She wiped them on the Lion. He batted at her nose with his paw.

Rachel rested her forehead on the Lion. The little beast purred like a cat. She could feel its body vibrating, such a glorious, comforting sound. It licked her face once. Its breath was very warm and smelled wonderfully sweet, like honeysuckles after a spring rain. When its rough tongue touched her cheek, the terror holding her chest prisoner unwound, melting away like ice around a spring bulb. Her lips parted in a sign of relief and gratitude.

An image rose up before her mind's eye of the woods beyond Stony Tor, on the far side of the wall of trees that made up the wards of the school. Rising up out of the center of the forest was a gorgeous old tree. It was noticeably taller than the trees around it.

Coming back to herself, Rachel blinked. With a growing sense of wonder, she realized this was her first vision. It was not a journey to another world, like the princess's, but it cheered her and brought an unexpected sense of hope. Rachel petted the Lion's back, all the way to its tufty tail. She rubbed her nose against its cheek. She felt better—until she remembered the question of whether or not Gaius knew about Valerie and the geas spell. Then she felt shaky again.

The Lion spoke in a powerful and calming voice that reached deep inside her and lifted her spirits, even parts that she had not realized had been drooping. "*Even in the darkness, the spirit of humanity burns brightly. When surrounded by evil, the good will show all the greater. If you meet a man, and he is lost, take his hand. Show him the way. You see the path and walk it already. Some just need to hear the sound of their footsteps upon the path to know it is different than the woods.*"

Awe caught away her breath. What a glorious image! But what did it mean? Did the Lion mean that Gaius was evil but could be saved, if she did not give up on him? Or did he mean something else entirely?

The Lion batted at some dust.

The door opened with a jangle, and Gaius arrived, his hands clasped casually behind his back. His gaze fell upon Rachel, sitting on her chair with her glass of water back in her hand, and his cheerful smile faltered. The dean waved him over and spoke with him briefly. Then, he walked over to Rachel, his footsteps echoing, his brow furrowed with concern.

He knelt in front of her and put his hand on her arm. Her skin tingled where his fingers touched her. "What's going on? You look upset. Were you attacked?"

Rachel shook her head solemnly. She looked him steadily in the eye and tried to speak very calmly. "No. I am okay. Gaius... Did you know...when you told me about the new kind of geas...did you know about Valerie?"

He frowned. "Know what?"

"That she was under this spell?"

"No, I didn't know! I swear!"

"Wh-what do you know?"

"I-I just knew that there was some new spell. A more advanced version of the old geas that can control you. I...can't tell you who I heard about it from. I am sorry. But I am almost a hundred percent sure the person who told me did so because he is trying to figure out if anyone was under it. I do not think he knows how to cast it. I also don't think he would cast it if he did... Well, I hope he wouldn't..."

Relief rushed through her like runners in the final meters of a marathon, leaving her weak. She did not bother wondering if he was lying. He looked so sincere and so worried. Rachel had a great deal of experience with people who dissembled, hiding or falsifying their emotions. This boy was not doing that.

He looked over at Valerie lying in the bed. Inclining his head toward Rachel, he whispered, "Is she going to be okay? I don't understand. I hadn't heard that a geas could actually hurt you."

"She tried to remember...tried really hard. When I found her, blood was coming out of her nose...lots of blood. She...she would have died if the little Lion hadn't come and got me."

"Little lion?" He blinked twice. "I don't even know what to think of all this. She must be very clever. I thought geases weren't something you could break yourself. I...am impressed. And confused. And slightly terrified."

"I am glad you told me about it, or I would not have understood what was happening."

"Someone actually cast a geas on a student?" Gaius asked, talking a little too quickly. His voice rose as he grew more alarmed. "Why would they bother? And why on her? Does this mean the people who cast it on her are different than the ones who tried to kill her? Or was it the same people, and they decided she needed to die? Was she no longer of use to them?"

Rachel paused for the space of three heartbeats, breathing deeply in an effort to slow her racing pulse. Should she tell him more? She did not want to betray her friends. Gaius was not an approved member of the Inner Circle, and she was the one who had pushed to have such a thing. On the other hand, no one had yet defined what qualified as an Inner-Circle-Only secret. Anything she told him about Valerie, the nurse and the proctor already knew. That meant it was not a secret, right?

She yearned so much for someone to confide in. Could Gaius be that person? On one hand, he might be evil. On another, the Lion urged her not to cut him—if she understood what the Lion was saying. On the third hand, she liked him. Even if he was evil, she still liked him. In fact, she realized slowly—her gaze resting on his soulful brown eyes, the perfection that was his lips, and the handsome curve of his jaw—she liked him *very much.*

Leaning toward him, until their faces were so close she could feel the heat from his cheek, Rachel whispered, "Valerie visited the Wisecraft offices in New York. She arrived early, but she was late for her appointment with the Wisecraft. What she was trying to remember was what happened in between."

"That's...disturbing."

"It gets worse." Her voice remained calm, but she began to tremble again. "Do you remember what Cydney said at the meeting, that one of my friends was a snitch? Well...Valerie suspects herself. She thinks that she's the snitch, but she can't remember what she did." Contemplating the indignities Valerie had suffered caused her to sway slightly.

Gaius laid a steadying hand on her shoulder. "I...don't understand."

"If Valerie is right," Rachel took another deep breath, "whoever cast the spell gave some kids in your dorm the control words to activate the geas. These kids—Cydney Graves, her friends Belladonna Marley and Charybdis Nott, that girl who cast that engorgement spell on me, Lola Spong, and probably Eunice Chase, too, considering she pinched Cydney for trying to say who the snitch was—have been making Valerie tell them things." Rachel's stomach clenched. Her voice grew louder, shrill. "Someone cast a spell on my friend and turned her mind over to these girls!"

Rachel broke off and wailed loudly.

"Um..." Disconcerted, Gaius let go of her and raised his hands—as if he did not have much experience with wailing girls. Stepping forward again, he awkwardly patted her shoulder. "There, there."

Rachel instantly quieted down, embarrassed. She was a little disappointed the boy had not pulled her into his arms. That was what her parents would have done. The thought of Gaius hugging her caused an entirely new kind of tremble to travel throughout her.

"Um...Sorry."

"Okay, what you just said...is not good," Gaius's entire attention was on what she had told him. He had not even noticed her apology. "Look, there's someone I've got to go tell about this. He...might be able to help. Or at least find out what is going on with the kids in my dorm. I'll be back in five minutes! I promise!" He turned and ran out of the Infirmary and down the path toward his dormitory. Before the door banged, the tiny Lion slipped out as well.

Chapter Twenty-Nine:
The Difficulty of Navigating
Without a Rudder

"YOU DON'T REMEMBER ANYTHING?" SIGFRIED SAT HUNCHED ON THE edge of Valerie's bed, holding her hand.

Lucky hovered above her. His flame-red whiskers twitched in distress. A healing melody issued from the purple and green agates set into the headboard beneath him. Little green sparkles swirled out of the gems and danced around the bed, bringing with them a sense of well-being. The green fire in the glass ball floating overhead flickered merrily.

Beside the bed, Rachel perched on the edge of her chair. Nastasia stood by her shoulder, gazing down with regal concern. Her golden curls waved in the breeze blowing through an open window. On it, Rachel could smell the scent of the wisteria that covered the gym as it mingled with the sandalwood and ubiquitous odor of disinfectant. Overhead, the chimes tinkled, jangling loudly whenever they became entangled with Lucky's long whiskers.

Across the Infirmary, the nurse and the dean talked quietly in one corner, one of the orangey-red curtains half drawn around them. Rachel glanced through the open front door and down the gravel pathway beyond, but there was no sign of Gaius returning. She looked around for a clock and realized she had not checked the time when he left. Had it been more than five minutes? It felt like a year and a half.

Valerie smiled at them blearily from her profusion of pillows. "No, I don't remember. Why am I here? The proctors asked me lots of questions, but they would not tell me anything."

Rachel hunched her shoulders. This seemed to be the trend with the adults, taking information without giving it. The lack of respect offended her innate sense of fairness.

Nastasia turned to Rachel, her face full of inquiry. "You found her. What happened?"

"First...your father. Any word?" Rachel reached up and touched the princess's shoulder lightly. The princess bore the familiarity with patient fortitude. She shook her head.

Rachel filled Valerie and the others in on what had happened.

"Nope." Valerie shrugged. "Don't remember this conversation at all. Are you sure you aren't making this up? Where were we?"

"In...the girl's bathroom on the second floor?"

Valerie squinted and then shook her head. "Sorry."

Rachel rocked her chair back. *Okay, that was terrifying.*

In the silence, the chimes jangled loudly in the breeze.

"Do you think..." Nastasia began, but she never finished. Her eyes rolled back in her head until they were entirely white. Siggy jumped up to support her, but the princess did not fall. Instead, she took a stumbling step forward. Her eyes returned to normal. Rachel rushed to her side and helped steady her, a hand on her friend's shoulder.

"I've..." Her chest rose and fell rapidly. She took a steadying breath. "I've just had a vision...I think. But not like before. I didn't go anywhere. I was right here. I think...it might have been a vision of the future."

"What happened?" Rachel and Valerie cried together.

"I saw Mr. Fuentes, the proctor. He came here, into the Infirmary. His eyes were odd, cloudy. He crossed the room toward us, casting cantrips. Black fire flew from his fingers toward Miss Foxx. Mr. Smith jumped in the way. He..." she gazed at Sigfried, her eyes widening in fear, "ended up on the floor. Not breathing."

"Mr. Fuentes tried to kill me, and Siggy saved me?" Valerie's voice broke on 'kill,' ending in a hoarse whisper.

Nastasia nodded. "I believe so."

Valerie choked out. "And Siggy...died?"

Footsteps echoed on brick. The front door was open. Outside, the handsome Hispanic proctor trotted up the two brick stairs that led to the entrance.

"Princess, should I attack?" Siggy turned to Nastasia, lifting his trumpet.

The princess stared at Fuentes, her face going pale. She looked rapidly around, as if searching for some authority to tell her what to do.

Fuentes strode into the Infirmary, grinning his customary cheerful grin. Rachel's legs tingled with suppressed excitement. She could not see Fuentes's eyes. Were they cloudy? Should she trust Nastasia's vision and risk attacking an adult—an adult she liked? Or play it safe and risk losing Siggy?

Make a decision.

A flick of a flame.

Choose or crash.

Fixing her gaze on the young proctor, Rachel whistled. Blue sparks flew from her mouth and shot toward the young proctor. The sound of it pierced the air, high and crisp. It blended with the blare of Sigfried's trumpet. Siggy raced across the beds, leaping from one to the next in his mad dash for the door. His eyes glittering with eagerness, he blew with all his might, his other hand reaching for his knife.

Rachel could not call up enough wind to knock a rock off a table, but the blast Sigfried Smith produced picked up Fuentes, carried him out the door, and threw him down the two brick stairs. The proctor tumbled backward amidst blue and silver sparkles. He slid along the gravel path, paralyzed.

Despite the roiling waves of trepidation churning within her, Rachel grinned in delight. She had frozen an adult!

Shouting in alarm, the nurse and the dean converged upon him. The princess had been staring at Fuentes. Now, her voice rose sharply. "Wh-what happened?

Valerie tried to rise, but dizziness assailed her. She put her hand out, as if to catch herself, and sank back onto her pillows. Lucky snaked through the air to where Siggy stood by the door, looking out. Rachel ran to join them. Fuentes lay motionless on the gravel walk. His hands were raised in an unfamiliar configuration. His eyes were milky white.

"Why is Carlos back here? I sent him to the City to bring back the Agents," the dean exclaimed, regarding the rigid young man. She turned on them. "Children! What did you do?"

"The princess had a vision that he was going to kill Valerie!" Rachel blurted out. "I think he's geased, too!"

The Dean looked at Nastasia. Her harsh expression softened, revealing the kindly grandmother beneath. Rachel recalled that the dean was a friend of the princess's family. "My child, is this true?"

Nastasia rushed across the Infirmary to join them. "Look at his hands, Dean Moth. That is the same gesture he made in my vision. Is it dangerous?"

The dean knelt down beside Fuentes, who was being fussed over by the nurse, and examined his hands. Blood rushed from her face. "Oh, my."

"That gesture is...bad?" Rachel asked.

"Yes." Dean Moth rose to her feet, brushed off her knees, and frowned down at the supine proctor. "Very bad. I am surprised he knows it. I have never met anyone who knew that particular cantrip who was not a truly black sorcerer."

Rachel stared down at him. "Maybe the villains who hypnotized him showed it to him."

The dean's eyes bore into Rachel. "You know, Miss Griffin, that is a very insightful hypothesis."

Dean Moth gestured. A great golden eagle flew from the roof off toward the gymnasium. There was a rushing sound. Mr. Chanson walked around the corner, smiling his mild, thoughtful smile. "You wanted me, Dean?"

"I don't understand," Nastasia whispered, as they gazed at the fallen proctor who lay like a tumbled statue. She was fumbling with her purse, pulling out her violin. "Why is he in such an unnatural position, as if he were still walking?"

"I paralyzed him." Rachel gazed at her handiwork with satisfaction.

"You?" Nastasia could not have looked more surprised if she had discovered a fish flipping about in her knickers. "Without an instrument? When—when did you learn to do that?"

"Evil Rumor Monger Number One taught me while you were at the YSL meeting," Rachel answered cheerfully. She glanced hopefully down the gravel path toward Drake Hall, but it was empty. Nervously, she shifted her weight back and forth. It had definitely been more than five minutes now. *Where was he?*

Glancing back, she caught an unpleasant expression as it flashed across the princess's face. Then, Nastasia's customary sweet smile returned. Glancing down at Fuentes again, Rachel played back Nastasia's reaction. The dark expression contorting the princess's pretty features was envy. Rachel squirmed. Nastasia had so many gifts; why would she resent Rachel's success?

"Hey! Watch out!" Siggy shouted, pointing toward Fuentes. "It's going to bite him!"

"Bite? Bite what, child?" The dean frowned at Sigfried. "There is nothing there."

The nurse and Mr. Chanson looked around but saw nothing amiss. Rachel, too, glanced this way and that but could not tell what Sigfried referred to.

"No, Dean Moth. I see it, too!" The princess drew her bow across the strings of her violin. A furious blast of wind blew something backwards. Lucky dived after it, fire shooting from his mouth.

Rachel stared in frustration, unable to see what was causing the commotion. Then, she thought back half a minute. In her memory, a black-eared snake had been slithering across the gravel toward Fuentes. It approached closely, flicking its jet tongue at the vein on the proctor's neck. The princess's gust of wind picked it up and flung it end over end along the pathway, where it rolled to a stop at the feet of a furious Dr. Mordeau. In Rachel's memory, the Math tutor's robes appeared to smoke, as if steam were rising from the black cloth. When Rachel stopped remembering back, Mordeau was still there, but her garments appeared normal.

With an angry jerk, Dr. Mordeau gestured with her Fulgurator's wand and knocked Lucky aside. He somersaulted twice, twisted in mid-air, and darted back to wrap around Sigfried. Siggy grabbed him and petted him, scowling petulantly.

A shiver ran up Rachel's spine. Had her friends not pointed the snake out, she would not have known to check her memory. She might not have known about the snake for hours, even days—long after it would have been too late to save Fuentes. Since Nastasia's reaction to her knowing the paralyzing spell had dismayed Rachel, she made the conscious effort to feel gratitude for her friends' keener perception. Envy was unworthy of some-one of her station.

"What is the meaning of this?" The Math tutor strode toward them, fuming. Her eyes narrowed as she regarded Sigfried and the princess. "Why are these students attacking my familiar?"

"My apologies, Melusine," the dean said brusquely. "The children are trigger happy from their recent success. They stopped a proctor who was under a geas. Kept him from harming a student. Apparently, they are now seeing enemies everywhere."

"It was going to bite him!" Siggy yelled, glaring at Dr. Mordeau.

"My familiar is a snake, Mr. Smith. It uses its tongue to sense the world. I sent it to discover what the commotion was about— so I would know how to be of help."

"My apologies," the princess lowered her head, quite contrite. Sigfried continued to glare, looking unconvinced.

Dr. Mordeau strode to the dean's side and gazed down at Fuentes. Displeasure darkened her face like roiling black thunderclouds. She snapped, "How could this be allowed?"

Rachel used a trick her mother had taught her. She gazed at the dean while keeping the Math tutor within sight. When Dr. Mordeau stopped speaking, Rachel glanced down and thought back to when the Math tutor had been speaking. She focused on Dr. Mordeau's face, recorded by her peripheral vision, bringing it to the foreground of her memory. This way, she could study the Math tutor's reactions without Mordeau being aware she was being scrutinized.

Clearly, the tutor was incensed, far angrier than she wished to let on. But was she upset that they had attacked her familiar? Or that they had stopped Fuentes? Rachel could not tell.

"Obviously, no one *allowed* it, Melusine," the dean's voice was firm. "As to how it could happen, I would like to know that myself. Colette, let's move him inside," she said to the nurse. To Nastasia, she added, "Child, if you have another such vision, please tell me immediately."

"I will, Dean Moth," the princess promised.

The nurse and the dean cast the *tiathelu* cantrip together and floated the young proctor into the Infirmary. Mr. Chanson walked beside them. Dr. Mordeau frowned severely. Then she stormed off, her robes flowing about her. As she passed out of the shadow of the trees and through a bright patch of sunlight, Rachel could see the steam coming off her cloak even with her natural sight. She glanced hopefully beyond Mordeau, but no lanky young man with longish chestnut hair hurried down the path toward them. She sighed.

"Look at that! There's blood!" Siggy grinned broadly as scarlet drops fell from the back of Fuentes head. "I got him! He won't attack my girlfriend again! Let's go tell her!"

He ran back to Valerie, who was looking pale, resting against her many pillows. Rachel followed more slowly, her gaze lingering upon Fuentes with concern. She recalled how he had protected her from Cydney and her horrid friends. She hoped fervently that he would be okay. As she watched, Mr. Chanson strapped him to the bed, in case he should wake up still under the influence of evil magic.

The front door banged open. Joy O'Keefe came into the Infirmary. She looked flushed, as if she had just been running. She was grinning foolishly.

"Miss O'Keefe, can I help you?" asked Nurse Moth.

"I think I have a fever," Joy announced. It was the fakest attempt to be sick Rachel had ever seen. Even Ian's purple spots had looked more realistic. Rachel cringed in embarrassment on the other child's behalf.

The nurse took her seriously. "When did this start?"

"This morning." Joy pressed her hand against her forehead and swayed. "I've been feeling ill since breakfast."

"Very well." The nurse waved her toward a bed. "Lay down, I will attend you presently."

Joy chose the bed next to Valerie. She jumped onto the mattress and sat there, her eyes dancing with excitement. Rachel had never seen anyone look so not unwell. Joy leaned toward the others. "So...what's going on?"

"It is dishonest to claim you are ill when you are not." The princess sniffed disapprovingly.

"If I had to wait any longer to find out what was up, I certainly would have made myself sick!" Joy replied. "So...what is going on? Tell me everything!"

"Not to start a new debate, but is Miss Price in the 'Inner Circle'?" Siggy asked, voicing the question that was forefront in Rachel's mind. "If you say it is okay, Princess, I will include her. I am your knight."

"Do you mean Joy?" Rachel asked, her face a placid mask despite her inward qualms. She did not want to share secrets with more people until they identified the snitch for certain. Valerie still had not recalled for certain that she had been the leak. On the other hand, Joy was the princess's friend, and Rachel did not want to interfere in Nastasia's budding friendship. She let out her breath in a silent sigh. "Her last name is O'Keefe. Under the circumstance, it would be rude not to include her."

"Miss O'Keefe, then. Whatever," Sigfried shrugged. "I wasn't paying attention to names. Back when we were all introduced, Lucky and I were busy talking about volcano pits—how to find the kind of place I need to nest and guard eggs. This is, of course, after I bite a mate on the neck and drag her there. He has been filling me in on the grown-up mysteries of life."

"Grown-up mysteries. Volcano pits. Right." Rachel stared at him, her face impassive, her eyes dancing with amusement. It was unlikely that Lucky's version of the mysteries of life were going to do Sigfried much good. She moistened her lips and wisely decided not to interfere.

Valerie and Sigfried began filling Joy in on what had occurred. Rachel glanced surreptitiously at the door for what must have been the four hundred and sixty-seventh time. Pin-pricks of nervousness ran along her arms. Where was that boy? It had been much longer than five minutes. Had he gotten caught up in something? Had he had trouble finding the person he was looking for? Had he intended to come back at all?

He had said he would come back. She would trust him and wait here.

As she listened to her friends, part of her mind wandered off with Gaius, wondering what it would be like when he kissed her again. Would they finally kiss each other? Should she even be encouraging him? Should she be running away? Next time she saw him, she decided, she would ask him if he started the rumor Valerie repeated—that they were boyfriend and girlfriend.

She was pretty sure he had not, but it would make a nice introduction to the topic.

Besides, it would be fun to tease him.

"Miss Griffin," the dean called from where she stood near the fountain.

"Yes, Dean Moth!" Rachel ran to stand before her. Beside them, the healing waters of the fountain gurgled and splashed.

Rachel looked up expectantly. It was a little intimidating to be in the presence of a legend. Dean Moth might be short of stature, but she had stood up to the worst of the worst when everyone else, except for Maverick Badger, had run away. She had battled Morgana Le Fay twice. She had led the students against the armies of the Veltdammerung, and she once single-handedly saved a group of children from a lightning-throwing storm imp. Rachel gazed at her with girlish admiration.

The dean might be short, but she still towered over Rachel. She leaned over until they were eye to eye. "Miss Griffin, I must ask you a question. This new geas you told Mr. Scott about—how did you come to know about it? Who told you?"

Oh, no.

Everything slowed down. The flicker-of-a-flame moment froze, becoming an eternity. Little bolts of electricity leapt along her arms. Her mouth went dry. Rachel had always been an obedient girl. She treated adults courteously. She loved them. She adored them. She wanted them to be happy.

Recently, grown-ups had let her down.

Rachel did not know how to make the decision currently before her. She was rudderless. She needed a person who could tell her whom she should trust, whom she should protect, whom she should betray.

Because she had to betray somebody.

That she understood. Either she must betray Dean Moth, one of the most famous, most respected figures in the World of the Wise—who, despite her great workload, had taken the time to find out who Rachel and Valerie's friends were.

Or she must betray Gaius.

The needle of her loyalty compass spun wildly, unable to find north. Faces of possible candidates for the position of captain of the ship of her soul swam before her. They all clamored in her head, all requested things of her, all asked for something.

Except for Gaius.

Only Gaius had given her information and asked nothing in return. She recalled the intense sense of kinship she had felt when they shared their mutual desire to live in Dee Hall. And the Lion had said…

As recklessly as a diver leaping off a cliff, plunging toward the frothy waves far below, without knowing how deep the sea was or whether rocks lay beneath the surface, she gave her allegiance to Gaius Valiant.

"Miss Griffin?" The dean repeated sternly. "I asked you a question."

Rachel swallowed convulsively. Drawing on courage as great as what must have been required of Dean Moth when she faced Morganna Le Fay, Rachel met the dean's gaze squarely and said: nothing.

The dean frowned severely. "Miss Griffin? Who told you about the geas spell?"

In Rachel's head, the gears of the machine designed to produce dutiful obedience to adults ground against each other. Their pressure weighed heavily upon her resolve, attempting to push her limbs, to work her lips. The desire to succumb, to submit, to answer, was nigh overwhelming. But she did not wish to lie to the dean, and she knew that if she started talking, she would not be able to stop. Silence was her only other option.

Grinding her teeth together, as if enough pressure upon them could break through the invisible resistance that oppressed her, Rachel fought the internal force attempting to compel her. She pictured Gaius very clearly in her mind. She reminded herself of how cheerfully he had removed the orange juice from her soaking robes. She remembered how he smelled when he stood close to her, like clean soap. She recalled how he had leaned toward her, smiling, as he murmured, "Have a good evening, Rachel."

She did not answer the dean.

It was the hardest thing she had ever done in her life.

The dean pressed her lips together until they became as thin as a pencil line. She turned away, disgusted.

Moments ago, that would have broken Rachel's heart; now her spirits leapt in victory. She had done it. She had faced the hardest trial of her thirteen years and triumphed. She had kept Gaius safe.

Rachel returned to where the others were talking quietly. She felt dazed and astonished. She had not even realized it was possible not to answer an adult. She had never tried anything like that before. Nastasia nodded to her kindly and walked over to where the dean stood talking to the nurse. She and the dean stepped aside.

Siggy leaned over and whispered in Rachel's ear. "Nastasia is telling the dean that as a friend of the family, she feels her loyalty to her must be greater than her loyalty to her new friends, however much she likes us. She is saying that she thinks the person who told you about the geas was an older student from Drake named Gaius Valiant."

Jagged pain cut through Rachel, as if a buzz-saw were shredding the lining of her stomach. She could even hear its revving scream in her mind's ear. How had Nastasia known that? Rachel had not told her.

Oh. Mentally, she slammed her head against a wall, groaning. She had told her friends that an older student had told her about the geas. Then she introduced them to Gaius at breakfast. Also, Nastasia had seen her leave with him the night before. She had even gone out of her way to tell Rachel that Gaius was wicked.

All the effort Rachel had made to protect him from betrayal; all that resisting of the turning of the gears of obedience; all that disappointing the world's most heroic Sorceress. All for nothing. Rachel felt as bleak as frozen winds sweeping across an arctic wasteland.

The princess joined them again. Rachel kept her face calm, as if she was unaware of the princess's betrayal. The knowledge of it, however, caused a sensation in her chest much like what Velcro must feel like when it was torn from its soulmate strip.

"So," Joy leaned toward Rachel, her eyes dancing with her eagerness, "Is it true that you are dating an older boy from Drake?"

"He's not my boyfriend!" Rachel shrieked. She waved her hands about as if to push the rumor away, her cheeks aflame.

"O...kay." Joy drew back. "Sorry I asked."

Nastasia opened her mouth to speak, but her eyes rolled up, going white again.

"Princess!" Joy leapt forward.

Rachel grabbed Joy's arm, holding her back. "Don't disturb her. She's having a vision."

They waited, tensely. This vision was longer than the last. Then, Nastasia's eyes returned to normal. The color drained from her face. "Dean Moth! I...I had another vision. Quick! Dr. Mordeau must be stopped! All of Drake Hall is under the sway of the new geas! Dr. Mordeau is about to take control of the Thaumaturgy students and send them out to commit a massacre!"

Chapter Thirty:
Visions of Evil Tutors
Dancing in Our Heads

ALL OF DRAKE HALL? RACHEL'S HEART STAMPEDED THROUGH HER chest. Gaius, too?

"Vision? What... Wait!" Dean Moth turned to Mr. Chanson, "Roland, bring my Thinking Glass! It's in the closet attached to my office."

"Back in an instant!" Mr. Chanson promised. There was a rush and a boom. Mr. Chanson was back, carrying an antique mirror framed in gold filigree. The Glass had a gold tint to it.

"See," Sigfried whispered, jabbing his finger repeatedly at the P.E. tutor. "I told you he could move super fast."

"Wow," Rachel mouthed back, gazing at the spot where Mr. Chanson was, wasn't, and then was again. The event momentarily distracted her from her fear for Gaius.

"What's that thing?" Sigfried turned his head sideways. "A looking glass?"

"No, a Thinking Glass," Joy replied.

"Thinking Glass?" Siggy asked. "What does it do?"

Rachel answered absently, her fear returning. "Lets you show other people your memories—if you know how to activate it. Father says they are tricky."

"How useful!" Valerie gawked at the mirror. "Can you imagine how helpful that would be in identifying suspects?" She frowned, her lips forming a thoughtful pout. "Why didn't they pull it out the first day and ask you all what the perp who tried to kill me looked like?"

"It's not very useful for law enforcement purposes," Rachel explained, "because you only see what the person pictures in their head. But yeah…I guess it would be useful for something like that…especially if I were the one doing the remembering."

"Why would it be better for you?" Joy asked.

Rachel blushed. She had forgotten that Joy did not know the secret about her memory. So far as she knew, Valerie did not either. She would rather keep it that way. She ignored the question.

Dean Moth crossed to join them, accompanied by Mr. Gideon and Mr. Tuck, who had just arrived. The dean performed a cantrip in front of the mirror. She drew all her fingertips together, making the same gesture Siggy had used to produce the skunk, and pointed from the princess to the mirror.

"*Oré!*" The dean commanded firmly. "Very well, Nastasia, Dear. Come here and touch the surface. This only shows what you recall, but often if a memory is fresh, the details will be fairly accurate."

Fresh? Accurate? What happened in other people's minds when their memories faded? The thought was jarringly disorienting.

The princess walked forward. The other children followed. Even Valerie got up and moved awkwardly toward where the mirror was propped against a wall. Siggy put an arm around her to support her. She smiled and leaned her head on his shoulder.

Nastasia lay her palm on the Glass. Images formed in the mirror. *Dr. Mordeau strode across the Commons, a dark scowl on her face.* The figure looked like Dr. Mordeau, and yet there was something about the image, the coloring of the sky, the shape of the buildings, that reminded Rachel of Nastasia. The effect was disturbing.

The Math tutor approached a group of students from Drake Hall. Her voice, speaking from the mirror, sounded like her but with an Australian inflection, apparently added by the princess's memory. *"Children, you will go and gather the following people for me: Eunice Chase, Magdalene Chase, Cydney Graves, Duryodhana Patel, Nazir Neferet, Mark Williams, Maleficent Rowley, Jasmine Grimaldi, Medea Volakov, Remus Starkadder, Jonah Strega, Heidi Arndt, Taka and Yuki Ishazuka, and Kremhild Schmitt. Tell them to report to your common room immediately. Even if they are in class."* The students ran off.

The scene shifted. Dr. Mordeau walked across the stone bridge that spanned the moat around the impressive edifice of Drake Hall. The solid granite dormitory had narrow windows, columns, odd square pillars that rose above the height of the roof, and a clock below its bell tower. Majestic stone lions flanked the wide stairs leading to the front door. One sat vigilantly. The other lay sleeping, its paws crossed.

Dr. Mordeau entered the dorm, swept down a curving staircase, and strode through a brick hall to the common room. Dark blue drapes blocked the small high windows. A dark blue rug covered the floor. There were two fireplaces, though no fire burned, sturdy yet elegant leather and oak furniture, and book-shelves between the curtains. A few students sat in armchairs, studying.

Dr. Mordeau strode in, wand in hand, a bone-white length with a tip of polished jet. She swept it across the room without saying a word. The tip glowed with a purple light. The students in the room stopped moving. Their eyes took on a dull look. Two of them had the same milky eyes as Fuentes.

Dr. Mordeau instructed them, "Wait here quietly."

They all waited.

The scene shimmered again. *The common room was now filled with children.* Rachel recognized Eunice and Cydney. *Magdalene Chase was the last to arrive. She clutched her porcelain doll, looking nervous.*

Dr. Mordeau said in a commanding voice, "Listen Carefully: Ve Vargo Derenti."

The students straightened. Their eyes glazed over white, except for two of the students. One was an older blond boy with bloodshot eyes. When the Math tutor spoke the words that activated the geas, he laughed out loud, harshly. Mordeau looked at him fondly and smiled.

"It is time, then?" he asked.

She nodded. He drew a wand from his robes, also bone-white but with a blood-red tip, and stalked out of the common room.

The other student who did not immediately succumb was tiny Magdalene Chase. Her eyes clouded and unclouded repeatedly. She pressed her hand against her forehead and moaned softly. A trickle of blood began to run from her nose. Dr. Mordeau turned and glanced at her. The Math tutor rolled her eyes. Then she casually pointed her wand at the tiny girl. A jagged bolt of black fire shot from the jet tip, striking Magdalene. Her eyes un-clouded, and she looked at the hole forming in her chest, shocked. Then, she collapsed, striking the floor face first.

Rachel screamed, pressing her fingers against her mouth in shock. Mr. Chanson laid a comforting hand on her shoulder.

In the mirror, the blond young man returned carrying a long ugly knife. He was smiling in an alarming manner.

Dr. Mordeau nodded at the gathered students. "Children, go forth and kill every student who does not carry a wand. I put the necessary spells into your gems. Merely paralyze the other Thaumaturge students. We can use them. This I Com—"

The back door to the common room banged open. Vladimir Von Dread stepped into the common room. Behind him were William Locke and Gaius Valiant. All three held their wands ready.

The dean's mouth narrowed, as if in disapproval. The nurse clucked in dismay, murmuring something about reprobates. Mr. Tuck and Mr. Gideon looked alarmed. Even Mr. Chanson frowned.

Rachel's heart attempted to drill its way through the armor of her ribcage. Had Gaius lied to her about not knowing about the geas? Had he known what was happening all along? Was he a willing servant of Dr. Mordeau? The dean obviously thought so. But, if so, why did he and the other two boys look so grim and resolute, as if they were going to their deaths?

Dread raised his arm until the sapphire on the end of his wand pointed at Mordeau's heart. Beside him, Gaius and William Locke leveled their wands at Mordeau as well. Dread's voice rang out, calm yet as unbendable as iron. "Doctor, I cannot allow you to use my students in this manner. Release them immediately, or suffer my wrath!"

The rush of relief made Rachel lightheaded. So Gaius was not Mordeau's lackey. Good for him. Beside her, the dean's moue of disapproval turned into a tiny smirk. Her left eyebrow arching up with wry amusement, Dean Moth murmured, "His students?"

Dr. Mordeau opened her mouth and screeched so loudly that it sounded like a roar. "Children! Kill them!"

Everyone began casting at once.

The scene shimmered again. It was still the common room in Drake Hall, but most of the students were standing like statues or lying face down on the floor. There were huge scars along the walls. One book case was ablaze. Gaius Valiant lay on his back, open-eyed and not breathing. William Lock lay on his face. He did not seem to be moving either.

Stark terror gripped Rachel, squeezing the breath from her lungs. Gaius lay motionless on the floor, dead. She had just elected to make him her most favorite person. Now he would die.

He could not die yet! She had not even had time to decide if she wanted him as her boyfriend.

Dread sat on the ground, breathing heavily, his back to a bookcase that was not on fire. Deep gashes slashed his body. Where his right arm should have been, he grasped a stump. Dr. Mordeau stood over him, her wand pointed straight between his eyes.

He spoke very calmly, his voice deep and resounding. "Victory is yours. Now you must slay me, for, otherwise, I will destroy you." Though her stomach churned with fear, Rachel could not help admiring Dread's resolve.

In the mirror, *Dr. Mordeau nodded curtly. "It is a shame, really."*

Black flame erupted from her wand.

The mirror went dark.

Rachel grabbed the dean's arm, her voice trembling. "The last vision took a couple of minutes to happen. We can still save them, right? Please!"

"Roland, guard the way to the common room in Drake!" The dean ordered, shooting Rachel a severe frown. A blur and a blast of wind, and Mr. Chanson was gone.

Relief flooded over Rachel for the second time. She let go of the dean's arm. Mr. Chanson would save Gaius. He would make sure everything was all right.

The dean continued, "Archimedes, I need you to go to the City. Bring back James Darling and Scarlett MacDannan. Of all the Agents, Darling is the one most likely to not be geased. I don't want to send you, as I fear it will be dangerous—that's where Miss Foxx got into trouble—but we need to break these geases. We cannot do this ourselves. Darling knows how. Be careful."

Mr. Gideon gave the dean a slight, wry grin, "If I come back without Darling and MacDannan, shoot first, ask questions later."

The dean nodded. The True History tutor departed at a run.

"I'll go with him." Mr. Tuck headed after him.

The dean shook her head. "No, Hieronymus. With Fuentes down, we have only Sanders, Stone, and Scott. Maverick Badger is off campus, picking up his wife, and Coal Moth is not back yet from summer vacation. I want you to gather the students who are in the White Hart Alliance. Pull them from their classes and put them on guard duty."

The White Hart Alliance! Rachel had heard whispers of the secret society devoted to protecting the World of the Wise. She knew little of the Alliance. Her parents were members, but they did not speak of it. She did know the story of the White Hart—how two brothers went in different directions hunting the legendary beast. They left their daggers in a birch tree. When one dagger rusted red as blood, the owner of the other knew his brother was in danger and went to save him. The heraldry of the White Hart Alliance was two daggers protruding from a tree, one whole, one rusted.

Mr. Tuck nodded. "I will collect them. There are five at the moment, right? Crispin Fisher's daughter, Marta, Agravaine Stormhenge, John Darling, and the orange-haired lass, Debussy. I can never remember who the fifth is."

A tiny thrill passed through Rachel at the mention of John Darling's name. She frowned, suddenly feeling oddly disloyal to another boy.

"It's Romanov, the crown prince," said the dean. Nastasia started.

"Ivan. Of course." Mr. Tuck nodded and departed. The dean and the nurse stepped over by the unconscious Fuentes and whispered together.With a start, she recognized the students they had just listed as the names from her father's letter.

"What are they saying?" Rachel asked Sigfried.

"Who cares!" Sigfried hissed back. "This is our chance. Nastasia, show Valerie the man who came looking for her."

The princess straightened and nodded, looking wan but lovely nonetheless. She lay her hand on the mirror again. An image of the false agent appeared, smiling blandly as he held out the white box that had contained the scarab brooch. The image looked something like him. It was wavy and unfocused; however, and so many details were wrong. Seeing the discrepancies made Rachel feel slightly nauseous. Nastasia removed her hand from the mirror.

Valerie's eyes grew big. "But...that was Mortimer Egg! He's a desk clerk. The guy who signs you in at the Wisecraft building."

"There's a boy in our class named Mortimer Egg," Rachel said. "Is this his father?"

"Why would a desk clerk want to kill you?" Joy asked. "Why would a desk clerk want to kill anyone?"

"Criminals come in all forms," Valerie assured her.

The princess frowned slightly and glanced over at the dean. "How negligent of the school to employ a Math tutor who is wicked."

"At least we know now," Rachel said fiercely. "Can you imagine what would have happened if Valerie had not remembered something and forced Mordeau's hand? She could have continued her evil all year. Instead, we found her out in the first five days!"

"Thanks to Valerie," Siggy gave his girlfriend a big grin. She leaned her head against his shoulder.

"I hope these first five days are not a reflection of what the rest of the year'll be like." Valerie tried to smile but fear warred with humor on her pale face. "Not sure I can keep up with this breakneck pace."

"Fear not, Milady," Sigfried vowed. "It will be my pleasure to rescue you every Friday!"

The dean crossed to where they stood, her face severe. "I am going to see that Dr. Mordeau is apprehended. I want you children to wait here. Do you understand me? Stay here!" She turned on her heels and set off for the door at a brisk pace.

Rachel ran after her. "Please! Let us come, too. Let us help."

The dean turned on her, scowling. "You can help by staying here. Out of harm's way."

Rachel slumped back to where the others stood. Her heart hammered with fear for Gaius. She hated being stuck here, unable to help. Then she straightened. Being stuck here could not keep her from figuring things out. The puzzle pieces that made up their current situation began whirling through her mind again, approaching each other, looking for bits that snapped together.

Frowning thoughtfully, she asked, "Does anyone know who the blond boy with the bloodshot eyes was? The one with the huge knife?"

Lucky spoke up from where he was wrapped around both Sigfried and Valerie, his head resting on Siggy's shoulder. "That's Mordeau's kid. The one who she lets pet people."

"Eww!" cried Joy.

"Does anyone know his name?" Rachel asked.

The princess touched the mirror. The boy appeared again, grinning his disturbing grin.

Joy tapped the edge of the mirror. "I know him. He's Jonah Strega."

"Oh." Rachel whispered. "Oh no."

"Why?" The others looked at her.

"Because Evil Rumor Monger #1 told me that he saw Jonah Strega talking to Valerie, but Valerie did not remember."

"Wait," Siggy's voice had gone oddly tight. "That guy Strega talked to my girlfriend? Did he do anything more than…" But his voice trailed off, because Valerie was holding her head and making a soft, horrible keening noise.

"I…I did speak to him. Or at least I decided to go talk to that boy. But what happened after that…I don't remember."

Sigfried pulled out his Bowie knife and stabbed the image of the blond boy in the mirror. The shiny blade making a *klunk-slick* noise as it slid across the Glass.

"I've found him. He is heading across the Commons for the building with the moat and the lions." Siggy's hand rested on his chest, where Rachel knew the amulet hung.

"That's Drake Hall," said Rachel. "I think he lives there."

Siggy's voice was unusually calm. "Lucky? Any reason he should live?"

The dragon growled, "So we can hear him scream?"

"Okay, we'll keep him alive for…" Sigfried faltered, his eyes bulging. "Oh no! I can see Mordeau! She's got her snake around her shoulders, and it's made her invisible, too! She just walked right by Dean Moth. The dean did not see her. Do you know that Mordeau's robes have steam coming off them in the sunlight?"

"That's probably why her classroom has curtains." Valerie murmured. "Um...I'm not feeling so well. I think...I am going to lie down." She stumbled back to her assigned bed, blood trickling down her lip again. Siggy went with her, with Lucky flying beside them, butting Valerie encouragingly with his snout.

Rachel asked, "Where is Mordeau going?"

"She is heading for Drake Hall," Siggy called back.

"No!" cried Rachel. All her fears for Gaius assailed her again. Her heart was beating so hard that she feared it would break out of her chest and fly off to help him without her.

"Do not worry. Mr. Chanson is there," Nastasia assured them.

"But...Mr. Chanson couldn't see the snake!" Rachel cried. "He won't be able to see Dr. Mordeau, either. She'll walk right up and kill him!" Her heart ached for the handsome athletics tutor. Turning to Siggy, she said, "Quick! Send Lucky! Warn him!"

Running to the open window, she put her hand out and cried, *"Varenga, Vroomie!"* It was a long shot, but she had left the window to her room open for just this purpose. According to what she had read about the cantrip, theoretically, this should work.

Halfway to the door, Sigfried paused and turned to Nastasia. "Confirm the order, Princess. Also, your knight requests permission to accompany Lucky to his fate. One familiar cannot hold off an experienced Sorceress."

The princess frowned, her perfect, pale brow contorting. "The dean told us to wait here."

"Go! Quickly!" Rachel shouted, furious with Sigfried for not acting immediately and with the princess for hesitating. "Don't you understand? The dean didn't know Dr. Mordeau could turn invisible. If we don't act, they are all going to die. Mr. Chanson! The students!"

And Gaius.

Siggy said, "Let's all get in the Princess's purse. Lucky can fly us to Drake Hall."

"Excellent idea!" Rachel cried. Her broom whooshed in the window. With a cry, she snatched it from the air and leapt on. "Jump in the purse, and I'll carry you. We've got to save them! Who's coming with me?"

Chapter Thirty-One:
Dire Occurrences at Drake Hall

Rachel sped across campus. The wind whipped through her hair, waving it like a war banner. Ahead of her, a stone bridge spanned the moat around Drake Hall, a massive and stark edifice of gray granite. Rachel bent low over her handlebars, her gaze locked on the heavy doors as she sped toward them at tremendous speed. Bracing herself with her feet, she let go and gestured with her hands.

"*Libra!*"

The doors trembled but did not open.

"*Libra!*"

Again, the thick oak trembled but did not swing open. The building rushed toward her, growing dangerously close. She thought of slowing, but the image of Gaius lying motionless on the floor hung before her. He was not going to die because she held back.

Rachel tugged the princess's purse out of her lower pocket and pointed the opening at the dorm. "Siggy! Open the door!"

"Rachel, slow down!" Joy's voice cried in fear.

"Open the door!"

"Slow down!"

"No!" Rachel shouted. The stone bridge flashed by beneath her. Only the stairs and the landing remained. "Open the door! As in with a cantrip!"

"But we're going to hit..."

Sigfried voice boomed, "*Libra!*"

The entrance flew open with tremendous force. The edge of the swinging door came directly toward them. In the bag, Joy screamed. Rachel did not so much as twitch. A three-dimensional diagram of the motion of the door and the trajectory of her broom sprang into her mind. It showed an inch and a half of leeway. Plenty of room.

She barreled forward at full speed. The tip of her broomstick missed the edge of the swinging door by an inch and three-quarters. The heavy oak of the door struck the stone of the building with a reverberating *krong.*

Rachel shot through the opening and into the dorm. Students thronged the foyer. She soared upward, bent low over her broom so as to fly above them. The breeze from her passing sent square black caps flying, tassels aflutter. She darted over the heads of some taller students, her foot brushing the hair of a tall girl with elegant bearing, who screamed. Then, she was speeding down the stairs, following Dr. Mordeau's path from the princess's vision.

The staircase led to a large brick chamber where four narrow corridors converged. Four thick pillars supported the vaulted roof. The odor of wood smoke permeated the air. The will-o-the-wisp globes were dim and far apart, filling the room with thick shadows. Rachel dismounted and let her friends out of the princess's purse. Her ears strained, but the thick stone muted all outside sound.

"Where is Mordeau?" she whispered to Sigfried, as he shimmied out of the opening in the handbag. Lucky swooped out beside him, his tail *swishing* through the air. Behind him, the Princess prepared to climb out, violin tucked under her chin.

Siggy paused, head cocked, and then said, "Around the corner of the corridor on the left, heading for Chanson."

"We've got to stop her," Rachel cried. Fear raised its smoky head, trying to cloud her thoughts. Rachel let her mind go calm and clear, as if she were flying.

Siggy turned to Nastasia. "Princess, there are two ways to get to that corridor. Straight through here on the left, or go down that last corridor and take two right turns. What would you like me to do?"

The princess's face went pale. She looked around at the brick room, confused and uncertain. "Um..."

"She just cast a spell at Chanson. He's petrified," Siggy reported what his amulet showed him. "She's about to do something else to him."

"How do you know all this?" Joy asked confused, struggling to get free of the purse.

There was no time to wait for Nastasia to make up her mind. People could die.

"Siggy, I am going after Mordeau." Rachel ran down the corridor Siggy had pointed out. "If I don't petrify her, at least I will distract her. Sneak around the other way and free Mr. Chanson with the Word of Ending cantrip. Leave Lucky here. He can tell me when you're ready."

"No! She will kill you!" Joy cried.

The thought that she might die did not frighten Rachel. It did not even disturbher. She looked back and met Siggy's gaze. Their eyes locked. Something burned in his eyes, something hotter than mere anger. An understanding passed between them, a mutual resolve. He nodded. Rachel nodded back. Sigfried ran off, down the other corridor. Rachel cast the *bey-athe* cantrip. When the crystalline shield glittered like a heat shimmer before her, Rachel moved to the corner.

"Okay. He's ready," Lucky whispered a moment later.

Rachel winked at the dragon. Stepping forward, she locked her gaze on the Math tutor, and whistled. Dr. Mordeau stood before Mr. Chanson, who sat slumped over in front of a doorway. The Math tutor spun and gestured with her Fulgurator's wand. She caught Rachel's spell and sent the stream of blue sparkles back down the corridor. The rebounding spell shattered Rachel's shield and hit her, freezing her in place.

She stood in the center of the hallway, exposed.

"How fitting," the Math tutor drawled, her voice deep and husky. She gazed at Rachel as if she were a curio in some pathetic amusement. "Your father destroyed mine. And now, I shall destroy you. How deliciously ironic."

Oh! That was why Mordeau hated her father! Rachel thought about the earred snake. Dr. Mordeau must be the daughter of the Serpent Master, one of the chiefs of the Morthbrood captured by Agent Griffin and his then partner, James Darling.

Mordeau raised her wand. Behind her, Sigfried shouted, "*Obé!*"

Mr. Chanson stirred. Faster than flickering flame, he slammed into Dr. Mordeau. The two of them went sprawling across the hallway. Siggy cheered. Rachel stood absolutely still, unable to move, her mouth still pursed as if to whistle.

From her position, Rachel could see both Mordeau wrestling with Chanson and the chamber where she had left her broom. The princess stood there, immobile. Her eyes darted this way and that, as if uncertain how to make a decision. Joy looked to her expectantly, waiting for Nastasia to tell her what to do next. As the two tutors struggled, Mordeau tore off her outer robe and threw it down the hall. The black cloth writhed and broke apart into dozens of sinuous shadows. Mordeau shouted, "Spread out. Find students with wands. Possess them. Use the wands to kill the others."

The shadows rushed by Rachel and up the stairs. Joy stared, open-mouthed. Pulling herself together, the princess took Joy by the hand and hurried down the corridor toward Rachel.

Siggy leapt and cheered, urging Mr. Chanson on. Rachel thought of fifty things she would like to do, or say, or suggest Sigfried do, but she could not move her paralyzed lips. Frustrated and impatient, she occupied her time by playing back her memory of the last few seconds. In her mind, Mordeau's black snake slithered down the hallway, heading directly for her. It glided over the square bricks that made up the floor, its black tongue flickering, its feather-like ears twitching.

Rachel willed herself to shout, to squawk, to squeak, but no sound emerged. She willed herself to move, to jump, to run, but no limb stirred. She willed herself to cast a cantrip, to whistle a wind, to do anything whatsoever, but no change occurred.

She was frozen, as helpless as a tree before a chainsaw.

The snake moved toward her. Remembering back, she broke the Obscuration that kept it hidden. She could see it coming for her. She stared at it, hypnotized, unable to close her eyes or look away. The snake hissed. It drew its head back, preparing to strike. Her heart beat quadruple time.

Thweeeek. The screech of bow on string cut through the silence. Princess Nastasia stood beside Rachel, her long golden curls blowing around her, her violin tucked beneath her chin. Twirling silver sparkles lifted the snake and threw it down the hallway. As the snake slid backwards, Lucky swept by and leapt on it. The two serpents rolled over and over, wrestling.

The princess tried the Ending cantrip on Rachel; then Joy tried. Neither of them pronounced it correctly—even though Sigfried had just used it. Rachel sighed mentally. It was so obvious to her. She had heard it once. She would never forget it. Apparently, it did not work that way for other people.

Mr. Chanson pinned Dr. Mordeau down. She squirmed but could not break free. Relief spread through Rachel. It was over. The villain had been captured. Gaius was safe.

Mordeau's body began to swell. She grew larger and blacker until the woman was gone, and a dragon rose in its place. Not a slender ribbon of a dragon, like Lucky, but a huge, scaly, black monstrosity that breathed out a gout of orangey-yellow flame seven feet long.

Oh no.

The dragon's fire smelled like rotten eggs. Rachel wanted to cough or pinch her nose, but she could not. She wondered how she continued to breathe when her chest did not move.

"Ace!" Siggy shouted. "I *knew* people could turn into dragons!"

Mr. Chanson leapt to his feet and barreled into the dragon at full speed. The orangey flames curled over his body. Not so much as a hair got charred. Rachel suspected that the rest of them would not fair so well, if the fire struck them. Who was Mr. Chanson? Or rather, what was he? How did he do what he did? He was fast as a flame, strong as a giant, and tough as a troll. Yet, she had yet to see him cast a single spell.

He was strong but not strong enough. He strained to lift the creature, but fifty feet of sinuous muscle and shiny black scales proved too much. The dragon lunged forward and grabbed Chanson in its mouth. He must not have made an appetizing morsel, however, because it spit him out again. He flew backward, landing sprawled. The dragon's tail lashed, slamming him into the wall so hard that he left a Mr. Chanson-shaped hole in the bricks.

Siggy gawked. "He went through the earth, under the moat and came up on the grass above. That's over a hundred and fifty feet!"

"Is he...dead?" Joy squeaked.

"Nope. He's moving. Has a pretty big bump on his head, though."

"Mr. Chanson must be relying on more of the new magic." The princess grabbed Rachel and began dragging her toward the corner. "He was knocked through fifty yards of rock earth and survived? There is nothing like that in the history books."

"Not even in True History?" Sigfried asked. To Rachel's surprise, his voice sounded right nearby. Apparently, he had come back after freeing Mr. Chanson.

Lucky's voice called, "Uh...Boss? The snake just bit me. Is that...bad?"

The great black dragon turned its head toward them.

Joy ran. Siggy took Rachel from the princess, swung her up over his shoulder, and lugged her around the corner. He set her down in the side corridor that led back toward the chamber with the staircase. Then he rushed back to check on Lucky.

Her nose itched. Her eyes felt dry. Her view consisted of six bricks.

"Nastasia? What are you doing here? I told you to stay in the Infirmary!" Dean Moth's voice echoed in the hallway.

"Mordeau turned invisible. She was about to kill Mr. Chanson!" Joy cried.

Nastasia nodded. "It is as Miss O'Keefe has stated. We knew that Mr. Chanson had not been able to see her snake. We feared for his life."

"I see," The dean snapped, annoyed. "Stay here!" As if an afterthought, she added, "*Obé.*"

Rachel's body sagged. She gasped, air rushing into her lungs. Turning, she took two running steps after Dean Moth, but the dean had stepped in front of the great dragon. She carried no wand, but lifting her hands, she began to chant.

Rachel bounced on her toes, wanting to call her back, to warn her about Dr. Mordeau's cloak and the danger to the other students. It was too late. Their duel had begun. Golden bands of light flew from the dean's hands, one after another. They encircled the dragon, who breathed fire back up the hallway. Dean Moth gestured again, and the fire curled around her without touching her. But the dragon had already broken the first few bands and was lumbering down the hallway. The hair on the back of Rachel's neck stood up. She had never heard of anyone breaking Glepnir bonds.

"We have to do something!" Rachel cried.

"The dean said to remain where we are," Nastasia reminded her sternly.

"But...we didn't tell her about the shadows!"

"Shadows?" The princess asked. "You mean the dark shapes that rushed by?"

"They came out of Mordeau's cloak. She sent them to possess students and kill people," Rachel said. "We've got to warn someone."

"The dean told us to stay here," Nastasia repeated.

The machinery of obedience clanked and strained in Rachel's head. The dean did not know that students were about to be killed, the same way she had not known that Dr. Mordeau could turn invisible. Surely, if she had known, she would have wanted people to be warned. It did not make sense to obey orders given by someone who did not know the situation, especially if the results would be that children died.

In her imagination, Rachel reached over to the lever that turned the crank of obedience-to-adults and removed the screws fastening it in place. The lever turned, but no gears moved. For the first time in her life, she felt free from the constraints of grown-ups.

Rachel grabbed her broom. "I am going to warn everyone."

"You can't. The dean said to stay here," Nastasia repeated firmly.

"And I am going after Chanson!" Sigfried called running down the other hall again, the one that would bring him out on the far side of the battle between the dean and the dragon.

"No, Sigfried!" Nastasia ordered. "I order you not to go, Mr. Smith!"

From where she balanced on her toes at the corner, Rachel could see Sigfried crawling into the tunnel Chanson's body had left behind, Lucky draped around his shoulders. So far as she could tell, Lucky was all right despite his evil snake bite. The body of the eared snake lay charred on the bricks.

Siggy did not pause when Nastasia called him.

Rachel raced back to the brick antechamber and jumped on her broom. "I'll be back!"

CHAPTER THIRTY-TWO:
THE MIDDAY RIDE OF RACHEL GRIFFIN

"ALARM! ALARM! ALARM!" RACHEL SHOT ACROSS THE COMMONS, shouting. "Beware! Alarm!"

Classes were in session, but the weather was beautiful, with a too-blue sky and a mild breeze that smelled of new autumn leaves. Many of those who had an open period, and perhaps a few who were supposed to be in class, had chosen to study on the lawn. Rachel rushed pell-mell, shouting and hardly looking where she was going. She nearly flew headlong into a peacock, whether a pet of the school or someone's familiar, she did not know. The creature screamed, an eerie, ear-splitting sound that reminded Rachel of a child yowling for help. This startled the other students and made them look Rachel's direction.

"Alarm! Mordeau's gone crazy!" She shouted. "She is sending the Thaumaturgy students to kill everyone! Alarm!"

Students gawked at her. A few started to laugh. Eunice Chase pulled out her Fulgurator's wand and fired a blast of greenish brown energy at Rachel. Her eyes were a milky white.

The sizzling beam shot toward her head. Rachel locked her gaze on Eunice and whistled. Blue sparks rushed toward her. Rachel bent close over her handle and rotated, flipping underneath the broom and shooting up on other side again. The horrid-smelling spell burnt the air where her head would have been.

"Look at her fly!" Evelyn March exclaimed. "I couldn't do that!"

A smile flickered across Rachel's lips. Serious again, she pointed a finger at Eunice, who stood frozen in the act of firing her wand, blue sparkles dancing around her body. "Look at her eyes! See how cloudy they are? Mordeau is possessing students and sending them to kill people! Anyone you see with eyes like that is possessed! Stop them!"

She sped through the trees, along the gravel paths that ran between the dorms on the western side of the campus. The pale pyramidal towers of Marlowe Hall flashed by. At her warning, the students playing croquet on the lawns of Spenser Hall scattered like startled doves. As she darted toward the spires of Dare, she shouted to those on the steps to retreat inside and block the doors against anyone with a wand. Then, she dodged white birches as she circled around to the back of Roanoke Hall.

Dark images rose up in her mind. She dismissed them impatiently, but as soon as one left, another took its place: Gaius lying on the floor, dead; herself dropping to her knees, clutching his limp body and rocking back and forth, wailing; herself dressed in the black crepe of mourning, going through the motions of her life as if in a dreary dream; herself as an aged spinster, explaining to her great grand-nephews and nieces how she had never married because, long ago, her true love had been slain.

Rachel blushed at that last thought. She had no evidence this boy was her true love; she was not even over John Darling. But the thought of Gaius dying, before she discovered whether he might be...

He was not going to die!

The birches parted, revealing the grassy area filled with sprouting tree stumps behind Roanoke Hall. Sitting in the middle of this field, rubbing an angry red bump on his forehead, was the P.E. teacher. Rachel leapt from her broom, landing beside him at a stumbling run.

"Mr. Chanson! Are you okay? Can I help you to the Infirmary?"

"No, no, child." He smiled up at her, rubbing his forehead. "I will be fine in a few minutes. Got the wind knocked out of me."

Rachel bent down and offered her hand, helping him to rise. "Sir...no offense, but you flew through fifty yards of earth. Are you sure you didn't lose more than your wind?"

"Must have been a tunnel here all along," he replied mildly. He started to stand, but paused on one knee, overcome by dizziness.

Laughter snorted out of her mouth in spite of her wish to restrain it. "Um. You left a Mr. Chanson-shaped hole in the *brick* wall, sir. Also, you move faster than I can see." Rachel leaned forward, her dark eyes dancing. "I think the time for pretending everything is normal has passed."

He tried again, rocking forward as he rose, clumps of dirt falling from his suit and half cape. Making it to his feet, Mr. Chanson ducked his head and gave her a sheepish smile. "Will you keep my secret?"

"Of course!" Rachel straightened and saluted. As she hopped back on her broom, she added, "I have more people to warn. I'll have to interrogate you about what you know about Metaplutons later."

"Meta..."

"Metaplutons," she called over her shoulder as she took to the air. "It's Mr. Smith's term for people who come from beyond Pluto ...people from outside. Like Lucky and the Lion."

Mr. Chanson gave her a very penetrating look. "You know a great deal for one so young."

"I pay attention," Rachel replied.

She shot off, barreling through the trees toward the dorms on the far side of Roanoke, rocketing by somber De Vern Hall. Ahead, a group of students had gathered on the pathway leading to Drake. Even with her naked eye, Rachel could see black shadows around them. A shadow surrounded a tall blond boy holding a wand. He turned and raised his hands, calling out a cantrip she had not heard before. "*Tur lu!*"

Vroomie stopped in mid air. The steeplechaser ceased moving, but Rachel did not. She flew from her seat, shooting forward. Her stomach tried to stay with the broom, but physics did not allow for that. The unfamiliar sensation of open air under her backside was disturbing. It was like that moment in a dream when you walked into a crowded room only to realize that you were naked.

Only, this was more like waking up to discover that you really were in a crowded room and you really were naked.

Gravel lay below her, promising a particularly painful landing. She could concentrate on saving herself, which was going to be uncomfortable, even if she succeeded. Or she could stop the kid who attacked her before he hurt anyone else. Or himself. She hated to imagine how it would feel to come out of a geas and discover that you had committed a murder. Even if others told you it was Dr. Mordeau's fault, would you ever believe it?

No child was going to have to live with that on her watch, not even a gangly boy from Drake.

Rachel gave the ground no thought. She fixed her eyes on the young man and pursed her lips, whistling. The shrill notes of the petrify spell pierced the air. Amidst blue sparks and the scent of spruces, the boy froze. Then, she shouted, *"Varenga, Vroomie!"*

The gravel path, with all its sharp stony points, rushed toward her. Four feet. Two feet. A foot and a half. Rachel tucked her head and somersaulted. Sharp pebbles pricked her painfully. Ouch. Ouch. Ouch. Grateful for her gymnastics classes, she came up out of the roll onto her feet.

As she rose, her hand closed around the polished handle of her broom, which had shot toward her when called. Swinging onto the seat, she leaned forward and snatched the wand out of the petrified boy's hand. Angling her broom toward the trees above, she shot upward.

Back in the air, Rachel slumped over her handlebars and rested her forehead on the handle. She had lived, and with only five or ten uncomfortable bruises. Thank goodness.

Beneath her, the other students clapped and cheered. Straightening, Rachel flashed them a split-second smile and waved. Then, she sped onward, shouting, "Alarm! Alarm! Petrify all students with wands!"

Continuing her Paul Revering, she shot past the yellow stone of Raleigh and the stone Scholars decorating Dee. In the distance, she could hear cries, shouts, and strains of music.

"Alarm! Alarm! Mad tutor alert! Students gone rogue," she cried as she passed fellow students. "Shut the doors of your dorms and don't let the Thaumaturgy students in!"

Lively music swelled from the trees ahead of her. Abraham Van Helsing, Conan MacDannan, and the other vampire-hunting boys from Dare stood side by side, defending a group of students, mainly girls. A circle of white sparkles spread out from their instruments, driving back the shadows that had been part of Mordeau's cloak. Rachel waved, and the boys grinned. Max Weatherby, the funny boy with the big chin, nodded over his flute and winked. Alex Romanov, the princess's brother, called out to ask after his sister. Rachel gave him a thumbs-up as she rocketed by.

She flew back across the Commons again. The young blond proctor, Mr. Scott, stood on the lawn, directing students into Roanoke Hall. As she flew closer, he waved her over, looking stern.

"Thank you, Miss Griffin. That is enough for now." He gestured toward the wide double doors. "Please join the others in the dining hall."

In her mind, she gave a swift kick to the geared contraption that created obedience to adults. It groaned and collapsed into a dusty pile of mental parts and fastenings, performing no function whatsoever.

"Yes, sir," Rachel saluted.

Without even the minutest qualm, she flew in the entrance, through the dining hall, and out the back door, where she soared upward and over the wall.

She saw the trees swaying and jumping before she heard the earth-rending crack. The ground in front of Drake Hall split open. The granite wall of the august dormitory cracked. The sleeping stone lion listed sideways. With a *whoosh*, the waters of the moat rushed into the newly formed chasm.

Up through the gaping tear in the earth came the black dragon. It writhed its way from the dirt, shook itself off, and spread its huge purple-black bat wings. Opening its mouth, it breathed a huge gout of foul-smelling flames into the pit behind it.

Through the flame rose the dean, carried by her golden eagle familiar. She held her hands up in an unfamiliar cantrip. The flames bent to either side of her.

The dragon and the dean squared off. Drawing itself back on its hind legs, like a winged-serpent rampant on a heraldic crest, the dragon roared out words. Its voice was surprisingly shrill for such a huge creature. "My servants, hear me! Kill the other two primary targets! I will take care of Dean Moth!"

Across the campus, shadows flickered, rushing away from the students and off toward some new goal. Rachel spun her steeplechaser, but she could not tell where they were heading. Terror grappled her limbs. She had no idea who these primary targets were. Valerie Foxx? But Dr. Mordeau and her assistant, Jonah Strega, had had Valerie under their power. If they wanted her dead, why wouldn't they have killed her then? Who else could it be? Mr. Chanson? Herself? John Darling and his sister, Wendy, the children of the other person who caught Mordeau's father?

From this height, she could see two members of the White Hart Alliance, Marta Fisher and Ivan Romanov. Both had been fighting students under the influence of the geas. Both paused and looked around, uncertain as to the threat.

If they did not know what to do, how could she—a mere freshman who knew only a meager handful of spells—be of any help? Panic threatened to highjack her body. If only she knew more magic. If only she knew who the other two targets were. If only she knew anything useful. But who could discern Mordeau's twisted mind?

In the midst of her frustration, she paused. She was very smart—otherwise she would not have been invited here a year early—and she had a perfect memory. What if she already knew the clues?

Rachel slowed her broom. She closed her eyes. She calmed her thoughts.

As rapidly as spells firing from a dueling wand, she drew on every reference she had ever encountered to Dean Jacinda Moth and Dr. Melusine Mordeau, the daughter of Eliaures Charles, the Serpent Master of the Morth Brood. The puzzle pieces whirled through her mind faster than fan blades.

Come on, Information. Come find me! No one loves you as much as I do!

Crispin Fisher and Maverick Badger—the other two heroes of the Terrible Years.

Oh, of course.

What if Mordeau wanted to kill the people at Roanoke responsible for the fall of her masters, the Terrible Five? That would be the dean, the head of the Proctors, and Crispin Fisher of the Six Musketeers. The dean was facing the dragon, and Rachel knew, while Mordeau probably did not, that Mr. Badger was not on campus.

That left Mr. Fisher.

Bending low over her steeplechaser, she shot off. She dodged the spires and bell towers of Roanoke Hall with consummate grace. Diving into a large loop, she flipped over half-way through, so that she barreled directly toward her Alchemy classroom.

Not all the windows of Roanoke Hall were the kind that opened. Luckily, these did. Barreling at the glass at high speed, Rachel let go of her handlebars and performed the Opening cantrip.

"Libra!"

The top slid down the tiniest bit. Her heart took off like a frightened rabbit. Forcing herself to take a calming breath, she prepared to try again. Flying through narrow openings was not something most people could do. Luckily, she had practiced this. She often darted in and out of windows at home. All she needed to do was open it about three times as far as she already had, and she could fit through.

"Libra!"

It opened another inch or two.

"Libra! Libra! Libra!"

The window budged no farther. No matter how loudly she shouted, it remained only a few inches open. Rachel was close enough to see inside the tinted glass. Toward the back of the room, students crouched behind the lab stations. Up front, an upper classman wielded a slender whip that gleamed like moonlight. Droplets flew from it as she flicked it backward. Some splattered on the pair of glasses that rested on the counter where Mr. Fisher usually sat.

Red droplets.

Rachel's eyes locked on the blood-splattered eyeglasses. The hairs stood up all along the back of her neck. Her heart lurched.

The window was now ten feet away, eight feet away, five feet away. It was not going to open. The young woman with the whip raised it again, preparing to strike. Rachel threw her arms in front of her head and drove her broom forward.

Glass shattered. Her broom spun. Her body struck the window's wooden muntins.

Her scream hurt her ears.

She whirled through the classroom, shedding shards and splinters. Her cheek ached. Her shoulder and back throbbed. Her leg burned. She did not care. Time enough later to assess the damage to herself—after everyone was safe.

The blond turned and raised her whip, flicking it at her, but Rachel was twirling too quickly even for the possessed girl to anticipate where she would be next. The whip sliced the air with a tremendous *crack*, grazing her ear.

Rachel screamed again.

Rapidly toggling the brass levers on her broom, she struggled to gain control of her spinning steeplechaser. The broom continued to rotate. She let go of her fears and slipped into flying mode, her thoughts calm. A three-dimensional picture sprang up in her mind. Rapidly, she calculated which forces needed to go where to achieve her goal. Throwing her weight far to the right, she crashed into the upper classman, knocking over the blond and her wicked whip.

The young woman fell backwards, striking her head on a lab station. Her body slumped to the floor. She twitched slightly, moaning, but did not rise.

The impact slowed Rachel's spin. With a shaky sigh of relief, she gained control of the steeplechaser again. She tried to whistle, but her lips would not purse. Raising her hands, she pointed two fingers at the young woman's weapon.

"*Tiathelu, Varenga!*"

Her voice came out hoarse and unrecognizable. Yet, the whip rose up and flew into her hand. She stuffed it into the large pocket in the bottom of her robe. Only then did she look around.

Two bodies lay on the ground, crisscrossed with long red welts. Mr. Fisher was on his back, gasping for breath, his face a web of cuts. Over him, as if he had thrown his body in the way to protect his teacher, lay Siggy's roommate, mild-mannered Enoch Smithwyck, the English boy from Japan whom Sigfried had called a wuss. Enoch lay very still, his throat a mess of blood and welts. His chest was not rising or falling. His eyes were open, glassy.

A horrible keening noise filled Rachel's ears. It took her a moment to realize that she was the one making it. From the back of the room, Wendy Darling and Sakura Suzuki rushed forward, clutching each other. Wendy ran over to the Alchemy tutor and fell to her knees, her hands pressed against her pale, pale face.

"Uncle Crispin!"

Mr. Fisher was not actually her uncle, but Rachel knew the two families were very close. Wendy's eyelids fluttered as if she might faint, but she took hold of herself and ran to the sink, looking for water. Sakura had stopped beside Wendy. Her eyes locked on Enoch's motionless form. She tried to swallow. Her dark eyes glowed with tears.

"No! Enoch! No!" Her anguished cry ripped through the room, like the shriek of a torn soul. Rachel remembered that the princess had seen that both Enoch and Sakura had come from the same alternate landscape. Her heart quivered. But she could not stop for pain. Or grief.

Using the technique that allowed her to hide her emotions, Rachel shoved her fear and sorrow aside. Glancing about, she took in the situation and rapidly ran through what needed to be done. She tried whistling again. Pain tore through her cheek.

On the floor, the blond groaned and reached a hand toward the back of her head.

"Tie up the upper classman! Or petrify her." Rachel called to the remaining students. "I'll get the nurse!"

The window was an unholy mess of sharp edges. Instead of leaving that way, Rachel shot out the classroom door, down the hallway, around the spiral staircase, and out through the back door of the dining hall. She rocketed up over the walls, heading directly for the Infirmary. Focused on her destination, she did not take time to look around, but she did turn her head rapidly from one side to the other. Later, she could review whatever had fallen under her gaze.

Something moved out of the corner of her eye. She did not pause. She barreled in the open front door of the Infirmary, screaming for the nurse. Nurse Moth came running, blanching when she saw Rachel.

"Don't worry about me!" Rachel leapt to the ground and shoved her broom at Nurse Moth. "Mr. Fisher. Enoch. Might be dead. Alchemy room." When that was not enough to launch the nurse, Rachel shouted, "*Go!*"

"Lay down, *Cheri*. The gems on the bed will begin the healing process." The nurse hopped on the broom and left. Panting and aching, Rachel played back her memory of the motion she had just seen out of the corner of her eye. She blinked and played it back again. It stayed the same.

Through the woods leading to the Infirmary, a little porcelain doll walked of its own accord, dragging the unconscious Magdalene Chase.

Chapter Thirty-Three:
Valiant Efforts

RACHEL LOOKED LONGINGLY AT THE BED WITH THE PRETTY GREEN and purple dragon-vein agates containing healing magic that glittered welcomingly in its headboard. She glanced around the Infirmary, taking in the sleeping Valerie, the unconscious and restrained Fuentes, the gurgling fountain, the orrery overhead. Sighing, she took a quick gulp from the healing fountain and splashed a bit of its icy waters on her face. Then, she headed for the woods and the living doll.

Rachel limped along the path. Her right leg did not want to work correctly. Her back hurt where she had somersaulted over the gravel, her shoulder still throbbed after striking the wood struts of the window. Her ear smarted where the whip had caught it. Her cheek burned.

Everything hurt. Worse, fear threatened to engulf her. What had happened at Drake Hall? Where was Gaius when the earthquake occurred? Where was Sigfried? Where were Nastasia and Joy? She had finally found friends. Would she be able to go on if they died, all in one day?

Mustn't think about it. Concentrate on the present.

Taking a deep breath, she forced herself to straighten up and walk with a smoother gait. After a few steps, she still limped, but it was less pronounced. She headed for the place where she had seen Magdalene.

As she went, she reviewed her memory, examining the other events that had been occurring on the campus while she had been flying from Roanoke Hall to the Infirmary. A number of skirmishes had broken out: Enchanter and Canticler students fought Thaumaturgy students, binding them with shining, golden Glepnir bonds to keep them from casting. Beside the reflecting lake, Seth Peregrine wielded a hockey stick, successfully holding his own against three older students. Near the path leading to Marlowe, students conjured bears and wolverines. Some of the conjured creatures attacked the Thaumaturgy students. Some wandered aimlessly. On the lawn near Drake Hall, a conjured bear fought a huge chestnut wolf.

In the middle of the Commons, a student from the princess's vision, a Hindu boy with longish hair, pointed his wand at a group of students. Rachel suspected he was Duryodhana Patel. Black light came out of the wand. Another child screamed. With a sensation like waking from a dream, Zoë appeared out of nowhere behind Patel and whacked him with her greenstone war club. There was a huge explosion of fiery red light. The words *Pow* and *Wham* appeared in mid-air as if traced in multi-colored lightning. Duryodhana Patel flopped over. The event had been too far away to have reached her ears, but in her memory, she could see the other students cheering.

Rachel heard the leafy slither before she saw the little China doll. The tiny porcelain figure was dragging her owner across the newly-fallen leaves. The doll was crying, which was an impressive feat, considering its face was painted. Rachel's heart leapt into her throat and stayed there. She had been so worried about Siggy and Gaius and the princess. Was Magdalene...

Falling to her knees beside the tiny girl, she was tremendously relieved to see Magdalene's chest rising and falling. Rachel's heart slipped back into her ribcage.

Magdalene was not dead.

"What happened?" she asked softly.

To her great surprise, the doll answered. Its voice was high and sweet. "She fight the geas. She resist it but cannot overcome. I know not how to help. I bring her to the nurse."

"Good thinking. Very good!" Rachel clapped her hands, smiling at the little doll. The concern on its face made it look so lost, so pathetic, that Rachel felt like crying. She felt so helpless, so...

"Wait! I can help!" Rachel jumped to her feet. She pointed at the other girl. "*Tiathelu.*"

Magdalene wobbled into the air. Rachel directed with her two fingers, moving her toward the Infirmary. It was much harder than the last time, even though Valerie had been bigger. She wondered if this was because she was exhausted. Bending, she snatched up the doll with her other hand, holding it to her chest, and moved forward. It was slow going. Twice, she dropped Magdalene. Several other times, she realized part of the tiny girl was dragging.

"Could you use some help with that?" A familiar voice drawled behind her.

Rachel's heart skipped two beats. She spun around, keeping her guiding hand in place.

"Gaius!"

He stood there, smiling down at her—looking cute, if smudged with dirt. She wanted to rush over and hug him, but she was too shy. Besides, she would have had to drop Magdalene. A grin spread over her face. Her whole body relaxed. She need not wear widow's weeds at a hundred and sixty after all.

"Gaius! You're alive!"

"So are you." He grinned. Then, his expression turned to concern. He reached toward her face but did not touch her. "Though you don't look..."

"Yeah, but I wasn't dead in the vision," Rachel blurted out.

"Vision? What vision?" he asked, alert. Then he slapped his forehead. "Some gentleman I am. Chatting while you're struggling. Here, allow me."

He gestured with his wand. Magdalene jerked into the air, floating a good three feet off the ground.

"Where are we going?" he asked. "Is she okay?"

"She will be. We're headed for the Infirmary."

"Infirmary it is," he replied, walking forward at a rapid pace, the floating form of the unconscious girl moving easily before his wand.

Rachel clutched the porcelain doll and followed. As they went, she told him the short version of what the princess had seen, about Fuentes, and then about Mordeau and Chanson.

The blood drained from his face. "So...Vlad and William and I...we would have died?"

"Yes."

"Um...thank you?"

"You are welcome." She curtseyed. "What happened down-stairs? Is Siggy there? Are Joy and Nastasia all right?"

"In Drake, you mean? There's still a firefight. The Princess of Magical Australia and another girl were a little ways from us. That princess packs a pretty good wind blast with her violin. She and the other girl kept the geased students from coming down the hallway. I didn't see the Dragonslayer kid. As to how things are going, Vlad and William are still fighting, I think. I got thrown out of the crevice by stupid Remus Starkadder. I tried to go back and help, but the proctors aren't letting anybody in. Then, I saw you. Speaking of which, we should probably hurry. Just in case there is something we can do back at Drake."

"I need my broom back. The nurse has it."

"I noticed you were limping. Did you get attacked?" he asked with concern. With a flick of his wand, he negotiated Magdalene up the staircase, into the Infirmary, and onto a bed. Rachel surreptitiously slipped the doll onto the mattress beside her.

"No, I assaulted a window."

"Um...okay."

Outside, they heard voices. Through the window, three women dressed in white, wearing wimples, could be seen hurry-ing toward the Infirmary.

"Visiting nurses! Nurse Moth must have called for help." Rachel ducked behind Gaius. "Hide me!"

"Hide you? But...you're hurt!

"Exactly. If they see me, they'll try to keep me here."

"And this is bad...why?" he asked sternly.

"They will stop me from helping people!" Rachel cried. When he looked skeptical, she cried while counting on her fingers, "So far, I've distracted Mordeau so that Siggy could save Mr. Chan-son—and the rest of you, warned people, and saved Mr. Fisher from a crazy girl who was beating him with an evil whip. I can still cast and do all sorts of things. I can't just lie here while my friends are in trouble. What if they die?"

Gaius snorted with amusement, but it was not a mocking amusement. There was respect in his eyes, as if he was im-pressed with what she had accomplished.

"Okay. But don't tell Vlad I did this."

He took her hand and hurried toward the back of the Infirmary. They slipped through the nurse's office, into a store room, and out a back door. Running around the building, they headed toward Drake. Rachel ran, even though it hurt. She gritted her teeth and made her legs keep moving. Every time something hurt, she told herself sternly that it was an injury that could be cured by healing enchantments. As soon as this was over, she would return to the Infirmary and the nurse would make her feel better.

"So you've had quite a day. Assaulting a window? Saving Mr. Fisher?" Gaius asked. "How did that happen?"

Rachel found herself panting. Between breaths, Rachel told him what had occurred.

"And...you figured that out by yourself?" His eyes grew wide with admiration. "Who Mordeau's targets were, I mean? I must say, I am rather impressed." The awed look he gave her went to her head like wine.

They headed through the woods, back toward Drake, leaves crunching under their feet. From ahead of them came crashes and shouts and the loud retort of a tree trunk striking the earth. The ground shook. Peals of thunder rolled down from Stony Tor, over and over, as if the Heer of Dunderberg could sense the chaos and chose this moment to test the boundaries of his prison.

A streak of red and gold came through the hemlocks. A voice called her name. Lucky wrapped around Rachel, snuffling her good cheek. His long, red whiskers tickled her neck. She touched him shyly. The dragon's downy fur felt as silky and fluffy as she had imagined. His long sinewy, serpentine body was very warm, as if he kept a furnace inside.

"Found her, boss!" Lucky called. "She's kind of beat up."

"Rachel! Are you okay?" Sigfried pelted pell-mell through the trees. "You look terrible! Did Mordeau get you? How do we get back inside? Joy's paralyzed, and some upper classman is burning the princess."

"Wha-what?" Rachel cried, horrified. She hugged Lucky more tightly. Gaius halted abruptly, alarmed.

Sigfried skidded to a stop just beside Rachel. His robes and hair were covered with dirt. "Some blond rotter—not Strega—has a wand pointed at her, and she's surrounded by flames."

"Real flames? Or phantom flames?" Gaius leaned forward intently. "Is the fire consuming her flesh and clothes?"

Sigfried tilted his head. Rachel knew he was examining the scene with his amulet. "No."

"Phantom flames." Gaius's voice shook. "You aren't supposed to use them on people. That's black magic. It's forbidden in most jurisdictions."

"Really? What jurisdictions allow it?" Sigfried blurted out, his eyes huge and eager.

Rachel shoved him. "Siggy! The princess!"

"You're not happy she's burning?" Sigfried asked, examining her face curiously. He did not look eager to see the princess hurt, just interested in Rachel's reaction. "Considering that she betrayed your boyfriend?"

"He's not my boyfriend!" Rachel shouted, certain from the rush of heat in her cheeks that her face had caught fire. "No, of course not!"

Gaius watched them both attentively. The temperature of Rachel's face subsided a degree. Gaius did not realize Siggy referred to him.

"This 'blond rotter'," Gaius asked, "was he tall with shoulder-length hair?"

"Yeah."

"Remus Starkadder. Same idiot who threw me out of there."

The three looked around but even from where they stood, they could see tutors blocking the doorway into Drake Hall.

Rachel's mind raced, searching for some way to help the princess. "Oh! What about the hole Mr. Chanson made?"

"No good," Sigfried replied. "Lucky and I tried to get back that way. It has collapsed. Even Lucky could not fit through."

"Could we fly down the crevice, if we had my broom?" Rachel looked back over her shoulder toward the Infirmary, but she saw no sign of Nurse Moth.

Siggy shook his head. "It's filled with water now. Beside, the nurse is still using your broom."

"I could go," Lucky offered. "I like water."

"Could you?" Rachel cried. "Go! Save Nastasia!"

Lucky took off like a bottle rocket, calling over his shoulder. "Okay with you, Boss?"

Sigfried nodded.

"The dragon talks," Gaius murmured weakly.

Rachel watched Lucky race toward the chasm in front of Drake Hall and dive into the waterfall created by the moat, as it flowed into the rent the dragon made in the earth. Rachel gnawed on her fist. Staring at the cracked edifice of Drake Hall, she regretted that her family did not belong to a temple and had no god to whom they paid homage. If only there were some outside power she could beg for help.

In the forest, something glinted golden. Rachel shaded her eyes and peered more closely. The tiny Lion sat among the hemlocks, washing his paw. He looked up, and their eyes met.

To Rachel, everything turned upside down. The Lion seemed enormous, larger than galaxies. Planet Earth, a tiny ball, rested on the pads of his paw. Atop this ball, she could make out the dollhouse that was Drake Hall—the front of the granite building with its crack and its stone lions, the roof, the far side, including several back doors.

Unguarded back doors.

Caw! Caw! The great black Raven dive bombed the Lion, the gleam of its blood-red eyes visible even through the trees. The vision ended. The world was back to its normal size and shape.

"Come on!" cried Rachel.

Despite the pain in her leg, she ran.

The three of them dashed around behind Drake. There were several back doors. The closest one led to the basement. A staircase led down to it. Rachel ran through the woods toward this door. To the right, among the trees, was a fenced enclosure with chickens and goats. A little beige kid pressed its head against the fence, gazing at them with its weird square pupils.

"Oh, cool! Animals," Rachel cried as she careened around the corner.

"For sacrifices," Gaius said offhandedly.

A shiver ran down the length of Rachel's body. She remembered why the other Arts did not care for Thaumaturges.

They piled across the stone bridge that spanned the moat and darted down the stairs, halting before a locked door. As Gaius fumbled for his wand, Sigfried moved his hands in the gesture for the Opening cantrip.

"*Libra!*"

The padlock sprang open with a *crack* and bounced off the door. Wand in hand, Gaius jerked back, impressed.

"Behind us!" Sigfried shouted.

Gaius whipped around and fired.

Grrrrrr. A blur of motion. Silver sparkles leapt from Gaius's wand and threw back a chestnut-colored wolf, just in time. Moments later, it would have struck Rachel. It came so close that the wind caused by the speed of its approach blew her hair into her face.

"I got this one," Gaius grinned like a fiend. He sprinted up the stairs, wand pointed at the wolf. "Come on, Fenris. Let's do this."

The wolf shivered and rose. He now looked like a lanky young man with spiky chestnut hair, dressed in black subfusc with the golden crest of Transylvania above his heart. He glared at Gaius and drew his own wand. Then, his eyes grew big, as if he had just realized who he was facing. Terror crossed his face. Turning, he ran, firing spells over his shoulder.

Gaius paused, leaned over the railing, and tapped Rachel on the chest. A mirrored shimmer spread across her body, fading quickly. Rachel recognized the reflective shield he had cast upon her before her duel with Cydney Graves. With a wink, he set off after Fenris, firing blue and silver sparks and bands of glowing golden light as he ran.

"Come on!" Siggy plunged into the darkness of the building. "This way!"

CHAPTER THIRTY-FOUR:
THE WILL OF THE VELTDAMMERUNG

SIGFRIED AND RACHEL RACED DOWN AN EXTREMELY NARROW STAIR-case and through a curving brick corridor, the slap of their footsteps echoing loudly. The air was dry and dusty, as if people seldom came this way. As they ran, Sigfried shouted out a play by play report, courtesy of his amulet.

"Lucky knocked into the blond idiot. The princess retreated behind a pillar. Joy is there. She's not moving. I think...she's paralyzed. Nastasia's okay. She's shaking, but she's not burned. She's got her violin under her chin again. She's not giving up. Good for her! She looks so grim.

"Wait! It's him! Strega!" Sigfried shouted. "His wand is out! He's sneaking up on Joy...who can't move. Lucky!" he screamed, his voice bouncing off the brick walls. "Lucky is moving toward him. Oh, Nastasia saw Strega. She's drawing her bow across her violin strings. Silver sparkles flying everywhere. Ace! Strega got slammed into a wall by a blast of wind. His wand went flying. Woohoo! Go, Princess! Oops! The princess just got paralyzed! Some skinny red-headed rotter did it."

Ahead, they heard voices, shouts. Bursting out of the narrow hallway, they skidded to a halt in front of a stone door. Siggy threw it open. Water flowed out, pooling around Rachel's new leather boots. She took a step forward and stopped in the doorway.

Beyond was a Summoning Vault, a vast stone chamber designed for calling up supernatural creatures. Four stone pillars supported the ceiling. Geometric designs—triangles, five and seven-pointed stars, all inside of circles—marked the marble floor. An altar stood toward the center, its surface dark from years of use. The chamber smelled of spellwork—spruce, cinnamon, and brimstone, along with the faint but distinct odor of dried blood.

Rachel recoiled. Wands were one thing, sacrifices another. She and her family disapproved of magic that required live offerings. This was not mere kind-heartedness. The path from Thaumaturge to black magician was short, and many strayed along it.

Strengthening her resolve, Rachel charged through the door. Across the chamber, students battled each other. In front of the far door, Vladimir Von Dread and William Locke stood in fencing stances, back to back, holding off a group of cloudy-eyed students. Sweat glistened on Von Dread's brow, and his chest rose and fell with the raggedness of his breath, but his expression was deadly calm. He looked like a young avenging god, firing an endless stream of spells from his wand without remorse.

Beside him, Locke regarded the events with a cool, rational demeanor. The only betrayal that this was not an ordinary day was one quirked eyebrow, suggesting that he found the proceedings fascinating from a scientific standpoint. Locke kept a series of three shields hovering in the air before himself and Dread. If a spell broke through one, he replaced it. Otherwise, he, too, fired spells at their opponents, though not as relentlessly as his companion.

Of the nineteen geased students in the chamber, a mix of boys and girls, three stood motionless, paralyzed. Two struggled inside Glepnir bonds. One hung in mid-air, slowly spinning in a circle. Two writhed, splashing on the wet floor, entangled in vines growing out of their clothing. Of the remaining eleven, Rachel recognized tall, blond, shaggy Remus Starkadder and the two Ishizuka brothers from the Knights of Walpurgis meeting. Remus led the fight along with two other college students: an angry young man with dark skin and a pale skinny young man with stringy red hair. The red-head had blood trickling down his forehead and was cradling his right arm against his chest.

Behind a pillar, though visible to Rachel, Nastasia and Joy stood motionless. The princess stood calmly, one arm outstretched. Joy's face was a mask of surprise, her hands lifted as if for a cantrip. Rachel wondered if she had looked like that when she was paralyzed. Beside them, Lucky hovered, hissing.

Water poured around Nastasia's and Joy's legs, its level rising. More rushed in from the open door behind Von Dread and Locke. In the distance, Rachel could hear a faint roaring that was growing louder.

"The moat," Rachel whispered. "This place's flooding."

Siggy ran into the vault, pulling out his trumpet. Sliding through the water, he blew a loud blast. Silver sparks picked up the young man with the stringy red hair who had paralyzed the princess and carried him a hundred-twenty feet, splashing and tumbling. He slammed into a wall. Everyone paused and stared—though Dread kept firing spells.

The gcased students fired back at Sigfried. Sigfried backpedaled, waving his hands and shouting. He tried to put up a shield or to perform the deflecting cantrip, but he mixed up the words and gestures. A multicolored swirl of sparks and lights struck him, twirling him in a circle, and throwing him hither and thither, until he ended up hanging upside-down from a golden band looped around his foot that hung in mid-air. He dangled back and forth like a pendulum, swearing foully, including some words Rachel had never heard. She wondered if they were truly bad swear words or if he had made them up. His golden hair waved beneath him, his trumpet falling from his hands. Lucky darted forward and wrapped around his master, breathing a huge gout of flame at the startled students. While they were distracted, Dread took out two of them. The remaining nine turned their attention back to Von Dread and Locke.

Nine against two, and yet those two were holding their own. Rachel moistened her lips, impressed.

Slipping away from the battle, she put her back to the cold stone wall of the foyer outside. Her heart raced. As she struggled to control her rapid breathing, she mentally reviewed the situation. Siggy, Joy, and Nastasia were all stronger sorcerers than she. However, thanks to Gaius, she knew the Word of Ending. If she could cross to where the girls were, she could release them. Unfortunately, they were across the wide chamber. Nor did she know how to free Sigfried. If someone zapped her that would be it. There would be no cavalry coming to rescue her.

Might there be something else she could do to swing the tide of the battle? She replayed what she had just seen, examining it from different angles. Remus Starkadder! Like his brother outside, the chestnut wolf, his eyes were not cloudy. He was operating far more efficiently than the geased students, firing four times for every one spell the others cast. If she could take him out, Dread and Locke could wipe up the rest with ease.

Pursing her lips, Rachel stepped back into the Summoning Vault and whistled, her attention focused on the Transylvanian prince. Her cheek ached fiercely, but the fountain water must have helped, because she succeeded despite the agony. Blue sparkles swept toward Remus. They struck the barely-visible crystalline shield that hung in the air around him but did not break it. Imitating Gaius when he dueled, she stood sideways to present a smaller target. Then, ignoring the eye-watering pain, she tried again and again and again.

The fourth time, his shield dissolved, taking her sparkles with it. She had gotten through but had not hit him. On her fifth try, Remus Starkadder spun around. With a leering grin, he parried her sparks, sending them toward Locke, who deflected them into a wall. Remus then turned his back on Rachel, returning to his fight with Dread.

Rachel frowned. He did not even think her a big enough threat to bother watching.

"Boss!" Lucky's voice cut across the distance.

Jonah Strega, blood dripping down the side of his face, his eyes gleaming manically, his teeth bared with some perverse hunger, crept up on the motionless Joy and the Princess. In his hand was his jagged, cruel knife.

"Strega!" Siggy shouted. He swung helplessly upside down, yet he still managed to unclipped the knife Valerie had given him and stabbed the air wildly in the other boy's direction. "Lucky, get him! Burn. Him. Now!"

Strega raised his knife and plunged it toward Joy's back. Quick as wildfire, Lucky darted between them. Drawing back his head, he breathed. A huge plume of brilliant red-gold flame shot into the older boy's face.

Strega's scream would echo in Rachel's nightmares. The smell of burnt flesh filled the chamber. One of the girls among the Drake students shrieked and covered her face, despite that her eyes were still clouded.

Rachel focused her attention back on Remus. She tried her spell twice more. Each time she whistled, he parried. He hardly even glanced her way. The third time, a flicker of annoyance crossed his handsome but brutish features. He volleyed her spell back at her.

The blue sparkles swirled toward her. Rachel prepared to leap out of the way. Then she paused. An idea struck her. The tell-tale whistle was betraying her. Remus could hear her spell coming. What if she could strike him silently? Biting her lip, she asked herself the all-important question: *Did she trust Gaius Valiant?*

Yes.

Drawing a very deep breath, she bravely stepped forward into the swirl of blue sparkles. Her rebounded spell struck her and played across her limbs. The scent of pine swept over her. Then, her body gleamed, mirror-like, as the blue glints bounced off the reflective shield cantrip Gaius had cast on her before he ran after the chestnut wolf. The blue sparkles flew back toward the Starkadder prince, striking him squarely in the back.

Remus froze, motionless, his wand arm still outstretched. With almost lazy grace, Rachel gestured at him, pointing with two fingers. "*Tiathelu.*" The wand leapt from his hand and flew to her. She snatched it out of the air and put it in her voluminous pocket, where it joined the whip and the wand belonging to the boy who had stopped her broom.

The distant roar grew suddenly louder. A hip-high wall of water burst through the far door into the chamber, knocking over two paralyzed students.

"*Keithwyth Selu.*" Vladimir Von Dread's voice boomed. He had moved to the center of the room. Warding circles and summoning triangles glowed a deep violet around him, gleaming under the water. He had taken off his right glove and drawn his fingertips together, gesturing at the approaching liquid wall.

The water trembled and rose. It formed a gigantic figure with a torso, crude arms, and a rounded head with simple features. Dread pointed at the remaining geased students. The watery giant surged forward. Strega, Joy, Nastasia, and Lucky disappeared beneath its living wave, followed by the paralyzed Remus and the others. Siggy kicked and jerked, his head beneath the surface. Then, he curled upward at the waist and drew his head out of the water, gasping and sputtering. Lucky burst from the surface and spiraled around him, helping him.

Dread gestured with his wand. The princess and Joy flew from beneath the wave into his grasp. He put them onto the dry altar. William Locke moved his right hand, index finger raised. Over the roar of the water elemental, Rachel could not hear him use the Word of Ending, but Nastasia and Joy moved again, gasping and sputtering.

Vladimir Von Dread gestured. The being of water moved backward twenty feet, leaving the geased students flopping and gasping on the floor. Walking forward calmly, Locke paralyzed those who were still moving. Rachel, too, crept closer. She gathered several dropped wands, slipping them into her pocket with the others.

The great living wave turned its head and looked at her. An eerie tingle slithered down Rachel's spine. She stopped picking up wands and backed slowly toward the door.

Von Dread's voice echoed in the vaulted chamber. "I can hold the moat in this form for some time, but I do not have the skill to dispel it. Can someone please retrieve Master Warder Nighthawk or one of the other competent tutors."

"I'll do it!" Rachel shouted. Ignoring the pain in her leg, she ran back toward the narrow staircase.

Outside, she spied Gaius Valiant striding toward her, grinning triumphantly. Dashing toward him, she grabbed his hand.

"Come on! Mr. Von Dread brought the moat to life, but he can't dispel it. He needs help. We've got to find the Master Warder."

Gaius's brows leapt up. "Wow! That's a rather advanced spell—even for Vlad."

They ran together toward the Watch Tower, deep in the hemlocks behind De Vere Hall. Before they reached it, they came upon the Lenai Lenape tutor, a tall man with craggy features and a nose like a bird of prey. He stood with his arms crossed, outside a circle of salt. Urd Odinson and Eve March, both young women from De Vere whom Rachel recognized from the Knights of Walpurgis meeting, stood beside him. Trapped inside the circle, a dozen shadows steamed in the sunlight.

"Sir. Mr. Von Dread summoned up something he can't put down. He needs help."

"Many people need help." Nighthawk's voice resonated deeply. Suddenly, his head shot up, alert. "Dread, you say? What did he summon?"

"The moat. He called it *Selu*. He said: *Keithwyth Selu. Keith-wyth* means 'come', right?"

His craggy face remained impassive, but his pupils widened a hundredth of an inch. Rachel suspected this was the equivalent of a scream of shock from other men.

"Where is he?"

"Southern Summoning Vault," Gaius stated.

With a curt nod to the two older girls, Nighthawk murmured something beneath his breath. A flash of light, and he was gone.

Rachel's jaw dropped. "I didn't know anyone could jump on campus!"

"A few people have been given..." Gaius cut himself off and shrugged. "It makes sense that the Master Warder for the school would have the keys to the wards."

"That's probably why Mr. Von Dread asked for him."

Rachel was limping badly now. Her leg hurt too much for her to force herself to run. The two of them walked slowly, still holding hands, Gaius looking down at her with concern. As they came around De Vere Hall, Rachel glanced to her left and froze. On the grassy area filled with stumps behind Roanoke Hall, a great black dragon faced off with the dean.

All around the two figures was destruction. On the pathway leading from the rent in the ground in front of Drake Hall, trees lay fallen. The earth was torn. A stand of hemlocks burned, crackling loudly. Black smoke billowed skyward, clogging the air with a smell that reminded Rachel of a paralysis enchantment.

Dean Moth faced the dragon, sweat pouring down her brow. Exhausted, she had tied herself to a tree trunk with a belt. The tree was not yet on fire, but one branch smoldered. Her hands were raised in a gesture Rachel recognized as a restraining cantrip. The dean panted, laboring to hold the monster in place.

Across from her, the math-teaching dragon struggled. Twenty Glepnir bonds lassoed the great beast. Even as Rachel and Gaius watched, they snapped, one after another. The cantrip restricted the creature's motion, but it could still move.

Gaius gulped. "I didn't know....Glepnir bands could break."

Rachel squeezed Gaius's hand tightly. Her gaze locked on the duel. "We've got to do something. We've got to help."

"What can we do?" he whispered, squeezing her hand back. "Our best bet is stay out of their way." He would have said more, but the tutors started speaking. Rachel shushed him.

"You have always been weak, Jacinda," purred the great black dragon, shrugging. A glowing golden band that had been encircling its shoulders popped, vanishing. "So pathetic. Too encumbered by principles. Too slow. Maybe you can find some students to cower behind, like you did last time."

"I did not set the Young Sorcerer's League on the Velt-dammerung. That was entirely Darling's doing." Dean Moth panted, straining to maintain her immobilization spell. "But I was proud to stand with them, Melusine. As you should have been."

"Proud?" raged the dragon, struggling against the dean's spell. "To stand beside those who undid my masters? Bah!"

"The Terrible Five were not worthy masters."

"Perhaps, but my new master is worthy. And subtle. So subtle that he hides in plain sight, and no one sees him. No one knows who he is."

"I know!" Rachel said softly, her eyes growing large.

"You do?" Gaius gawked.

"His name is Mortimer Egg," she whispered. "He works as a desk clerk for the Wisecraft. Hiding in plain sight. He's the man who tried to kill Valerie Foxx."

"That's...quite extraordinary," Gaius murmured, impressed.

The dragon struggled. Two more golden bands snapped, one around its middle and one that had been securing its legs. "My new master knows a marvelous spell. The price is high, but it's quite worth paying. What are a few traumatized infants, a few lost worlds, compared to what we seek to achieve? Soon we shall succeed. Then the true Veltdammerung shall occur. This damaged world shall end, and a new, grander one shall rise in its place!"

"And how shall this new world differ from our current one?" Dean Moth asked disdainfully. "Let me guess: the Wise shall rule the Unwary. You know from your study of history that this doesn't go well for either of us."

"Rule? What care I for power over the meager minds of mundane men! Yet, people will beg for us to lead them, when they discover we can give them what they truly desire!"

"And what is that again?" The dean's voice dripped with sarcasm. "Wealth? Beauty? Extra pairs of shoes?"

"Resurrection of the dead."

Surprise jolted Rachel. She stood straight up. Could it be done? Could she have her beloved grandfather back?

Even the dean started, though she recovered quickly. "Not possible, Melusine. Necromancy is a failed Art."

"I am not speaking of necromancy, Jacinda, but of true resurrection."

"No power on Earth can accomplish true resurrection!" the dean stated fiercely.

"Not on Earth." The dragon laughed, a deep, grating sound. "But my master is not from the Earth, Jacinda. He is from beyond the edges of our world. Where do you think all this new magic comes from? Who do you think is bringing it?"

Rachel's breath caught, her heart banging against her ribs. *Mortimer Egg was a Metapluton!* Was it just Egg? Or was the entire Veltdammerung—the organization devoted to the Twilight of the World—from Outside?

"You sneer," The dragon continued, "but don't you also wish to live in that future? What if we could bring back *your* dear ones?" The dragon leaned its horned head toward the dean. Its sapphire eyes glittered. "What if we could resurrect Jasper Hawke?"

"How...could you know of that?" Dean Moth gasped, her voice strangled by her shock.

"You goody-goodies are not the only ones who have visions. Wouldn't you like him back? Your star-crossed love? It is unlikely that he is in a good place now."

"W-why would you say such a thing?" the dean asked thickly.

"Come, Hawke hardly had clean hands."

"He died a hero!" Dean Moth ground out through clenched teeth.

"Certainly he did, defeating Bismarck's sorcerers...alongside Aleister Crowley and General Blaise Griffin," sneered the dragon.

Rachel stiffened at her grandfather's name and leaned farther forward. Her palms were slick with sweat, but Gaius's hand still grasped hers firmly. The solid presence of the boy beside her brought tremendous comfort.

"Crowley, I give you," the dean replied. Her face was unnaturally pale, and her voice was failing. "But Griffin never went astray."

"Oh? In the last century, no act has been so great a boon to those who walk the Dark Path as the weakening of the Eternal Flame when Amelia Abney-Hastings broke her Vestal vows."

"That's my grandmother!" Rachel whispered.

"She was a Vestal Virgin?" Gaius asked, surprised.

"I...," Rachel tried to swallow, "didn't know that."

"I don't know much about it," Gaius asked slowly, "but...when Vestal Virgins break their oaths, doesn't something bad happen?"

Rachel nodded, finally swallowing with some difficulty. "The Eternal Flame—that white and gold stuff? It loses some of its efficacy to harm wickedness and not hurt innocence."

"Ah. So that's..." Gaius paused.

Rachel wet her very dry lips. "Bad."

"One can't blame her, under the circumstance," the dragon purred. "Who among us could have endured what he did and kept going as bravely? And yet, you can hardly hold him up as proof that your dear Jasper is not twittering about in Hella's Kingdom, the plaything of some vengeful god. Wouldn't Hawke be better off alive and walking beneath the daystar?"

Dean Moth did not reply. Her face glowed with sweat, her breath uneven. Rachel feared the dean would faint. Only five golden bands restrained the dragon now. What would happen when the last one broke before she could cast more?

Rachel leaned forward on her tiptoes, her legs trembling. But she could hear nothing. They were both silent. She replayed her memory of the conversation she had just heard. What was

Mordeau talking about? What had happened to her grandfather? What had been difficult to endure? She jammed her jaws together angrily. How dare the dragon insinuate that Blaise Griffin was anything other than the best of men!

Wrath coursed through her. Rachel glared at the transformed math tutor. Her fingers curled into fists. In a burst of anger, she pursed her lips and whistled. Pain flared, blinding her briefly. Yet, she succeeded. Blue sparkles swept through the air and danced around the dragon. Her enchantment was weak. It only held the great beast motionless for less than a second before it tossed its horned head and shrugged off two more golden bonds.

An instant was all the dean needed.

"*Muria! Muria! Muria!*" Dean Moth shouted, free to release her restraining cantrip and conjure. Three times, she drew her hand down, fingertips pressed together. Above her head, her golden eagle cawed and fanned its wings. The underside of its outer flight feathers were silver and glittered in the sunlight.

A bolt of lightning woke into existence, striking the dragon, who screamed in pain and outrage. Thunder ripped the air, which sizzled and smelt of ozone. Rachel gawked, tremendously impressed. Conjuring electricity was extraordinarily difficult.

The dragon's limbs jerked randomly. It howled in pain.

After the lightning, crackling white fire traced with gold struck the beast. Rachel gasped. Beside her, Gaius's jaw dropped. They glanced at each other, shrugging. Neither of them had ever heard of anyone conjuring Eternal Flame. The dragon screeched, a horrendous, shrill sound. Its flesh scorched. The odor was similar to grilled steak but richer and strangely disturbing.

"That's odd." Gaius's brows drew together nervously. "Didn't the dean say the Word of Becoming three times?"

A *whistling* made them look up. A meteor plunged toward the earth, its flaming tail burning behind it. Gaius scooped Rachel into his arms and bolted into the woods.

Rachel curled against him. She could feel his muscles straining, his heart thundering in his chest. She clung to him, her arms around his neck, and felt simultaneously terrified, embarrassed, and pleased. Over his shoulder, she could see the duel. The dragon looked up an instant before the meteor smashed it to the ground.

Then the shock wave hit.

The force of it lifted Gaius and threw the two of them five yards across the forest floor. He tried to hold onto her, but Rachel flew free of his arms. As the ground rushed at her, she ducked her head and somersaulted, rolling across the dry leaves. Rocks stuck into her back, jarring her spine. When she came up onto her feet, Gaius was lying on his stomach, spitting out dirt and leaves.

Behind them, the great black dragon lay splayed beneath the steaming fallen rock, twitching. As they watched, it shimmered and turned back into an unconscious woman, lying partially under the meteor. Untying the belt that had held her to the tree, the dean moved her hands rapidly, shouting out cantrip after cantrip. Golden bands, and sparkles of three different shades of blue encircled the math tutor. Then, Dean Moth collapsed, falling to her knees, panting.

Other tutors arrived, surrounding the unconscious Dr. Mordeau. To the south, through the trees, Rachel could see Siggy, the princess, and Joy tumbling out of Drake Hall. Above them, Lucky darted joyously through the air. Nighthawk, Von Dread, and Locke followed more slowly, deep in conversation. Farther away, music played. Green healing sparks swirled across the campus. A few danced around Rachel, lessening the ache in her cheek, back, and leg.

Rachel and Gaius rose unsteadily to their feet. They took a few ragged breaths. Then, Gaius grinned.

"We're alive!" he cried. Catching Rachel about the waist, he lifted her into the air and swung her around and around, shouting: "We won!"

GLOSSARY

Agents – Magical law enforcement. Agents fight magical foes, both human and supernatural.

Alchemy – One of the Seven Sorcerous Arts. It is the Art of putting magic into objects.

Bavaria – a country that exists in the world of the book but not in our world. It is known to both the World of the Wise and the Unwary. It is ruled by the Von Dread family.

Canticle – One of the Seven Sorcerous Arts. It is the Art of commanding the natural and supernatural world with the words and gestures of the Original Language.

Cantrip – one word in the Original Language, i.e. a Canticle spell.

Cathay – the Democratic Republic of Cathay, a country that exists in the world of the book but not in our world. It is known to both the World of the Wise and the Unwary. It is ruled by an elected council.

Conjuring – One of the Seven Sorcerous Arts. It is the Art of drawing objects out of the dreamlands.

Core Group – a group of students, usually from the same dorm, who attend all their classes together.

Dare Hall – the dormitory at Roanoke Academy that is favored by Enchanters.

De Vere Hall – the dormitory at Roanoke Academy that is favored by Warders and Obscurers.

Dee Hall – the dormitory at Roanoke Academy that is favored by Scholars.

Drake Hall – the dormitory at Roanoke Academy that is favored by Thaumaturges.

Enchantment – One of the Seven Sorcerous Arts. It is based on music and includes a number of sub-arts.

Fulgurator's wand – a wand with a spell-grade gem on the tip that is used by Soldiers of the Wise to throw lighting and to hold other kinds of spells.

Gnosis – One of the Seven Sorcerous Arts. It is the Art of knowledge and augury.

Heer of Dunderberg – Storm Goblin locked up with his Lightning Imps in a cave in Stony Tor on Roanoke Island.

Jumping – a cantrip that allows the practitioner to teleport.

Magical Australia – a country that is only known to the Wise. It is ruled by the Romanov family.

Marlowe Hall – the dormitory at Roanoke Academy that is favored by Conjurers.

Morthbrood – an ancient organization of practitioners of black magic. During the Terrible Years, the Morthbrood served the Terrible Five.

Mundane – without magic. Refers both to the modern technological world and to those who cannot use magic. It is possible to be mundane and Wise, if one has no magic but is aware of the magical world.

Obscuration – a subset of Warding. It allows for the casting of illusions that hide things and trick the Unwary.

Original Language – The original language in which all objects were named.

Parliament of the Wise – the ruling body of the World of the Wise.

Pollepel Island – the name the Unwary call the island they see in place of Roanoke Island. It is also called Bannerman Island.

Roanoke Academy for the Sorcerous Arts – school of magic on a floating island that is currently moored in the Hudson near Storm King Mountain.

Scholars – practitioners of the Art of Gnosis.

Sorcery – the study of magic.

Spenser Hall – the dormitory at Roanoke Academy that is favored by Canticlers.

Terrible Five – the leaders of the Veltdammerung, who terrorized the World of the Wise during the Terrible Years. They consisted of: Simon Magus, Morgana Le Fay, Koschai the Deathless, Baba Yaga, and Aleister Crowley.

Thaumaturgy – One of the Seven Sorcerous Arts. It is the Art of storing charges of magic in a gem.

Thule — a country that is known only to the World of the Wise. It occupies the section of Greenland that is, in our world, occupied by the world's largest national park (larger than all but 32 countries.)

Transylvania – a country that exists in the world of the book but not in our world. It is known to both the World of the Wise and the Unwary. It is ruled by the Starkadder family.

Tutor – the term used for professors at Roanoke Academy.

Unwary – one who does not know about the magical world.

Veltdammerung – Twilight of the World. The organization that served the Terrible Five during the Terrible Years. It consisted of the Morthbrood and of supernatural servants.

Warding – One of the Seven Sorcerous Arts. It is the Art of protecting one's self from magical influences.

Wise – those in the know about the magical world (as in the root of the word 'wizard'.)

Wisecraft – The law enforcement agency of the Wise. The Agents work for the Wisecraft

World of the Wise – The community of those who know about the magical world.

READ ON FOR A SNEAK PEEK OF

THE UNEXPECTED ENLIGHTENMENT
OF RACHEL GRIFFIN
VOLUME TWO:

THE RAVEN, THE ELF, AND RACHEL

ONE HOUR LATER...

CHAPTER ONE:

THE UNFORESEEN DIFFICULTIES

OF RETRIEVING A BROOM

"THEY AREN'T LOOKING!" RACHEL GRIFFIN GRABBED SIGGY'S ARM and tugged. "Let's go!"

They dashed past the *No Students Allowed* sign and raced up the spiral staircase, their footsteps echoing against the stone steps of the Watch Tower. Siggy's legs were significantly longer than hers, and he soon raced past her.

"Do you think the proctors will find us up here?" she gasped, trying to keep up.

"We should have a few minutes," Sigfried Smith replied over his shoulder, taking two steps at a time. Like Rachel, he spoke with an English accent, though his was of a much lower class. "First, they have to interrogate the princess. Do you think she'll break under torture? Of course, she blabbed about your boyfriend with no provocation. They hadn't even made her go without food for a week, or used a thumb screw, or anything."

"Gaius Valiant is *not* my boyfriend!" Rachel hollered.

"Shhh!" Siggy hissed. "They'll hear you!"

Embarrassed, Rachel clamped her hand over her mouth. From underneath it, she replied, "They don't torture students here at Roanoke Academy, Siggy. It's just not done. Did they really torture you at the mundane orphanage where you grew up?"

Siggy's voice became hard as flint. "Let's not talk about it. It's not something a girl would want to hear."

"I want to hear," Rachel responded earnestly. "I want to know *everything*."

They pelted up two flights of stairs, speeding through rooms containing cabinets and barrels filled with items useful for warding away the supernatural. Rachel noted chalk, salt, stones with a hole in the middle, red thread, and a barrel overflowing with dried daisy chains. A bag of weed killer lay open beside the barrel. She wondered if that was a warding material, too, or if the tower was also used for storage.

Ducking through the opening in the stone ceiling, they burst out into the belfry. The air was damp and smelled of the straw that covered the rock slabs of the floor. A set of huge tubular chimes hung from the ceiling. Beneath them, in the center of the belfry, stood an Obscuration Lantern, a brass contraption taller than Rachel. It was as large as a lighthouse lamp and topped with an enormous cut-crystal globe.

Eight tall arches were set into the thick stone of the belfry. Half of them were open, containing no glass. Outside, to the north and east, stretched a forest of virgin hemlocks. The setting sun shone in the west, bathing the straw on the floor in a rich golden hue and gleaming off the brass of the lantern. The other four arches contained mirrors, each tinted with a hint of color. Rachel recognized the green one as a talking glass and the blue one as a walking glass. Of the remaining two, one was tinted with the same golden hue as the thinking glass in the Infirmary. The final was purple and spiderwebbed with cracks. She did not recognize it.

As they topped the staircase, they were reflected in the tinted glass: two children emerging from the opening in the floor. Both wore muddy and ripped academic robes of matte black, the kind that had been worn by scholars since Medieval days but which mundane Americans now wore only for graduations. The first child was a tall, extremely handsome boy with golden curls and bare feet. When he smiled, the gleam of his teeth was bright enough to blind passing geese. Behind him ran a panting little Asian girl, much younger-looking than her thirteen years. Black shoulder-length locks flew wildly about her face.

Patting the back of her head, Rachel found nothing but hair. Somewhere—perhaps when she crashed through a classroom window to save her Alchemy tutor—she had lost her black and white polka dotted bow. In the mirror, her reflection simultaneously patted the back of its head, seeking its lost bow.

They sighed in unison.

"Quick," Sigfried urged, peering down the stairs behind them, "we only have a little time before they notice we're missing."

"Oh! Right!"

Crossing to the south window, Rachel threw herself onto the sill, panting. The campus of Roanoke Academy for the Sorcerous Arts stretched before her. Beyond the tall spires and towers of the main hall that housed the college and the Upper School, she could see bits of the reflecting lake, the long green lawns of the Campus Commons, and, to the side, the paths leading to the seven dormitories, three to the west and four to the east. Farther yet, she could catch glimpses of monuments and fountains, the lily pond, and the Oriental Gardens.

There was still a great deal of commotion on the Commons: students rushing to and fro; proctors rounding up wrongdoers; tutors—as Roanoke Academy called its professors—helping the injured. Among them, Rachel caught a glimpse of Nurse Moth astride her orange Ouroborus Industries Flycycle—a device that had as much in common with an old fashioned broom as an automobile has with a horse-drawn carriage. The nurse's hands were raised in a cantrip as she floated a patient toward the Infirmary.

"I see the nurse!" Rachel leaned forward excitedly. "She's on her own bristleless."

Sigfried peered over the staircase and looked down. Rising again, he called, "The coast is clear! Go for it."

Rachel stretched out her hand and shouted, *"Varenga, Vroomie!"*

Siggy joined her, gazing out at the campus over her shoulder. "Is your broom coming?"

"Can't see it yet. It can take a minute or two."

"What's that noise behind us?"

They both spun around. The giant lantern rattled. A chill slithered up Rachel's spine. She and Sigfried exchanged glances.

"Why is it...doing that?" she whispered.

"I'll look." Sigfried did not move. Absentmindedly, his fingers came to rest on the chest of his black academic robes. Underneath the cloth was his mystical, all-seeing amulet. "It's an animal. A rat, maybe? Brown and ugly."

Rachel crept across the straw, circling close to the damp, mossy stone wall. She craned her neck. A small, brow, rat-like animal with a long slick tail worried at the brass pedestal of the lantern. Comparing the creature to pictures in encyclopedias she had memorized, she whispered, "Looks like a muskrat."

"What's it doing?" he asked.

"Don't know. Maybe there is food inside."

"Maybe it's someone's familiar."

"No." Rachel shook her head. "If it were, the pads on its paws would be silver."

The lantern flared. Multi-colored flames flickered and leapt within the crystal globe. Glints of red, blue, and green danced over the hanging chimes, the straw, and the rough stone walls. Mingling with the warm gold of the sunset, they transformed the drab stone belfry into a wonderland. Both children paused, awed. Rachel's lips parted in delight.

"How beautiful! But we should probably..." Her voice died.

The muskrat had turned its head. Its eyes were the same milky color as those of the children who had been under the control of their wicked Math tutor, Dr. Mordeau. Rachel thought back five seconds. She replayed her memory of what she had just experienced. In her perfect memory, a tall, black shadow, which her eyes had not shown her, hunched over the little animal. It was not a solid human-shaped shadow, such as the wraith that used to follow Upper School junior, Mylene Price. It had a more slender shape, like the shadows that had come from Dr. Mordeau's cloak.

"Siggy!" Rachel shrieked. "Stop that muskrat!"

Fixing her gaze on it, she whistled.

A tingle of energy welled up in her body, running from her toes and fingers, through her limbs, to her lips. Excitement and giddiness gripped her, but she kept her face as calm as a mask. Silver sparkles emerged from her mouth, flew across the distance, and pushed the muskrat three feet across the straw.

Rachel grinned and clapped her hands. She had only been at school for five days, yet she had improved so much. She could now push something the size of a muskrat with a wind she summoned with sorcery. Her practicing was paying off!

Sigfried pulled out his trumpet from the voluminous in his robe and blew. A wind swirling with the same silver sparkles picked up the muskrat and swept it another twenty feet across the belfry and out of a window into mid-air. Rachel sighed. It had taken her hours of practice to be able to push that creature just a few feet. Siggy was a natural.

Running to the western window, Rachel shaded her eyes against the glare of the setting sun and thought back. In her memory, she tracked the progress of Mordeau's shadow-creature. It abandoned the muskrat as soon as the animal was thrown from the tower and took off for the south. Watching the little animal fall, Rachel hunched her shoulders in anticipation of the poor thing splatting on the stump-filled field below.

Only the muskrat never hit the ground.

Out of the hemlocks to the north shot a serpentine shape, about twelve feet long and covered with golden fur. Its long whiskers, the mane that ran along its length, and the puff on the end of its tail were flame red. Ruby scales coated its underside. Short horns curled above its almost wolf-like head.

"Go, Lucky!" Siggy cheered his familiar and best friend. "Get it!"

A plume of fire shot out of the dragon's mouth. The flames struck the falling creature. It let out a horrible screech. With one large gulp, Lucky swallowed the muskrat. Rachel cringed. She felt sorry for the poor thing: abused by Mordeau's shadows, tossed out a window, charbroiled in mid-air, and then eaten.

Siggy whooped.

Rachel turned away with a sigh of sad amusement. Chiding Sigfried for his lack of sympathy would do as much good as scolding the wind for blowing.

Boys were like that.

Crossing to the lantern, she knelt before the large brass key that controlled the flame. Tipping her head back, she watched the dancing colors—red, blue, purple, green—as she rifled through her mental library, calling up from her perfect memory any information she had ever encountered about such devices. She reviewed a manual she had glanced at once on how to refill the oil in an Aladdin lamp, an encyclopedia entry on the history of chandeliers, a book on lighthouses and how they worked, the time she had come upon...

Ah! That was what she needed!

Carefully, she recalled the time she had come upon her father lighting the Obscuration Lantern in the small turret atop her grandfather's tower at Gryphon Park, her home back in England. The spirits the lamp commanded had loomed about him in a circle. The moment she had come bursting up onto the tower roof, however, he had dismissed them. She played back the memory twice, frowning. He had sent her back downstairs before turning off the lantern.

Well, that was no help.

"Which way do I turn it?" she murmured.

"Righty tighty, lefty loosey?" Siggy offered, squatting beside her.

"Does that apply to Obscuration Lanterns, too?"

"Is that what this is?"

Rachel nodded.

"No idea what that means." Sigfried shrugged. "Remember, I didn't grow up in your World of the Wise. I'm unwary even for an Unwary."

Rachel giggled at that. "Okay, well…" She paused, thinking how best to explain. "You know we're on the Island of Roanoke, right?"

"Are we?"

"Yes…" She eyed him skeptically, wondering if he was joking. "Remember how the 'lost' colony of English sorcerers uprooted it and turned it into a floating island? So they could escape persecution from England? They sailed it around the world for several centuries. Then, it became grounded here in the Hudson River. You remember all that, right?"

"No."

"But…" Rachel gazed at him in frustration, an uncomfortable tingle making its way across her shoulders. The notion of forgetfulness always disturbed her. "Mr. Gideon told us this in True History class."

Sigfried looked as if he were so bored it was causing him pain. "You mean True Napping class? If it does not teach us how to brew poison or throw fireballs, what good is it? I plan to learn a cantrip so I can sleep with my eyes open."

Rachel took a long slow breath. "Okay…Um…The short version. We are on Roanoke Island. Only the Unwary, the mundane folks—if they look from the bank of the Hudson River or an aeroplane—they see Bannerman Island, a fake image kept in place by a Sorcerous Art called Obscuration. Got it so far?"

"Maybe." Siggy tossed his bowie knife and caught it again. It gleamed in the late afternoon sun. Glints of blue and green and purple flickered across the blade. "Is there going to be a test?"

Rachel threw up her hands in exasperation. *"Eecks! Eegrec! Zed!* What do you remember? You must remember something!"

"Really? Why is that?" Sigfried scowled at her. For a moment, like unexpectedly catching a glimpse of the scorching sun between the clouds of an otherwise overcast sky, something painful and sad burned in his eyes. "Everything I had been taught before this week is wrong. Every fact I learned about the world. Every law of physics. Every historical event. All wrong. Even the things that the Wise Guys are telling me are apparently wrong—at least if my Metapluton theory is correct: that there is another secret world manipulating our world the way we manipulate the Unscary—the Wiser than the Wise.

"If everything I remember is wrong, what is the point of remembering any of it?"

Rachel sat extremely still, her heart thumping oddly. The concept of not remembering disturbed her, partially because she was not exactly sure what people meant by it. She occasionally neglected to check her memory and thus missed an appointment or did not do something she had promised to do. That was a temporary oversight.

But forgetting? She tried to picture what that might be like but failed.

"Magic shock." She shook herself, pushing away her discomfort. She continued solemnly, "Can't tell real things from story things. It happens sometimes when sorcerers have been raised in the mundane world."

Siggy shrugged again and gestured at the giant lantern. It burned away merrily, sending glints of purple and blue dancing over their faces. "So...what is this thing again? Is it important?"

"Okay...even shorter version," Rachel gulped. "This lantern casts magic shadows. These shadows—these servants of the lantern—can be instructed to create illusions, called Obscurations. The enormous chimes above us are part of the Obscuration magic, too."

"I don't understand. It does...what?"

Rachel paused, collecting her thoughts. "You turn on the lantern and call up its servants. You instruct them as to what kind of illusion you want."

"And the muskrat turned on the lantern...why? Because it thought there was food inside?"

"No! It was possessed! By one of the things that came out of Mordeau's cloak. It was trying to turn off the illusions and wards that protect the school."

"You mean the protections that keep out wraiths—like the one we fought? And evil teachers—like the one we fought?"

Rachel giggled in spite of the seriousness of the matter. "Er…yeah. Only that was one wraith and one evil tutor, and they snuck inside. Beyond the wards, there are a whole lot more waiting. If the wards ever come down, they can all rush in. *And*, the Unwary would see us."

Sigfried glanced eagerly out the western window—where the peak of Storm King Mountain rose in the distance, above the trees—as if he expected to see a horde of specters and malevolent instructors preparing to rush the campus. From the gleam in his eye, he was already imagining what fun it would be to watch Lucky charbroil them.

Rachel rubbed her temples, which were threatening to ache. "We need to turn this lantern off without calling the—"she formed the gesture for the *taflu* cantrip—middle fingers curled, outer fingers extended, thumb across the middle fingers—with both hands and crossed her arms in front of her, so that the repelling gestures blocked her mouth from the supernatural world. "*Tenebrous obscurii*, the Obscuration spirits. One way turns it off. The other way, if you turn it the whole way…calls them. Which we don't want to do."

"Why not?"

"Because we are not their master."

"Will these *tenebrous obscurii* know we're not in charge?"

"Don't call their name!" Rachel cried.

"You did."

"No! This gesture—*taflu*—makes it so that supernatural creatures can't hear me! Please don't say their names. We don't want them to come!"

A soft sound, like the whispering in the tombs of the dead on All Hallow's Eve, came from around them. Dark figures rose from the floor until they stood as tall as men, solemn cloaked figures with deep hoods. They seemed to be made of solid darkness— not insubstantial forms such as the wraith or the shadow that had possessed the muskrat. Standing near the outer wall, they formed a circle around the lantern and the children, staring inward.

Cold fingers of terror touched the back of Rachel's neck. She clutched Sigfried's arm and swallowed.

"What're they?" he hissed.

Rachel opened her mouth. Then, raising her finger to her lips, she shook her head wordlessly.

Ignoring her warning, Sigfried turned toward the nearest figure and made a shooing gesture. "Hey, whatever-you-are. Obsceney-thing, or whatever you are called. Stop what you are doing and go! Scat! Vamoose!"

The shadowy hoods all turned toward him, simultaneously. A dozen sibilant voices spoke in unison: "Master Warder, we hear and obey. Everything we do, we shall stop. "

No. No. This was bad!

Rachel threw up her hands in a *stop* gesture and shouted, "Maintain! Maintain!"

The *tenebrous obscurii* turned their many hoods toward her and paused, as if puzzled.

She raised her hands and held them exactly as her father had in her memory, when he had dismissed them at Gryphon Park.

"Oyarsa! Taflu!"

The shadowy cloaks shivered. Silently as black moths under a new moon, they sank into the stones of the floor. The moment they were gone, Rachel raised the index finger of her right hand and spun in a circle, shouting out the Word of Ending cantrip over and over.

"Obé! Obé! Obé!"

They did not reappear. Rachel drew a ragged breath of relief. Then, she turned and glared at Siggy, tapping her foot.

"What? Why was that bad?" Siggy asked innocently.

"You told them to stop protecting the school!"

"Oh." Siggy thought about this and then shrugged again. "It would have been exciting if wraiths and black magicians had rushed the campus."

"Not today, Sigfried," Rachel said solemnly. "We just got done fighting geased proctors, possessed students, and a Math-teaching dragon. People got hurt. I think," her voice shook, "your roommate might be dead."

Siggy's face went pale. "Ian MacDannan? Or Enoch the Wuss?"

"The *wuss*, as you call him." Her voice felt too thick to obey her. "He threw himself in front of our Alchemy teacher."

Sigfried scowled. "Who hurt him? I'll have Lucky burn his face."

"It was a crazy possessed girl."

Siggy threw up his arms. "Why does it *always* have to be a girl?"

"Okay..." Rachel turned back to the Obscuration Lantern and pulled up her long sleeves. She took a deep breath. "Here goes...something!"

Lunging forward, she turned the lantern key all the way to the left. The flame sputtered and died away. The multi-colored lights dancing around the tower flickered and vanished. The golden glow had faded as well, as the sun had sunk farther into the western sky.

The wonder was gone. They stood again in drab straw, their images reflected in a cracked mirror. With a sigh of mingled relief and regret, Rachel slumped forward and rested her forehead against the lantern's column. She drew back with a yelp. The brass was hot.

Whoosh.

Through the southern window flew Vroomie, obedient to Rachel's call. Shouting for joy, she grabbed her steeplechaser, a wonder of polished dark wood and brass, and hugged it to her. It was, in her humble opinion, the most beautiful bristleless flying broom in the world.

"Mission accomplished!" She flourished the broom victoriously, leaping toward the stairs. "Come on! Let's go tell the proctors: the shadows from Mordeau's cloak are still on the loose!"

To Be Continued....

ACKNOWLEDGEMENTS

THANK YOU TO MARK WHIPPLE, JOHN C. WRIGHT, AND WILLIAM E. Burns, III who breathed the life into the original story.

To Virginia Johnson, Erin Furby, Bill Burns, and Brian Furlough, who helped iron out the bumps, and to my husband and my sons, Orville and Justinian, for playing along— and particularly to Juss, for wearing a lightning imp under his cat.

To Erin Furby, Ginger Kenny, Carman Finestra, Anne-Marie Droege, Cherry Vanderbeke, Katherine Peterson, Laura Taylor, Emily Leverett, Merry Muhsman, April, Jubal, and Jeremiah Freeman, Susan Furlough, and Von Long for slogging their way through the early drafts, and, in particular, thank you again, to Carman, Cherry and Stephanie King for correcting some of my Americanisms.

To Anna "Firtree" MacDonald and Don Schank, for making it readable, and to Danielle Ackley-McPhail for believing in me.

To Dan Lawlis, for being the perfect artist and to my dauntless husband, John C. Wright, Esq., for taking the time to draw.

To my brother, Law Lamplighter, who listened, and to my mother, Jane Lamplighter, for listening, too, and for making dinner on Thursdays, so I could write.

ABOUT THE AUTHOR

L. JAGI LAMPLIGHTER IS THE AUTHOR OF PROSPERO LOST, PROSPERO *In Hell* and *Prospero Regained.* She is also one of the editors of the *Bad-Ass Faeries* Anthology series. When not writing, she reverts to her secret identity as an at-home mother in Centreville, Virginia, where she lives with her husband, author John C. Wright, and their four children, Orville, Ping-Ping, Roland Wilbur, and Justinian Oberon.

CPSIA information can be obtained at www.ICGtesting.com
Printed in the USA
BVOW03s2224121114

374765BV00002B/104/P